I SERVE

A NOVEL OF THE BLACK PRINCE

BY

Rosanne E. Lortz

ANNO DOMINi CREATIVE

ISBN-13 978-0-9792145-4-7
ISBN-10 0-9792145-4-8

Publisher: Anno Domini
Printed in the U.S.A.

3 5 7 9 0 8 6 4

For you should be certain of and hold firmly to the belief that you have no other course of action to take except to remember that if you love God, God will love you. Serve Him well: He will reward you for it. Fear Him: He will make you feel secure. Honor Him: He will honor you. Ask of Him and you will receive much from Him. Pray to Him for mercy: He will pardon you. Call on Him when you are in danger: He will save you from it. Turn to Him when you are afraid, and He will protect you. Pray to Him for comfort, and He will comfort you. Believe totally in Him and He will bring you to salvation in His glorious company and His sweet paradise which will last forever without end. He who is willing to act thus will save his body and his soul, and he who does the opposite will be damned in soul and body. Pray to God for him who is the author of this book.

– Geoffroi de Charny's closing instructions to knights from *The Book of Chivalry*

TABLE OF CONTENTS

1

THE WOMAN IN THE CHURCH
December, 1360

*I*t was an unusual sight these fifteen years and more to see a man traveling the road alone—especially a solitary Englishman in the heart of the French countryside. But the peace treaty had recently been signed at Bretigny, and on paper at least there was friendship between the people of the lion and the people of the fleur-de-lys.

The traveler looked about thirty years of age, with a well-knit frame that sat easily in the saddle. One glance at his arms proclaimed that he was a knight, but his arms were not as recognizable as his rank. The shield showed a silver bolt of lightning across a sky black with thunder, or to put it in tournament cant, a field sable emblazoned with a chevron argent. It was not a famous crest. A herald of some worth might look this emblem over and still fail to tell us the chevalier's name. The solitary condition of the rider also spoke to his humble estate. No squire accompanied the knight. He led no packhorse and carried only a small bundle pillion.

The road from English Calais had been quiet as a cloister. It was near Christmastide, and the winter wind had begun to breathe upon the fields. The knight had many friends in Calais, but he had declined to stay Christmas with them. When they pressed him, he confessed that a burden bore heavily upon his soul. Even though the war had halted, he had a personal quest that lay unfulfilled. He would not explain the nature of the quest, but folk whispered that it had something to do with the small cedar box that he carried carefully wherever he went. It must be a relic, they said, and his quest must be a pilgrimage. Perhaps he was bound for the pope's palace in Avignon, or even for the Holy Land. Others claimed that his quest was of a less spiritual nature. They had heard him ask after the whereabouts of a certain lady— one Jeanne de Vergy. Assumptions ran rampant about the relationship between the two. The knight was known to be unmarried, and though he had at one time paid court to an English maid, perhaps he had re-sworn his homage to this French Jeanne. Although both sets of speculations would prove spurious in the end, they were true in some small measure. He *did* treasure a cedar box and he *was* seeking the aforesaid lady.

Jeanne de Vergy lived in the hamlet of Lirey, a village to the south of Calais that sat on the outskirts of Troyes. The knight was accustomed to travel, and though the weather had grown chill, the road was not hard. Towards the close of the sixth day he entered Lirey, and chancing upon a roadside inn, he accosted a local gossip to ascertain his destination more exactly.

"Lady Jeanne has a house in the southeast corner of the village," said the host of the inn. "But you'll not find her there. Not while there's candles left to burn in the church vestry. She spends all day on her knees in front

of that sheet in the gold box. Pious, you think? Maybe—
but not if you hear the bishop talk. A clever fake, he calls
it—the work of some godless charlatan! And if the lady's
not to blame for foisting it on the church, at least her
husband is—God rest his soul!"

The knight crossed himself in silence at the mention
of the dead. Then, bestowing a groat upon his loquacious
informer, he betook himself to the church at the center of
town. The plaza outside the church contained a few suspicious onlookers, their curiosity and animosity piqued
by the stranger's presence. They were wary to approach
the knight, but by means of another groat judiciously
dispensed, he induced a young villager to look after his
charger. While the French folk gazed inquisitively, he
removed the cedar box from the bundle behind his saddle.
Then, like one of the Magi that Saint Matthew writes of,
he went gift in hand into the dwelling of Christ.

The walls of the little church stood weightily in the
old Roman style, with narrow slits for windows that
barely admitted the fading light of the wintry afternoon.
The seating in the nave would accommodate few. The
altar beyond the transept was small. However, a costly
triptych painted with gold and vermillion gave evidence
of a wealthy donor in the parish. The knight passed
beyond this screen into a forest of burning wicks. The
corridors of the sanctuary had been silent and gray, but
beyond the altar the walls of the apse glowed like a phos-
phorescent sea. Arranged around a small niche, the candles illuminated an honored reliquary. It was fashioned
of dark wood and richly inlaid with gold and ivory.

Enchanted by this glory, the knight barely noticed
the worshiper kneeling on the flagstones. There was

little enough to notice. She was a drab, unprepossessing creature with eyes nearly larger than her face. These eyes were her most intriguing and most attractive feature. Her pupils flickered in the candlelight, but the gaze never wavered from its rapt contemplation of the reliquary.

"Lady," said the knight softly, after his own eyes had adjusted to the hazy glory cloud that overspread this place, "Are you Mistress Jeanne of Vergy?"

The bright eyes turned to him and without rising she answered aye.

"I bring a great treasure," said the knight proffering the small box he carried.

"A treasure?" she repeated, and her tone changed to one of warmth and welcome. "The Lord will bless you and cause his face to shine upon you. He is worthy of all treasures a man can give." She rose, took the box in her hands, and started to place it before the reliquary. The knight shifted awkwardly before her fervor, and his words fell out in a torrent.

"Nay, there are other treasures better fitting for the Lord of heaven and earth," said he. "The treasure I bear is of little value to any save one. The widow of Geoffroi de Charny is the proper one to receive this gift. And you, if I mistake not, are she."

She looked puzzled, almost disappointed that the box in her hands was a gift for her, instead of a tribute to the gold-encrusted reliquary in the niche. He bid her open the box. She loosened the catch and lifted the lid.

Out fluttered a strip of orange satin embroidered with golden stars. The edges were slashed jaggedly as if it had been cut from a larger piece of cloth. Here and there it was speckled with dark red, the dew of a battle long past. It was a tongue of flame torn from the mouth of a dragon. It was a handful of fire wrested from the hearth of the gods. "How came you by this?" she demanded, and staggering a little, she sat down on a nearby pew. "This was his. This was his! Were you there when he met his end?"

"I was there, I was close by—would to God that I had been far from that place! I was not the one to strike the blow, but even so, it was my hand that killed him. Afterwards, I returned to the place where he lay. I took the thing he most honored to place in the hands of the one he most loved." The knight inclined his head lower to speak to the lady, for though she was of middle age, she was as small as a yearling doe.

"But you were his enemy! France's enemy! You say that he was slain by your own hand. Why should you come all this way to bring a scrap of fabric to Charny's widow?"

"Exactly for that reason, lady—because you are *Charny's* widow, and whatever was Charny's, that I shall honor, for I loved Charny as I have loved few other men."

"What is your name, sir knight?" she demanded almost disbelieving, for her husband was beloved of few Englishmen.

"Sir John de Potenhale," the knight replied.

"Ah," said she, and knowledge lit up her face like a paper lantern. "He was your prisoner."

"Aye, yet also my liberator," replied the knight. "My enemy and my prisoner, my counselor and my friend. Your husband was all these to me and more."

"He spoke of you once or twice," said the lady, "but not enough to satisfy a woman's curiosity. Come, you must tell me your story. An Englishman that knew my husband—knew him and loved him—bears a story that my ear longs to hear." She motioned to the wooden pew begging him to sit down and commence the tale.

The knight hesitated a little. "It is a long story with many threads. Where would you have me begin? Shall I tell you of the day I first met your husband?"

The lady smiled and shook her head. "No, you must begin as he would have had you." Her companion looked a little puzzled. Surely he must know which day Charny had held as significant as birth, as sacred as baptism, and as solemn as death. She prompted him with a question. "Where is it that the story of a knight must start?"

"With his knighthood," replied the man, and setting himself down upon the wooden pew he began his tale of arms, of death, of love, and of honor.

2

THE LANDING OF
THE CONQUEROR
July – August, 1346

*I*f you would hear of my knighthood, you must first hear of my passage to France, for the one turns upon the other as tightly as a door upon a hinge. It was the fifth of July, 1346, when we set sail, an army of wooden-hulled castles bound for Gascony and France. The forecastle of each fighting cog was crammed with vibrant pennants, high-mettled horses, and eager Englishmen. Our king had determined to be master of your France, but the sea proved to be its own master. Almost as soon as the fleet weighed anchor, the wind began to breathe heavily like a thickset man climbing a hill. The ruffled water pushed back against the coast, and the cogs could make no southwestern progress.

Originally, the king had designed to go down from Cornwall and round the tip of Brittany. Our fleet would carry us southward along the French coast till we reached the sun-kissed lands of Gascony. The ships would enter the sheltered mouth of the Garonne River, and we would disembark on the wharfs of Bordeaux. Gascony was the ideal landing place, for at that time, Gascony was the only piece of the continent still honoring its sworn fealty to our English sovereign. A small expeditionary force led by the Duke of Lancaster had already landed there and was awaiting our arrival. Once the king's army united with the garrisons of Gascony and with Lancaster's men, we would fall over the border into France with all the power of a mighty waterfall. Then let the usurper of France lift his head in astonishment! Then let the house of Valois tremble for its ill gotten gains!

The sea, however, seemed to be on the side of French Philip. For five days we tossed about like butter in a churn. Whenever the perseverant pilots took the ships a league or two beyond land, the watchful waves cast us back on the coast of Cornwall. Our English king was a masterful man, but he knew when to cry *Deus li volt* and let circumstances have their way. "If the wind will take us to Normandy," said he, "then to Normandy we will go."

So the plan for Gascony was abandoned, and having submitted ourselves to the will of the sea, we found a calm southeasterly passage to the coast of the Cotentin. This beachfront, jutting out from Normandy like a gnarled thumb, boasts the second shortest crossing between our lands. It is a place well acquainted with launches and landings. On a shore not far from this one, the Norman duke William once readied an invading army bound for Pevensey, Hastings, and the English crown. Now, eight generations later, his Plantagenet descendant had returned to be a conqueror in his own right.

It was mid July, but the water of the channel was still as cold as a mountain spring. The cogs had all beached, and upward of fifteen thousand men were clamoring to disembark. They were not the only creatures champing at the bit. Untrammeled at last, the mettlesome steeds were half-crazed from the cramped conditions aboard the ship. But before the shore could be fully attained, a foot-wetting awaited them. "Here, boy!" said my lord Chandos. "Take my horse!" "Gently, gently," I breathed, patting the heaving withers of my master's destrier. I had been Sir John Chandos's squire for a year now, and the horse knew me well, a friend from frequent saddlings, combings, and feedings. I guided him firmly into the boiling surf, keeping a soothing hand on his neck all the while. Once on dry ground, he ceased his nervous plunging and waited quietly while I brought my own nag onto the sandy shore. I was one of the first to disembark; I waited on the strand for some time as the rest of the bellicose passengers splashed their way to the beach.

The crowded docks at Cornwall had given me no leisure to survey the full scope of our company. Here the empty shore of the Norman coast displayed them to their full advantage. I saw scores of archers tromping loudly through the surf, holding their longbows above their heads to protect them from the wet. The men-at-arms sang out lustily as they stepped onto dry ground, thanking the Holy Trinity that they had reached terra firma at last. The knights came ashore in full battle gear having donned their crests at the first sight of land. The flamboyant reds and yellows on their coats-of-arms sparkled as brilliantly as the salt water surrounding them.

Once each ship had surrendered its inmates, we crossed the dune that separated the sea from the countryside. The roar of the surf grew fainter, and the hubbub of men grew louder. I saw that many were beginning to unload their packs.

"Shall we arm ourselves and ride?" I asked eagerly, for in those days I knew as little of strategy as a boy brought up in the monasteries. I knew only that we had come to fight the French, and now that we were in France, I wished to do battle.

"Nay, nay," said my master Chandos patiently. "We must settle our forces and pitch camp first. We'll not go riding off into French territory willy nilly without drawing up into proper formation and sending out a scouting division."

"Indeed," I nodded sagely, trying to conceal my inexperience by assenting to what must have been common knowledge.

"And then there's the little matter of finances," said Chandos with a gleam in his eye. "It's many a fancy farthing to collect an army of this size. His Majesty must see about raising some of the gold before we find ourselves up to the neck in gore."

"But surely it would have been easier to raise the money in England?" I asked puzzled.

"For any ordinary tax, yes," said Chandos with a shrug, "but this shield fee is just as well paid on foreign soil as not. It is a tax the nobles will not grudge, for it can only be demanded of them once in a king's lifetime."

The shield fee, as you may know, is the sum that each English knight, baron, or noble owes to our king when his eldest son receives knighthood. Edward, the young Prince of Wales, was in our company and had not yet felt the accolade upon his shoulder.

I had seen the prince several times from no great distance, for my lord Chandos was on familiar terms with the royal household. He was a dark, comely youth, taller than me by nearly a head. He was young to be made a knight, a fact I knew full well, for it had been borne in on me since birth that the prince and I were of the same age. But he was a prince and a Plantagenet—and at the same age his father had been crowned king of England. A man of lowlier parentage might expect to wait four more years to receive the spurs, or even longer if it were not a time of war. A man of my parentage might never be knighted at all.

"It will be a great thing then for the prince to be knighted," said I, a little enviously, "if His Majesty can turn such a profit off of it."

"Mind your tongue!" said Chandos, in response to my pert words. "It is a great thing to be knighted no matter the circumstances or the compensation. I'll warrant a pup like you would give your eye teeth for such a chance."

"Lord! And give up being your squire? Not I!" I spat on the ground in mock contempt, but he and I both knew the truth. I would give up far more than my eye teeth for the accolade and the spurs.

The knighting took precedence over setting up camp. The king and his nobles mounted a small hill that straddled the seashore and the countryside. The Earls of Warwick, Northampton, and Arundel were there and Sir Walter Manny, the king's favorite baron. They stood solemnly on the hillside, making a wide circle to encompass the ceremony that was to come. The men-at-arms and lowlier folk waited below, uninvited to the ceremony.

Chandos, as usual, followed in the king's train. And strangely enough, he bade me accompany him, insisting that my presence was necessary to carry his shield and a certain important scroll.

I hefted the shield over my arm and pocketed the scroll in the breast of my jerkin. As other squires looked on brimming over with youthful jealousy, I bore my lord's shield to the crest of the hill. And thus it came to pass that I stood no more than ten paces away when the king unsheathed his sword to knight his firstborn.

Edward, our king, was in the height of his powers in the year of the invasion. Both the salty breeze on the prospect and the prospect of imminent conquest had combined to augment his handsome virility. He was thirty-four years old, tall, fierce, and majestic.

Kneeling on the ground before him was a younger copy of himself. The lithe, long-limbed Prince of Wales had none of the Flemish softness that characterized his mother Philippa. He was made of the same stern stuff as his father and his Plantagenet ancestors, rods of iron that could smash their enemies into pieces like shards of pottery. Men of this race do not kneel to others and so it was a remarkable sight to see his royal highness with head bowed and knee bended before his king and father. It has been fourteen years since the day of the prince's knighting, and since then I have only seen him kneel to one other.

In days of peace the ceremony would have lasted far longer. The prince had spent years in preparation for knighthood, and it seemed a pity that it should pass in an instant, like a puff of smoke, like a ripple in water, or even like a violent sneeze. First, there should have been the ceremonial bath. The warm, scented water would purify his body while two older knights instructed him in the purity of heart a knight must possess. Then, there should have been the vigil. Throughout the darkness of the night, he would prostrate himself before the light of the chapel's altar in humble prayer. And on the morrow, in the great hall of Westminster, he would walk fearlessly through a staring crowd of gentlefolk to receive a stately tap with the flat of a sword.

To be knighted on the fields of France was another matter. It was all over in a moment. The words were said, the tap was given. Two grizzled knights, my master Chandos and his boon companion Audley, advanced to buckle the ceremonial golden spurs onto the prince's heels. And then arose the newest knight in Christendom, Edward of Woodstock, Earl of Chester, Duke of Cornwall, and Prince of Wales.

"You are a knight now," I heard the king say to his son, "And as such, you may confer the same honor on those whom you will."

"Aye, highness," said Sir Walter Manny, whose counsel was respected by king and commoner alike. "And besides conferring this honor upon your nobles, you must also set about creating a household of your own warriors. A royal must have none about him but belted knights; no half-fledged squire should wait attendance upon you."

The prince nodded in compliance, and Chandos advanced toward him. "I have a list of half a dozen young lords who would be grateful for such preferment."

I removed the scroll from the breast of my tunic. This was my moment to come before the royal notice! The prince extended a gloved hand, and at a word from my master, I deposited the scroll inside his open fist. He gave me a simple gramercy and I resumed my place behind my master, an insignificant caterpillar in this grand assembly of butterflies.

"They are worthies all," the prince commented dryly, his eyes overglancing the list presented, "of good parentage and suitable age. Let them advance in turn." At a word from Chandos, the stage was set to admit another initiate into the inner circle of chivalry.

William Montague, the young Earl of Salisbury, was the first to receive knighthood from his royal highness. A slim youth of fair complexion, he was two years the prince's senior. His father, the old Earl of Salisbury, had served the king well both in France and at home. The previous earl had been a formidable captain in the war against the Scots. For his valiant service, Edward had given him the Isle of Man as a reward. The old earl did not enjoy his new domain for long. When he returned to England, he jousted poorly in a tournament at Windsor and fell in the lists. He never recovered from his wounds. The Isle of Man, as well as the rest of Salisbury's estates, passed into the hands of his young son, William Montague. That was two years before the present campaign. Now, in a quiet way, the new earl was rapidly earning the respect that his father had accrued with a lifetime of arms. It was rumored that the king had a brilliant marriage in store for him.

The second to receive knighthood was Roger Mortimer. This youth, much of an age with Salisbury, was grandson to the infamous Mortimer who seduced the mother of our king. On account of his progenitor's perfidy, Mortimer's lands and titles had been stripped from his house when he was still in the cradle. His own father had died just a year after his grandfather met the noose. Fortunately for the kingdom, young Roger's character was cast in a more honorable mold than that of his forbearers. Now, at the age of eighteen, he was beginning to restore the honor that his grandfather had tarnished, and he would eventually reclaim the title Earl of March with his valorous exploits in France.

The prince was not thrifty with his accolades, and several more youths entered the halls of knighthood that day. Like Salisbury and Mortimer, most of them were already lords in their own right. They had their own households to attend to, their own vassals to manage, and their own companies to collect.

"Highness," interjected Sir Walter Manny once again. "May I be so bold as to nominate some squires worthy of an accolade from your hand? They are of good but lowly parentage. You have left most of your own household in Cornwall, and it would be fitting for our newly knighted prince to elevate some new knights to serve as his attendants."

Overhearing these words, I stifled my overwhelming desire to fall on my face like the prophet Isaiah and cry out "Here am I!" I was a squire, and my parentage was lowly enough. My father was a plain man-at-arms who had never felt the accolade. My mother was a waiting lady, of poor but honest means. To become a knight of the prince's household was a boon I could hardly hope to receive, but even so I dared to hope it—until Chandos frowned and shook his head at Manny.

"Nay, Sir Walter," said my master. "Let be, let be!"

"Aye," said Audley, agreeing with Chandos as was his wont. "No more knightings!" Audley's voice was as harsh as a crow; his black humor made him easily distinguishable in any crowd. He was a short, stocky man with close cropped hair. The grey which had started to tinge my master's black hair had already liberally sprinkled Audley's sandy head. Both Chandos and Audley were of the older generation. They had fought the Scots under the second Edward; they would fight the French under the third Edward.

"Wait until the men have matched their mettle against the French," said Chandos. "Then's the time to be noticing worthy squires, for then's the time they'll prove their worth."

"You hear these two old bloodhounds?" said the prince to Walter Manny. "There is no gainsaying their wisdom. I'll rest my sword a little, and when I use it again for a knighting, there shall be blood upon the blade."

Sir Walter Manny shrugged but made no protest. It was in his nature to think of the lower ranks, for it was out of those lower ranks that he himself had once climbed. Sir Walter had come over from Hainault with Queen Philippa nineteen years earlier when first she wed our king. In those days Manny was no more than a humble meat carver. His was the hand to bring the venison and veal to the royal table, to separate the pheasant thigh from the pheasant breast, and to keep the royal trenchers fully laden. But though his birth promised no advancement, his competence and fidelity augured great things. The young king Edward soon paid heed to his wife's careful carver; he noted him, knighted him, and nurtured his advancement. Sir Walter proved himself an able soldier in the wars against Scotland. Sir Walter proved himself an able sea captain in the skirmish off the coast of Sluys. And Sir Walter would soon prove himself an able field commander in the invasion of France itself. But the invasion, as yet, was hardly underway; the knighting was finished, the fighting had yet to begin.

"Come," continued the prince to the men surrounding him. "We've tarried long enough upon this hill. With my father's permission, we'll adjourn these ceremonies and repair to camp. I've a mind to eat my first supper in this land of our Norman fathers. Mortimer, Salisbury, have you stomach?"

"Aye, highness," said the young Earl of Salisbury with a ready smile.

The prince fell into step with these two companions, and the rest of the company slowly wended its way down the hill. The newly made knights stepped gladly into the prince's pavilion, while I trudged heavily to Chandos's quarters, bearing a shield that was not my own.

The seashore camp rose with the summer moon and set just as quickly. On the following morning, we rolled up every ell of canvas and sought out more comfortable quarters. The nearest town was Saint-Vaast-La-Hougue, easily visible from the prospect where the prince had been knighted. Here was our first glimpse of the French!

We advanced upon the city in martial array. The inhabitants had spotted the high masts of our beached ships. Our coming was expected. The governor of La Hougue had hastily collected a small force of men, but they scattered like dried grass before the blast of our mighty army. We took possession of the town with scarcely a drop of bloodshed; indeed, most of the town folk had deserted the place at the first sign of our landing. That night we lay in more comfortable beds than we'd had on ship or in the field.

Both the governor and the few remaining French were anxious and assiduous to please; I found to my pleasant surprise that I could swagger about the streets like a grand milord ordering whatever I wished and taking whatever I desired. The men-at-arms were wild with excitement at this capture of a French citadel. By nightfall they had ransacked every house, opened every coffer, and extorted from every citizen.

The looting fever did not leave me untouched. I joined a company of English soldiers pushing their way into an inn. A frightened Frenchwoman begged us not to hurt her children. I saw two tousled urchins hiding behind the wood counter. "Open your strongbox!" shouted one of the soldiers. She fumbled with the keys at her waistband and, trembling, deposited them in his hands. The soldier shared out the coins to all in our troop with quickly snatched, uneven handfuls. I placed them eagerly inside my purse, a leather bag that was nearly always empty.

It was my first taste of plunder, and it was sweet as honeyed cakes. I wanted to go up and down all the streets, enter all the houses, threaten all the villagers, open all the cabinets. But Chandos kept me busy running errands throughout our stay in La Hougue. I had messages to carry to detachments of soldiers, reports to bring to His Majesty's headquarters, and victuals to procure for my master. One handful of silver coins was my only memento of La Hougue.

When we left the town on the following day, one company of the army stayed behind. At first, I thought that Edward meant to garrison the place and keep a foothold on the Norman coast for transport or retreat. But I had scarcely gone half a furlong before I saw—and smelled—the reason for the company's delay. They had orders to destroy the place; La Hougue caught fire like a row of hayricks, the first casualty of France's folly in resisting our most puissant monarch.

As we began our southeasterly march, raiding parties fanned out over the countryside cutting a wide swath of destruction. After the smoke of La Hougue was behind us, the king had given orders that no town was to be burnt, no churches sacked, and no women or children harmed on pain of life and limb. The king's officers, however, turned a blind eye to the enforcement of these decrees. I never saw one of our English arraigned and convicted for crimes against the peasants. It was popularly understood that any resistance on the part of the French abrogated the king's concern for their life and property. And as every village was sure to have a few resisters, every village was in danger of sword and torch. More than once the noontime sky glowed as red as sunset.

I rode out with Chandos every morning, and he, as often as not, rode escort to his highness. Our band was nearly always the first to break camp and assume the vanguard. The prince was but a new knight, but he had been playing the soldier since he could first hold a sword. He commanded his company with ease and confidence, commandeering cattle, loading wagons with provender, and spreading fire as freely as seed corn.

We continued our southeastern course through Normandy and then turned eastward sharply before entering the county of Anjou. As the prince and his company were riding out that day, we reined up sharply upon a small outcropping. All around us waved fields of yellow broom. "Look!" said Audley loudly. "It is your highness's flower." The prince smiled wryly. He reached for one of the taller shrubs, carefully maintaining his seat on his black charger. His fingers seized the yellow broom; he snapped off a single blossom and tucked it jauntily into the top of his basinet.

I looked questioningly at Chandos.

"It is the *planta genista*," said he, "the yellow broom. The house of Plantagenet derives its name from these yellow flowers. Here Geoffrey of Anjou fixed the sprig of broom into his hat—just before fixing his interest with Maud, the Conqueror's granddaughter. And now the heir of Anjou has come to claim his rightful inheritance at last!"

We marched a fortnight at easy stages preoccupied with pillage till the easterly road took us at last to Caen. I had seen London while in Chandos's service, but even so, I was unprepared for the splendor of the city that stood upon our path. London may have been larger, but Caen was of a surety more magnificent. The river Orne divided the city in two parts, like a chain of braided silver across the waist of some magnificent monarch. On the westerly side stood the citadel, two ancient abbeys, and a few small suburbs; on the easterly side lay the heart of the city, replete with handsome houses and glittering gold.

The citadel, we knew, was impregnable. Built by the Conqueror before he conquered England, Caen's castle was one of the strongest in France. Our great-grandfathers had seen the inside of these walls and had good reason to prize their prowess. Four generations ago, the English had held Caen; but like the rest of Normandy, Caen had been ceded away in the reign of John Lackland. The strength of the castle was now a weapon in the hands of our enemy.

To speak of the citadel's strength, however, was to say little of the city's. Caen itself was unwalled, with no natural defenses save the river and a bothersome but passable marsh. Separated from the main city by the Orne, the castle could give little aid to the citizens that sat in its shadow. The Orne proved a faithless friend to the French in another way; as our army approached the vicinity of Caen, our ships—which had been trailing our progress through any accessible waterway—anchored just off the outskirts of the city, waiting like birds of prey to engorge themselves with looted valuables.

I was in the van with the prince when Caen was sighted. We could have halted and waited for the rest of the army to draw up—indeed that was what Chandos advised—but instead, the prince quickened our pace, and we entered the west side of Caen at a headlong gallop. The sight of Caen had excited his blood, and the prince was hot for battle.

I was eager for the coming encounter but also anxious. Here was our first real battle. We had met the French before now, but all of those minor skirmishes had been like practice in the tilting yard. Who knew what lay behind this perimeter of houses? We would ride down upon them, rein up, and what then? The melee would be joined and I would kill or be killed in turn. I had crossed swords with half a dozen men in the course of our raids, but the enemy was always outnumbered, and the kill had never been left to me. The furious pounding of my horse's hooves was echoed by the frantic pounding of the heart in my chest. The wind blew full in my face, and my mouth was dry with apprehension.

But contrary to expectation, the western half of Caen was as empty as a drunkard's purse. The inhabitants had either cloistered themselves behind the high walls of their castle or crossed the bridge to the main part of the town. Our company scoured the streets but found no sign of soldiery. We regrouped out of range of the castle's archery for new orders.

"Highness," said Chandos, anxious to avoid pressing forward to the bridge without support from the main army. "We'd best secure this side of the river."

"Aye," said Audley.

"There's the two abbeys," said the prince, looking up at the spires that adorned the skyline. "We shall set up a headquarters there and wait for my father the king to advance."

"Well chosen, highness," said Chandos and at a word from the prince, we entered the *Abbaye-aux-Hommes*, while Audley and another contingent secured the sister building, the *Abbaye-aux-Dames*.

The streets outside had been silent enough, but their silence was the outside kind that allows a man's shouts to slice cleanly through the air. The silence inside the abbey was different. It swallowed up your voice with stone and drowned your words in their own echo. The abbot had not fled to the citadel with the rest of the town folk. He met us as we entered and asked the peace of the Lord upon us.

"Amen," said the prince, and he crossed himself. "And may the Lord's peace return upon this house. Is there lodging here for Englishmen?"

"Aye," said the abbot simply. "There is lodging here for all who call upon His name whether master, man, or beast. The brethren will minister to your needs." He clapped suddenly, and there appeared two men in the Benedictine habit. "Give them whatever they require," he told his followers, and with a courteous inclination of the head he was gone.

Chandos sent me to the stables to seek accommodation for our horses. The abbot's words had reached the Benedictine ostler before me, and I had little to do but bid him make ready to stable our mounts. I besought another errand, but Chandos had none for me, and with my time my own, I crossed the cloister with rapid strides to explore the interior of the church.

The closest door to the church opened into the transept. On either side of me stood small chapels, full of paintings and carvings, one of them housing lit candles before an ornamented tomb. I wondered briefly whose body the chapel housed but was distracted by my desire to see the full prospect of the church. I walked forward to where the arm of the transept joined with the body of the nave. Behind me the rounded arcade shot up straight and simple, with columns that reached toward a vaulted heaven. Before me the altarpiece stood stately and substantial, demarcating the holy of holies from the pews of the lowly worshipers. Above me the light from the clerestory windows sifted down gently, a glory cloud of golden dust that bathed the stone in color and set my face alight.

"The only thing wanting is a heavenly choir," said a voice beside me, and turning I saw that his highness had come in beside me with footfalls too noiseless to notice.

"Aye, highness," I said and bowed a little awestruck, for I had never had private conversation with the prince before this time. He was tall, of his full stature then at sixteen years of age, whereas I would not reach my height for another four years. He was still in battle dress, as was I, and the cascading light from the clerestory illuminated his armor while his face appeared dark.

"Shall we explore the apse?" the prince asked. I mumbled a quick assent, and following his easy stride, circumambulated the altar piece. Here the windows clustered thickly like a bunch of ripe berries. The ornate moldings and rose windows proclaimed that the apse had been constructed later than the main body of the building, perhaps as recently as twenty years ago. The prince led the way, examining the carvings. I followed a step behind in respectful silence. He did not walk aimlessly, however, and as we peered into each vaulted corner he looked about sharply as if he were searching for some especial treasure.

"It is not here," said the prince shaking his head.

"What do you seek, highness?" asked I.

"The Conqueror's tomb. This was his church, you know. He built it with the same stones as that citadel yonder. And he came here to be buried when he met his final hour."

"It was an inauspicious funeral, if I remember the story aright," said I.

"Aye," said the prince, and he caught my eye with something of a smile. "The monks could barely lift the great man's corpse, he had grown so corpulent in later years. And the mourners had no sooner begun to wet their eyes, than cries of 'Fire! Fire!' filled the air. So all the citizens of Caen went out to save their city from flames, and King William might bury himself for all they cared."

"But the monks stayed behind!" I reminded him. "They stayed behind to put him in his coffin."

"Pity the coffin was so small!" said the prince, and at that we both laughed aloud, for we both knew the story—that when the monks had gone to place the Conqueror in his stone sarcophagus, they found that his bulk had not been reckoned with, and the box had been hewn too small. The fire put them in a great hurry, however, and instead of taking the sensible course of waiting for a stonemason to mend matters, they tried to force the body into the opening. William's flaccid body had burst open, sending out such a great stench that it chased away all whom the fire had not frightened. Thus was the ignominious end of the lord of England and Normandy.

But though we might laugh at the crass nature of his departure, it did nothing to diminish the achievements of his life in our eyes.

"There was a small chapel off the transept," said I, remembering where I had first come into the church, "with candles and a stone box. Perhaps his tomb lies there."

We retraced our steps and found the place; the inscription on the tomb confirmed my supposition.

HIC SEPULTUS EST
INVICTISSIMUS
GUILLELMUS
CONQUESTOR,
NORMANNIAE DUX,
ET ANGLIAE REX,
HUJUSCE DOMUS,
CONDITOR,
QUI OBIIT ANNO
MLXXXVII[1]

The words proclaimed that we had found the Conqueror at last. The box was bare besides this, no effigy, no scrollwork, no evidence of his greatness besides this simple listing of his titles and achievements.

"He is as alone now as at his burial," said I. "A pity his lady could not be buried nearby so that at least his tomb might have company."

"Ah, but she is!" said the prince. "This whole abbey is his tomb, and the sister abbey, the *Abbaye-aux-Dames* that lies across the way, is the tomb of his lady Matilda. They were cousins, you know, on his father's side. Some say he bullied her into marrying him, and threw her to the ground by her hair until she consented. But others say she chose him of her own accord, and it was her father who disliked the match."

---

1   Here is buried the most undefeatable William the Conqueror, Duke of Normandy, and King of England, and the builder of this house who died in the year 1087.

"Cousins?" said I. "I wonder that the pope did not forbid it. If they had lived now, 'Consanguinity!' would be all the cry in Avignon and a king's ransom required before the ban could be lifted and the banns pronounced."

"It was the same in William's day," said the prince, "though at that time Peter still ruled from Rome instead of Avignon. The pope tried to negate the nuptials, but William was a determined man. He would have whom he would have, be she cousin or no. When the pope insisted on the mortality of such a sin, he paid the pope a princely price. You are standing in the portals of his penance. This abbey for him, that abbey for her. And with these two edifices their sin of marriage was effectually effaced. If we step over yonder to *l'Abbaye-aux-Dames*, you may see where she lies buried."

Before we could pursue this course, however, a messenger strode swiftly in and fell on one knee before the prince. "His Majesty is encamped outside the town, your highness, and bids you attend him at a council of war."

"Send him my compliments and assure him of my prompt arrival," replied the prince, and almost before the messenger had departed, the prince disappeared as noiselessly as he had entered leaving me alone in the great vaulted tomb of *Guillelmus Conquestor*. I did not stay long by myself in the church. There was still a battle to be fought and a city to be taken. And when Caen had capitulated, there was the rest of France. King William might lie at peace in this church, but King Edward and all his men would remain at war until France finally yielded to her rightful king and lord.

❖ ◆ ❖

The inhabitants on our side of the Orne had fled, but the Caen on the easterly side of the river showed no signs of yielding. Word trickled over that the Comte d'Eu had recruited militia from the surrounding countryside. These raw locals along with a small company of knights were prepared to wage bitter resistance against our troops. As Constable of France, the Comte d'Eu was a powerful noble, second-in-command only to the king. Philip of Valois had finally taken our invasion seriously enough to raise something of a defense, for Caen was too rich a plum to let fall into English hands undisputed.

The attack was slated for sunrise. I had spent the evening furbishing Chandos's harness and inspecting the gear for ourselves and our mounts. The blackness passed anxiously, for myself and others in the camp, and it was still night when we rose to meet the day. The king and all his nobles heard mass before the sun showed its florid face, and the army, which had encamped in the fields outside Caen, drew up in marching order. Our greatest impediment was the river, and we expected to struggle hard to gain the crossing points before we could engage the enemy within Caen.

To our surprise, however, the enemy was not in Caen, but had come over the bridge to meet us. Ranged in battle formation on the western side of the Orne, there stood nearly four thousand men; no more than a thousand looked to be knights or trained men at arms. Our men numbered four times their total force, and as we saw their motley band, our formation grew tighter, our pennants waved higher, and our spirits rose.

We were still three furlongs away when their line began to waver. A shout went up from our men, and their line disintegrated completely. A frantic Frenchman wearing blue with golden stars—presumably the Constable—rode up and down their fleeing ranks. He cursed them roundly and adjured them to hold fast, but it was to no avail. These French were no soldiers; they were farmers, shepherds, and vinedressers. Their spirits had shriveled within them at the first sight of us, and now they dispersed in a crazed rush to cross the river and return to the eastern half of the town.

Our own commanders gave us free rein. We charged forward trying to reach the head of the bridge and cut the fugitives off from the gatehouse. Knights, archers, and men-at-arms rushed madly into the fray, hacking down the fleeing French with indiscriminate blows. Separated from Chandos by the swirling mob, I dismounted my horse in the melee. Once on the ground the tide of moving bodies swept me along. My eyes focused in on the blue surcoat with golden stars; I pushed toward it dealing blows to the right and left. Before I knew where I was headed, the blue surcoat had disappeared and I found myself at the foot of the gatehouse.

The bottom of a tower is a good place to be as long as there are no archers above. I set my back against the wall and held my ground against all comers. To my left stood a big Englishman with a neck like a bull. He had one eye with a jagged scar across the lid and nothing but the white of the eyeball inside. His shield showed the map of England surrounded by a silver border. A troop of a dozen men or so ranged themselves round about him, and I saw that he must be a baron of some small standing.

The fugitives were frantic now, with passage across the bridge being their only hope of survival. I blocked blow after blow with my shield, slicing at men who came too close or beating them down with the pommel of my sword. "Have at them, boy!" grunted the man with one eye. "Skewer the bastards!" He lunged and panted like a mastiff, snarling all the while out of the corners of his mouth.

The battle was all in our favor. As more and more of our men reached the gatehouse, the sloping banks of the river ran red with blood. "Shall we give them quarter?" I asked, seeing a few Frenchmen fall to their knees with their hands above their head.

"Quarter?" bellowed the big man. "We give no quarter!" He spat as he said this, tripped a fleeing Frenchman, and sliced cleanly through the back of his neck. I shrugged wearily and hitched up my shield, anxious for the butchery to end.

"Sir Thomas!" said a voice from a place above.

"Eh?" said the big man, looking about him in bewilderment. His men shook their heads in confusion. None of them had called his name.

"Sir Thomas!" sang the voice again.

"There, in the tower window!" said I, and a flash of blue and gold peeked out.

"Who knows my name?" bellowed the big man. "Who calls me?"

"It is I, the Comte d'Eu," said the man in blue.

"And I, the Comte de Tancarville," said another voice, slightly higher pitched, from within the recesses of the window."

"You are Sir Thomas Holland, are you not?" said the Comte d'Eu. "We fought with you in Prussia. You were with the Teutonic Order then."

"Aye, in Prussia!" replied Holland, dropping his jaw in amazement. "I recognize your voice. You are Raoul of Brienne. You saved my skin more than once from the infidel."

"And now I'm asking you to save our skins from your infidels," replied the Comte d'Eu, the honored Constable of France. "They seem resolved to slaughter us all without regard for rank or quality. Come up to us in the tower so that we may surrender to you and save ourselves alive. For even prison is better than the dishonorable death that awaits us below."

"It shall be done!" said Holland, saluting the window with exaggerated courtesy. He ordered his men to cut a path to the tower door, and once there to guard the door below while he ascended. "Let no one pass, either French or English. These counts will fetch a pretty penny, and I'll share their ransom with no man."

I watched Sir Thomas Holland bludgeon his way through the crowd till he reached the door of the tower. Then he climbed its uneven stairs to secure his captives while the struggle slowed to a halt on the ground below.

I will not describe in full the remaining efforts we English made to gain Caen, but suffice it to say that the burghers were stubborn and our efforts were considerable. The city was unfortified on the outside, but each house was its own fortress. The door of every home became a barricade, and the upper story a battlement from which women and children could hurl makeshift gunstones. Our men suffered more from the French citizens in the streets than we had from the French soldiery in the field.

In one irate moment, His Majesty stormily ordered that the entire population be put to the sword, but a few choice words from his counselors dissuaded him from this purpose. This grudging clemency, and also the futility of their cause, eventually convinced the citizens to open their doors. The town was plundered with grim determination. The soldiers entered every house, questioned the inhabitants, examined the cupboards, and stripped the walls bare of their trinkets. The king issued a new edict forbidding the citizenry to be harmed, but edicts were not a language that soldiers understood; I heard the screams of many women that day.

Sir Chandos and I scoured the city in the company of the prince. His highness had charge of his own detachment of soldiers, and he sent them systematically through the riverside streets to search each house from top to bottom. The prince always treated the citizenry courteously, but his will was inflexible and he took all that he found despite their pleading. In our company most of the plunder was designated for his highness's coffers. It was no small thing to pay the wages and supply the food of such a large expedition. The prince himself was required to bear the expense of the men levied from his own estates. The forced contributions of the French would defray some expenses.

In one rich burgher's house we came across an ornamental vase, covered in gold and brilliant blue enamel. The rim was scalloped evenly all around like the petals of a flower. The vase was the size of an infant child and just as fragile in its constitution.

"This vase is very old," said Chandos reverentially, "and of Byzantine origin. These French folk must have purchased it from a Crusader."

"It is exquisite," said the prince, and he raised it gently in his hands. "Everything else must go into the common pot, and the merchants will stir it up into money for the men. But this beauty, this I shall keep. She shall be an heirloom in my family, a keepsake of my first campaign."

Our fleet, as I told you, was anchored upstream on the Orne. Glad to hear that we had obtained the town, several ships put in at the docks where they were loaded stem to stern with plunder. The prince had the vase wrapped carefully and sent aboard, and with it the other loot our company had secured. Our takings from the city of Caen were so extensive that the hulls of our ships could barely encompass all the treasure. Edward ordered the fleet back to England to unload the booty. The army spent five days in Caen to make sure we had licked the platter clean, and then we too abandoned the city to continue our eastern march.

The luxurious spoils of Caen whetted our appetite for more. Many hoped that Paris would be our next conquest, but the king, as we learned later, had set his sights north of that on the city of Rouen. We had been in France well over a fortnight now and had yet received no word of French Philip's intentions. He had lain very quietly, waiting like a thrush in the hedge till the hounds pass by. But as we neared *l'Ile de France* and nosed about his nest a little, Philip began to rouse himself.

The first sign we received that Philip had bestirred himself was an embassy from the pope. For over fifty years now, the pope has had his seat at Avignon, and for over fifty years, the English have mistrusted whether Peter's successor still holds the keys. The rock upon which the church was built has sat in Rome for over a millennium, and it cannot be carted over the Alps like a cask of wine or a wheel of cheese. The removal of the papacy to France effected the removal of the pope's independent judgment. Your French pope sits in the French king's pocket, and this our king knows well enough. But though he might wish to, the English king cannot disregard the pope entirely; though his spiritual authority is dubious, his temporal authority is indisputable. An English king who disregarded the mandates of the pope would face the wrath of the Holy Roman Emperor as well as the wrath of France.

Edward received the cardinals courteously and just as courteously refused their offers to broker a peace. Their embassage gained nothing for us but the delay of a day; but for Philip of Valois, this delay was a boon from heaven. Guessing our plan of cutting north, Philip set spurs into the sides of his royal army and reached Rouen before us.

When our scouts realized Philip's position, Edward ordered us to fall back. Our troops numbered just over fifteen thousand and Philip's at least four times that many. The reports of the French strength began to dishearten our men, and the enthusiasm from the sack of Caen disappeared entirely. But although the men had fears, there was no talk of retreat the way we came. We had burned such a wide swath of land in Normandy that there would be no supplying our army on a return march. Only two pathways lay open to us. We could plunder Paris in

Philip's absence, or we could cross the river Somme and unite with our Flemish allies in Picardy.

At first, His Majesty seemed to have settled on the former stratagem. With Philip patrolling the ramparts of Rouen, our army strode southwest, paving a highway of burned fields into Paris. The French army proved as mobile as our own, however, and we had no sooner reached Poissy, on the outskirts of Paris, than we received word that Philip had returned to his capital.

To hunt a lion in his own lair is a dangerous under-taking for the hunter, and Edward was not unmindful of the perils. Paris could not be taken with Philip there. Choosing discretion as the better part of valor, we hur-riedly crossed the Seine and went northward on winged feet. The prospect of uniting with our Flemish friends seemed more and more inviting. But Philip, by now, was accustomed to sniffing at our heels. The Seine was an easy stream for him to leap, and he brought his army northward, dogging our steps for ten days and sending challenge after challenge to bid us turn and fight.

"Think you we will engage the French?" I asked one night as I oiled Chandos's cuirass after a long day's ride.

"Aye," said he, "there's no shaking them. We'll fight them soon enough, but when we do it will be in a place of our own choosing with the advantage on our side."

"We had the advantage of the terrain in Poissy," said I. "That's where the first challenge came. Why didn't His Majesty form battle lines there instead of waiting to wear out our men with these forced marches?"

"There's more to having the advantage than terrain, boy," said Chandos with a knowing grin.

"What else is there?" I asked.

"There's the advantage of knowing you are in the right. That's the advantage His Majesty seeks, and that's why we do not turn to give battle. Not until the Somme is crossed. Then we know we have God's favor—at least that's what Bradwardine, the king's chaplain claims."

"But why should crossing the Somme matter so much?" demanded I. "This whole land of France is the king's by right. We shall prove this with our bodies before heaven and all of Christendom, and the just Judge will look on no matter where the battle is waged. Why should Bradwardine split straws as to location?"

"In truth," said Chandos, "the whole of France does belong to our sovereign by right of inheritance through his mother. God keep the English from having such sickly sons as the French! Their old king, Philip the Fair, had three sons; and all of them died without begetting so much as a halfwit manchild to wear the crown after them. But their sister Isabella, she was more valiant than them all—albeit with the malice of Satan in her breast! She mingled her blood with the Plantagenets, and bore a son the like of which France has never seen. A second David, a second Alexander, a second Julius Caesar! This son, our King Edward, is the only true grandson to the Fair Philip, while this Philip of Valois who claims to own the throne is nothing more than a third cousin of bastard stock. So aye, the whole of France does belong to our Edward.

"But there are many in France who would deny this," continued Chandos. "They say that Isabella's child cannot inherit, and that Philip of Valois has better claim since it lies through the paternal line. They claim that the crown of France cannot pass through the line of a woman—a brazen falsehood as their own annals will bear warrant. But once we cross the river Somme there can be no contest. That county, the county of Ponthieu, belongs to Edward in more ways than one. It was his grandmother's possession. It was his mother's land, and she passed it to him by direct inheritance. Let the lawyers argue away every other county in France, but Ponthieu at least is Edward's. There we will turn to face our adversary, and there may God defend the right!"

It pleased me to know the reason behind our flight, and I wondered how much of this explanation other squires would get from their masters. "We may reach the Somme tomorrow," I remarked, as I finished cleaning Chandos's cuirass. "Think you the prince will follow your advice and make new knights after the battle?"

"Mayhap," said Chandos with a sleepy grunt as he removed his tunic. "But winning the battle is more to the point. There'll be no knighting if the day goes against us. Go to bed now, boy. Sleep sound, fight hard, speak true, and you may yet be a knight if you stay alive."

3

THE PRINCE'S SERVICE
August, 1346

I will pass over our crossing of the Somme in a far shorter time than it took us to pass over. The river which we sought so eagerly almost became our place of battle. Philip's army caught up with us at the ford; for a time Ponthieu seemed unattainable. Arrows filled the air as thick as gnats before the army and the baggage train could reach the other side. Though unwished for, the skirmish at the ford was a valuable experience for our men. The colossal size of Philip's army had intimidated us at first, but now that we had tasted the flavor of Philip's army we found it raw and unseasoned. The archers shot short, the horses ran shy, and the foot soldiers fought little better than the farmhands we had butchered at Caen. Philip's army may have been superior to ours in size, but it was inferior in all else.

"No more running," said Chandos as we entered the undulating hills of Ponthieu. "Now we turn and fight." As usual, Chandos knew the mind of the king. Edward led the army as far as the forest of Crecy and cried halt on a ridge overlooking the valley. It was a well defended spot. The forest and a little brook protected our right flank. The village below the ridge protected our left. From our vantage point we had both a view of Philip's approaching army and the ease of downhill momentum if it came to a charge.

Night approached and the king ordered every man to look to his armor and to his soul. The tents around Crecy were unusually wakeful, owing to the imminence of Philip's arrival. Morning came for most before the sun had risen. Bradwardine, the king's chaplain, recited a special mass for the king and his nobles and offered them communion. The army also heard mass. Following this there was a round of murmured confession such as I have never heard before. The men dredged up all the sins of past and present from the dark recesses of their hearts to receive absolution before the time of peril. They confessed sins from long ago committed against fathers and mothers at home in England; they confessed sins from a month past of theft and rapine perpetrated in France.

My own list of sins, so it seemed, was far less black than the sins of those around me. I could think of few sins to make confession for—a guinea pilfered from Sir Chandos when my own purse had run low, a deliberate lie to cover up my laziness the night I neglected his horse— but my own lack of sins to confess worried me more than a packload of evil. The men around me had lists an ell long of sins both mortal and venial. Perhaps I was forgetting crimes that ought to be confessed. I poked and prodded my memory fearing to die unshriven. A nagging thought arose in me that perhaps I ought to make confession for each guinea or bauble I had extorted, for each terrified fugitive I had cut down in retreat, for each woman's scream that I had heard and ignored. But every time the thought of guilt assailed me, I swallowed it back down my throat like a lump of bread. These were the necessary evils of war, and there was no need for me to make confession of such things.

Whether or not he had finished confession, each man repaired to his place when the alarum sounded. "We are assigned to the prince's body," said Chandos as I fitted him for battle. He extended his arms to the side so that I could fasten the points of his breastplate. With this secured, I placed the pauldron on his shoulder and secured his mail all the way down to his gauntlets.

I was pleased that we were to be bodyguards for his highness. "What division will the prince be in?" I asked as I unfolded the surcoat which would cover Chandos's armor. It was blue, bright blue, the color of a cloudless summer sky. And on the breast of the coat was embroidered an image of the Blessed Virgin surrounded by rays of silver.

"His Highness is the commander of the first division," said Chandos. "He holds the right flank beside the forest and the brook."

"Commander?" asked I in some surprise, for though he was of royal blood, he was still a youth of my own age. He had never taken part in a battle of this magnitude. I wondered that the king should charge his heir with such responsibility—and such risk.

"Commander *in nomine*," said Chandos with a smile. "He has Warwick and others to assist him. The king has charged Audley and me to guard his body as if it were our own."

"And the right flank is best protected," I reasoned, "by virtue of Crecy forest."

"Aye, best protected," agreed Chandos, "but also closest to the Somme. When Philip crossed the river, he'll come our way first; we'll bear the brunt of the attack I'll wager."

"Who leads the other divisions?" I asked.

"The second belongs to the Earls of Northampton and Arundel," replied Chandos. "They're to our left with their withers pressed against the village. And the third belongs to His Majesty. It's to be held in reserve behind the other two companies."

"If we do our duty, we'll not need the king's men," I said spiritedly, trying to boost my own confidence.

When we reached our place on the line, we found that the men had already assumed their positions. The archers, who made up the majority of our company, arranged themselves two or three deep in front of the men-at-arms. There was no shortage of English archers in our expedition to France; King Edward had made sure of that. When he had first laid claim to the crown of France the king sent out edicts to prepare for a future invasion. One edict demanded that all children, whether noble or common, be taught the French language; this ensured that our men-at-arms would be at home in a land with a foreign tongue. Another edict encouraged practice with bow and arrow. The king commissioned shooting games in each shire and awarded prizes to the archer most supremely skilled. Play with the quarter-staff was all but abandoned as the young men bent their backs to string the longbow. Farmers turned foresters, robbing the wild geese of their tail feathers and the wild beasts of their skins. Thanks to Edward's edicts, the men of England had become masters of the longbow, and the muster of archers at Crecy more than doubled the men-at-arms standing behind them.

As the enemy advanced toward us, the longbowmen would exercise all of their skill in bringing them down. When the enemy advanced too far for comfort's sake, the line of archers would split in the center and form two columns on either side of our division. From there they could rake the enemy's flanks while our men-at-arms waited for the French horse to close the distance for hand to hand combat. But it was the French who must close that distance; we would not advance. In front of our line, each man had dug a small pit about as deep and as wide as a man's forearm. The French horses which survived the breast-piercing onslaught of the archers would have to contend with the foreleg-twisting trap of the pits.

The sun was just beginning to ascend into the heavens when we ascended the ridge and found our place beside the prince. Grey clouds were forming in the north; they threatened to blot out the sun and water the land before the day was through. The men-at-arms had all dismounted as instructed; the prince, one of the few solitary figures on horseback, sat tall above the rest. He wore a suit of armor that I had never seen before, black and sharp like polished obsidian. His visor was up and I saw his eyes searching the field like a falcon wheeling above a rabbit warren. It was the same keen expression his face had born in *l'Abbaye-aux-Hommes* when he searched for the Conqueror's tomb.

"They will not be here till at least midday, highness," said the Earl of Warwick in a calm voice. Warwick was twenty years the prince's senior. Accounted one of the best captains in the English army, he had been the king's

Marshall for the past three years. It was on account of this experience that he had been assigned to the prince's division. The prince's pennant with the Plantagenet lion was the largest banner over our company, but Warwick's red pennant with the yellow bar held second place beneath it.

"Since we've time on our hands," said the prince, "let the men sit and serve out something to break their fast. It benefits us nothing to fight on empty stomachs."

"The storm will break on us sooner than Philip does," said Chandos, looking up at the ominous clouds gathering in the north. "We shall all be a good deal wetter before the afternoon is out."

"Highness," said Warwick deferentially, also looking upward at the sky, "when you give the orders to serve out rations, let the archers also look to their bowstrings. A wet bowstring sends a weak arrow."

Shriven, supped, and posted at the ready, the English army waited on the crest of the hill for all of the morning and into the afternoon. The sky sent down fitful showers of summer rain while the lightning and thunder fought their own battle over the territory of the sun. The noise was terrible and a few horses were frightened. "The heavens themselves portend our conflict!" remarked Audley with irony.

When the rain abated, the sun returned in glory, brighter for having been obscured a while. Our army faced east, and the light poured in from behind us; it illuminated the field of battle and shone full in the faces of the advancing foe. Philip and his army of sixty thousand men had arrived at last to do battle on the plains of Ponthieu. From half a mile away, I could pick out their great red-orange standard fixed on a lance and flying overhead. It was the Oriflamme, the battle flag of the French kings. Philip had unearthed it from the vaults of Saint Denis and brought it to Crecy, hoping that its golden stars would shine brightly on the house of Valois and that its tongues of fire would speak victory for the French. I wondered who carried the Oriflamme that day, for only the pick of French chivalry were allowed to touch that hallowed banner.

No sooner had we sighted their troops than the battle began. The French did not advance in any regular order. From the hill opposite, it was difficult to tell whether they had any leadership at all. Our men, on the contrary, were still arranged in tight formation. At one word from the prince, we arose from our seats on the ground, gripped our weapons, and girded up our loins.

"They are disorganized!" said I, and my anxiety at being so grossly outnumbered began to abate a little.

"So is an avalanche," replied Chandos soberly, "but it can still crush whomever it falls upon."

A large company of crossbowmen broke off from the rest of the French army and headed for our ridge at a run. "Here come the Genoese," said Chandos. "The French were always wont to hire their bowmen."

"Best to hire an Italian," boomed Audley, "because a Frenchman always aims crookedly."

"With arrows as well as with words," said Warwick with a laugh.

"Good God, these fellows are excitable!" said Chandos, as we watched the Genoese come forward. They ran across the field in short spurts, using most of their energy to send up a great hooting and howling.

"If bravery was located in the lungs, why then these Italians are the bravest men alive," said the prince.

Again they ran forward and again they stopped to taunt us with their cries. For our part, no man said a word, but each stood silent with hand on sword or arrow on string. They came on a third time, and this time they let loose a volley of arrows as well as a volley of shouts. I saw one or two of our men flinch, but the bulk of the barrage fell short. Not a man fired in response; stoic silence continued to reign across our lines.

"Their bowstrings are wet from the thunder shower," declared Chandos assessing the cause behind the ineffectual volley. The Genoese had halted now in the field, winding their crossbows for further fusillades. The prince looked questioningly at Warwick, and the earl nodded gravely.

"Let the archers stand forward," ordered the prince, and his voice assumed an unusual roughness. "And on my mark, let them fire in unison."

Signals circulated throughout the line, and the company commanders barked out his highness's orders. The archers fired directly on cue, using the full strength of their longbows to put their arrows in flight. I heard men say later that the sky looked like it was filled with snow. The shafts flew so thick that they snuffed out the sun like a candle. The Genoese wore armor on head and breast, but it was as much use to them as a satin doublet.

Our arrowheads pierced through the plate like a tailor's needle through a lady's gown.

The English silence was broken now, not only by the cheers of our archers but also by the thunder of our new engines. The king had brought several cannon from England; we had carted them across Normandy all the way to this battlefield. The engines themselves were metal instead of wood, and when lit on fire they shot great iron balls and sent out a deafening rumble.

The arrows and gunstones did their work. A wail went up from the wounded Genoese, and they tried to exit the field of battle in even more disarray than they had entered it. The French king, however, would not let his mercenaries earn their pay so easily. French horsemen leaped forward impeding the Genoese in their flight and urging them to remember their duty. But soon it became apparent that the crossbowmen had lost all heart; they would not return to the ridge no matter how much urging they received. With swords turned into scythes, the French horsemen began to cut them down. The Genoese, instead of being an asset, were now an obstacle that must be removed.

"Send me a volley into their horse," commanded the prince. The English archers complied. The riot beneath the ridge grew louder as the neighs of stricken steeds combined with the groans of dying men. Philip sent more men into the fray, attempting to overcome the accuracy of our archers with the sheer magnitude of his host. Through unflagging perseverance, several companies of their mounted knights crossed the sea of confusion to reach our lines. Our archers broke ranks immediately and retired to the flank; their arrows were no match for armed riders in such close proximity. Our men-at-arms braced themselves for the onslaught. The hidden pits slowed the French horses down a little, but it was still a thunderous clash when their host met ours in hand to hand combat.

"Montjoy and Saint Denis!" they cried.

"England and Saint George!" was our response. It was well that our archers had felled so many of their knights; we had more than enough to do with the ones who reached us. I laid about me right and left with my sword, fighting frantically to keep the Frenchmen off and to stay near my master's side. Chandos fought more coolly, with his experienced eye trained on the prince all the while.

"God's blood!" roared Sir James Audley, after we had been immersed in the melee for half an hour or more. "This battle presses thicker than marsh fog."

"I can keep near him no longer!" said Chandos, and indeed, the rushing tide of men had swept between us and the prince. His highness was still mounted, but the jet-black brilliance of his armor had dulled to an earthy red. Only a few of our knights kept pace with him as he cut deeper and deeper into the lines of the enemy.

"He's fearless as his father!" cried Chandos, as the prince urged forward his horse to cross swords with a knight twice his girth. In a moment more we could barely see him; our whole company was pushed back and engaged in hard battle.

"Shall we send for help?" demanded Audley.

"What says Warwick?" replied Chandos.

But Warwick was as separated from us as the prince, far to the right of the fray. "Boy!" said Chandos quickly, "Do you see Warwick over yonder?"

"Aye," said I confidently, and pointed him out where he stood.

"Go to him. Ask him how the battle stands from there. And tell him we cannot keep the prince in blade's range of his bodyguard. If he will, bid him send for the second division to come to our aid."

It was no easy matter to reach Warwick. The slope of the hill had liquefied from the rain, the blood, and the heavy trampling. I slipped several times in the mud as I dodged here and there to avoid encountering the enemy. One little man-at-arms gave chase and I was forced to delay my mission to parry his blows. But the mud proved as treacherous to him as it had to me. His legs lost footing and I drove my sword into the joints of his armor, right where the breastplate meets the helmet.

After dispatching this assailant, I looked again for Warwick. I sighted the red pennant with the yellow bar fluttering nearby. But before I could reach it, I heard a familiar bellow and glimpsed the one-eyed bull making the sound. Behind me stood Sir Thomas Holland, the man who had captured the Constable at Caen. His shield hung carelessly in his left hand while he struck out fiercely with his right. I stepped backwards before I was trampled or cut in two. "We are friends!" cried I. "Leave off, man!"

"You are English, boy?" Sir Thomas cried in disbelief. "Sweet mother of God! Then take a stand! All this scurrying about is for mice—or Frenchman. Turn around and fight the enemy, you poltroon!" I understood now that he thought I was trying to flee the field of battle. Seizing me by my collar, he shoved me toward the foe and gave me a hearty kick to the buttocks. I grimaced painfully and choked down rage at this treatment. It was useless to protest—the niceties of my mission would be lost on this baron filled with bloodlust. Unable to explain, I thought it best to escape his custody. I made a half-hearted attempt to engage the enemy before us, keeping Sir Thomas's lumbering form in the corner of my eye. He turned to engage a mounted knight, and they grappled together in the mud. Once I saw that he could no longer bother me, I took to my heels again. This time I reached the red pennant with the yellow bar.

The Earl of Warwick was panting heavily when I overtook him; the company surrounding him looked weary and bedraggled. I recited my master's message bidding him wind the horn to summon the second division. .

"The second division is already with us!" he exclaimed, and he gestured further down the line to where the earls of Northampton and Arundel had joined the fray. The battlefield here looked much the same as the patch of ground I had come from. The French pushed against us strongly while our men fought back fiercely, summoning up valiant vigor from weary limbs. Warwick's countenance, instead of bearing its normal, placid composure, looked harried as a housewife with unexpected guests. "There's no help for it," he said. "We must send to the king." I waited by his side while he sent one of his knights to discover Edward and desire his aid. I was still waiting by his side when the knight returned, alone and unabashed.

"How comes this?" demanded Warwick. "Did you find His Majesty? And did you deliver my message?"

"I found him on the northern prospect beside a windmill," said the knight, "and in truth, I gave him your message most plainly. 'Sir,' said I, 'The Earl of Warwick and the others who surround your son are vigorously attacked by the French. They beg you to come to their assistance with your battalion. If numbers should increase against the prince, he will have too much to handle.'"

"And what answer made the king?" said Warwick.

"He answered this: 'Is my son dead, unhorsed, or so badly wounded that he cannot support himself?'

"'By no means,' replied I, 'Thank God! But he is in so hot an engagement that he has great need of your help.'

"Then the king fixed his eye on me sternly, and said, 'Return to those that sent you. Tell them not to send again whatever may happen, and not to expect that I shall come as long as my son has life. I command them to let the boy win his spurs. God willing, I am determined that all the glory of this day shall belong to him and to those who are in charge of his care.'"

At the relation of these words, Warwick's eyes glinted brightly and I saw his soul stir within him. "His Majesty is right," said he. "This day belongs to the prince and to us. What need have we of help? Return to your master, boy," he said to me, "and bid him stand fast and cleave unto his charge."

This refusal on the part of the king to send aid dismayed me at first, but it was not long before I saw the wisdom of it. From his vantage point beside the windmill, the king had judged the battle more accurately than those down in the thick of it. The enemy's strength had begun to ebb. The victory was ours; we had only to claim it. I looked about the battlefield until I spotted the Virgin Mary, embowered in blue on the surcoat of Sir John Chandos. He had regained his position beside the prince, and I darted through devious paths to rejoin them.

"They are turning!" cried Chandos. "By St. George, they are turning!" It was even as he said. The French knights had taken to their heels, for few of them had horses left to ride, and were beating the same ignominious retreat for which they had earlier punished the Genoese. Our archers, who had formed up on the flanks of our army, began to ply their skill once more. It was a rout, a total rout, and Philip recognized it. Instead of castigating his fleeing troops, he ordered the orange Oriflamme furled. The great banner disappeared from view, and we heard the lugubrious horns of France sounding a retreat. The day was lost for Valois.

But as the French companies and commanders left the battlefield in such haste, a strange sight met our eyes. Five enemy knights, undeterred by the general retreat, were riding toward our lines. Four of them had arranged themselves in a square, and their horses were attached with ropes to the bridle and trappings of the fifth horse which rode in the middle. Tethered as he was to the others, the rider of the middle horse did not need to hold the reins of his own horse to guide it. Both of his hands gripped a great broadsword, and though he bobbed a bit unsteadily, he managed to keep his saddle. Upon his helmet he wore a crown and a plume of three white feathers. These same feathers were painted on the shield that hung at his side, and beneath them was a motto, though I could not make out the words.

The prince and all of us about him looked on in amazement to see this strange company advance upon us. "What foolhardiness is this?" exclaimed Audley. "Do they not know that the battle is as good as over?"

"If I mistake not the crest," said Chandos, "it is John, the king of Bohemia. Our scouts spoke true when they said that many Germans had come to help Valois against us."

The Bohemian king and his strange bodyguards continued to advance picking their path carefully through the bodies that littered the field. In one uneven place, the horses stumbled over a hollow in the ground. The king nearly lost his seat until the riders reached out and steadied him in his saddle.

"Why does he ride thus?" I asked, looking perplexedly at the ropes that bound the central rider to his companions. Chandos shrugged and Audley turned away. The prince alone responded to my question.

"He is old and he is blind. That is why they lead him thus. But his spirit is not as shrunken as his body. He has sworn to serve Philip in battle against us, and eyes or no, he will strike a few blows for honor's sake. He is a brave man, this king. It is my wish and express order that he not be harmed."

But even as he spoke, a flock of arrows arched heavenward and descended on the handful of Bohemians. Their wounded horses neighed and fell. The blind Bohemian king went down like a great cedar tree when an ax is put to its roots.

The prince uttered a little cry; I sprang forward instinctively. "He is still alive!" said I, but I had not reckoned with the Welshmen.

Wales, as you may know, fell into English hands in the reign of the first Edward, the grandfather to our present sovereign. Edward made Wales English by an act of violence, and the Welshmen in our army are a particularly violent breed. They fight for England now, but the bitter edge of their spirit is as keen as the long knives they carry. In battle, they run amidst the enemy's horses striking upward with quick thrusts. When the battle is strewn with fallen knights, they run among them and cut their throats. Many French nobles were finished this way at Crecy, and we lost more than a dozen ransoms from the rancorous rapacity of our Welsh brethren.

When the Bohemian king was felled by the archers, I immediately ran forward to succor him. The prince, who was mounted, arrived there ahead of me, but the Welshmen had been there even before him. The blind king lay motionless on the ground, his heart pierced by a Welsh knife through the armhole of his corslet. His hands still gripped the broadsword; the bridle of his horse was still tethered to the horses fallen around him.

"Here lies a noble lord," said the prince as I came up beside him.

We were not the only Englishmen on the battlefield. All around us, our archers and men-at-arms had begun to loot the bodies of the French dead. A swarthy young fellow darted in among the Bohemian king's retinue and began to strip off valuables like a tanner skinning a dead animal.

"Have a care, you!" cried I as the looter began to root around the fallen king's corpse. I sprang forward and cuffed the man. He would have traded blows with me, but he saw the company I kept and resigned himself to cursing before he slunk away. My blow had knocked his plunder from his hands; on the ground I saw the plumed ostrich feathers that had erstwhile crowned the Bohemian's head. I picked them up.

"Highness," said I, and I fell on one knee before the prince. "The spoils of the fallen belong to the victor."

The prince dismounted and took the feathers in his gloved hand. He looked them over with reverence. "I take them not as spoils but as inheritance, for I will honor these feathers as surely as if mine own father had bequeathed them to me. What says the motto on his shield?"

"*Ich dien*," said I, sounding out the German with some difficulty.

"*Ich dien*," repeated the prince. "*I serve*. Old and eyeless he was, yet he served his master well and performed his duty. My sight remains, and I can only hope to serve as bravely as he. *Ich dien*. It shall be my motto henceforth."

He looked at me, still kneeling. "And you," said he, "You serve Sir John Chandos, do you not?"

"Aye, highness," said I. "I am his squire."

"What is your name?"

"John Potenhale."

"Then," said he, drawing his sword, "rise *Sir* John Potenhale, knight of England and—with your master's permission—knight of my own household."

"He has that permission," said a clear voice. Glancing behind me, I saw that Chandos had come up behind us on the battlefield. Chandos gave me a friendly nod and I saw that he did not in the least begrudge the good fortune that had befallen me. I smiled gratefully at my old master in wordless thanksgiving for all his years of patronage. Then I turned my eyes to my new master, eager to do him some service.

"Well then, Sir Potenhale," said the prince with a smile, "you are mine to command. And the first act of service I demand from you is to order prayers to be offered by all of our men in the field. Instruct them to give thanks to the Holy Trinity, for the victory we won today was not through our own strength. And when you have done this, find my father the king. Tell him the enemy is fled, the battle is won, and I await his further instructions."

Both the precociousness of my knighting and my entrance into the prince's household were wholly unexpected events for one of my station. I was not born a nobleman. My father was a man-at-arms with no great estate; my mother had been waiting woman to a lady, but she was a steward's daughter and unendowed to boot.

But though my ancestors were not knights, our family had martial blood in its veins. My grandfather had lost his life fighting against the Scots; my father had lost his leg fighting against the French. My father's name was William Potenhale. The limb under discussion was severed at Sluys, the first great battle our king waged against

Philip. My father was boarding the French flagship when it happened. The enemy was intent on boarding as well, and the iron grappling hook they tossed aboard the English vessel pinned his leg to the rail. The leg was mangled beyond repair, and it was a marvel that he lived when the surgeon removed it. He returned home crippled in body and cramped in soul. The battlefield was in his blood, but no noble would take a maimed man into their garrison or regiment.

With the sword his only skill, my one-legged father was forced to lean on his wife's relations. My mother's people were from Herefordshire; we moved there and tenanted a small croft that my mother's father had stewardship over. I was ten years old at the time, old enough to work the fields like any serf or hired plow hand. I swung a scythe at harvest time and sweated among the hay ricks. Sometimes, my grandfather brought me with him when he administered the lands of the estate. Sometimes, he took me to the manor house when he surveyed the rent rolls. The landowner himself was rarely present. My grandfather told me that the master was too great a man to stay long on his estates. The king demanded his attendance and so he traveled around the England with the transient royal household, only stopping in Hertfordshire when the court came close.

My father, too crippled to follow the plow himself, raged against this activity on my part. "You'll make the boy unfit for anything but field labor," he complained to my grandfather. Even though the hammer of war had broken his own body, he had no desire for me to be anything else but a soldier. With me, the line of Potenhale warriors must continue or become extinct. "He must learn to swing a sword, not a scythe. His arm must heft a shield, not a bag of meal."

At evening time, when the day's labor had concluded, my father would hobble out of doors with me. There he would bid me strike with a wooden blade at a fence post, as the squires do on the wooden pels of the practice yard. "Strike harder!" said he. "From beneath! Now turn about!" My mother would watch from the door of the house, small wrinkles forming in her brow. Women never feel the stirrings of the march in their breast or the call of the trumpet in their soul. She had seen what a life of arms had brought to my father, and though she never spoke it, she hoped I might someday become a steward in my grandfather's footsteps.

One summer's day, when I had reached my twelfth year, my grandfather brought news that the owner of the estate had returned for a few short days. My father looked at him sharply, and in cryptic language said, "Now God be praised! The boy is of age now, Thomas,"—for Thomas was the name of my grandfather—"and what better time to put him forward than the one at hand?"

My grandfather frowned a little and rubbed his wizened forehead. "I have said that I will ask, but the request is a great one and unlikely to be granted. You are not of noble blood. Your father was no knight. What call should my master have to take in your son?"

"Well were you named Thomas," replied my father fiercely, "for you do nothing but doubt when the way is laid out plain in front of you. Aye, I am no nobleman, but your master was no nobleman himself. He was knighted for his worth and not his name, and so too will be my son." He turned to me. "Boy, ready yourself! Your grandfather is taking you to the manor house, and if God be willing, you shall not come back here again."

The landowner was in his prayers when we arrived. I remember the stoop of his broad shoulders before the image of the Blessed Virgin on the altar. The dust of travel still coated him but it could not dim the bright blue of his surcoat or the silver face that shone upon it. "Ah, Thomas!" the master said when he had arisen. "It does me good to see your face. The tenants are as quiet and the house as orderly as I could ask. You have done your work well in my absence."

"Sir John," said my grandfather humbly. "I am glad that my work finds favor in your eyes, for I come before you to beg a boon."

"Speak it," replied the master.

In short, halting words, my grandfather humbly beseeched that I might enter the house as a page, be trained in service later as a squire, and someday—if the Holy Trinity willed it—become a knight. Then, before Sir John could muster any objections to receiving me, my nervous grandfather nearly buried his request with a pile of them. "The boy has his wits about him, but he's none too clever. He works hard, but he's awkward and clumsy to boot. His father was a fighting man before he lost his leg, but there's not a drop of noble blood in his veins or the boy's."

"Thomas, Thomas," interrupted his master with a broad smile, "It is well that you are no merchant, for a seller should not decry his own wares. I am the buyer here. Let me be the judge of the lad.

"Come here, boy," he said, addressing me. Forward I came, head lowered and jaw clenched like a servant expecting to be beaten. "What is your name?" he demanded.

"John Potenhale," I answered gruffly. I peered up through my eyebrows to see a kindly face, ringed with grey around the temples. His black beard had a touch of silver and so did his voice.

"John Potenhale, do you want to enter my service?" asked the lord of the estate.

"Aye," said I, but it came out harsh and forced for my mouth was as dry as sand from Araby.

"Can you fight?" he asked.

"A little," said I remembering the wooden fence posts and my father's instruction.

"Can you read?"

"A little," said I for my mother had taught me my letters.

"Can you pray?"

I looked up in surprise and stared him full in the eye. "Aye, I can pray right well."

"That is good," said Sir John, "for however well you wield the sword or however well you trim your pen, it is the favor of heaven that will prevail. Perhaps you have the makings of a knight in you." He turned to my grandfather. "Very well, Thomas. I will take him as a page. If he proves apt, he may go further."

"Gramercy for your kindness," said my grandfather in utter astonishment at the success of his mission.

Sir John bade me remove to the manor immediately and gave me into the charge of his lady wife. I had left little behind at my parents' croft save a tunic, a dagger, and a pair of shoes. My grandfather brought my small bundle to the house and bid me adieu. When I would have thanked him for the place he had got me, he shook his head. "Nay, no thanks to me. It is your father who deserves the thanks, for I would not have importuned Sir John if your father had not importuned me so frequently. 'Ask, ask!' he says, and 'No, no,' say I, till at last my resistance wears through like a padlock beset by a file. If I had my will, you would be steward after me, for I have no sons of my own to take my place. But your father's will is stronger than my own; and he has the right of it to send you where he pleases, for the duty of a son is to serve the will of his father."

With these words, my grandfather left me. I would see him again a few short times, but his days in Herefordshire were numbered and death came on swiftly the following winter. My own days in Herefordshire were shorter than his; Sir John Chandos was not one to linger in the countryside when the king's court had entered the city. I traveled to London with his household when he went thither to wait on Edward.

The cautions my grandfather had delivered concerning my dullness and ineptitude proved but little true. I learned quickly and eagerly the duties pertaining to a page. Sir John's lady took a liking to me; she was a stately woman with no children of her own. She took me in hand and remedied the churlish manners of my upbringing. She was one of the most learned ladies I have ever known. In two years' time, she taught me to read in my own tongue, the tongue of the French, and the tongue of the Church.

You may know that in our country, the English tongue is used by the common folk, French is the speech of castle and court, and Latin is the language of the monks and scholars. A knight must know all three languages: Latin, for how else would he confer with God's servants? French, for how else would he speak with other knights? English, for how else would he command his serfs and the lower men-at-arms? And besides all this, the king threatens every year to change the language of Parliament to the English tongue, for he likes it not that the governance of England must be discussed and debated in the tongue of our enemy.

With my tongue trained in courtesy and cant, I was ready to exercise the rest of my body in arms. Sir John allowed me to join the ranks of his squires. The practice yards were my new schoolroom, and I learned the sword, the axe, the mace, the halberd, and the lance. At times, Sir John sparred with me himself, but for the most part my matches were with fellow squires under the supervision of a grizzled, old master-at-arms. I came into my strength early and was broader by a span than the rest of the squires my age. By the time that Edward assembled his invasion force, I had become squire of the body to Sir John Chandos. Someday, I hoped to receive the accolade, but I had never dared hope that it would come from the hand of the prince.

4

THE IMPREGNABLE FORTRESS
September – December, 1346

The Sunday following Crecy's battle we spent in reckoning up the dead. The day after that we spent in burying them. The count of the dead was prodigiously in our favor; for every twenty Frenchmen, there was only one English corpse. The king congratulated the prince on the victory and commended him on the choice of his new crest. "A fitting motto," said the king, "for you have served me well this day."

The prince accepted the praise calmly, but I saw that he was remarkably free from elation. I questioned him about this later when we retired to our tents. "Highness," said I diffidently, still overawed by my new position of familiarity with the prince, "How comes it that you are not more glad of this victory?"

He trained his dark eyes on me. "I am as glad as any Englishman," he replied.

"But why not gladder," asked I, "since you had the command of such a victorious enterprise?"

"The command?" he asked arching an eyebrow in disbelief. "Who picked our battle ground?" said he. "Who composed our divisions? Who devised our for-

mation and defenses? Who sent and withheld reinforcements when the battle was finally joined?"

"The king," said I slowly. I realized now how little
the prince had to do with the direction of the battle.

"And therefore I am as glad as any Englishman,"
said the prince simply. He snuffed out the candles and
retired to his bed, less happy in commanding a victory
that would astonish Europe than I in my newfound belt
and spurs.

In my service to my new master, I still had frequent
opportunity for conversation with my old master; Sir
Chandos was never far from the prince's person. "God
be praised, boy," said Chandos kindly. "You've earned
the accolade younger than I." His graying beard wagged
as he reminisced about the winning of his spurs.

"It was not such a glorious time for England in those
days," said the grizzled knight. The Scots had beaten us
at Bannockburn and declared their independence. And
while Isabella and Mortimer were conniving to take the
throne, they swept over our border and laid waste to
the North. The Bruce and his highland robbers took
full advantage of our weakness. Our king was imprisoned—or dead—no one knew which. Young Edward
had been given the crown, but it was Mortimer who
gave all the commands. The English captains did not
trust him, and we could not hold the line against the
Scots. The Bruce forced England to fall to her knees
and come to most humiliating terms. Mortimer handed
young Edward the pen, and he signed away his rights to
the crown of Scotland. That was at Northampton. And
it was in such a time, at that ignominious treaty, that I
received the accolade."

"But you, boy," continued Chandos, "you've come into your knighthood when England blooms her brightest. Children yet unborn shall talk about the feats done at Crecy's battle by the Prince of Wales and his doughty band. And to be knighted by the prince himself—methinks you were born under a lucky star."

"The prince himself takes no credit for the victory," said I, and I recounted to Chandos how the prince disparaged his own role in the battle.

Chandos nodded knowingly and little lines of laughter appeared around his mouth. "That is like a Plantagenet," said he, "Both to desire the sole command of the enterprise and to dismiss any undeserved adulation. They will not abide flattery, even though the truth be unfavorable to them. There is a story about the first Edward that illustrates the character of that family.

"They say that a Florentine farmer once conceived the plan of visiting King Edward, for he had heard that the King of England was the greatest, most magnificent monarch in all the world. He sold all that he had for the journey. He traveled far, and he traveled long, till he came at last to the shores of England and found Edward sitting in his court and playing a game of chess. The weary Florentine fell on his knees before the king and poured out these words: 'Blessings on the hour and moment that led me here, so I could see the most noble, prudent, and valorous king in Christianity! I count myself more fortunate than any of my peers now that I am here where I can see the flower of kings. If I were to die now, I could face it without much sorrow, because I am standing before that most illustrious crown which attracts all men, as a magnet attracts iron, to view its dignity.'

"The king, hearing this panegyric, leaped up from his chair and took hold of the farmer from Florence. Without a word, he threw him to the floor and showered him with so many kicks and punches that the poor man was black and blue. Then the king returned to his chess game. The wretched farmer, meanwhile, began to think that his entire journey had been wasted. 'O miserable day!' he groaned aloud. 'Curses on the ill-conceived plan that brought me to this place. I thought to see a noble king, but instead I see an ungrateful, unappreciative one, a king filled with vices instead of virtues, a man who returns bad for good. When I lauded and honored him, he beat me so harshly that I do not know whether I will ever have the strength to till my fields again.'

"The king heard these denunciations and rose from his chair. The farmer trembled violently, for if the king had beaten him for speaking well of him, how much more would he harm him for speaking evil? But the king, instead of laying a hand upon the Florentine, called instead for one of his nobles and ordered him to bring a robe of costly fabric. 'Go,' said the king. 'Lay this rich garment on the shoulders of that man in return for his true words, for I have given him a rich beating in return for his false ones.'

"The Florentine farmer, still trembling, received the robe, and when he returned home he showed it proudly to all—a reminder that the Plantagenets value truth over obsequious truckling."

"I will bear this tale in mind," I said appreciatively, for I desired to keep the goodwill of the prince and advance in his regard if I could.

◆ ◆ ◆

The spades had no sooner turned earth over the corpses at Crecy than Edward gave orders for the army to march. Our way was already set. We had humbled the hamlets of La Hougue and sacked the city of Caen, but these had been taken merely because they were in our path; Edward had held no special enmity towards them. There was another city, however, which Edward loathed and longed to lay low. Toward that city we now turned our face. We traveled northwest by easy stages, burning and plundering as we proceeded, till we came at last to our destination—Calais.

Calais is a city seated on the threshold of the sea. The salty waters of the channel lap at her gates, and the sea birds nestle in her crenelated ramparts. She is close to England; on a clear-skied day a clear-eyed man might glimpse the cliffs of Dover from atop her walls. She is also close to Flanders. If we could occupy this outpost, we would have easy access to our Flemish allies.

But although Calais's strategic location played a part in the king's decision to take her, another motive weighed heavier in his thoughts. Calais was a poison-tipped thorn. She jutted out from the coast like a cunning nettle, and our vessels could never sail close to her waters without being scratched. Untold numbers of English ships had lost their cargoes to the rapacious pirates that holed up in this den. Edward hated Calais, and his hatred was stocked with so powerful a fuel that it kept alight for the many months it took to achieve the city.

If you have been to Calais, you know that it is a heavily fortified town. On the north side of the city is the sea; the three remaining sides discourage attack with two water-filled moats. From the tremendous height of Calais's walls—double-ringed and as impregnable as the virtue of Diana—the haughty inhabitants stare down at you. They say that Julius Caesar built these walls; if so, then they are well worthy of his illustrious memory, for it was not till a year after we came and saw them that we were finally able to conquer them.

Upon our arrival at Calais, Edward summoned a council of war. The nobles discussed various methods of taking the town and then dismissed them each in turn. The height of the walls precluded any attempt to scale them, and indeed, his majesty was loath to waste men on such an unpromising enterprise. We had the means of erecting siege engines, but some doubted whether the marshy ground surrounding Calais was firm enough to support them. This maleficent marsh also forestalled any hope of tunneling underneath the walls. Only one course of action lay open to us; we must starve the city into submission.

Deliberately and methodically, Edward encompassed the landward side of Calais with troops and a palisade. On the harbor side of the city, he created a rampart of English ships, a "wooden wall" like that of Themistocles. There would be no going in or out. Calais was shut up on all sides like a fox which has gone to ground.

We had lain there no longer than a month when word arose that Philip of Valois had regrouped his humiliated army and planned to descend upon us and raise the siege. He had brought sixty thousand men to face us at Crecy. Men said he had doubled that number to raise the siege of Calais.

As rumors ran rampant and estimates of the approaching army grew higher and higher, our own numbers dwindled. The yearlong contract that bound many of the men-at-arms had run its course. More must be pressed into service. His Majesty sent to England commanding a levy of a thousand men. The prince himself demanded that a company of two hundred be sent from his Welsh estates. New companies of men swelled our ranks, and the camp outside Calais grew larger. "English Calais," the men were beginning to call it, for indeed our tents presented the appearance of a small town. Life in our camp was much like living in a provincial town, for though a few soldiers were employed in foraging or patrolling, the rest had nothing to do but eat, sleep, drink, play at dice, and wait.

Though the English soldiers outside Calais sat idle, the English soldiers back home were busy enough, especially those in the north. "The Scots are rattling their spears again," said the prince to me one day, after having spent several hours in conference with the king. "They've swept over the border into Northumbria, looting and pillaging."

"I thought your father had secured peace with King David before we left," said I.

"Aye," replied the prince, "but Philip's convinced him to break the treaty. France has but to snap her fingers and Scotland will dance. No one ever accused the Bruces of being too trustworthy. Their word is as light as a feather when they can feather their own nests."

"Will we give up the siege and return home?" I asked, unsure whether this new development would curtail our stay at Calais.

"Indeed, I daresay Philip hopes as much," said the prince. "But I think we will disappoint him if we can. An absent Edward does not mean a helpless England. My father has commanders in Northumbria who will meet the Scots foot to foot, and—God being our helper—we will have the Bruce begging for terms by Michaelmas."

The prince's trust in the Northumbrian commanders proved to be well founded. The Scots received a sound drubbing and retired in disgrace over the border while Edward quaffed wine in his tents outside Calais. The diversion had failed. If Philip wanted Edward to budge from France, he must come in person to drive him away.

November came and went, and still the fabled French force did not materialize at Calais. Other visitors besides our new recruits crossed the channel to enlarge our camp. Queen Philippa, weary of her husband's absence, joined us, bringing with her a court of ladies-in-waiting. With the advent of these ladies, the lavish pavilions which housed the king and his nobles became more lavish still. The tent town became even more town-like, as knights and ladies paid visits and entertained each other with fetes and parties.

For the French inside the walls, however, fare had become frugal. Philip's failure to succor the town gave the governor there cause for grave concern. News trickled out to us that the citizens had begun to ration their supplies.

One morning, late in the year, the prince and I were riding in tandem along the palisade. He was seeking his father, to report the success of the foraging party that had just returned. I sighted the king half a furlong ahead holding parlance with Sir Walter Manny. The blue and red of Edward's jupon flamed brightly in the gray morning. Manny, attired in the more subdued raiment of gold and sable, still stood out sharply in the brown landscape. I thanked the Lord that the French archers were little wiser than scullery maids, for if English archers had held those walls, they would have fired straightway upon such promising targets.

As we drew near to the king, the prince suddenly reined in his horse. His eyes fixed on the distant city like an eagle's eye upon a rabbit. "Potenhale," he said suddenly. "If my eyes do not deceive me, yon gate is opening at last." We stared through the mist—for it was a wet morning—at the surrounded city. As he had said, the gate was opening, and a herd of cloaked figures stepped slowly outside. They were not soldiers, for there was nothing martial in their bearing. From the size of them, I could see that many must be children.

"What means it?" asked I in astonishment. "Do they surrender?"

"Nay," said Sir Walter Manny, for he had heard my question. He fingered his long mustache with an ungloved hand. "See, the gates are closing behind them." We stood silent for a minute and watched the unsteady procession wending toward us like a crowd of lepers.

"Ha!" said the king, and he clapped his hands savagely. "Here come their weak, their women, and their worthless ones. Their governor has turned them out."

"Aye, sire," said Manny with a grin. "What further sign do we need? They've run short of food at last."

The bedraggled band came nearer. The figures in the mist began to take on clear forms. Many of them were women. Some held wrapped bundles in their arms, and from the faint wails that penetrated the mist, I surmised that they were holding their infants. Here and there, old men leaned upon sticks, with crooked arms too withered to hold a sword. They were too weak to defend a wall and so the walls refused to defend them.

What would become of them? The faces of the young girls took on a white pallor as they approached our lines, and they pulled their cloaks around themselves tightly.

"The enemy has come out to us at last," the prince said with gentle irony. "Shall we give battle or allow them to pass through our ranks?"

"Let them pass, let them pass!" said the king with a smile. "What harm can these poor folk do?" The expulsion of these town folk had cheered him like the first break of sunlight after the gloom of a storm. He was disposed to be generous.

"Part ranks!" shouted Manny, as he galloped toward the palisade. The soldiers made a gap for the now-homeless French folk to pass through. Their departure augured well for the siege; the hour was surely at hand when the famine in Calais's belly would gnaw through the ties that bound her to Philip.

"We shall hold Christmas in Calais!" said the king, and when the army heard of his words, they gave three cheers for His Majesty's soon-to-be triumph. But like so many of our fondest hopes, this prediction fell afoul of fate. His Majesty's Christmas was to be spent in the field. There were still many months to come before Calais would capitulate.

◆ ◆ ◆

The prolonged camping at Calais threw the men together in far closer quarters than they had been during our march across France; the enforced idleness of the siege magnified petty disputes. Tempers began to rub raw like a horse which has been too long in saddle.

It took some time before I felt the oppression of the ceaseless siege. At first, the excitement I had at joining the prince's household colored the whole world with leaf of gold. As a belted knight, I was no longer the invisible squire that merely fetches, carries, and curries the horses. I attended the prince wherever he went and, although I was still a subordinate, could converse on easy terms with his coterie of friends. William Montague, the earl of Salisbury, was a general favorite with the prince and could always be counted upon for a game of backgammon. Roger Mortimer was a particular friend of Salisbury's and though he lacked the bonhomie of the earl he had a sharper mind for debate. And then there was Sir Bernard Brocas, the curly-haired jester of the group. He never failed to make the prince laugh or amuse him out of his fits of seriousness. Besides these three, there were others that surrounded the prince. Sir John Chandos and Sir James Audley brought their graying heads to the prince's table, and the king himself occasionally supped with his offspring.

There were a few men, however, who were not welcome at the prince's table. Of these, Sir Thomas Holland was one. I had not been raised near the court, and it was no easy matter for me to distinguish between men who were great and men who merely wished to be. The difference between deserved dignity and odious pretension was, for the most part, lost on me. Yet, even I could see that Thomas Holland had grown overbold since his capture of the Comte d'Eu and the Comte de Tancarville at Caen. The clink of golden ransom in his purse had procured for him a fortune far higher than that to which he was born; and the adulation for this feat had worked on him like heady wine.

Holland was a big, bluff man, some twenty years older than I. He was coarse of feature and expression—though many women found him handsome and artful enough. His father had been a baron in Lancashire, beheaded during the tumultuous reign of the second Edward. Holland himself was a belted knight and in younger days had seen battle near the Euxine Sea. It was there that he had gained the scar that cut across his brow and had lost the sight of his left eye.

When he returned from the east, Holland sought employment as seneschal to the Earl of Salisbury. Here he was competent. But his days with the Teutonic knights had whetted his taste for battle, and this avocation for violence could not be satisfied in the managing of meadows, manors, and rent rolls. When King Edward made his first sortie into Flanders, Holland enlisted with drawn sword. When King Edward engaged the French at Sluys, Holland thrust and parried aboard ship. And when King Edward turned to fight the enemy at Crecy, Holland commanded a company in the prince's division.

Embroidered with Holland's colorful storytelling, his capture of the French Constable at Caen had become the stuff of legend. He had cornered the two counts outside the gatehouse and chased them up the stairs of an enemy tower. A battalion of French archers rained down arrows from up above, but he had brushed their shafts aside like drops of water and continued the pursuit. When he reached the landing at the top of the tower, they had both turned on him like lions. Two of the mightiest knights in France—or the world for that matter—had encountered him with drawn sword. But Holland was undaunted! A second Roland was he! Blow for blow he met them, turning their swords like a mighty anvil, till at last he forced them to their knees. Then they pleaded for their lives—like runaway serfs begging not to be returned to their master. And Holland being a merciful man did not put them to death as they deserved, but instead, brought them before his lord and master King Edward.

So spread the story of Holland's fantastic feat. The Constable could have disproved the story had he seen fit, but he only shrugged generously and allowed Holland to have his glory. Many thought Holland's newfound swagger to be as savory as a mouthful of sand. Of these, William Montague was one—Montague who treated the whole world as a friend and yet found no friendship in his heart for Holland. The earl had grown to manhood with Holland as his father's steward, and it liked him not that Holland should salute him now as an equal. "God's life!" I heard him mutter to the prince, "How much better for all of us if this fellow had been taken by the Comte d'Eu instead of the Comte by him."

The prince himself treated Holland with a cold courtesy. It was meet that prowess be honored but unsuitable that pretension be humored. One day as we rode outside the walls of Calais, looking for any sign of weakness, Holland came alongside the prince and saluted him.

"God give you good morning," replied the prince with a curt nod. He would have ridden on, but Holland urged his horse forward to have speech with him.

"Your highness played the man right valiantly in Ponthieu," said Holland in an avuncular tone. I had been but newly admitted into the prince's retinue, but I bridled at the sound of such familiarity. "You fought like a bonny lad, and I was right proud," continued Holland. "God knows that this campaign has been the making of both of us."

"It may have made you, sir," said the prince coolly, "but it has made me nothing other than what I was born to be." His beardless chin jutted out with indomitable defiance, and the hauteur of his bearing compensated for the sinews that his youth yet lacked. Holland flushed angrily, and his horse fell back into line beside me. I rejoiced in his confusion, and adopting my master's demeanor, shot a frosty glance at him.

"The Prince of Wales is a right haughty lord," Holland observed. I could see that he did not remember me from Caen or Crecy, and knew me only as the prince's attendant. To him, I was but a newly belted knight of obscure origins.

"And well he should be," said I sharply. "Not only is he heir of both England and France, but he has also proven himself the most puissant knight of the realm. You call him haughty, but he has good reason."

"If he has good reason," Holland quipped, "then why does he keep a churl like you about his person? Answer me that!"

My face flamed hot, for I knew well how clumsy and unfit I was for his highness's service. "As to that, I cannot answer, for the prince chooses whom he will and takes whom he desires."

"Does he indeed?" mocked Holland. "It is a fortunate man that can choose whomever he will. The prince, I think is not so fortunate—at least not in the matter of women. I'll wager that there's one there he desires that he cannot take."

The prince had never spoken to me of the fairer sex, and I knew not whether Holland was speaking from certain knowledge or simply throwing darts at random. I was inclined to think the latter. "Methinks your words are something too insolent," I replied hotly.

"Softly, softly, young sir," said Holland, in a voice calculated to incite me further.

I swallowed hard, trying to keep my wrath inside of me. Images fluttered in my mind like washing hung on a line. I remembered standing side by side with Holland with my back against the tower while the Frenchmen shouted to him from above. "Softly?" asked I. "Softly, you say? As soft as the blows you delivered at Caen when the Comte d'Eu yielded before your mighty prowess? Aye, you were a rare paragon of valor that day, when you strove so doughtily to climb a set of stairs and receive the surrender of two of the best knights in Christendom!"

"Insolent pup!" cried Holland, and he would have sprung at me had the prince not been so near. I half-regretted my words as soon as they left my lips. For though the French counts had rolled into Holland's hands like ripe berries from a bush, that was not to say that he would have gone to no trouble to obtain them. Whatever else Holland might be—rude, belligerent, and self-serving—he was not in the least cowardly.

"Have a care, Potenhale," said Holland, crowding my horse with his own and snarling through clenched teeth. And with that he pulled away, leaving my anger to age and ferment like wine in oaken barrels.

◆ ◆ ◆

Fortunately for me, I soon found pleasanter thoughts to dwell on than my rancor at Sir Thomas Holland—for what could hold more pleasure than thoughts of a beautiful woman? Among the ladies that had crossed over from England in Queen Philippa's company was Joan of Kent. She has a part to play in my tale, so it is necessary that I should tell you somewhat of her ancestry and upbringing.

Joan was a granddaughter of the first Edward, and thus a cousin to our own king. Her father was Edmund of Kent. He had remained faithful to his unfortunate half brother, the second Edward, when most of the nobles had decamped to Edward's wife Isabella. That French she-wolf, along with her lover Mortimer, soon contrived to rid the world of her husband.

It was through Isabella that Joan's father Edmund also met his end. First, she imprisoned him claiming that he disbelieved in his brother's death and was plotting to restore him to the throne. Then she ordered his execution. Edmund was beloved, however, and none besides the queen wished him dead. For five hours he waited at the block because no one would handle the axe to be his executioner. Isabella raged and cursed but still no one would cut off Edmund's head. At last, she sent to the Tower for a convicted murderer, and, in return for a pardon, he agreed to sever the head of her brother-in-law Edmund. Little did she know that in less than a year's time, her own son would ask her to answer for the deaths of his father and his uncle.

All men know how the third Edward removed his mother from power and slew her lover Mortimer. It is less well known how he befriended those whom she had cast down. Edmund of Kent had left three fatherless children, the youngest of which was barely out of the womb. Edward himself had just produced his first son, and his tender young wife Philippa offered to nurture her husband's cousins along with her own babe. And so it was that Joan of Kent became a member of the king's family, to be raised alongside her royal cousin as befits the granddaughter of a king.

The first that I saw of Joan was when the prince bade me bring a message to her. "You shall find her in my mother's tents," said he, and he produced a scroll that I was to deliver into no hands but her own.

"But how shall I know her?" I asked, for I had never laid eyes upon the lady, and I feared that I would somehow miscarry through ignorance.

"How shall you know her?" the prince repeated, and he laughed as if I had voiced some monumental stupidity. "She is accounted by all to be the fairest lady of England, and if you know her not by that, then God help you!"

I traced my way through the maze of tents to the royal pavilions that belonged to Queen Philippa. Winter was coming on apace and the sharp wind had chased all the royal ladies indoors. I stepped into the anteroom of the pavilion and begged an inquiring damsel to see the lady Joan. "Who are you, sir?" she demanded with an

arched eyebrow, and I blushed fearfully and mumbled
something about my service to the Prince of Wales. "Ah!"
she said with her hauteur unabated, and she floated away
with such a fluid motion that I could discern no steps in
her stride.

I waited for some minutes, gazing with wonder at
the delicate tapestries that hung the wall of the tent.
The first panel showed two men fighting. There was a
great disparity in size, but the smaller man had beaten
the giant and was wounded in the attempt. "Marhault
is slain," I read in the stitchery. In the second panel the
wounded man was traveling to a new land, and there
a woman with hair of red and gold sat by his bedside
and applied a cordial to his lips. "Isolt, the healer," said
the caption. More and more pictures followed. The man,
having been healed, returned home on a ship, but his
king bade him sail back again to the strange land whence
he had just come. He took the woman into his ship and
together they shared a cup of wine. The warrior's king
received the woman, and wed her to himself with a great
marriage feast.... But in the panels that followed, I saw
her not with the king, but with the man whom she had
healed.

Footsteps sounded in the room behind the curtain. I
skimmed through the pictures in a hurry, seeing that the
woman with the red-gold hair returned to the king while
the warrior whom she had healed departed for another
land. The last panel showed a tower above the sea, and
on the sea below, a ship approached....

"Do you like my tapestry?" asked a clear voice, and I
turned sharply like a man caught in some shameful act.

"It is all folly," the voice continued, "for Tristan was never meant to have the lady."

"Yes," I said with a sheepish grin. "But it is noble folly, for I have never seen anything so beautiful."

The voice originated from a little woman, plump and coming on to middle age. Her face was simple and complacent like a tame spaniel, but this simplicity did not extend to her dress. Pearls embroidered her close-fitting bodice and the cut gems on her sleeves twinkled like stars. I stared at her a moment, convinced that she must be some great lady. But I could see that she was no Joan of Kent, for she was of no more than average beauty. My errand was not to her.

"Please, lady," I said. "I have an errand to the lady Joan."

"So I have heard," said the lady. "You bring a message from my son."

"Aye, Majesty," said I as I fell to one knee, for with those words I comprehended that I was in the presence of Queen Philippa.

"Come, sir," she said, and stretched out her hand. "Give me the scroll. I will bear your message and give you gramercy for it."

I swallowed. "I thank you for your kindness, sweet lady, but your son has commanded me to place this letter only in the hands of the lady Joan."

She looked at me with surprise. "Methinks you are bold, sir, to rate the commands of your master above the commands of his mother. Nevertheless," she said, with soft words that displayed fixity of purpose, "you will give the letter to me. The lady Joan is my attendant and will not complain of it—that I promise you."

There was little to do but comply. I delivered the scroll into Her Majesty's plump hand and with a gracious smile she left me. I hung my head, ashamed that I had failed to carry out the prince's commands. Still, I determined to have one more look at the tapestry, for my eyes had barely brushed over the last scene when the queen had entered.

In the tower above the sea, the warrior lay on his bed—but whether sick or dead I could not tell. Below the cliffs, a ship had nearly reached the beach, a ship with a white sail. And on the ship was the woman with hair of red and gold. She had come to see her warrior once again, but was she too late to heal him?

As my eyes feasted on this picture, it seemed that the tapestry itself had come alive, for two of its panels parted and a girl stepped out of its borders.

"Sir Knight!" she whispered in a soft voice. "Come hither, at once."

She was lithe and slender as a flower stalk and her hair flamed red and gold like a field of poppies. The prince had said that Joan of Kent was the fairest maid of England, and my mind misgave me that this might indeed be she. I followed her awkwardly into a little room behind the curtain. The closet was small and narrow, and she drew very close to me so that I could catch her murmurs. "Speak low," she warned me, "for we must not be heard."

"Are you the lady Joan?" I breathed.

"No," she said, and she laughed as if my question had been a fine joke. "I am called Margery, but I serve the lady Joan. You are the prince's man, are you not?"

"Aye," said I. "He sent me with a message for Lady Joan, but the queen took it to deliver to her."

Margery scowled; a sharp line shot between her brows as when marble is struck by a chisel. "Aye, she'll deliver it," said the girl scornfully, "as willingly as the French will deliver up Calais. You were a pretty fool to give it to her."

My blood ran hot to hear these words, and my hand fingered the sword belt that sat on my hips. "I could not well refuse it to her," I said defensively.

"Nay, and since you've failed in your commission from the prince, you cannot well refuse to undertake a second commission from the lady Joan." She placed her arms akimbo as she said this, and I could feel her breath warm on my face.

If she had been a man, I should have been angry with her, but as it was, my only wish was that she should not be angry with me. "I shall do any honorable service that the lady requires," I said, trying to bow, but there was barely room for it.

"Sweetly said, Sir Knight," said Margery, and producing a scroll from her sleeve she placed it in my hand and closed my fingers around it. "Guard this well, for it is worse to lose a lady's letter than a gentleman's."

I flushed to the roots of my hair. She treated me like the veriest page boy, and yet, if her face did not belie her, she could be no older than I!

"Why do you linger?" she demanded. I dropped my eyes to the floor. There was no answer to be made. I tucked the scroll into the breast of my tunic and looked about me sharply as I lifted the flap of the tapestry and left the women's pavilion.

When I returned to His highness's tent, I found him playing at chess with Sir Bernard Brocas. The board and the pieces belonged to the prince and were a particularly treasured possession. They were of Moorish construction, carved ivory embedded in a base of gold. The pawns were the height of a grown man's thumb, and the king weighed as much as a sling stone in your hand. The prince kept them in an inlaid box of rosewood and acacia, so ornamented that one might mistake it for a reliquary.

It was a favorite pastime of his to play at chess. I had carried messages from him before to Chandos, to Audley, and to Sir Walter Manny, begging them attend his highness in his pavilion for a match. It was rare that a man could get the better of him. Chandos had done so once, and I knew that the prince acknowledged Bradwardine, the king's chaplain, as his master in the game. But for most men, the prize of prevailing over the Prince of Wales was as unattainable as the golden fleece.

I had seen the prince and Brocas play before and knew that Brocas was insurmountably outclassed. In the game of chess as well as the game of warfare, Brocas could think no further than two steps ahead. He was an impulsive man, quick to speak, quick to smile, quick to frown, and slow only in apprehending the consequences of his actions. This the prince had known since childhood. And since childhood, the prince had sought to remedy this defect in his friend.

"Have a care, Bernard," the prince said as I came in. "Do you not see that if you advance your pawn thus, you shall leave your knight exposed and my queen shall take him?"

Brocas's dark brows pressed against each other as he encountered the prince's eye across the chess board. "Highness," he said petulantly, "Methinks it is superfluous for you to ask another to play, since you mean to play for both." He knocked over his king with a disrespectful flick of the fingers. "There, I have done. You have won, which is what you wished, and I have saved you a half an hour of your time."

"Not so long," said the prince, triumph glinting in his eye like the sparks from a fire. With a few deft motions, he showed Brocas how victory would have been his in three moves.

"Ah, Potenhale," said the prince becoming aware of my presence. "You gave the lady my missive? What said she?"

I was unsure at first where to begin, and a little bewildered by the presence of Brocas, but the prince bade me tell him everything and I saw that he kept no secrets from this friend of his childhood. My story stumbled over itself several times as I related to his highness each detail of the mortifying episode. I left out nothing besides the haughty manner in which Joan's maid had received me.

The prince was not overjoyed to hear my tale. He did not storm as his father would have done, but his displeasure with me was apparent in the curling sneer of his comely face and the harsh edge to his voice. "You have miscarried in the worst of all ways," he said shortly. My shoulders drooped sadly, and I wanted to crawl backwards out of the tent like a dog who has received a cuff from a beloved master.

"Don't berate the poor man so," said Brocas, who had recovered his good spirits at the same time that the prince had lost his. "Forsooth, what was he to do in such a pass? As a wise man once said, 'Do you not see that if you advance your pawn thus, you shall leave your knight exposed and the queen shall take him?' Well, here is your pawn returned to you, and it will do you as much good to berate him as it will do me to berate this chess piece."

I expected the prince to bridle at this, but he took the rebuke right calmly and gave me his hand in token of forgiveness. "So my letter is lost," he said thoughtfully, "but you say that you have another."

"Aye," I said eagerly, and fumbling in the breast of my tunic, I pulled out the scroll that Margery—beautiful Margery!—had put in my hands. The prince's hands split the seal with haste. He leaned closer to the candles on the table, and I could see his lips forming the words that lay on the page though he did not speak them aloud. What manner of things had she written, the lady Joan? And how came it that her handmaid could produce a letter in answer to the prince even before her lady had received one?

"Now God be praised!" the prince said after a moment, and his countenance metamorphosed completely from fire and brimstone to gentle rain. He quartered the letter with crisp, neat folds and placed it in his own tunic. My erstwhile unforgivable error seemed to be forgotten entirely. He gave me a golden guinea from his purse, clapped me upon the back, and called me a second Hermes. Then with a farewell to Brocas, he exited the tent stepping lightly over the threshold and whistling a merry tune.

5

THE SURRENDER OF THE CITADEL
January – August, 1347

Spring came to Calais bringing rising sap, shooting buds, and returning birds; but the one thing it did not bring was the termination of the siege. The high walls of the town loomed before us with the same impregnability they had possessed in September. It had been six months, and we were no closer to attaining the prize.

The ladies had grown fretful and talked of leaving again for England. But there would be no leaving without the queen, and she was determined to lay her head down on the same pillow as her lord and husband. Philippa's short, plump figure had grown plumper still in the past months. The prince confirmed my unvoiced suspicions when he noted that his mother was with child. She would allow none of her ladies leave her at such a time, though God knows that the experience was common enough to her. It was the twelfth child she had carried, and there have been more since Calais.

Calais's recalcitrance was wearing on more than just the ladies. The king's mood was ugly, and all the nobles were on edge. When Calais's governor had expelled the feminine and feeble from the town in early December, His Majesty had assumed that the end was near. He had only to maintain the siege and Calais would capitulate. The siege had been maintained, and yet the town still held out. It was incontrovertible, it was incomprehensible, but it was fact. The only explanation was that the town was still receiving supplies from somewhere.

The blockade had not been breached by land, but the wall of wooden ships proved to be a porous palisade. Suspicious that the town might be receiving supplies from the sea, the king increased the numbers of galleys and cogs that lay across the harbor. Now barely a minnow could pass through the water without a cry of alarm and a hoisting of the sail.

The king's suspicions were well founded. The French for some time now had been smuggling in food at night in flat-bottomed barges. The increased vigilance on our part made their midnight runs impossible now. After the barge captains made several abortive attempts that nearly cost them their lives, they forsook the enterprise. No amount of gold was tempting enough to lure them back through the teeth of our English sharks. And so Calais was shut up as she should be, with a cordon drawn around her as tight as a tourniquet; the flow of life was cut off at last.

Shortly after the cessation of the food-smuggling, the gates of Calais opened once more. This time a crowd nothing short of two thousand persons crawled out of the ramparts. It was the same sort of feeble folk as before— women, children, and old ones, all too weak to wield a sword or wind a crossbow. The siege had begun to pinch unbearably, and Calais had expelled two thousand more bodies with useless hands and hungry mouths.

But the careless clemency with which the king had greeted the last group was spent. Calais had cost him too much money and too many months. Whatever debt the city owed him, these poor folk would now pay.

"Shall we open the palisade?" asked Sir Walter Manny, hoping to let the town folk pass through unmolested.

"In God's name, no!" said the king. "They'll gain no grain from this maneuver. Drive them back from the lines. They must re-enter the town and share the food and fortune of their friends."

The palisade bristled with archers, and they fired a few warning shots at the émigrés. That halted them. I saw them debating amongst themselves, though none in this ragged band seemed to hold any leadership. We fired again, and the volley sent them scurrying away. In a moment's time they were back at the base of the wall, looking up for succor like a hurt child clinging to his mother's knees. But the gate which had opened to release them was no longer open to receive them. The cries or entreaties of the turned-out two thousand had no power to turn the winch that raised the portcullis. A man's head appeared on the height of the gatehouse tower. He had come to address the refugees. The words he spoke were lost in the distance which separated us from the town, but the people below heard him well enough. A dreadful keening arose from the motley crowd and they held up their hands in supplication.

"Their governor has refused to readmit them," I heard Manny report to the king. "Shall I give the order for the palisade to be opened?"

"God forbid that I should prove kinder than their natural lord," replied Edward stonily. "There shall be no passage through our lines. They shall re-enter Calais or sink to shades in its shadow. Calais has tried my patience for too long—let her surrender when she will, there will be no quarter given to man, woman, or child. They shall all perish like these brutes."

As nightfall approached and the town folk saw that their governor would not relent, they turned about again and pressed toward our line. But the king's word held firm, and warning shots from the archers repelled them like stones thrown at a stray dog. There was no choice for them but to keep their distance. Hungry, homeless, and hopeless, they lay themselves down to sleep in the limbo between the lines of battle.

It was a wretched week that followed. Already weakened by the scanty rations in Calais, the trapped refugees now rooted in the mud like pigs, searching for any trace of vegetation that could be crammed into an empty maw. Their famished frames moved haltingly, and their eyes gaped dully like the sinkholes of the surrounding marsh. Most of the company lay down in a huddle till the weakness of hunger shut their eyes forever. But ever and anon a few frantic members of the company, those who refused to acquiesce to their inevitable fate, ventured toward the city or the palisade. From the city there was only silence, but from the palisade there was always a sharp-tipped volley of arrows, no longer just a warning, but actual measures of defense to keep the forlorn French from rushing upon our lines.

The sight of this cadaverous company corralled by our lines sickened me to my stomach. I had seen death at Caen and death at Crecy, but this was something worse than death. One twilight, while the prince and I paced the lines, I heard the bloodcurdling, guttural groan of a refugee who had chosen the pain of the arrow over the pain of the belly. Nauseated by the sound, I turned to His Highness in appeal. "Think you that His Majesty will finally relent and allow them to pass?"

"Nay," replied the prince. "The only feast they'll ever attend is a feast for the ravens."

"But why, in God's name?" I demanded.

"He is teaching these burghers a lesson, and the French remain stupid to all but the harshest of schoolmasters."

"But there is no honor in this!" said I. "*You* would not do such a thing."

"You think I would not?" asked the prince, and he cocked his head to the side a little, as if pondering the idea. "Perhaps you are right; perhaps I would not have given this order. But then, I have not spent a hundred thousand guineas to achieve this place. A man's conception of what is honorable may shift a little when his purse is in danger of depletion."

"Then you admit it," I cried out, "that to starve this wretched band is something short of chivalrous!"

"Have a care, Potenhale," said the prince. He drew into himself suddenly and the frostiness of his tone reminded me of my place. "My father is considered an honorable man by all, and peer to the greatest monarchs of Christendom; it is not for an obscure knight barely belted to question the judgment of a Plantagenet. Have a care, Potenhale."

❖ ◆ ❖

It was not until the summer that Philip finally came, with a mighty force to relieve the suffering citizens of Calais. By this time, the French burghers had tightened their belts to the last notch. We had apprehended one courier from the town who (in a letter to Philip) lamented that the town folk had eaten every cat, dog, and horse within the walls; if succor did not arrive soon, they would be forced to partake of human flesh or else give up the city.

Some of Calais's couriers must have slipped through the English blockade bearing this same message, for Philip gave up his indolence and arrived at the end of July. Encamping his army on the marsh, he left nothing but a hill between his lines and ours. His first action was to request a parley, and—since the Holy See was always wont to intervene on his behalf— sent two cardinals to sound the current of English intentions. Edward bristled a little, as any Englishman would at emissaries from the Francophile pontiff. But he acknowledged himself favorable to a parley, and two tents were pitched on the wasteland between our two armies.

Diplomats from both countries convened in the common ground. On our side were Sir Walter Manny and Henry, the grey-bearded Earl of Lancaster who had just quitted his post in Gascony to join us at Calais. On Philip's side were the dukes of Bourbon and Athènes, as well as Geoffroi de Charny. You will note, milady, that this was the first time that I caught sight of your husband. At the time I did not mark it much—it was merely the faint outline of a man at a quarter league's distance. But my later history with him caused me to recall this instance and inscribe it with a chisel on the walls of memory.

Neither my master nor I was present at the parley, but the English emissaries were buzzing like hornets when they returned. I stood behind the prince's chair in His Majesty's tent while Manny and Lancaster told their tale.

"We told them we could only conclude general terms of peace," began Manny, "as Your Majesty authorized us—"

"But God's life!" broke in Lancaster. "They would have none of it. The Bourbon fool insisted that we must lift the siege entirely before they would even lisp the littlest offer of a truce."

"We remonstrated with them," continued Manny, "and Sir Geoffroi de Charny hinted that Philip's offer of peace would be an even trade of Gascony and Ponthieu in return for Calais and the surrounding country."

"—And this Charny said everything as solemn as an abbot," seethed Lancaster, "as if Your Majesty does not already hold Gascony by right of inheritance and arms. Give us Gascony? Why, then, we'll give him Paris as a present, since we're to be making presents of land to those that already own it."

"And what said you to this offer?" demanded the king.

"I made bold to say that it liked us not," answered Manny. "I insisted that our most wise and puissant sovereign would never trade the sweet kernel of Calais for husks and chaff like Ponthieu."

"And France's reply?" asked the king.

"Since we would make no guarantees to lift the siege, their graces the dukes of Bourbon and Athènes would have given up the parley, but Charny begged leave to tender another offer for your consideration. To prevent the great loss of life which would inevitably occur should our two armies engage in battle, Charny suggests a trial by combat. Each lord would select four champions to defend the honor of his army. The winners would take Calais; the losers would withdraw."

"And what answer made you to that?" said the king.

"No answer," replied Manny. "I would know your good pleasure."

The king turned to his assembled council. "Lords, good sirs, what think you of this offer?"

"Folly!" croaked Audley, and Chandos nodded his concurrence. It was rare to find the minds of these two out of concert with each other.

"We have the advantage," reminded Chandos. "Philip knows he cannot raise the siege, or why would he throw out such a fantastical offer?"

"And yet," interjected Bradwardine, "trial by combat has its merits." Bradwardine was a cleric and the royal chaplain, but the king often used him for matters of diplomacy. Besides his abilities in church and court, he was renowned in all the Paris schools for his sharpness of intellect. He was a prominent astronomer and a preeminent mathematician. The "Profound Doctor" was one of his nicknames and the sobriquet suited him entirely for he was as deep as he was learned.

"What merits does trial by combat have?" demanded the king.

"Four that I can foresee," replied Bradwardine, and he began to itemize them on his fingers. "First, immediate termination of the siege; second, proof to the world which side divine justice has taken in this quarrel; third, reduction of the loss of life that a battle would entail; and fourth, relief for the miserable citizens of Calais."

"Three worthy reasons," replied the king, "though your fourth deserves no consideration."

Bradwardine shrugged and folded his hands. "Then consider only the first three, but also consider Charny's offer, for it is a sound one both for us and for the French. We cannot remain another winter in the field, and here is a way to end the siege swiftly."

"But Majesty," expostulated Lancaster. "You are ignoring the drawbacks of such a proposal! Four of their knights against four of ours? The French peasantry may be of poor mettle, but their chevaliers are considered the best in Europe. Choose our champions as carefully as you may, they could still be outclassed. Nearly a year's work would be lost and all in an hour's time."

"Better to fight Philip in the field," agreed Audley. "We'll have our archers then and you know the work they did at Crecy."

One by one, the nobles voiced the same opinions as Lancaster and Audley. The prince alone remained silent, resting his chin on his gloved hand and listening intently to both Bradwardine and his opponents. Perhaps he disagreed with the prevailing current of opinion, or perhaps he merely wanted to learn in silence.

The king listened to his nobles' clamorous objections for a time, then silenced them with a wave of his hand. "Soft, soft," he said. "I have heard you all and heard you well. But I would also know the opinion of another. Come now, what says the Prince of Wales? Shall we send out our champions or shall we wait in the field?"

His highness paused a little space then answered slowly. "In truth, Your Majesty, I do not know the better course. Master Bradwardine has spoken well and worthily, but the concerns of your nobles are also weighty. I must beg leave to refuse judgment, for I do not know the course you ought to take."

"Well enough," said the king quietly, but he seemed a little disappointed at his offspring's reticence in this matter. "You have not been long in the field, and perhaps it is best to defer your judgment."

The king then gave his opinion of the matter. Little to my surprise, the king was of the same mind as his men. Turning to Sir Walter Manny and Henry of Lancaster, he said, "Go back to Geoffroi de Charny and bear this answer: *The fingers of England are around the throat of Calais, and we will not let go to swat at gnats. If Philip would raise the siege, let him use all his strength. We are prepared to stand against him in the field. That is the only trial by combat which we will endure, and may God defend the right when our two armies meet.*"

As the emissaries departed, the council also dispersed; the king and all the nobles left the pavilion. But the prince caught Bradwardine's eye, and the two lingered behind to have speech once the folds of the tent fell shut.

Bradwardine was a short man, advanced in years, well-fleshed, and wearing the tonsure and habit of a clergyman. Despite his rotund appearance, his fingers were curiously long and slender with the calluses of a frequent writer. He smiled at his highness, the benevolent smile of a familiar confessor who had heard the prince's sins since childhood and never failed to grant him absolution.

"Your reasons were well founded," remarked the prince. "Had you carried the day, this day might have given us Calais."

"Aye, highness," said Bradwardine, "but His Majesty knows best the risks he is willing to undergo. He takes the safer course in this, and perhaps that is wise."

"Wise indeed," said the prince, and he stood silent a while musing.

"What would your highness have done in such a case?" asked Bradwardine, echoing the question that the king had put to the prince earlier.

"I do not know," answered the prince again, then he frowned as if the question—or his inability to answer it—distressed him in some way. "Come, Bradwardine, you are an astute judge of character. What would I have done in such a case?"

"Nay, highness," laughed Bradwardine. "I know you less well than you think, and less well than when we landed at La Hougue a year past. The battlefield changes a boy into a man and changes one man into another. The Prince of Wales at seventeen is a different creature than the Prince of Wales at sixteen; if you cannot sound the dictates of your own heart, then no man can read it for you."

"Perhaps I know a man who can," rejoined the prince. "Potenhale! You presume to know what I would or would not do. You said that *I* would have let the refugees pass through our lines. Tell me, what would I have done in this case? Would I choose the safer course or would I send my champions into the field?"

I hesitated, unsure if I should brook the prince's displeasure by another disagreement with his father's policy. "Methinks the safer course is surer, but also not as full of glory. What would King Arthur have done in such a case? What would Charlemagne have done? They would not withhold their champions in the face of an honorable challenge. Perhaps it is to the advantage of our safety to decline the offer, but is it not also to the advantage of our honor to accept it?"

The prince smiled. "Predictable Potenhale—you and Charny are cut from the same bolt of cloth. I know what you would have done. But what of myself? What of myself? Can any man tell me?" He sighed, a little sadly it seemed.

"You shall find your way soon enough," said Bradwardine comfortingly, "or if you do not find it, it shall be thrust upon you. The world is changing, methinks, and these are not the days that Arthur and Charlemagne knew. When a yeoman's arrow can fell an armored knight, when Peter's successor can pontificate from a French see, then all hierarchy is unbound and all order is overturned. And in such a time, prince, you are called to serve. What wonder then if the way should be hard?"

"Sweet Bradwardine," said the prince affectionately. "The way may be hard for me, but you always find the truth of a matter."

"Ah, truth!" said Bradwardine, and his eyes shone bright and sharp like two cut gems. "Have you heard of my latest writings, highness?"

"Nay, I have not heard," replied the prince in amusement at Bradwardine's excitement.

"Then, if you will indulge an old man's humor I will tell you and this young sir of my latest insoluble."

"Insoluble?" repeated the prince. "Is anything unsolvable for a man with your keen logic?"

"Aye," said Bradwardine with a smile. "For here's a proposition that defies logic."

The old clergyman turned to me. "Sir Potenhale, how if I were to say to you that this statement is false."

"What statement?" asked I, a little puzzled.

"The statement itself," said Bradwardine. "This statement is false."

"Why, then I would bow to your superior intellect and agree with you."

"You would agree that what I say is true?" asked Bradwardine.

"Aye," said I, "for you are a truthful man."

"So, you are saying that if this statement is false then it is true?"

"Why, no!" said I. "I said that I agree with you. So if you say that the statement is false, then it must be a false statement."

"But if it is a false statement to say that this statement is false, then the statement must be true," said Bradwardine.

"And," interjected the prince, "If the statement is true, then it is of necessity false."

"But you are going in circles!" I cried as my head began to spin like a wooden top.

"Aye," said Bradwardine, and he gave a deep throated chuckle. "And no matter how many circles you go through, the statement is unsolvable. I have several more like that one, but they're all of the same kind. My latest writings are concerning the nature of such statements."

"But what is the purpose of such a thing?" I asked, still bewildered.

"It has no purpose in and of itself," replied the prince with a laugh. "It is merely a grinding stone for Bradwardine to whet his mind on so that his intellect may stay sharp enough to deal with substantial matters—like the merits of listening to French ambassadors. But come, Potenhale, we must not stand merrily about. The alarum has a logic which cannot be denied, and it may sound any minute when Manny and Lancaster return from the French parley."

◆ ◆ ◆

Philip's response was less martial than we English anticipated. Just as Chandos had surmised in council, his fear of raising the siege was greater than his fear of losing Calais. When Charny, Bourbon, and Athènes returned with Edward's refusal to lift the siege or send out champions, Philip lacked the manpower to man the field. Since we would not treat with him, he resigned himself to retreat. His soldiers, who had established camp on the hill opposite us, put away their tents as quickly as they had pitched them and disappeared into the west.

The citizens of Calais had been filled with elation at the approach of their king's pennants. Now they plummeted to the nadir of despair at his departure. Their store of hope was as empty as their larders. They lifted the white flag and entreated a parley. Sir Walter Manny crossed the limbo between our lines to speak with their governor. The king, meanwhile, stood at the edge of the palisade waiting to hear the news from the town. The chief men of the army stood roundabout, and on the king's right hand stood the prince with me in attendance.

"Majesty," said Manny when he had returned from the ramparts. "I have spoken with Jean de Vienne, the governor of the place. The famine in the city has become unbearable. Both the citizens and the soldiery are ready to surrender to you. They stipulate only this condition— that you allow them to leave the city unharmed."

"Unharmed?" repeated the king, and he laughed incredulously. "I have sworn to the contrary, Sir Walter, and there is not the slightest hope or prospect of my changing my mind."

"My lord," said Sir Walter, and he advanced closer to the king to reason with him in lowered tones. "These men have been set by their natural lord to defend this place. If you punish them with death for their obedience, what example will you set? Whenever the French take a city or fortress of ours, they will butcher us likewise, and our men will go less cheerfully to their posts with the fear of what may come. Consider, Majesty. Consider!"

Warwick, Lancaster, Chandos, and Audley added their remonstrances to Manny's, and the king proved at this time that he was not altogether deaf to counsel. "My lords," he said at last, "My anger burns in me against this people, but I do not want to be alone against you all. Sir Walter, go back to Calais and tell its commander that this is the limit of my clemency: six of the chief citizens of the place are to come out, with their heads and their feet bare, with halters around their necks, and with the keys of the town in their hands. With these six I shall do as I please; the rest I will spare."

Manny returned to Jean de Vienne with these terms. It was a hard word for him to hear, but the French governor accepted; he had no choice.

I wondered at first how they would choose the six citizens. I supposed they would use a lottery, for surely no man would offer himself to certain death for the assuagement of the English king's wrath. But in my surmises, I underestimated the selflessness of Calais's citizens. We learned later that when their governor announced the doleful news to the town, the town folk stood a while in grieved silence. But then, one after another, six of the wealthiest men of the place stepped forward as sacrificial lambs. And with the prayers of the people upon the heads, they put ropes around their necks and delivered themselves into the hand of the English.

The king, by this time, had retired to his tent. Sir Walter Manny led the burghers through our lines to Edward's quarters. It was a strange procession. The six men had stripped to their shirt sleeves and removed their caps and shoes. They wore their hempen halters as proudly as a chancellor wears his golden chain. Their hands gripped the iron keys devoutly like a bishop carrying a chrism. Our English soldiers stared in wonder at Manny's captives; many fell in line behind the procession to see what would become of the wretched men. By the time Manny reached the courtyard in front of the king's tent, a great crowd had assembled to hear the judgment of Edward.

At first, the king said nothing, but only glared fiercely at the burghers. His spirit was too vexed within him, for he hated the people of this city as a shepherd hates the wolf, as a sailor hates the shoals, or as a farmer hates the locust. The six men fell down on their knees before him and clasped their hands in supplication. "Most noble lord," said one of them, "we surrender to you the keys of the town and the castle, to do with them as you will. We put ourselves entirely in your hands so that we may save the remaining inhabitants of Calais, for they have already undergone great suffering. We pray you by your generous heart—have mercy on us also!"

These pitiful words had great effect on the English beholding the scene. I looked about me and saw that Manny's cheek was wet with tears. Audley too, that harsh cynic, had eyes that were far from dry. The king, however, remained untouched. He continued to glare at them savagely, his heart so bursting with anger that he could not speak.

At length, he opened his mouth to pronounce this doom. "Strike off their heads immediately!"

The burghers moaned a little, but it was the noble lords of England who made the greatest outcry. "Noble sire," begged Manny, "curb your anger. You have a reputation for royal clemency. Do not perform an act which might tarnish it and allow you to be spoken of dishonorably." Mortimer murmured his assent to Manny's words, and Salisbury fell to his knees in supplication beside the burghers.

But the king, if it were possible, became angrier than ever at these attempts to thwart his will. He ground his teeth together and clenched his fists. "That is enough, Sir Walter," he barked. "My mind is made up. Let the executioner be sent for. The people of Calais have killed so many of my men that it is right for these to die in their turn."

A sigh went up to the crowd, and I looked to where the prince stood, hoping that he would raise his voice to intervene. But the pity that flowed from Manny was well hidden inside the prince. His arms crossed stoically across his chest and his eye was unclouded with tears. But even as the prince stood silent, the crowd on the other side of the square parted. A lady clad in brightest green came forward with slow steps, and when she had drawn near before the king, she fell to her knees.

"Ah, my dear lord!" said she, and I saw at once that it was Queen Philippa. Sir Walter Manny, her former meat carver, had no doubt apprized her of the desperate situation. Her light brown hair was bound back in gold nets, and the full fabric of her bright gown draped heavily over her rounded belly. "Sweet sir," she said winsomely, and pregnant as she was, she lay in the dust before His Majesty. "Ever since I crossed the sea at great danger to myself, I have never asked a single favor from you. But now in all humility, for the sake of the Son of the Blessed Mary and for the sake of the love you bear me, I ask that you will be merciful to these six men."

The king groaned aloud, and I saw that a battle was being fought within his soul. His fondness for his queen was common knowledge, but so also was the implacability of his vengeance. His breast swelled in torment, with a heart as divided as the blue and red surcoat that he wore. "My sweet lady," he said as his mind came to a merciful truce. He stepped forward and raised Philippa to her feet. Her head barely came to his shoulder and her two hands fit easily into one of his. "Upon my soul," said Edward, "I most heartily wish that you were anywhere but here. But you have entreated me in such a manner that I cannot refuse you. So, although I do this against my will, I do it nevertheless." Reaching down, the king grasped the hand of one of Calais's citizens and placed the man's fingers in Philippa's palm. "Here, take them. They are yours to do with as you please."

Philippa thanked her husband joyfully. Her plump arms encircled her lord's neck while the crowd of Englishmen gave a huzzah for their bonny Flemish queen. Sir Walter Manny dried his eyes and brought the six Frenchmen to the queen's tent where she fed them, clothed them, and sent them away in safety.

But though the lives of Calais' citizens had been spared, no other clemency was granted them. The king, whose vengeful plans had been foiled so forcibly, spent the rest of his energy in forcibly expelling the inhabitants of Calais from their homes. I led a small company of men throughout one quarter of the town to perform the eviction. Many of the citizens were glad enough to leave the desolate city, but the unwilling folk we turned out with kicks and curses. The French soldiers were happy to lay down their arms—especially since many of them were not French at all, but Italian mercenaries like the Genoese at Crecy.

"How is the English pay?" demanded one fellow, as I took his sword and bade him make his way to the gate. He was a tall man who seemed to have some prominence among the mercenary group. He was lean from hunger, and his sharp, shiny face eyed our ranks inquisitively.

"The pay is well enough," said I. "But there are enough English to fight for England, and our king does not put his trust in foreign hire."

"Ah, well," said the Lombard, "If the English will not have us, we'll find the French again." And as he turned about to join his companions, I saw that his ears had no lobes, but were joined curiously to his face like the handle of a drinking cup. *"A più tardi!"* he said, but I doubted that I would see him again.

6

SICK AT HEART
September – October, 1347

e did not know it at the time, but the capture of Calais marked the end of our campaign in France. Though Philip's army was not doughty enough to dislodge us, there were forces more powerful than he to send us scurrying homeward. An evil wind had blown in from the east and brought with it the pestilence. Araby and Italy had felt it first. At the same time as we entered Calais, the plague entered the kingdom of France. There were stories of cities in southern France that had sickened and died overnight, with half their people laid to rest from this evil pestilence. In Paris the schools closed their doors, and scholars from all over Europe fled home to their own countries.

But, pardon me, Madame—I jump ahead of myself. I will tell you of the plague and the distresses it caused all in good time. First, however, I must return to Edward's army and tell you of the celebration that followed the surrender.

We had camped outside of Calais for nearly a year; no wonder then that the streets were rife with revelry when at last we possessed them. The king ordered that masses of thanksgiving be said in all the churches. The prince himself spent a whole night in vigil giving thanks to the Holy Trinity for the victory.

The soldiers received their thanks as well as the Almighty. To the common men-at-arms Edward dispersed a bounty of golden coin; for the knights and nobles he held a grand fete. He sent raiding parties throughout the countryside; they commandeered the meat, bread, cheese, and wine that French Calais had been lacking for so many months. The same city that had starved for so many months under the rule of King Philip would now see eating, drinking, dance, and song under the rule of King Edward.

The prince had been in a particularly pleasant mood the week following the cessation of the siege. He seemed determined to enjoy the sights of the city from the inside, for he would leave his quarters for half a day at a time, and when I looked for him he was nowhere to be found. I ascribed it at first to his excitement at entering Calais, but Sir Brocas found another cause for his good humor. "His highness is a free man again," he remarked as we waited for the prince outside his quarters. He had bid us meet him there when the bells rang None and here it was nearly Vespers.

"Free from the siege?" I asked.

"No, free from La Brabant!" said Brocas laughingly and he grimaced like a gorgon at the name.

"Why, who's she?" I asked.

"She *was* his intended," said Brocas. "But her father's just broken off the match and wed her to the Count of Flanders instead. The king is furious, of course, but I daresay his highness is glad for the reprieve. They say the lady is a shrew and ill-favored at that."

"But if Flanders is England's ally," said I, "is it not unwise of the Count to take the lady that was promised to our prince?"

"Nay, it is not the Count that is our ally, but the artisans," replied Brocas patiently. "And that is no wonder, when their looms are all supplied with English wool. The Flemish guilds are for us, but the Count of Flanders favors the French. He rode with Philip against us at Crecy even while his own people were supporting us in Picardy."

"And Brabant?" I asked, confused about the tangled alliances of the lowland countries. "Whose side does he take?"

"The Duke of Brabant has always fawned on Philip, but His Majesty assumed that this union with the Plantagents would bring Brabant into the English camp. Brabant and Flanders would put two arrows in our quiver to hedge in the eastern border of France."

"But the prince cannot marry Brabant's daughter now."

"You say true," said Brocas, "unless it were possible for a lady to have two husbands. Now Brabant's daughter is in bed with Flanders, and Brabant is in bed with France."

"And the prince makes his bed alone," said I.

"Aye," said Brocas with a wink, "though I warrant there are more than a few maids who would gladly keep it warm."

"What is this bawdy talk?" demanded the prince who had materialized behind us as quietly as a hunting cat.

"We do but pass the time, highness," said Brocas saucily with a shake of his curly locks, for the prince had kept us waiting long.

"You had better pass the time in dressing yourselves," said the prince curtly. "The hour approaches for my father's fete." We took his exhortation to heart and sought our rooms to change our raiment.

In my years of service with the prince, I have often been amazed by the lavishness of his attire. The costume that his highness chose for the fete, however, was unparalleled in its opulence. His doublet was all of black and secured down the front with a row of perfectly matched pearls. The sleeves of the doublet were close fitting and buttoned with rubies and sapphires. A golden belt sat low upon his hips, with carvings of lions inset on dark enamel. The doublet ended midway down his thigh with a pair of red hose covering the rest of his leg. At the base of this costume, a pair of leather buskins jutted out with martial acuity. On these, the shoemaker's awl had been as hard at work as an Italian's paintbrush. A delicate tracery of leafwork, as elaborate as any rose window, adorned the shoes from heel to point. Over all of this splendor, the prince cast a black cloak scalloped along the edges; he pinned it to the side with a great brooch that bore the crest of the Plantagenets.

You may ask how the prince managed to obtain such fantastic attire in a foreign land when our army, only a week since, and lain encamped in the field. Such a question could only be asked because I have not done full justice in describing our "English Calais." The camp itself had every sort of cooper, cobbler, and carpenter that a man might desire; there was no reason that the prince should lack a tailor simply because he tarried in the field.

The prince, when procuring his own raiment for the revelry, had not neglected to provide for his retainers. My own suit of green and gold was far less dazzling than his highness's costume, but still the finest clothes I had ever worn. I adorned myself with particular care, for the fete was of particular interest to me. The ladies who had come over from England had not gone back again. Joan of Kent was sure to be at the ball, and in her train was a maid with red-gold hair with whom I longed to have further speech.

We were late coming to the ball. The musicians had already struck up their carols as we entered the doors of the hall. It was too near to the sea for flowers, so the room had been garlanded with greenery from the marsh. But the bright costumes of a hundred ladies made up for any lack of flowers, and my eyes flickered over shapely forms in red, yellow, and green joining hands in their own garland as they danced.

The king and his fair consort sat on a dais overlooking the floor. Her majesty, Queen Philippa, was too far advanced in pregnancy to partake in the revelries of the ball, but the intricacy of her costume must have made up for her forced inactivity. Her short figure was encased in a mosaic of gemstones, and the golden coronet upon her headdress sparkled with the vivacity of the dancers. The queen smiled softly to see her eldest son enter, and I followed my master to her side where she greeted him with a kiss.

"What a sight you are, my son! As handsome as you are brave."

"But neither as handsome nor as brave as my mother is beautiful."

She laughed a little at his compliment, and bade him sit by her and talk a while. The prince dismissed me with a nod, and I set out to find the fairest flower in the room, by which you must understand that I mean Margery.

The lady Joan of Kent was dancing, always dancing, for no sooner would she gratify one lord's wish, than another would whisk her away into the *estampie*. Just now, she was with William Montague, the earl of Salisbury, and I saw Mortimer hovering patiently in the background waiting to engage her hand. It was no wonder that Joan was so sought after by men. Her violet eyes met theirs frankly and innocently, her rich coils of hair glowed like honey, and her curving figure swayed gracefully to the tune. I was less enamored with Joan than most but I kept a wary eye out for where she might be, for I suspected that wherever Joan strayed my sweet mistress Margery would not be far off.

I spotted Margery seated snugly against the wall. She was dressed in the blue of a cloudless summer day. Her gown was simple; the bodice and sleeves molded tightly to her form and a great cascade of fabric fell down from her waist. I stepped before her a little tremulously, blinking stupidly like a mole come into the sunlight.

"The prince's messenger boy!" she said with a laugh, and her red-gold hair nearly shook loose from the gold netting that confined it. "You are late," she said reprovingly.

"I am honored that milady should notice," I said, for from her words I supposed that she must have been looking out for me.

"There is little that I do not notice," said she. "For instance, I notice that you do not wear my color."

I glanced down at my yellow and green doublet in some confusion and saw that it did sort poorly with her blue gown. "If milady had sent word of what she would have me wear, I should have contrived to find another costume."

"Ah," said she, "But I feared that if I sent a message, you would have lost it or given it into the hands of another."

"You are too cruel, lady," said I, flushing with mortification.

"Cruel, but not too cruel," she said gaily. I saw that it was her pleasure to laugh at me.

"I had thought to find you dancing, lady," said I.

"That is surely unlikely," said she, "for I have taken a vow."

"What manner of vow is this?" I demanded.

"That I shall dance only with a man in green and gold, and gentlemen of this description are scarce."

"Why, here's a lucky chance," said I, "for I have the very outfit to match your vow." I held out my hand to her so that we could join the circle.

"Ah, but my vow was very clear that I must dance only with a *man* in those colors," said she. "I see none such here."

My beardless face flushed once again. I would have answered her hotly, but her attention had turned elsewhere. A man in a great red doublet stood before her and begged her to enter the dance with him. It was Thomas Holland, that one-eyed knave who had captured the Comte d'Eu. His decorated clothing displayed the degree that his fortunes had improved since Caen, and his full face displayed the self-satisfied leer that had always betokened it. Margery lowered her gaze when he addressed her, and the light in her eyes was snuffed out like a guttering candle. "Sir Thomas," said she, "I do not mean to dance tonight."

"Natheless, Margery," said he, imperiously, "I think that you will dance with *me*." I listened to hear her sharp retort, but nothing came. She rose without a word and put her hand in his. "Good girl," said Holland, as he led her out into the circle, complacent and preening like an overfed cat. The musicians struck up another carol, and I watched Holland put his arm about her waist. My throat began to burn with anger, but the anger was not at Margery.

The king himself was fond of dancing, and he usually joined in a carol or two at the side of his fair consort. But Queen Philippa, as I have told you, was indisposed to dance that night, and so the king led out two or three of the other ladies in turn. As the evening wore on, I saw the king take the hand of his cousin Joan. Montague had already bespoke her for the dance, but he graciously gave way to his sovereign.

The prince, who had spent the evening at the side of his mother or in speech with several of his father's captains, approached me with a glass of wine and inquired after my enjoyment of the festivities. "You do not dance, I see?"

"No," said I shortly. Margery had disappeared after her dance with Holland and I was in no mood to pay compliments to another lady.

"So," said the prince, and he seemed abstracted in thought. "Sir Walter Manny says that my father means to withdraw from Calais with all speed."

"Is the truce then concluded?" I asked.

"Soon," said the prince, "for the French are of no mind to fight with this foul pestilence sweeping their land. And His Majesty's of no mind to stay in France and fight the infection as well as Philip. We'll keep our gains and retire, then come back again when the black cloud is gone."

I grunted in agreement, but the prince saw something amiss in my countenance. "Methinks that there is a black cloud hanging about *you*, Potenhale," said he. "What has put you out?"

"This fellow Holland...." I burst out, but I'd no sooner said it than I saw that the prince was not listening.

All around us a stream of perplexed brows and inquisitive eyes had turned toward an alcove in the southwest corner of the hall; the prince's own gaze had followed the same path. Thither, at the conclusion of the last dance, King Edward had escorted his fair cousin, and there they still stood. Or rather, there the lady Joan stood, while is majesty knelt on the flagstones beside her, picking up what seemed to be a scrap of linen.

"Sweet Mary!" murmured Sir Bernard Brocas, who was standing close by me. "'Tis the lady's garter."

A lady tittered on my right. From somewhere in the crowd, I could make out Audley's harsh croak—"it were a right cousinly duty, to put the garter back on the lady's leg."

On the other side of the room Sir Walter Manny manfully manufactured conversation with Thomas Bradwardine. "Simple truth is a luxury that the warrior does not know...."

"Hussy!" breathed a lady in red and silver, the same lady who had been guarding the door the time I entered the queen's pavilion.

"Hush," breathed another, with a graying head of hair.

Queen Philippa, from her seat on the dais, placidly and pointedly directed her attention elsewhere.

But though Philippa chose to ignore the pretty scene in the alcove, it was there that the crowd as a whole had focused its attention. The actors in the corner continued their play. King Edward, laughing, stood up and in his hands he held a piece of lace. "The spoils of war," he jested merrily and then tied the garter securely around his own leg. General laughter followed; a few gentlemen applauded as if they were viewing a rude burlesque.

The prince stood like one transfixed. His fingers, vine-like, wound tightly about the half-filled flagon in his hand. His eyes were as wide as a full moon in harvest. His jaw had tightened with such force that I doubted it would ever open again. "God in heaven!" he breathed between clenched teeth. "And is this why he bade me not to touch her?"

Someone came close to the prince and gripped his wrist warningly. It was Brocas. "Quiet, highness!" he said, and the prince said no more.

The king, meanwhile, had at last become aware of the staring crowd. He posed nonchalantly with hand on hip, extending the leg that now held the garter. "Cousin!" he said to the lady Joan, "Your beauty has overpowered them all. Look, they stare like men bewitched!"

Joan stood silently, with her eyes on the floor and a warm tinge of red lighting up her golden complexion. "Please, sir," she said softly. "Do not make a shame of me before all these people."

"Shame?" echoed the king in an expression of surprise. "Why, what is shameful in this? The lady has dropped her garter and I have picked it up. Is there any harm in that? Ho, Bradwardine! You are my confessor. Have I aught to confess for removing a lady's garter from the floor?"

"I cannot say," said Bradwardine straightforwardly, "since I do not know how the lady's garter came to be loosened. But there are many here who think that something shameful has come to pass. Do you not see it in their faces?"

The king gazed around the room slowly, meeting every eye and matching every stare. "Is this then what you all think, that there is something shameful between myself and the lady Joan? As God is my witness, there is no shame here. The real shame lies in you. Shamed be him who evil thinks!"

At this rebuke, the crowd began to blush along with the lady in question. Some turned their heads immediately, trying to pretend that they had not noticed the king's conduct. Sir Walter Manny stepped forward, offered the lady Joan his arm, and gallantly escorted her to a chair. The king dropped the subject entirely, and began to rally Bradwardine about his latest writings. Slowly, conversations began to resume.

His royal highness, it seemed, was the only one unable to conveniently put the episode out of his mind. Brocas, however, performed a friend's office, and cajoled the prince outside into the open air. A moment later, Brocas reappeared. "The prince has returned to his quarters," he said to me. "He requests you to tell his mother that he is unwell and to take leave of her for him."

I nodded and made my way to the dais. King Edward had returned there before me and, in low tones, was exchanging words with his lady. I stood at a respectful distance, but by careful concentration I could just make out their words.

"You are not angry with me, my love?" said the king.

"Nay, lord," answered Philippa. "But the common folk are foolish in their talk. Have a care or rumors will fly so thick that no man will wed my sweet Joan."

"That would be a great pity," said the king, "for I have a marriage in mind for her already."

"Indeed?" asked the queen. "I had hoped that you would turn this affair over in your mind. How soon will the match take place?"

"Soon enough. We leave Calais within the fortnight. I can announce the betrothal on our arrival in England."

"That is well," said the queen, "yet sooner would be better still; I have had much ado to keep him from seeing her. He kept to himself well enough as long as the Brabant betrothal lasted, but now, alas...."

The king shook his head in displeasure and murmured something I could not catch. I had stood there too long for my own comfort. Anxious to avoid being labeled an eavesdropper, I stepped forward noisily and fell to one knee. "What is it, sir?" demanded the king.

"Your Majesties," I said, addressing them both, "his royal highness the prince feels unwell and has retired to his tent. He sends his regretful apologies that he cannot attend the remainder of your fete and takes humble leave of you both."

"Please God he not be taken with the plague!" said the queen, a mild terror audible in her voice. "I will have my leech sent for, and any care he needs shall be provided."

I assured her that he had shown none of the symptoms common to the pestilence, neither spots nor swellings of any kind. She bade me look after him well, and on her word of dismissal I turned about to leave. The hall was crowded and it took some skill to thread my way through the dancers. I was not sad to leave early; the ball had been nothing but frustration for me. But as I went out the door I could not forbear taking one last look behind me to see Margery in her sky-blue dress; she was seated on a bench and frowning heavily as she watched Lady Joan dance with Sir Thomas Holland.

The king, as events transpired, did not wait to evacuate to England before betrothing the lady Joan. Sir Brocas was the first to have news of it. He came in suddenly while the prince and I were at breakfast and stood about woodenly until the prince asked him what was the matter.

"Here's a small to-do," said Brocas with a demeanor of forced calm. "It seems that our friend William Montague has been monstrously valiant in the course of this campaign. And His Majesty, to reward said valor, could think of no better way than to unite him with the house of Plantagenet."

"Indeed?" said the prince with arched eyebrow. "And how is such a union to take place."

"By matrimony."

The room grew warm with silence

"What is the lady's name?" the prince asked softly, but I think he knew the answer before he spoke the question.

"It is your cousin, Lady Joan of Kent," replied Brocas. "She and Salisbury are to be married upon our return to England."

The prince hesitated. "And the lady Joan? How does she like the arrangement?"

"They say that when His Majesty told her of this proposed marriage, she fell upon her knees and entreated him not to force her into this marriage. She said she was willing to do anything to avoid it—even willing to take the veil and join a nunnery. But your father would not relent, and in the end she said she would be obedient unto his will."

The prince's face was like a mask. He heard the news impassively with nary a motion or a sound. I murmured something vague about seeing to the horses and stepped out of doors into the autumn air.

I was still standing outside when Margery came, heavily cloaked and walking swiftly. Her net of red-gold curls was covered completely by her thick hood. The ivory of her face was even paler than usual and her cheeks looked drawn and haggard.

"Are you sick, lady?" I asked, thinking anxiously of the few cases of plague that had begun to spring up around Calais.

"Nay, only sorrowful," said she.

"Wherefore?" asked I.

But she shook her head and would not answer. Instead, she handed me a missive and drawing the cloak tighter about herself continued down the street.

I brought the scroll into the tent. The prince read the letter swiftly; it could have been little longer than a few sentences. Then he turned to me and said in earnest, "I have a message to send in return, Potenhale. But I cannot write it, for it must not miscarry. Can you remember my words and repeat them exactly to the lady Joan?"

"Aye, highness," said I. Slowly and carefully, he sounded out the message. I repeated it back to him five times before he was satisfied.

When I reached the quarters of Queen Philippa's waiting women, I was accosted by the same haughty damsel who had sent the queen to seize my letter at the pavilion half a year ago. She wore the same red and silver colors that I had seen her in at the ball.

"Ha!" said she. "You are the prince's man, are you not?"

"Aye," said I.

"Well then, what do you come here for?" she demanded.

I cudgeled my brain a little, knowing that it would take all my wits to gain access to the lady Joan. "I cannot help but come here, sweet lady," said I. "The queen of my heart resides in this place—and where the beautiful sun shines, there the adoring plants will turn their faces."

"Then you do not come on the prince's behalf?" the lady asked suspiciously, and I saw that she had been warned to repel all messengers from him.

"Nay, I come on my own errand," said I, "for I would see the cruel mistress who has captured my heart."

"Why call her cruel?" asked the damsel. I had piqued her curiosity.

"For she uses my love cruelly indeed, and when I come to see her she swears she will not see me."

"What is the name of this cold-hearted lady?" asked the doorkeeper in red and silver.

"I will not tell you," said I. "For you will only make a mock of me."

"Nay, Sir Knight!" she protested. "How should I mock you?"

"How?" I declaimed passionately. "You'll scorn and flout and spread it about that John Potenhale loves Margery, and alack, she loves him not."

"Margery?" said the damsel, and she gave a high pitched laugh like tinkling bells. "You spoke the truth when you said your love was cruel, for Margery Bradeshaw is as cruel as a sultan to her suitors. You are right that she will not see you.

"But come, Sir Potenhale," the damsel continued, and a conniving look came into her eye. "I like your face. And I swear I'll bring you to see hers whether or not she'll grant you audience. If she spurns your suit, at least you'll vex her sorely and put her out of countenance. For she has a way of vexing me that should surely be repaid."

The damsel bade me follow her; I passed through a collection of chambers and corridors only to come back outside into a small enclosed garden. "There is your paramour," said she, "in attendance on the lady Joan. I shall bring you to them and then leave you to plead your suit."

Joan and Margery were seated on a stone bench, making use of the pale autumn sun to ply their needles.

They looked up as we approached; their fingers ceased to work and they rose to their feet in greeting.

"Who is this young sir that you bring us, Eleanor?" asked the Lady Joan in dulcet tones.

"His name," said the damsel pertly, "is Sir John Potenhale, but I do not bring him to you Lady Joan. He is here to place his heart beneath the heel of your wench Margery. God help him or she'll crush it entirely!" This said, the damsel smirked maliciously and flounced away, no doubt greatly satisfied by the confusion and choler evident on Margery's face.

"Well then," said Lady Joan, putting away her needlework and gazing from Margery to myself. "I shall walk over yonder, Sir Potenhale, and allow you to speak with Margery unhindered."

"Nay, my lady," said Margery swiftly. "I will hear no protestations of love whereof I am the object."

"Then you are fortunate," said I with a little bow, "for I have no such protestations to make." I turned to Joan. "Forgive the deception, lady. It was necessary to gain access to your person."

"Who are you, sir?" asked Lady Joan, astonished.

"He is the prince's man," interjected Margery, "if a man he may be called." Now that my true mission was revealed, the scarlet cast to her cheeks had melted away into her usual sauciness.

"Then he is not your lover?" asked the lady Joan, still confused about the introduction Eleanor had given me.

"Nay," said Margery, "No lover of mine. But that was a right clever ploy, sirrah, for sidling past the dragon that guards our gates."

"Saints be praised that I thought to use it," said I, "though my conscience misgave me to tell so many lies."

"I'd rather hear you lie and say you loved me than have to hear the same words spoke in truth," said Margery coldly. "Deliver your message." She extended her hand to receive a scroll.

"Aye, an' you ladies will sit down again, I'll deliver it soon enough, for my message sits in my mouth and will come sooner to your ears than your hands."

Without further ado, the ladies seated themselves and I recited the prince's letter. I can still remember the exact words that I said that day:

TO THE SWEET AND MOST BEAUTIFUL JOAN OF KENT,

From Edward of Woodstock, Earl of Chester, Duke of Cornwall, and Prince of Wales.

Cousin,

Today it was announced that His Most Royal Majesty, Edward III, has affianced you to William Montague, the Earl of Salisbury. Common report and your own letter have communicated your aversion to this marriage. You have entreated me to speak to the king on your behalf, but ere I do so, I must entreat you, by the kindness you bear me, to answer this question that I put you, namely: on what grounds do you disrelish this marriage with Salisbury? Is your *dislike rooted in his own person, or does it spring from a liking already formed for another? If you, sweet Joan, will but answer me in this matter, I shall know how to direct my steps.*

Peace be with you,
Edward

When I had finished reciting this letter, the lady Joan burst into tears. Her breast heaved wildly like the swells of a wind-tossed ocean; she continued to cry for full on five minutes while I watched awkwardly and wished desperately to be elsewhere. Margery put her arms around her lady and held her comfortingly against her bosom.

"Should I leave you, lady?" I asked timidly, when the storm seemed a little stemmed.

"Nay, Sir Knight," said the lady Joan in between sobs, "for you must bring back my answer to your lord—though in truth, I hardly understand what I am to say."

I ventured to elucidate the letter in my own words. "The prince would know for a certainty whether you dislike Salisbury's suit because you wish to wed another."

"Wish to wed another!" she repeated wildly and began to sob afresh. "What shall I tell him, Margery? What shall I tell him?"

"Tell nothing!" said Margery fiercely. "There may yet be no reason to despair. Wed Salisbury today, tomorrow, or in a fortnight and I will contrive to make the rogue hold his tongue."

"How now!" I cried, becoming sensible of some intrigue. "You are a strange friend to my lady Joan! Why urge her to wed Salisbury when she holds him in such distaste? I think Salisbury must be a fiend to force his suit on an unwilling maid!"

"Nay," said Lady Joan forlornly. "The earl of Salisbury is a good man. He deserves better than one such as I. Better to take the veil than enter a makeshift marriage, for once I enter the cloister none can drag me away from its walls."

"So Salisbury does not please you, or else pleases you too well," said I, unable to understand the logic behind her rejection. "But be that as it may, there are more husbands to be had than Salisbury and Christ!"

"Aye," said Lady Joan and her eyes grew wide. "There are more husbands to be had. And therefore, I beg you— tell your master, by the love that he bears me, that he must ask me no more questions, but only entreat the king on my behalf that I may be allowed to join the Benedictine sisters."

There was no more to be said. I left the ladies in the garden and found my way back to the entrance. The damsel who kept the door inquired after Margery's reception of me. I moaned a little and hung my head; that seemed to satisfy both her curiosity and her spite. The entrance into the street was dark and narrow, and I nearly stepped into a fellow as I turned the corner.

"Ho there!" cried an offended voice. An apology was on my lips before I realized the speaker. "Have a care where you walk, boy!" replied the speaker ungenerously and I found myself face to face with Thomas Holland.

"What do you here?" I demanded curtly.

"I come to offer my congratulations to the lady Joan," he said. "No doubt you have the same office—or perhaps you've come to offer your master's congratulations since he cannot bear to utter them himself."

I gritted my teeth, enraged that such a viper should know of my master's affections. "I wish you were not a Christian," said I, "then I could cut out your heart without compunction."

"Mighty words from a mere lackey," said Holland, and the scar across his left eye flamed purple. "It is well for you, Potenhale, that other matters claim my attention at moment. Save your rooster crowing till we roost in England, and if the heralds can stomach your impudence, I'll meet you in the lists at tourney."

7

THE DUST OF DEATH
October, 1347 – August, 1348

I never knew whether the prince took up Lady Joan's plea before the king. But whether he did or not, it is certain that the king was of no mind to be swayed. He ordered the marriage to be celebrated at Martinmas, and within a week of the ball the convoy at Calais lifted sail.

The crossing to Dover was stormier than usual. Our fleet lost several ships. The king exclaimed that whenever he crossed over to France the weather was fair, but whenever he returned to England it was as foul as an old witch. His memory was somewhat at fault, however, for the trip to France had been as difficult as the departure. I was minded of our frustrated crossing a year and two months past, wherein we spent five failed attempts to reach Gascony and shipped instead for Normandy and La Hougue.

Despite mishaps along the way, the crossing was eventually achieved and we entered London with all the pomp of a Roman triumph. Joyful citizens lined the streets and called blessings on King Edward's head. "O woeful bloodshed!" said one of the songs. "Presumptuous pride cast Philip down! Trust in God has raised Edward up! France bewails the day of sorrow, England delights in the day of Joy and Consolation, which Our Lord Jesus Christ has deigned to grant her. Praise and honor be to Him forever and ever."

Our English people gloried in the triumph we had achieved, but even more so in the spoils that we brought back from the continent. There was not a noblewoman who did not profit from our pillage. French clothes, French furs, and French jewelry decked every lady's body, while French furniture, French pillows, and French goblets decked her home. The sweethearts of the lower orders received gifts from their men as well, till every woman in England went appareled in foreign trinkets.

Lady Joan's marriage followed fast upon our return. The alliance had political ramifications beyond the mere union of a man and a woman; Salisbury would join to Kent, and the two earldoms would become one. The ceremony was to be celebrated in the chapel of Westminster Castle. The king, queen, and all the royal family would attend, for Joan was a cousin—almost a daughter—having been reared in the royal nursery.

The prince and I went early to the church. We met Montague outside the gate. His face was flushed with pleasure and excitement, and well it should be, for today he would wed and tonight he would bed the most beautiful woman in England. He greeted his highness with a radiant smile and clapped him on the back in friendship.

"God give you joy," said the prince, forming each word distinctly like a man speaking an unfamiliar language.

We went into the church and found our seats. Stratford, the current Archbishop of Canterbury, entered.

The pallium swung gently from his shoulders as he took up his place before the altar. As the highest prelate in the land, it was his privilege to preside over this marriage mass. When the time was right, the bride and groom processed through the nave. Montague's thin arm held Joan's rapturously; her face had a nervous smile. The choir began to intone the Kyrie, but a disruption in the rear of the chapel put all their notes out of joint.

"Hold there!" bellowed a voice. A hushed whisper suffused the chapel as the onlookers turned their heads to see the intruder.

"Who halts the service of the Lord?" demanded Stratford with indignation.

"It is I, Sir Thomas Holland," said the man, and he came forward down the central aisle of the nave.

"What reason have you for such an outrage?" asked the archbishop.

"Only to say that this marriage is an outrage and there must be no wedding."

A general gasp filled the room. "Explain yourself, sirrah!" said Stratford sharply. "Is there some impediment of which we know nothing?"

"Marry, yes," said Holland. "But not on the gentleman's part. It is the lady who cannot be wedded today, for she has already taken another as husband."

Every eye turned to Joan, pure and virginal as the Madonna in her blue dress.

"What is the name of this alleged husband?" asked the archbishop.

"His name is Sir Thomas Holland," replied the intruder, "that is to say—myself!"

"Upon my soul!" said Montague with a hoarse cry. "I have heard enough from this rogue. He seeks to bait me with these spurious accusations. He was my father's steward and has always been at odds with me. Envious dog! What ear would believe that this beauty here could mate with such a beast as you?"

"Madman," said Holland coolly. "I speak no more than the truth."

"I will not hear you!" said Montague. "Archbishop, continue with the mass."

The king, in his royal mantle, stood up slowly. "Stay," he said. "This matter must be sifted a little ere the marriage can proceed. Lady Joan," he said somberly, and his words were as heavy as the lid of a granite tomb. "You have heard Sir Thomas's avowal. Is it true that this man is your husband?"

Joan's face was ashen. She said no word.

"You must answer," said the king. "Is this man your husband?"

"Yes," said Lady Joan. "God help me, he is." And when she had said these words, she swooned away entirely. Montague caught her before she fell and set her down gently on the flagstones. A tempest of red hair pushed him away, and I saw that Margery was at her lady's side, rubbing her wrists and calling her gently by name.

"This is some trick!" cried Montague. "How comes it that the lady is married to you but none of her guardians here know of it? You did not wed her lawfully, that I'll wager."

"I can produce the priest," said Holland with a sneer, "if you'll give me leave to pen a few lines to your estates in Salisbury. It was the same priest that wed your mother to your father—and if my marriage be something less than lawful, then your birth is something less than legitimate."

Montague let out an inarticulate cry of rage. He laid his hand on his dagger and would have sprung at Holland, but the prince came up behind him and pinioned his arm behind his back. "Let go!" said Montague to the prince. "I will have his blood."

"Nay," said the king sharply. "You shall not. We will investigate this matter thoroughly and evaluate all the proofs. If Holland speaks true, then he shall have the lady. But if he speaks false,"—the king's brow grew dark as a thundering sky—"more men than Montague will cry for his blood."

The matter was under examination for nearly a fortnight, and this is the story that was unearthed. The marriage between Holland and Lady Joan had been contracted seven years ago. At that time Holland was but newly returned from the Euxine Sea where he had achieved glory in the ranks of the Teutonic order. There was scant work in England for his sword. The war with France was barely underway, and Sluys had not been fought yet. Holland sought employment wherever he could find it. The old Earl of Salisbury admitted Holland into his household as his seneschal and the one-eyed knight took on the duties of a steward.

Lady Joan was twelve years old at the time, mild, biddable, and easy to please; her beauty had not yet blossomed into the glorious flower of later years, but the budding girl was fair enough to turn men's eyes. The Earl of Salisbury had daughters of an age with Lady Joan, and Queen Philippa allowed Joan to spend a summer in Salisbury's household. Holland enchanted Joan with his suavity, his scars, and his savoir-faire. She listened to his stories with shining eyes and felt his hungry gaze with guilty pleasure. When Holland talked of love, Joan did not rebuke him; and when he took her by night to see the priest, she did not say him nay.

Holland, it must be understood, had no desire at the time for the marriage to be made public. He had little to recommend himself besides a reputation for valor. If the marriage were known, Joan's guardians would use all means in their power to have it set aside. The intervening years, however, and especially the lucky captures at Caen, had advanced him in both fortune and prestige. As a trusty baron of His Majesty, he was nearer to Joan's equal. He had intended to promulgate the marriage at the end of the French campaign, but the news of Joan's betrothal to Salisbury had overset his plans entirely.

Joan also had good reason to cloak the marriage in secrecy. Her rapid removal from Salisbury's household released her from the spell which Holland had cast upon her. Instead of admiring the seneschal, she began to loathe him for his coarseness. She was overcome with shame and remorse over the marriage and filled with dread lest anyone should discover it.

But although she might deplore her entanglement with Holland, she knew that she was not at liberty to marry another. When the king affianced her to Salisbury, she had resisted the betrothal with all means in her power. Yet she also knew that if she revealed the true reason behind her reluctance, the first marriage would become public. She would be forced to enter Holland's house as his wife. For this reason, she had maintained silence until the wedding day, in constant terror that

Holland would reveal the dreadful secret, and hoping against all reason that the second marriage would cause him to keep silence about the first.

The king heard this story with good grace. "And has this marriage been consummated?" he demanded.

"Nay," said Holland grudgingly. "But that can be remedied soon enough."

"But the priest, the bride, and the groom all affirm that the ceremony took place?"

"Aye," said Archbishop Stratford, "They have each sworn a sacred oath to that effect."

"Then there is little to be done," said the king, "save to give the lady to her lord. You are a fortunate man, Holland, to come off so well in this matter!"

"Aye, Majesty," said Holland with a self-satisfied leer.

"But what if the lady will not have him?" demanded Montague.

"She has already said that she *will* have him," said the archbishop, "seven years ago in the blessed sacrament."

"But what if she refuses?" Montague persisted.

"Why, I suppose that the only thing to be done then would be to appeal to the pope," replied Stratford. "He may annul the marriage, though I hardly think it ought to be set aside because the fickle female has changed her mind."

The prince and I were with Montague when the archbishop mentioned this course of action. "What think you, highness?" demanded the young earl. "Shall I send to the pope?"

The prince shook his head sympathetically. "Nay, friend, you do but prolong your pain. Have the tooth drawn, and the fever will subside."

"God's eyes!" said Salisbury vehemently. "You do not understand, highness. I cannot abide that another man should be her husband."

"I understand well enough," answered the prince, and methinks that he understood better than Salisbury could ever know. The prince sighed sadly. "The pope is better pleased with England now that the truce is signed, and mayhap he will show us a gracious countenance. But even so, it is not yours to decide whether to appeal. It is the lady who must decide in this."

I was deputed to deliver the message to the lady Joan. But when I came to her house, they told me that she was sick in bed and would see no one. I asked then for Margery and she met me at the door. I told her what was afoot and bade her find out if the lady Joan desired to send to the pope or no.

"I know her mind already," said Margery, "and she is sick to heart at the thought that she must be Holland's wife. Send to the pope, and though he be French, I'll pray a thousand *pater nosters* for his soul if he can save her."

"She could have saved herself," said I. "If she had denied the marriage, Holland's words would have fallen to the ground. They would have said the priest was in collusion with him, and her story would have swept the field and all before it."

"Aye," said Margery. "But should a woman be less honorable than a man? She will not lie to save her life. Though, in truth, the penance she will do for the truth must be a thousand times greater than the penance she would have done for the falsehood."

"But," said I, determined to carry my point, "the Holy Writ finds falsehood in the very nature of a woman,

and what is found in nature, can be but venial at worst.
Ask the Hebrew midwives and Judith if deception is not
the best course."

"But they lied to save others, and not to save themselves," said Margery, "and so they can be excused of
wrongdoing."

"You are too clever for my advice," said I with a
smile. "Give my greetings to your mistress and tell her
my master shall send to the pope. And if God be for
us, the marriage shall be annulled with nary a lie to be
said."

"Who is your master today?" Margery asked. "Does
the prince send you or Montague?"

"Both," said I, "for the prince stands Montague's
friend in this matter."

"Ah?" she said with eyebrows raised. "I had not
thought to find the two so close. He is a true friend
indeed." She gave me her hand in farewell, and for the
first time, we parted with goodwill for one another.

*In the days of King Arthur, there was a state
of lasting peace throughout all of England. He
increased his court by inviting very distinguished
men from far-distant kingdoms to join it. In this
way he developed such a code of courtliness in his
household that he inspired peoples living far away
to imitate him. Even the man of noblest birth
thought nothing at all of himself unless he wore
his arms and dressed in the same way as Arthur's
knights. At last the fame of Arthur's generosity*

*and bravery spread to the very ends of the earth;
the kings of countries far across the sea trembled
at the thought that they might be attacked and
invaded by him, and so lose control of the lands
under their dominion.*

Thus runs the story told by the good bishop Geoffrey of Monmouth. If he is to be believed, King Arthur extended the domain of England all the way across Europe to the very gates of the city of Rome. Our own King Edward had similar ambitions. And since he desired to possess both the resplendent reputation and the expansive empire of Arthur, it seemed good to him to organize his household in the same way as the heir of Uther Pendragon.

Two years before Crecy, our good King Edward had held a tournament at Windsor. It was called a tournament of the Round Table, and there the premier knights of England played at being Lancelot, Tristram, Galahad, and Perceval. As they smote each other with lance and sword, Edward swore that he would one day re-establish Arthur's old order of knights, the Knights of the Round Table.

The king chose St. George to be the patron saint of this future order. St. George, as you must know, is the favorite saint of England, just as St. Martin is the favorite saint of France. Any Frenchman who has fought our forces will have heard them bellow this good saint's name as a talisman against the foe. It was St. George who appeared to King Richard in the Holy Land and gave him victory over the Saracens. Some say that Richard himself intended to make an order of knights in honor of the saint, but he did not have time to establish the order before his short reign gave way to his brother's.

There was no expectation that Edward's reign would be too short for such an enterprise. He settled on Windsor Castle as the headquarters of the new order. But Windsor must be made worthier ere it housed its new inhabitants. The old building had stood virtually intact since the time of Edward the Confessor. Our Edward commissioned William of Wykeham to renovate the keep and to construct a chapel suitable for the ceremonies which would take place. The new architect was given free hand. He replaced the low, heavy ceiling of the old chapel with pillars as long and slender as the lance of St. George, and arches as sharply pointed as the spear that he carried. The vaults of the roof fanned out like the wings of the dragon, and colored glass bathed the nave in a fiery glow of light.

The chapel was completed while the king was in France, and in the new year following our return, the king was ready to establish the order. He chose St. George's Day, the twenty-third of April, to inaugurate it, and on that day he summoned the chief peers of the realm to assemble at Windsor Castle. There they sat in the great wooden chairs along the sides of the chapel, like a council of bishops in martial dress. Thomas Beauchamp, the Earl of Warwick, was there along with his younger brother John. Henry of Lancaster came, and Sir John Chandos, and Sir James Audley. Sir Thomas Holland was there, but he was placed far away from the Earl of Salisbury since blood was still hot between them. Roger Mortimer sat beside Salisbury, a happy man having just recovered the barony that his treasonous grandfather forfeited. The

Captal de Buch, a leading noble from Gascony, had been invited to participate. All of our companions from Crecy were there—all save Sir Walter Manny. Ever useful and ready to serve, Manny had remained behind in Calais to keep a close eye on the tenuous truce with France. But what Manny missed now, the king would make up later, for he was admitted to the order in the year following.

I, as you must apprehend, did not partake in the ceremony, but was allowed to stand quietly in the chapel corridor and observe the proceedings. The king entered in all his royal panoply and took the governing seat at the head of the chapel. The colored light poured down upon him from the patchwork of stained glass windows giving his radiant robes an even brighter hue. He wore a gown of russet under a mantle of blue. A blue garter bound his right leg and a blue sash slung low across his breast. A chain bearing a medallion encircled his stately neck, and on the medal was engraved a picture of St. George trampling the Libyan dragon.

The prince, seated on His Majesty's right hand, was the first to receive the regalia of the new order. The king's squires came forward and fastened garter, sash, and medal upon him. Then turn by turn the knights received their trappings, twenty-six in all including prince and king. The Archbishop of Canterbury had come to Windsor for the occasion, and the knights of the new order knelt bareheaded before him as he celebrated the holy mass.

Afterwards, they went to dine, and there I was permitted to join them at last. The feast honored the martyrdom of St. George, but also the choosing of the Knights of the Garter. Each of the knights felt honored to be a part of the privileged twenty-six, but for some of them the name of the new order was confusing in the utmost.

"What part has female gear with arms?" demanded Henry, the Earl of Lancaster. "And for men to wear a garter.... 'Tis womanly! No true knight of Arthur's court would abide such folly."

"Nay, there's precedent in it," said Chandos. "Sir Gawain wore a lady's girdle when he left the Green Knight's castle."

"But he wore the girdle to show that he kissed the lady," said Audley wryly, "and our king wears the garter to show that he didn't."

The allusion to Lady Joan was only too clear. Several of the men guffawed loudly. Salisbury flamed red and walked away clumsily like a man just woken from deep sleep. The prince kept his countenance but there was no levity in his eyes.

"Perchance the garter of our order has naught to do with that incident at Calais," said Warwick delicately.

"Examine your medallion," replied Audley, "and see if there can be any doubt of the matter."

The Earl of Warwick turned the medal of St. George over in his palm, and there on a scroll beneath the image were carved the words, *Honi soit qui mal y pense*. "Shamed be him who thinks evil of it," he read aloud. They were the very words that the king had spoken the night of the ball in Calais. Audley laughed triumphantly.

"Perhaps," said Warwick, manfully grasping at straws, "this motto reinforces our sovereign's claim to the crown of France. 'Shamed be him who thinks evil of it,' which is to say 'Shamed be him who thinks evil of Edward's claim.'

"Perhaps," said Lancaster doubtfully.

"Aye, perhaps," said Chandos with a gleam of mirth in his dark eyes. "But that explains the motto and not the garter."

"Perhaps it is not so much a garter as a strap," continued Warwick, "and symbolizes the fastening of our points of armor, thus signifying that a knight of our order must always be armed and ready to uphold Edward's claim to the French crown."

"Upon my soul," said Audley, "you are too clever by half, Beauchamp. 'A garter is not so much a garter as an armor strap.' Ha! An' I listen to you, I'll soon swear that an apple is not so much an apple as it is a tennis ball, and an arrow is not so much an arrow as it is a monk's pen. Leave this scholar's talk and say like a plain man that a garter be a garter. And I, for one, care not a whit that the garter belongs to Lady Joan, for she's the bonniest lass in England and has more husbands than one to swear to the truth of that."

The Italians say that the black death came from the Turks. The Germans call it the Italian infection. In England, we blame the French, for the disease was theirs before it was ours. It was the plague that precipitated the truce and hastened our homeward journey from Calais. But when we fled from the plague to England, we found that the plague would not be shaken so easily. It followed on our heels like a stray dog, loath to depart for prayers or curses. The harbor towns were affected first. The sickness almost denuded Dorset of inhabitants. Devon, Somerset, and Bristol came next, then Gloucester, Oxford, and finally London.

At the beginning of the disease, the sufferers were afflicted with great swellings upon the more shameful parts of the body, some like an ordinary apple in size, others like an egg, or others small as a cherry. These swellings were so hard and dry that, even when they were cut with a knife, hardly any liquid flowed out. The deadly lumps, in a short time, spread all over the body. Then the symptoms of the disease changed form. Black or livid spots erupted on the arms and thighs, sometimes big and scattered, sometimes little and close together. They were the sure sign of death to whoever had them. No physician, no medicine was of any use.

The plague was all the worse because it traveled from the sick to the well as easily as fire catches dry wood. Any form of communication with the sick gave the disease to the well and both died in misery; but also, mere contact with the clothes, or anything that the sick had touched or used, seemed to carry contagion with it. Many, eager to preserve their own lives, shunned all contact with the stricken. Brothers abandoned brothers; fathers and mothers abandoned children. But the Almighty rarely rewarded them for this desertion; more often than not, their flight was too late to save themselves.

Your own country France suffered as much or more than mine, so you will believe me when I say that of every two men in England, only one was left alive; the nobles lost less, the commoners lost more, and the clergy suffered worst of all. The graveyards of our ancestors were too small by far, so new fields were chosen where the dead might be buried.

The prince and I were at Berkhamsted when the plague first lifted its head in England. He had large estates there, and though like Chandos he completely relinquished their management to a steward, from time to time he tarried there a week to remind the tenants of their fealty. We had heard but little news of the pestilence, and the prince determined to go to London and enter the lists of a tournament there. The trip down through the country-side was filled with rumors of strange happenings. As we neared the metropolis, we observed many travelers going the opposite way, some driving carts laden down with all their household possessions.

A low mist hung over London as we came up the Thames by barge in the early dawn. The docks and wharfs stretched out cold and empty like the hand of a dead man. As our rowers neared the landing, I moved forward holding the lantern at the front of the boat; the space lit by its feeble flame was small enough for a man to fold his arms around. No one came to tie up our boat. The prince bade me call for the harbormaster. We had often poled up the Thames since our return from France, and I knew the master of the royal dock by name.

"Will Tyler!" I shouted, but my voice fell to the bottom of the boat against the thick wall of fog. "Will Tyler!" I bellowed, "Do your duty, curse you, and haul the line."

The soft shuffle of bare feet indicated that someone was present. I tossed the heavy rope into the gloom and was rewarded by a gentle pull from the dock. The boat secured, I leapt onto the wharf and looked about me to chide the harbormaster. "You've kept His Highness waiting, Tyler."

"I beg pardon, sir," said a small voice. In the mist, I discerned a tousled head, atop a leather jerkin far too large for its wearer.

"Where's Will Tyler?" I barked.

"Here, sir."

"I mean your father."

"Dead, sir. Dead one week."

"Why, how is this?" I demanded. "And has the city commissioned no new harbormaster for the royal dock? God's life, this is a sorry state of affairs...."

The boy blinked stupidly and scratched his left armpit. The prince, who had disembarked by now, considered him quietly then halted my harangue with a raised hand. "You have done well, Master Tyler," he said simply.

"Thank 'ee, sir," said the lad, his lip trembling a little, and his mouth dropped all together when he recognized the crest of the Prince of Wales.

"Here is a florin for your trouble," said the prince, and he tossed a bright gold piece to the little urchin. "And mark you, Tyler, if you grow tired of playing harbormaster, then you must come to my estate at Berkhamsted, and I will see about a place for you in my household."

"Yes, sir. Thank 'ee, sir. If my mother be willing, I will, sir." The lad tucked the florin into his oversized tunic, and with an awkward bow, rushed unsteadily to the harborside cottage, doubtless to share the news with his one remaining parent.

"You are too generous, Your Highness," said I.

"It is my pleasure to be generous while I am able. You are right, of course, that he will be a trouble for my steward, but I do not think it will come to that." His eye followed the boy who had tripped, risen, and taken to coughing. Then, unaware that he was being watched, the boy began to scratch himself in a most indecent manner. "He will not live the week," said the prince simply. And it came about that his prediction was most true, for the next time that I was in London, I inquired of the boy and found that the plague had taken him not three days after our landing.

The prince himself was seemingly immune to the curse. The lintel of his door was marked (with whose blood, I do not know), and though retainers, men-at-arms, and even his own sister perished in the pestilence, the avenging angel passed over him. The king and queen were likewise spared, and indeed, nearly all of the nobler members who had fought in the French campaign.

But for any Christian, whether sick or well, the streets of London were no healthy place to be. London had always seemed cramped and dingy—especially after the splendors of Caen and Calais—and the scourge which beset the city only increased the squalor of the place. If a man did not contract the plague, he must contend with the stench that attended it. All about the city the dead were thrown into open pits by relatives too sick or too frightened to carry them farther. If a man could overcome the stench, he must fend off the insanity that had overcome London's citizens. While some citizens cloistered themselves in their homes to fast and pray, others ran riot in the streets, drinking, laughing, singing, joking, and doing whatever they willed. All laws, human and divine, were flouted. A man was in as much danger from cutthroats and cutpurses as he was from spots and contagion.

The tournament that we had come to London to participate in was cancelled because of the plague. We tarried a day, and then left the way that we had come. But Berkhamsted was too close to London for comfort, and within a fortnight the prince retired to his estates in Wales.

This change of venue pleased me well, for Wales was no more than a day's ride from my parents' home in Herefordshire. I had not visited Chandos's estate since my days as his squire, and I longed to display to full advantage the spurs I had won in France. Only then could my parents take proper pride in their son who had become companion-at-arms to a prince. His highness established himself comfortably on his lands and then gave me a week's leave. I armed myself for the short journey, carefully polishing the insignia upon my shield. I had left a boy; I would return a man, entering the nineteenth year of my life and the third year of my knighthood.

It was the same wooden house that I had left behind, though the thatch was as threadbare as a pauper's jerkin and in sore need of repair. A thin wisp of smoke came from the chimney and I rejoiced to see that the place was inhabited. As I turned down the lane toward the cottage, a wizened old woman stepped out of the trees and came face to face with my mount. The horse started violently; I calmed him and berated the old hag for coming so suddenly into the way.

"Better sudden than saddened," she cackled.

"What do you mean?" I asked.

She answered in a lilting tone of gaiety, "I must be quicker than the pest, if I'll stay quicker than the rest."

I saw then that her brains were addled and would have pushed past her in the road. But she called out after me, "Have a care, stranger! The devil's spouse is in that house."

"Devil's spouse?" I asked, befuddled. "What's she?"

"A horrid hag you call the plague."

I reined in my horse and crossed myself fervently. "Are you sure?" I asked, for I had heard of few cases of the Black Death in the rolling pastures of Herefordshire.

"As sure as any, sir," the rhyming witch replied, but when I plied her further with questions, she mumbled incoherently and darted back into the woods.

I frowned in consternation, unsure how to proceed. If the house had plague, it was folly to enter it. But who knew whether to trust the words of such a crazy beldame? I looked again at the house and saw the smoke curling up from the chimney like the tail of a cat. The plague may have entered the cottage, but someone there still had life enough to add wood to the kitchen fire. I could not leave without venturing further.

I called out when I came to the clearing in front of the house. A man answered me through the door, with a voice that grated like the chains in a well. "For Christ's sake, begone!"

"I seek William and Miriam Potenhale!" I said. "Are they here?"

There was a moment's pause. "No," answered the voice.

"Are they alive?" I asked.

"What is it to you?" demanded the voice.

"They are my kin."

I heard a rustling inside and it seemed like the voice was nearer to the door now. "What is your name?" the man asked.

Sir John Potenhale," I answered.

"Ah," said the voice plaintively, and the cottage door swung open to reveal a gaunt, hollow-eyed man. His right leg ended just below the thigh, and he leaned helplessly on the frame of the door.

"Father!" I exclaimed gladly, though I recognized him more by his crippled leg than by his altered face.

"Not a step nearer," he croaked as he saw that I had begun to dismount. "The plague has been in this house—I'll not have it take you as well as your mother."

"Is she dead then?" I asked, and when he nodded I felt a heavy weight like a millstone begin to bear down on my chest.

"How did you avoid it?" I asked.

"I did not. The pestilence grew on me before it touched her body. Yet she would not leave the house and stayed to nurse my sickbed. I had given up all hope except for death to come quickly. I do not know how many days I lay there, insensible with the fever. But when I awoke, the swellings had subsided, and your mother—God rest her soul!—had died in the bed beside me."

"God rest her soul," I said mournfully.

"Aye, God rest her!" said my father, "For she's had little enough of rest in this world. She toiled night and day to see to the food and comfort of a worthless cripple, and I with this useless stub of a leg have outlived her at the last. I should have died in her stead."

"You could not choose to take her place," said I.

"I should have taken her place years ago," said my father. "I should have taken her place of humility, of service, and of love. But instead I chose to pursue a life of pride and glory—I took up the arms of an earthly lord instead of the cross of a heavenly king. And for my sins—and for the sins of others—she has paid the price. Aye, for this plague is a punishment on our land, a woe on our war-mongering king, a scourge on his stiff-necked nobles, and a curse on the complacent clergy. It is the bane of sinners everywhere both in impious England and the lands round about."

"Peace," I said. "You are raving."

"Peace, you say! Peace, you say! But there is no peace. This pestilence is the hand of God and it will not be lifted till the English people humble themselves in the dust before Him."

"The plague has addled your wits," said I. "I will not hear you."

"Miserable sinner," said my father, and his eyes rolled wildly in his gaunt and frenzied face. "Once I took nothing but pride in your advancement. I gloried in your prowess and your preferment at the hands of Sir Chandos. But this too was sin and for this your mother was stricken. I see the same pride in you, and for this you will perish with the rest of them. If only I had taken you at birth and sent you far from me. If only I had given you to some holy hermit or cloistered you away from the world. Then, maybe then, you would have sought the fear of the Lord instead of the honor of men, and your soul at least would have been saved." He laughed hoarsely, and out came the same devilish cackle of the old woman that had met me on the path.

"Is everyone in this place mad?" I cried out in terror. I had overcome my fears at the battles of Caen and Crecy, doing my duty with sword and buckler despite the gnawing worries in my throat. This new fear was overmastering. I put spurs to my horse and took to the road as if a pack of snarling wolves were at my heels.

My poor horse worked hard that day, for I barely gave him time to breathe on the path back to Wales. My father's hollow laughter was ringing in my ears, and the terror of it nearly blotted out the sorrow I felt for my mother's death. There was no one to reason me out of the indescribable horror that had overwhelmed me; no one save myself. "So," I said pensively, "I have no mother, and my father is a madman. Is that the hardest thing that could befall a man? I still have my honor, I still have my place, and there are worse things that a man could do than serve a prince." With these words, I calmed myself, and by the time I reached the prince's stables my nerves had steadied a little.

I hoped to find the prince's household a refreshing haven after the nightmare that had confronted me at home; I soon discovered, however, that ill fortune had attended the house in my absence. Brocas and the prince were closeted together when I came in, and his highness's steward told me that they desired my attendance. I entered the prince's chambers and bowed. A stiff silence pervaded the air like fog over an impassable fen. Brocas was sitting stolidly, with none of his usual banter or jests. His highness walked to and fro with a harsh stride, hands clasped behind his back.

"Potenhale," said the prince sharply without any words of greeting. "Have we still that vase I took at Caen?"

"Aye," said I, remembering the scalloped beauty inlaid with gold and blue enamel. "It is here in Wales. You bade me send it to your steward."

"Then bid him send it now to my cousin Joan," said the prince, "and with it a message that I am, as I have always been, her humble servant." With these words, the prince turned on his heel and strode abruptly out of the room leaving Sir Brocas and I alone.

"Why, what has happened?" I asked aloud. "And why is the prince sending Lady Joan the vase? It was his favorite treasure, a keepsake of his first campaign."

"The pope has ruled at last," answered Brocas.

"Yes?" I asked in earnest expectation.

Brocas shook his head ruefully. "Salisbury's appeal is denied, the first marriage is upheld. Joan goes to Holland's home within the week, and with her the vase as a wedding gift."

8

A TRIAL OF VALOR
September, 1348 – August, 1349

The plague continued to work its will in England, but the prince could not stay forever at his estate in Wales. We rejoined the royal household to celebrate Christmas, and the celebrations, though not as lavish as the season before, were gay enough to dispel the pall that the pestilence had cast upon the court. The prince's money flowed as freely as water; he bestowed magnificent jeweled brooches on his mother and sisters and rings and clasps on all of his attendants. True, the rent rolls of his estates had suffered in the last year—for many of his tenants had perished in the plague. But the prince's expenditures never had any proportion to the amount of his income, and he continued to live as luxuriously as the Plantagenets were wont to do.

In the spring of the following year, the queen gave birth to another child, and for that occasion the king held a great tournament at Windsor. In bygone days, the royal family and their retainers would have lodged comfortably in the castle, but now the place was as full of craftsmen as a guild fair. William of Wykeham, the king's master architect, had begun his renovations of the castle proper, and handymen, hammers, and hoists filled the air with creaks, bangs, and shouts. The prince elected to lodge in the field, and we spread his pavilion near the plain where the tournament would be waged.

I had participated in tournaments before—there was one at Lichfield shortly after our return from France—but the Windsor tournament was the grandest I had beheld. The king presided over the tournament, dressed in a bright green robe embroidered with pheasant feathers. He sat on a dais beside Queen Philippa watching the jousts that honored the arrival of their newest progeny. King David of Scotland attended, having patched up a shamefaced peace with England after his treacherous attacks of two years ago. Most of the Garter knights were present. The field also held the Comte d'Eu and other French prisoners from Crecy. Their captive status was no hindrance to a friendly trial of arms; the English knights welcomed the chance to try their prowess against the French who—even in our land—are reckoned the most puissant chevaliers in all of Europe.

The spoils I had earned in France were long since spent, and without the prince's aid I would never have been able to enter the lists. His highness, however, outfitted me for the tournament at his own expense and paid the herald fees so that my shield could hang beside his own. My first round of jousts was as successful as I could have wished. I challenged Sir Stephen Cosington, another knight whom the prince had recently attached to his household. We were of similar mettle and experience. On the first two passes we broke our lances upon each other, but on the third pass, I hit him squarely in the center of his helmet. My opponent slid backwards off his crupper and the heralds awarded me the victory. By right of tournament, Sir Cosington's steed and armor were forfeit to me, but I bestowed them back on him again, for he was a courteous knight and we shared the same master.

The prince's first joust was against Roger Mortimer, the Earl of March, but I never saw the outcome of the match. While the prince's squires were helping him mount, I glimpsed red hair in the stands; my eyes searched frantically till they lighted upon Margery. The company she was in did not surprise me. She was still in faithful attendance on her unfortunate mistress. Margery sat in a small chair behind the Lady Joan.

The pope's decision had been unwelcome, but the Lady Joan looked radiant as ever. Her hands rested gently upon her stomach while her violet eyes darted about taking in the spectacle and her golden complexion glowed with life and interest. Perhaps her new husband had not proved so dreadful an ogre as she had feared. The new Earl of Kent—for Thomas Holland had assumed that title by right of his wife—sat beside Joan, his large frame sprawled carelessly over the bench. He had altered not at all. The same smug smile spilled over his face while the scar across his brow bestowed a hint of savagery in his mien.

I longed to enter the stands and speak with Margery, but my desire faltered a little at the thought of encountering Holland. At our last meeting in Calais, he had bidden me look to my sword when next he saw me at tournament. I had seen him fight at Caen and Crecy, charging like a bull at the hapless Frenchmen and decrying the need for any quarter. I was not anxious to engage him in the joust.

But desire to hold speech with Margery won over in the end. While the prince broke lances with Mortimer on the field, I climbed the stairs till I came quietly behind Margery's bench. I touched her on the shoulder. "Sir Potenhale!" she said with a sharp intake of breath, and I fancied that there was a note of excitement in her voice.

"Aye," said I, a little sheepishly. "It has been a long time since I have laid eyes on you."

"Not long since I saw *you*," she replied, "for I watched you break lances with Sir Cosington not half an hour since."

"Ah, you have been watching me, lady?" I asked, pleased to know that she had been in the stands for my triumph.

"No, I was watching Sir Cosington," she replied, "for methinks that the man needs more watching than you—he is so apt to fall and hurt himself."

"Methinks my lance may have had somewhat to do with his fall," I said smilingly. I took her hand in mine.

"Why, how now, sir!" she said. "You are very bold." She drew her hand away, but not as quickly as she might have had my touch been unpleasant.

"If you will not give me your hand," said I, "then give me something else that I may wear into the lists."

"Why should I?" she said.

I determined to speak my heart. "Because I would have all men know that I hold Margery Bradeshaw to be the fairest of all women and the queen of love and virtue."

"Does not your conscience misgive you to tell so many lies?"

I winced a little, remembering the words I had spoken in Lady Joan's garden at Calais when I had denied being Margery's lover. "The only lie, lady, is to say that I do not love you, for—upon my soul—you have captured the castle of my heart."

She stared at me in silence, and I think that her scorn melted a little. "Well, Sir Potenhale, I will grant you *a* favor. You shall have my glove. But I do not say that I shall grant you *my* favor, for that you must earn with more than words." Saying this, she unfastened her glove of crimson and placed it in my hands. "Do not lose it, and may it bring you luck and victory."

I thanked her and turned to go, but the movement of my rising caught the eye of the Earl of Kent. "Potenhale!" said Holland, demanding my attention as one would that of a servant or a dog.

"Sir Thomas," I said, acknowledging him and bowing stiffly.

"I see you have been fortunate at the tournament thus far."

"Aye," I replied, contriving to keep the red glove clenched tightly behind my back and out of his view.

"Then you will have no fear to meet me in the lists," he said, and his left eye flickered open with its missing pupil. "I think I promised you a merry joust when next we met in England. I arm for the games this afternoon, and I have contrived with the heralds so that my first bout will be against you. Will you be ready?"

"I will be at your service," I answered steadily, though inside my heart had begun to pound with unaccustomed ferocity. I would not—I must not!—falter in front of Margery. Holland dismissed me with a wave, and I departed without a backward glance.

By the time I descended from the stands I saw that the prince had finished his three jousts with Mortimer. "Did you win, highness?" I asked.

"Aye, I unhorsed him," he said with a tone of surprise, for he assumed that I had been watching the trial.

"God grant that I do the same to Holland," I answered, and I began to bind the red glove to the crest of my helmet.

"What is this?" demanded Brocas; he had pitched his tent beside the prince's and now came over to hear our conversation. "You are to joust with Holland?"

"Indeed," I said, with an air of false nonchalance. I could see the look of concern in their eyes. Holland was a giant of a man, and though I had increased in girth since my days as a squire, he weighed nearly four stone more than me and was reputed to be a valiant adversary.

"I shall lace your points," said Brocas impulsively. The prince said nothing. But he gripped me firmly on the shoulder, and I saw that like myself he wanted nothing more than for Holland to come tumbling off his horse into the dust of the tourney grounds.

The afternoon came quickly. We ate a light repast, and then Sir Bernard Brocas made good on his promise, playing squire and arming me for the joust. He was tightening the laces of my helmet when the heralds called my name. "Whose glove do you carry, Sir Potenhale?" he asked slyly when he saw my helm, for I had not yet told anyone of my attachment to Margery.

"Why, none other than Queen Philippa's," I replied roguishly.

"Pray that the king does not recognize it!" he riposted, then laughed merrily and urged on my horse with a slap. I lifted my lance and rode into the lists to encounter the Earl of Kent.

Thomas Holland looked even larger in the field than he had in the stands. His magnificent warhorse was caparisoned in silver, and the image of England blazed confidently on his shield. My own horse had few trappings, and my shield was as simple as my birth. When I was first knighted, I had no family crest to assume. The prince bade me make one, and I had chosen a silver chevron on a sable field. I had been knighted at Crecy, and the storm which preceded the battle had put me in mind of this crest. The shield was a sky black with clouds, and the silver chevron a bolt of lightning. Now, as we aligned our horses for the joust, the symbolism struck me as painfully one-sided. What could one lightning bolt hope to do against the whole of England? The herald ordered us to take our marks, and with one wave of the flag, we were charging at each other with lances lowered.

I had unhorsed Sir Stephen earlier with a blow to the helmet, and I aimed now for the little flat spot, just above the bridge of Holland's nose guard. My aim was true, but as I felt the tip of my lance connect with my opponent's helmet, a crash of splintering wood erupted on my chest. Holland had broken his lance on me. I managed to keep my seat with difficulty; I continued on to the end of the barrier, then wheeled about to see if I had unhorsed him. His smiling face greeted me, and I saw that instead of knocking him off his horse as I had intended, I had done nothing more than knock the helmet from his head. Holland was awarded three points for the broken lance, and I returned to my side of the lists to receive a fresh lance from the hands of my volunteer squire.

"His helmet laces must have been loose," said Brocas with a frown. "If I were Holland, I would thrash my squire, for he does his job ill. But it was a good hit. Once more the same, and you are sure to overthrow him."

The second pass was uncannily similar to the first. Taking Brocas's advice, I aimed again for the center of Holland's helmet. Just as before he broke his lance upon me, and when I turned about, I saw that only his helmet had fallen to the ground. I gritted my teeth in anger and walked my mount slowly to where Brocas stood.

The king's dais was close by the field, and as I passed by I heard Chandos expostulating with His Majesty. "He does not fight fair!" said my old master. "Why is not his helmet as well buckled and laced on as young Potenhale's? Tell the heralds that Holland must be on equal footing with his adversary."

"Let him alone," replied the king. "In arms every man takes whatever advantage he can. If Sir Potenhale thinks there is any advantage in fastening his helmet in such a manner, he may do the same. Though for my part, were I in the field, I would lace my helmet as tightly as possible—for Holland takes a great risk to go exposed in such a manner, and it would serve him right if he lost his second eye to the tip of Potenhale's lance."

Brocas was livid with anger when I returned to receive my third lance. "Now, by the holy rood," he exclaimed, "his helm is loose on purpose. You must strike for the breastbone and unhorse him that way. God willing, he'll play the same trick with his breastplate, and it'll flap loose while you drive your lance through his heart."

I waited for the herald's flag and then burst forward for the final joust. I thought briefly of striking at his helm again, wondering if that was the stroke he would now least expect. But at the last minute, better judgment made my lance point swerved downwards, and I caught him on the center of his breastplate. My lance shivered and splintered into a thousand shards, but I hardly noticed the shock of that impact. Right as I hit Holland's armor, I felt my body thrown backwards from a mighty blow to the forehead. Holland had found the flat spot on my helmet; and since my basinet was firmly laced, when it fell it took my body to the ground as well. Holland had unhorsed me.

I heard a mighty cheering erupt in the stands, but my closed visor showed me nothing but the sky above. The victorious Earl circled his horse to where I lay on the ground. "It's a mercy that your horse is a better tilter than you," he sneered, "for I will be adding him to my own stables."

I groaned and tried to rise, but my head was swimming so badly that the light soon faded into blackness.

◆ ◆ ◆

When I awoke, I found that it was already night. I was lying on cushions in the prince's tent, and his highness was seated at a table some little distance away from me penning a letter.

I sat up and rubbed my head a little ruefully.

"Ah, you are better!" said the prince, and he bade the servants fetch me something to eat and drink.

I remembered then how I had been defeated by Holland, and I groaned in frustration. "I am afraid that I have lost the horse your highness bestowed upon me."

"That is no matter. I will give you another," replied the prince. "But you have lost more than just your horse. The heralds awarded Holland your armor as well."

"My armor!" I exclaimed, and my countenance fell, for attached to my helmet was something more precious to me than a horse from the purest bloodlines.

"I did not let him take this," said the prince quickly, and he placed a crumpled red ball in my hand. I unfolded it and saw Margery's glove, dirtier and more wrinkled than when she had given it to me that morning, but still a keepsake that I could not bear to lose.

"Gramercy, your highness," I said fervently, and placing the glove to my lips, I kissed it.

"You will thank me twice when you see what else I have to give you," said the prince, and to my utmost surprise he dropped a second red glove upon the bed where I sat.

"Whence comes this?" I demanded in surprise.

"Its owner was here to see you," replied the prince. "But you were still in your swoon so I sent her away again."

"What said she?" I asked.

"She said that you bore as much watching as Sir Cosington and warned me not to send you into the melee tomorrow."

"She seems tender toward my safety."

"Mayhap," said the prince with a smile, "or perhaps merely doubtful of your prowess."

"You will not heed her, highness?" I asked anxiously. "I shall enter the melee tomorrow?"

"You have no armor."

"I shall beg or borrow some."

"You have no horse."

"Your highness has promised me another."

"You meet my objections well. But there is one more objection that I must put forward—I have promised your shield and your name to another. Allow me the loan of your lightning bolt for the day. I swear to you that the bearer shall not dishonor it."

The prince's request was cryptic, but I granted it without further thought. I presumed that he meant to fight incognito on the morn. Oftentimes at tournament, his opponents in the melee were loath to engage the crown prince. They would turn to the side when they encountered him in the press or refuse to strike when he charged upon them. By wearing the coat-of-arms of a young and relatively obscure knight like me, he would be met with no such reticence. The harder he pressed upon his enemies, the harder they would press back on him; and the greater the skill he displayed, the greater would be their desire to unhorse him.

Although I would not be participating in the melee tomorrow, it was impossible for me to sit in the stands and enjoy the event with the other spectators. If I were recognized, the masquerade would be evident immediately; the news would spread rapidly that the knight with the silver chevron was not the true Sir John Potenhale. And yet the idea of sitting quietly in the tents while the rest of the knights took the field liked me not. I fumed a little, till happily, I conceived a way to see the melee. If the prince could pass incognito tomorrow, why not I? I conferred with his highness on the matter, and we determined that the best costume for my disguise was that of a monk. Under the heavy cowl of a Benedictine, I could watch the games with the rest of the public. I might even get the chance to sit close to the lovely visitor who had bestowed her gloves so freely.

The next order of business was to procure a monastic habit. The prince and I set off on foot for St. George's Chapel. When the king had instituted the Order of the Garter with its twenty-six members, he had also engaged twenty-six poor knights as adjuncts of the order. These military veterans were maintained by the king's bounty, their sole responsibility being to pray for the wellbeing of the Garter knights. All of the poor knights took this responsibility very seriously; some of them even adopted monastic rules and dress, hearkening back to the military religious orders of our grandfathers' time. The prince jokingly called them the "Templars" and confidently assured me that we could root out a monk's habit from among their possessions.

The chapel, when we entered it, was not empty; but instead of the grizzled veterans we expected, we found a lady kneeling before the altar. The prince recognized her at sight. At first, he would have drawn back, but thinking better of it he advanced and addressed her by name.

"Peace be with you, Joan."

She looked up a little startled. Her cheekbones colored, and her hands fell away to the side from where they had been clasped over the curve of her stomach. "And with your spirit," she replied.

"What do you pray for?" asked the prince.

She hesitated, and then encountered his dark eyes with an appealing gaze. "For my child," said she.

"So, you are carrying a babe then?" asked the prince looking at the slight swelling beneath her full skirts.

"Aye," said she. "He will come with the winter."

"God give you joy of him," said the prince gently.

"I pray he is as sturdy a babe as Prince William," said Joan, referring to the royal infant whose birth the tournament celebrated. "I did not see your mother the queen when she was churched, but I hear she could not refrain from smiling and that the infant cried lustily all through the mass."

"Aye, he has a hearty will for life," said the prince, "unlike the last manchild she bore." For the infant that Philippa was carrying at Calais had died not a fortnight after his birth.

"Is it true that you stood godfather to him?"

The prince laughed. "Yes, and a pretty penny it cost me. Now, I am not only bound to be his spiritual guardian but also bound to make presents to each of his nurses."

"But if I remember aright, you have never begrudged a show of largesse. Would you refuse to be godfather if you were asked again?"

"That would depend on the one who asked. A mother's request is not to be denied."

"What of a cousin's?"

"You would have me be godfather to your child?"

"Yes," she said, "if you are willing."

"And what of your husband?" asked the prince. "Does he wish me to be father to your child as well?"

She blushed at the phrasing of his question. "My husband thinks only of preferment, and it is a great thing for one's son to be godchild to a future king."

"Well then, I shall not say you nay. Send word when you are to be churched, and if I be not in France, I shall be there to hold the child and speak the vows."

The lady Joan took the prince's hand and kissed it, then would have resumed her prayers; but the prince—amidst all of the cares surrounding him—had some care still for the retainer whose arms he was appropriating. "Lady," said he, "Since I have granted your request, I have one to ask in turn. I have in my household a holy man on pilgrimage from his abbey. I have convinced him, albeit against his will, to attend the melee tomorrow. May I recommend him to you and allow him to sit in your box to behold the events?"

"Indeed," she said, a little puzzled. "My ladies and I would be glad to converse with a holy one such as him."

I had remained silent in the background throughout the prince's conversation with his cousin, but this new arrangement seemed fraught with mishap. Both Joan and Margery were acquainted with my voice, and I had no hope of speaking with enough erudition to convince them of my saintly calling.

"Highness," I objected, "I am sure the holy man—in light of his vows of celibacy—would be averse to mingling so freely with women. No doubt he can find his own place in the crowd...."

"Nay," said the prince, "I have it on good authority that our holy brother is quite accustomed to having speech with the daughters of Eve. Indeed, he is aptly suited to the task of elucidating doctrine to devout young females. It fits him...like a glove.

"However"—the prince continued, taking pity on my panicked face—"tomorrow will be a special exception to his verbosity. The good man has taken a vow of silence as part of his pilgrimage, and he may not speak till he reaches Canterbury and kisses the flagstones where the martyr's blood was spilled. When he sits with you, you must content yourself only with his presence, cousin, and do not try to ply him with conversation."

Lady Joan looked perplexed at this peculiar request, but she assured the prince that she and her maidens would respect the holy man's vow of silence. The prince kissed her hand in return, and we left the beautiful lady to her prayers. The monk's habit, as the prince had conjectured, was easily obtained from one of the poor knights at the chapel, and we retired to our tents to recover from the day's exhaustion.

◆ ◆ ◆

I awoke with the morning light but found that the prince—and my shield—had already vanished from the pavilion. I struggled into the monk's robe, pulling the hood close about my face. The cloth was coarse and stiff. It rubbed roughly against my skin, and I frowned to find it so unlike the soft linen clothes I was accustomed to wear beneath my armor. The hempen strand I tied about my waist felt curiously light; I missed the weight of the sword belt and the familiar tap of the scabbard against my leg. I said a short prayer of thanks to the Holy Virgin that my father, when he was in his right mind, had trained me to be a knight and not a clergyman.

As usual, I could not remember my father without a cloud of despair overtaking me. In the nine months since I had visited his forlorn croft, I had thought about his words often. His fierce denunciations of all that I valued had cut me to the quick, and the only way to remove his lunatic laughter from my mind was to distract it with pleasanter daydreams. My sweet mistress Margery was one such opiate. I mused awhile on her comely face and form, no doubt indecent thoughts for the wearer of a monastic habit. Then, tucking Margery's crimson gloves into my breast, I set out to watch the *melee à cheval*.

Yesterday's event had been the *joust à plaisance*, and for that the herald's work is relatively simple. He arranges the competitors in pairs. Each match consists of three jousts, with points being awarded for breaking the lance tip, breaking the lance, or especially unhorsing one's opponent. The victorious knights are paired with other victors, and the number of competitors is whittled down in successive rounds of elimination. Holland eliminated me from the tournament, but it was not long before he also met his match; he was unhorsed in the first joust by the very man he had brought to England as a prisoner. The Comte d'Eu displayed all the finesse that your French knights are renowned for, and in the end he was crowned as victor of the event.

For today's event, the *melee à cheval*, the herald's work is not so simple. First, the wooden stakes must be set around a field large enough to contain the charging horses of the mock battle; then, the body of competitors must be divided into two companies of roughly equal numbers and strength. The judging of the melee is the most difficult part of the event. The herald and his companions must keep sharp watch on all corners of the battlefield, so that they may disqualify any knight who has been struck three times with an opponent's weapon. In olden days, our English knights fought with sharp points in the melee, and many were the deaths that occurred at tourney. But ever since the days of Edward I, only blunt weapons have been permitted. Knights who receive three blunt-bladed blows must yield up their horse to the one who vanquished them. Then the squires of victorious knights descend upon the battlefield like carrion crows to seize their masters' spoils and ride them to safety. Complete mastery of the field or the waning light of evening precipitates the end of the melee, and the heralds award a crown to the most puissant member of the winning team.

When I reached the tourney field, the heralds had already posted the names of those assigned to each team. I scanned through the list, happily noting that Sir John Potenhale was in opposition to Sir Thomas Holland, the Earl of Kent. My shield was in better hands than my own, and I smiled to think what a hard time Sir Thomas would have of it, should he attempt to encounter me in the field. The prince's name was in the same column as my own, and I wondered if he would inform the heralds of his withdrawal or leave them to wonder at his absence in the melee.

Attired in my Benedictine habit, I made my way to the stands where an audience had begun to gather. Joan and Margery had arrived before me, closely mantled in the chill morning air. "Welcome," said Lady Joan when she saw me appear beside them. "We are pleased to have you as our guest, though we will not press you with words." I inclined my head in greeting, taking care to keep my hood drawn forward over my eyes. Then, at a word from Lady Joan, I took my seat at the right hand of my beautiful mistress Margery.

The royal stands where our party sat were filled mostly with women today. All of the nobles and knights were engaged in arming themselves for the battle to come. Even the king was absent; he had lain abed too late to see the start of the tourney. The queen was alone on the dais, though she assured the heralds that the king would join her in good time.

At last the knights had armed themselves. The two companies arranged themselves in battle lines upon the field while the trumpets blazoned the beginning of the day with tones as golden as the climbing sun.

"Do you see him, Margery?" the lady Joan demanded.

"Aye," said Margery and her white hand flamed out like a beacon, indicating one of the knights who had just ridden in on the south end of the field. I could not tell for a certainty what man she pointed to, but it was assuredly not her lady's husband. Sir Thomas Holland was in the opposing company, and the image of England glinted brightly on his shield in the other corner of the enclosure.

"And there is thy champion as well," said Joan with a smile, pointing out the silver chevron that I knew so well.

Margery frowned. "Nay, no champion of mine."

"Has your heart cooled so quickly?" asked Joan in a tone of gentle reproof. "It was but yesterday that you gave him your glove and thrust aside all maiden dignity to visit him at his tents."

"But look to his crest, milady!" said Margery. "He does not wear my favor."

I looked in dismay out upon the field. There was the knight with the lightning bolt shield, but his steel cap was as plain as a hermit's table. I cursed myself for a fool. I should have taken care to give one red glove to the prince instead of hoarding them both in the bosom of my monkish gown. The only consolation I had was this: the enforced dumbness on my part had lulled my fair companions into assuming my deafness as well. I must make the most of my fortuitous seating arrangement by eavesdropping assiduously.

The flags fell to the ground and the melee commenced. A cloud of dust filled the air as soon as the riders put spurs into their mounts. For a time, little could be seen in the center of the field. But when the riders had thinned—with the most inexperienced knights walking shamefaced and horseless to the corners of the field—the cloud of dust also abated. I squinted anxiously and saw that the lightning bolt was still intact. Sir Potenhale was encountering the Earl of Warwick now, and astounding him greatly with the force and dexterity of his blows.

But as I surveyed the field, I saw something which puzzled me not a little. There was the prince's crest, the three ostrich feathers waving triumphantly over the Bohemian king's motto. I marveled to see the prince and Potenhale in the field together and wondered whom his highness had recruited to fill his own armor. Whomever he had found, he was a brilliant fighter, for the man on the prince's mount fought as well or better than I had ever seen his highness fight.

"Look at my cousin!" said Joan, clapping her hands in delight. "He is magnificent."

"And yet," said Margery in astonishment, "I doubt not that Sir Potenhale is his equal in arms. I had thought him a mere stripling, but look! He has unhorsed the Earl of Warwick and defeated both Sir James Audley and Lord Stafford."

"Aye, he fights like one of the French knights. But fie on him for not wearing your favor!" said Joan affectionately.

"Nay, the fault is mine," said Margery solemnly. "I was something too disdainful in my speech with him. It has always been my way, and I am heartily sorry for it now."

The battlefield cleared even more, and I saw that Sir Thomas Holland was still in the saddle. His team was sorely depleted, however, and it was unlikely that they could hold the field much longer against the fierce onslaught of the prince and Sir Potenhale. It was only a matter of time before Holland encountered one of those two paladins.

The current of the melee threw him into the path of the prince. Holland urged his horse forward to cross blades with his highness, but at the last minute the prince pulled away and declined to engage him. At first, I was half angry with my master for not giving Holland such a buffet that he would remember it all his life, but then I remembered that another man wore the prince's crest.

"Blessed Mary, I am glad he did not hurt him," said Lady Joan breathlessly, speaking of her husband for the first time that day.

Sir Potenhale, when he encountered Holland, was not so kind or forbearing. He advanced on the earl and, rising up in his stirrups, dealt him such a blow that he slipped swooning from his saddle. If my impersonator had been using sharp edges, I doubt not that he would have cloven his brain in two.

I glanced inquiringly at the two ladies to see how Holland's fall had affected them. Margery's eyes glittered brightly, though she said nothing in deference to her mistress's feelings; Joan herself had paled considerably, and her hands cupped protectively around the child she carried in her womb. Holland's swoon was short lived, however. By the time his squires reached him, he had regained his footing and was able to walk out of the battlefield leaning on their arms. Joan's face resumed its golden merriment, and she made no move to go down to the pavilion where her husband was being attended by a physician.

Holland's fall marked the beginning of the end of the melee. Just as the beginning blows had augured, the team containing the prince and Sir Potenhale swept the field of all its opponents; the sun had not yet reached its pinnacle when the heralds declared the victors. The king, contrary to Queen Philippa's expectation, had not arrived in time to see the conclusion of the melee; so Sir

John Chandos held the victor's crown and prepared to bestow it upon the champion of the tournament.

Chandos conferred a while with the heralds, then addressed himself to the audience. "Lords, ladies, and good people of Windsor, the feats of arms that we have witnessed today are without parallel in Christendom. And in this garden of chivalry, there are two flowers that have bloomed the brightest." Here he bade Edward, Prince of Wales, and Sir John Potenhale stand forward. "I would that I could divide this crown between you, but the victor's crown is for only one knight to wear." The crowd waited in breathless excitement to see whom Chandos had chosen.

"Sir Potenhale, unfasten your helm," he said. A great roar of applause suffused the field. I looked to Margery to see if she smiled, but her face was a riddle I could not read. In obedience to Chandos's words, the knight with the silver chevron came forward and removed his basinet. His head was uncovered now, and out streamed a mane of dark hair around a closely clipped beard. I had thought to be the only man unsurprised by the revelation, but now my own eyelids pulled back sharply. Those nearest to the dais gasped; Sir John Chandos fell to his knees before the one he had chosen to crown. "Your Majesty," he said reverently, for there in the arms of John Potenhale stood King Edward, the sovereign of England and France.

The prince, meanwhile, had removed his own black helmet, and I saw that he had fought in his own name. The loan of my shield had been for one even greater than he. And what was more than that, it was the prince himself who had refused to encounter Holland in the melee. I marveled at this forbearance, but then ceased to do so when I remembered Holland's fall and Joan's frightened hands cupped around her unborn child. The prince was wise to forbear.

"What think you now, Margery?" said Joan excitedly. "It was the king all this while and not your paladin."

I looked anxiously in Margery's direction. I feared that she would be displeased. Her perception of my valor had been built to such heights and then torn down again in but a few brief moments. Unexpectedly, I saw her face lit by a smile as radiant as the victor's crown. "I am well pleased," she said fervently, "for though it was not Sir Potenhale who won the field, it was also not Sir Potenhale who refused to wear my favor."

Her words inspired me with a new confidence, and while Margery and Joan's heads were bowed in quiet conversation, I rose on silent feet to take my leave. They did not notice my movements, and before I slipped out of the stands I slipped my hands within my habit and laid a parting present upon the chair that I had occupied. When Margery looked my direction again, instead of a tongue-tied monk, she would find the crimson glove that she had left at the tents of her champion. I smiled to think of her surprise.

◆ ◆ ◆

The summer of 1349 came and with it no relief to the pestilence. The prince and I had occasion to visit London and found it even ranker and more wretched than in the previous year. The physicians had given up all hope of balancing the humors in the stricken ones, and many clergymen refused to minister last rites to the dying for fear of contracting the illness themselves. Radical and ridiculous theories abounded as to the cause of the catastrophic sickness. Some blamed over-eating. Others claimed that the disease was contracted by carnal relations with an older woman. Still others continued in their convictions that the plague was the hand of a God upon an impious and undeserving generation.

It was there in London that the prince and I encountered the flagellants. We had attended mass at St. Paul's Cathedral, reputed by all Englishmen to be the most beautiful church in Christendom. But as we came out blinking into the warm sun of the courtyard, we saw that a great crowd had filled the streets as if there was a troupe of jugglers to be seen. When the prince and I pressed forward, we found that the cause of the disturbance was far less festive. A procession of men, perhaps a hundred in number, marched solemnly down the thoroughfare. They wore white robes with white hoods, and on them flamed a cross as red as blood. As they reached the courtyard in front of the cathedral, the line of robed men looped around to form a circle. In unison, they removed their hoods and stripped their garments down to the waist. Their backs were striped like the back of a skunk or badger and red with unhealed wounds. Then, in ominous silence, the circle of men fell to their faces upon the ground, arms outstretched in the form of a cross.

The bishop of London had exited the cathedral in our wake, anxious to see the cause of the commotion within his see. "Who are these men?" the prince demanded, "And what do they here?"

The bishop frowned thoughtfully. "They are the flagellants, highness. I have not seen their like in England before, but I have heard tell of their presence in Italy, France, Germany, and the Low Countries. This company has come over from Friesland, no doubt to spread their sect throughout our country. Their words are a dangerous heresy. They say that they possess a heavenly letter from the Almighty which foretells the impending destruction of this world. They claim that they alone can avert this judgment, and their procession here is to atone for the sins of mankind."

"What works will they do to atone?" I asked curiously.

"Watch and see," said the bishop, and he had hardly spoken the words before the flagellants rose to their feet. One of them, presumably their leader, began to chant out a verse in German while the rest of the half naked men responded in the refrain.

"What do they sing?" I asked, unsure of the meaning behind their foreign words.

"They bid us remember the suffering of Christ," answered the prince, "and battle the harder to put off the sin of this world."

I saw that each man had untied the flail that hung at his side. It was a leather strip, weighted down with iron spikes. Still singing, they began to march about in the circle. The steady pulse of their song was mingled with the steady flick of their wrists as each man administered the lash to the bare shoulders that walked before him. When they had finished the verse of their song, they prostrated themselves again. Only their master stood upright. He went around the circle bidding them pray to the Lord for mercy on the people, for mercy on their friends, for mercy on their enemies, for mercy on earthly sinners, for mercy on sinners in purgatory. They rose to their feet and stretched their hands to the sky, then marching as before they reapplied the lash.

This continued three times, till at last their master came forward into the center of the circle. He bore a scroll in his hands, and opening it he began to read in a loud voice a letter which he claimed to have received from an angel. Christ, the flagellant declared, was angry with the depravities of man: with his pride, with his ostentation, with his blasphemies and his adulteries; with his contempt for the Sabbath day, with his neglect of the Friday fasts, and with his usury toward his brethren. Already, God had punished the earth with a plague more dreadful than any that had come before, but men still refused to repent. For this reason, Christ, the righteous Judge, had determined to slay every living thing upon the earth.

The flagellants moaned and sobbed at this dreadful news—though no doubt they had heard it before. Some of the Londoners joined into their frenzied wails. Restrained by my proximity to the prince, I made no noise, but this did not mean I was impervious to the terror of the proclamation. Fear wrapped around my throat like the coils of a snake and I found myself overcome by a sickly fascination with the flagellant's words.

The master continued the scroll. Though our sins lay against us, the Blessed Virgin and the angels had interceded for us, begging the Son to supply mankind with one last chance. Moved by these appeals, Christ had agreed that if men abandoned their evil ways and did penance for their sin, he would postpone the fiery judgment they deserved. The land would bring forth its fruit again and the pestilence which polluted our land would vanish like the night air before the rising sun.

This was the penance that Christ had decreed. Those who wished to save the imperiled world must desert house, position, wife and family and join with the flagellant brethren. For thirty-three and a half days, they must proceed from town to town publicly performing the rites of self-flagellation in memory of the thirty-three and a half years that Christ suffered on this earth. Only through this act of contrition would Christ extend his mercy, the plague be lifted from our land, and the final judgment be averted.

"Watch now, and see if these fanatics will gain any converts," said the bishop of London, apparently unmoved by the awful threats of the letter from heaven. "In Strasbourg, after a performance such as this one, nearly a thousand men joined their brotherhood. But I do not think our English people are made of such craven or unnatural sentiment."

He was right. The grand master of the flagellant order had begun to call for new recruits from the crowd, but though the spectacle had affected the Londoners, none were willing to offer their flesh to the flails of the flagellants. They shook their heads to the master's repeated entreaties and kept their eyes uncomfortably on the ground. His vituperations grew wilder then, and he denounced them for a perverse generation who deserved the destruction that was to come. When this had no effect, the master ordered his men to resume their habiliments. Placing their white robes upon their bloody backs they returned the way they had come.

"So much for these madmen," said the prince. "You say that their heresy is a pernicious danger, father, but it seems that few are inclined to believe it."

"Aye, few in England," said the bishop. "But their words are far more potent in the southern lands; they have turned many people against our Mother Church which—in their perverted minds—has nurtured the sin of the people within her own bosom. I hear that Pope Clement has outlawed their sect and Philip has forbidden them to practice public flagellation within French domains on pain of death."

"My father need make no such decree," said the prince confidently. "Our English are too sensible a race to subscribe to such teachings." The bishop nodded, but my countenance must have looked doubtful. The prince arched his eyebrows in concern or perhaps contempt. "How now?" he asked. "Surely, you do not believe their ravings, Potenhale?"

"I hardly know what to believe," I said truthfully. Behind the white hood of the flagellant master, I could feel the distorted face of my father reviling the sin of the world which had brought such judgment upon my innocent mother. A father's grief is a more powerful demagogue than even the rites of the flagellants.

9

A KNIGHT'S TREACHERY
September, 1349 – January, 1350

The continued virulence of the plague in our land seemed to confirm the words of the flagellant brethren. The prince retreated again to his lands near the Welsh border, and I, as usual, danced attendance on him. My duties were few. I served him at table, rode with him in hunting, and yawned in silence as he heard the complaints of his tenants. With little to distract me, I often fell into a dark and meditative mood. My father's words hung heavily between my ears and the picture of the bloodied flails swung painfully before my eyes. If my father were right, I must forsake the world for the sake of the cloister. I must forswear my knighthood to swear the vows of a monk. I must choose between losing Margery—and every hope of bliss in this life—and losing my eternal soul in the life to come.

I confessed my fears to the prince one night—fears that our shedding of blood had caused divine justice to shed the blood of our people, and fears that a life of chivalry had unfitted me for salvation.

He stared at me curiously and fingered the new growth of his dark beard. "You are afraid then," said he, "that I have required you to do deeds in my service that are worthy of damnation?"

I saw then that he had understood me not at all. "Nay, highness, it is not my service to you that I question, for you have always been a right honorable master. It is the service of every knight that I question, and the soul of chivalry that I doubt. Christ says He will know us by our deeds—what good can a man of the sword do?"

The prince modulated his voice patiently, like one explaining a lesson to a child. "There are three estates that men may hold in this world," said he. "Some are men of the cloth, some are men of the field, and some are men of the sword. The man of the cloth saves all others by preaching God's word. The man of the field saves all others by providing them with bread. And the man of the sword saves all others by warding them from the foe. Each estate is useful to the others, and each estate is honorable before God."

I listened to his monologue with respect but with little confidence. His words were merely a mechanical recitation of arguments I had heard before. The prince was my master in many things, but in the understanding of holy things his birth gave him no advantage. "You say that my estate is honorable before God. Is it truly? I throw handfuls of guineas for a herald's fee while the poor die hungry in the streets. I redden my sword with the blood of villeins to prevent the stain of cowardice on my scutcheon. I fight in quarrels that are not my own to gain a name for myself among men. Can God look kindly on one such as I?"

"You are overwrought," said the prince.

"Better to be overwrought now then overwrought in the Day of Judgment! But while I am living, there is still hope. Until the plague has got a hold of him, a man may get a hold of heavenly grace and change who he has been for something better."

"Will you become a monk, then?" asked the prince in disbelief.

"Perhaps," said I, in a tone of misery.

The prince frowned. "Your father abbot will no doubt object to a certain crimson keepsake you carry about you; I hear tell that monks must mortify the desires of the flesh."

"Aye, there's the rub," I said, and my hand went instinctively to my bosom where I carried Margery's favor. I sighed bitterly and hung my head. I had the words of two men to convince me—my father and the flagellant—but the prince and all the world continued to deny that the cause of judgment could be found within ourselves.

While these tormented thoughts crept through my mind like a crowd of lepers, the greater torment continued to afflict the land. The hand of the Almighty lay heavy upon us, and He proved to be no respecter of persons. Stratford, the archbishop of Canterbury, was struck down, and scarcely before a second could be raised up he also succumbed to the infection. When the monks of Canterbury met to bemoan the fallen and elect a third prelate, they chose Thomas Bradwardine, chaplain to His Majesty. The king was loath to let Bradwardine quit his side—indeed, the monks had proposed him ere now, and His Majesty had blocked the appointment—but he finally acquiesced to this nomination. Bradwardine repaired to Avignon to receive his pallium from the hands of Peter's successor then returned to London to tend a dwindling flock. Despite fears of returning again to the unhealthy town air, the prince's household made its way thither to receive the new archbishop's blessing.

I, for one, was particularly glad of our journey to London. Bradwardine, of all men, would have the answer that I needed. Bradwardine could make distinctions the breadth of a hair. Bradwardine could split true from false as easily as cracking a walnut. But we had not yet reached the outskirts of the city before we heard the news. The plague had claimed its third archbishop. He was not dead yet, but a few days time would sort that.

"Miserable Bradwardine," said the prince, "to see the death of a beggar for the sake of a beggared see. His mind was too fine for this world, and where shall we find another like it?"

Without any further delay, the prince would have had us all return on the road we had just traveled. But I had come to see Bradwardine, and see him I would before the grave claimed him wholly. I begged the prince's patience and besought his leave to desert his train for a day.

"It is madness to go near him," said the prince.

"Then I must risk it," said I, "for I am already half mad with uncertainty. And sick though he is, he may provide me physic."

The streets of London were emptier than I had ever seen them, and I felt that the citizens there had succumbed to the same despair that held me in its grip. I cast about a bit, and collared a spare and threadbare journeyman striding intently past the wharf. At first, he hung his head disinclined to speak with me. But when

I dropped a groat into his hand, his tongue loosened a little; he pointed out the place where the archbishop was housed.

"But, sir," he said, "you'll not be wanting to go there, for the devil's been there afore you."

"Then I'll send him about his business," said I, "for the devil's no fit company for a cleric."

I made for the house where Bradwardine was lodged and let myself in. The servants had all fled at the first sign of the plague, and there was no one to direct me to his room.

"I am seeking Master Bradwardine," I shouted. "Is anyone here?" First there was silence; then a faint rasping sound. I looked up to the top of the stairs and saw a corpulent body creeping slowly along the floor, pulling itself across the floorboards like an inchworm across the dirt. It was Bradwardine, devoid of his books, his vestments, and his dignities, as wretched as any simpleton who cannot count on his hands.

"Water!" said his hoarse voice. "For Christ's sake, give me water!"

There was a barrel with a dipper just outside. I filled the dipper and carried it up to him, and at arm's length poured the water through his cracked lips.

"God will requite you," he said, and he gasped a little as he spoke. From here, I could see the little pustules that had formed about his neck, dark and malodorous like rotting plums. A panic seized me, and I wished to be gone before the pestilence should seize me as well. The wretched man spoke again. "I recognize your face, John de Potenhale, kind and young, and a little foolish as it always was. Why have you come here? Do you seek death? It is before you."

"I seek knowledge," said I. "And if you die, it must die with you, for you of all men can most help me."

"I am past all help. I am past all knowledge." He coughed a little, leaving a glaze of blood-tinged sputum on the floor beneath his face. "I go before the true and awful Judge, and what misery will be mine if my works are not approved. I have given my life to enigmas and equations, to futile argument and fruitless disputation. I have fed my philosophies but not the hungry; I have clothed my syllogisms but not the naked.

"And you," he continued, and his eyes grew large with terror, "are you not also in fear of the judgment? You are a man of blood, and will you approach the Almighty's throne unwashed?"

Without my asking, he had poured out a draught of the knowledge I sought. "What must I do?" I asked, and in my fear of perdition I forgot my fear of the pestilence and gripped his plague-ridden shoulder.

"What must you do?" he repeated, and his eyes grew wide and wild. "What *can* you do? The harvest has been gathered in and the grain must be separated from the chaff. Repent, for the kingdom of God is at hand. Or repent not, for the kingdom has already passed you by."

"Is this the truth?" asked I, but he was raving now and I could not get him to answer me directly. "Is this the truth?" I demanded, and began to shake him in frustration. He closed his eyes and then opened them as if he had recognized me afresh.

"What is the truth?" I asked, and I may have said it with a sob for my soul was a-prickle with terror.

"Who can say what truth is?" he answered. "If it is true, it is false. If it is false, it is true. Have you not heard me say it? 'This statement is a lie!'" As the insoluble rolled off his tongue, his parched mouth opened in a horrible, croaking cry. His eyes rolled back wildly into his head. He twitched suddenly, gave a little moan, and was silent. This may very well have been the end of him, but I did not stay to find out.

By fast riding, I rejoined the prince and his retinue before they had stopped for the night.

"How is Bradwardine?" said his highness.

"Dead, I think," said I, and I gave a little shudder.

"Then he did not resolve your troubles for you?" asked the prince.

"No," said I. "By the time I arrived, his own trouble was too great for him."

"A pity," said the prince shortly, and I was glad that he did not ask more of me.

The third witness had spoken.

It was the Feast of Saint Andrew in England when news came that Lady Joan of Kent had given birth to a son. The prince sent a handsome parcel of gifts and on the appointed day arrived at Canterbury to stand godfather to the child. The infant Thomas was small and unremarkable. Not so his parents. The lady Joan, if it were possible, had grown in beauty and brilliance since the birth of her child. Holland—never a beauty to behold—had grown in bulk since last I saw him; his corpulence caught the eye as a windmill catches the breeze.

I glimpsed Margery at the baptism. She sat beside the wet nurse in the stall of the church. As I gazed at her, the same passion that I always experienced welled up in my breast. But in front of the picture of her face, the archbishop's black pustules, the flagellant's swinging flail, and my father's lunatic laughter interposed themselves. When the service was over, she caught my eye and smiled in welcome. I turned and went the other way—stuffing her memory deep down into my bosom beside the crumpled red glove that I carried.

For two years the plague had kept our countries at truce and the truce kept us from each others' throats; but your people had not forgotten the fall of their fortress by the sea. After concluding the siege of Calais, you will remember that the king had expelled its inhabitants and peopled the place with our own. Walter Manny, one of His Majesty's favorites, had received a grand manor in the town. He took up residence there when the rest of us headed home to pass the pox to our own country. The governorship of the town went to a Genoese captain, one Aimery de Pavia. I knew little of this Aimery, and to my knowledge had never laid eyes on him. Reportedly, he had done His Majesty some small service during the evacuation, and this had secured him the appointment as governor when the army quitted the town. For two years we had held the city in peace, and since neither the plague nor the truce had terminated in France, there was no reason to believe that we would not continue to hold Calais.

After the baptism of Joan's little son Thomas, the prince had hurried to join the royal household for the season of Our Lord's Advent. We met the king in Hereford and had tarried there for some days when winged rumor alighted and built a nest in the eaves of the court. Calais, so the story ran, was in great peril. True, her walls still stood impregnable, her storehouses still overflowed with grain, but the fidelity of her governor had ebbed like the tide. Aimery de Pavia had contracted with the French to sell this pearl of great price.

Edward received this intelligence with great emotion. The hot anger that had blazed for the six burghers was nothing compared to the inferno that awaited Aimery de Pavia. "Send for the dog!" were Edward's words. "Let us see if this Lombard will dare lie to our face."

The summons sped across the channel, and Aimery arrived with the first of the snow. He was ushered immediately before his impatient interviewer and a concerned council. The fading winter day left little light in the hall, and the furrowed brows all around me were as dark as the sky outside. Lancaster was there, and Audley and Chandos. Mortimer, Brocas, and others filled the periphery. On the king's right hand sat the prince, and I, as was my wont, stood silent behind my master's chair.

Aimery walked in with short, cautious steps for a man of his height. He had a lean face, sharp and shiny like hewn quartz. His eyes glittered dangerously from deep-set sockets, and as I glanced him over, I saw that his earlobes were curiously joined to his jawbone. There was no question but that I had seen him before—my mind misgave me that it was at Calais. Yet why should that surprise me, for he was the governor of that town.

"How now, governor!" demanded the king. "What tale is this which reaches our ears? Have you not crassly conspired with our cruelest enemy? Have you not deviously devised to deliver up Calais, that child which we brought forth with so much travail? Answer me, governor, for I have heard tales told of you that would make Brutus blush and Cassius livid with loyal feeling."

The Genoese governor stepped backward awkwardly, then fell to his knees on the floor of the hall. "Your Majesty," he began, licking the taste of fear from off his lips, "In time of war, it is not unknown for lies to be circulated by the enemy...."

"Do you then call Sir Walter Manny a liar?" demanded the king. He pulled out a parchment bearing the seal of that baron and flung it fiercely on the floor. It was not without reason that the king had left such an excellent correspondent in Calais. "By God's eyes, you shall tell me the truth of this matter, for I will have it out of you one way or another."

"Your Majesty," the Genoese groveled. "I see that all of my actions have been reported to you; I can only pray that my motives received as thorough an exposition. As you have heard, the French commander has made me an offer. In exchange for a sum of gold, I am to open the northwest gate of Calais, admitting by night a force of Frenchmen large enough to slaughter the sleeping garrison and occupy the city. This was the offer from the French."

"And what made you for your answer?" said the king.

"Your Majesty, I am your loyal servant, even as all these,"—he gestured helplessly at the circle of lords, but received scant encouragement. "God forbid that I should profit from perfidy. And yet, a cunning fox may serve his king as well as an honest hound. My first thought was to spurn this offer under my heel, but a revelation came to me, seemingly from heaven. Would it not better suit

Your Majesty's cause to accede to this plan? To lure the French in with fair words, then clap the gates shut and betray them to their own ruin? Your Majesty,"—here, the governor rose to his feet and held out his palms in appeal—"I answered France as would best serve England. I have made an appointment to betray Calais."

The room was as silent as a charnel house. The tribunal of nobles waited grimly for their sovereign as he fingered his beard in thought. Beads of sweat began to gather on Aimery's brow, and though the affair was of little moment to me, I gripped the wooden frame of the chair before me so tightly that my knuckles went white.

"So," the king said at last, and the word fell like a millstone into a pond, "it seems that you have done well, governor."

His stern features relaxed into a smile and he began to speak with the enthusiasm of a stripling schoolboy. "Is it not a good jest, my lords? We shall have their gold, and they'll have been gulled in the bargain. Prithee, governor, what price have they set on the city?"

"Twenty thousand crowns," said Aimery.

The king sneered. "So little. God knows I paid ten times that sum to achieve it. And what has proved so costly in the getting shall not be lost for lack of watchfulness. You say that you are preparing an ambuscade for these marauders. Describe to me, governor, your force."

"My force is even as you have left it to me, one thousand men disposed about the walls, and...."

"Not enough, by heaven! We must reinforce you," said the king.

"Aye, majesty!" agreed Roger Mortimer. He had caught some of the king's fervor and was leaning forward with an earnest smile. "An' it please you, I'll plant my escutcheon at the head of this reinforcing party."

"Your boldness pleases me right well," said the king, "but there are others who must be waiting to entreat the boon of command."

The words were pointed, and I felt a great many eyes turn to the chair in front of me. "How now?" said the king, when his son said nothing. "Do you not covet the glory of this enterprise?"

"Aye, I covet glory as much as any man," replied the prince, "but I would know my enemy before I throw down my gage. Who has tendered this treachery to you, governor? Come, I must know the fellow's name and quality!"

"Your highness cannot fail to know the man. It is Geoffroi de Charny with whom I have compacted."

"Charny!" said the king, and he laughed mockingly—for madam, you must forgive me, but he did not rate your husband highly.

"Was it not he," demanded Mortimer, "who asked us to set aside our vantage during the siege and engage the French in equal numbers, four of their knights against four of ours?"

"Aye," boomed Lancaster, "and I could regale your ears with half a dozen tales of Charny's follies. A knight for damsels and tourneys, but no true soldier. You'll have little enough to fear from this enemy, if he plays the gallant goat as is his wont."

"On the contrary, my dear Lancaster," said the prince, "I have heard tales as well as you, and I fear that this Charny is as shrewd as he is gallant."

"If he is so cunning," replied Lancaster, "then why was there no evidence of it at Crecy?"

"He was not at Crecy," replied the prince. "Though if he were, Philip's men may not have advanced in such a pell-mell fashion. Shall I tell you where he was? He was fifty leagues to the west at the city of Bethune. Our Flemish allies were there in force with plans to take the city; Charny contrived to hold them off, with only two hundred lances in his command."

"Impressive," said Lancaster grudgingly.

"Aye, most impressive," said the prince. "Our governor was not wise to cross crooked blades with such a man. But be that as it may, Calais must still be held at any cost. Give me the command, sire, and I will not disappoint, though ten such Charnys turn all their gilt to guilty stratagems."

And so the king bestowed the command of the expedition upon his son, the prince. Yet as he did so, he hesitated a little, and it seemed that he was loath to let the leadership pass from out of his own grasp. It had been over two years since our last engagement with France, and Edward of Windsor was not a tame lion to sit meekly at home when others were in the field. The prince received his commission and orders to sail with the tide. But how much authority the prince would truly have, I will show you later, for this expedition turned out much the same as the field of Crecy. Though the prince might be named commander, his would not be the hand to hold the reins.

Later that night, I waited table for the prince, and after I had cleared the flagons, he bade me reveal my thoughts on the Genoese governor.

"He was astonishingly foolish," said I, "to enter into such a compact with the French with no word thereof to His Majesty."

"He was astonishingly shrewd," said the prince, "to confess it without reserve when word of his deeds had flown abroad."

"You think then, that his original intent was not a stratagem to deceive the French, but an act of definite betrayal?"

"Aye, I think that if Sir Walter Manny had not eyes in his head and ink in his pen, then a month's time would have seen Charny's flag on the ramparts of Calais and Aimery's purse filled with traitor crowns."

"And thinks the king the same?"

"Aye, I read as much in his face."

"Then why did His Majesty not beard this Lombard to his face?" I demanded, for the thought of Aimery's double-dealing stuck in my craw like half-chewed gristle.

The prince smiled at me with a look both sage and careworn, and it came to me then that though we had been the same age at our knighting, the experiences of the last four years had grown him up to a wisdom that did not come with years. "My father knows what mold of men his servants are, whether of honor or dishonor. And who can say whether the vessels of wrath are not as serviceable as the vessels of mercy? He has played us false, but he is found out. And with the help of God, we shall make him play us true or else smash him to pieces altogether."

I remembered the thought that had come to me when Aimery had first entered the hall. "I have seen this fellow before," I said. "He was at Calais, and yet, I think that he was not of our company."

"Your memory serves you well," said the prince, "We were outside the walls, and he inside."

"In the pay of the French?"

"Aye, until they could pay him no longer. My father offered better pay, and so the Lombard-turned-French has turned English."

"Well, we shall pay him out his full deserts," said I, with a vehemence that my voice had lacked for many a fortnight.

"Is this the talk of a Benedictine novice?" demanded the prince with an air of mock piety, and he clapped me on the back with affection. "This Aimery must be truly wicked, my friend, to make you forget your intended vows. Methinks we are in danger of losing not only Calais, but also your immortal soul."

We made the crossing to Calais by night. The fog was thick about us, and we were muffled in great coats both to keep out the chill and hide our quality. Our identity and purpose must remain hidden even from Calais's garrison if it were to remain hidden from Calais's enemy. The prince had begged Roger Mortimer to second him on the expedition, and that noble had agreed ungrudgingly, bearing no rancor that the standard would not bear his pennant. Besides Mortimer, few others of note had embarked in our flotilla. The prince and Mortimer kept to the cabin in our ship, accompanied by one tall, heavily cloaked man, whom I took to be either Lancaster or Chandos. The rest of us were exposed to the elements for the voyage, and many of the men slept for the duration of the trip.

It was early morning by the time we disembarked, and Aimery de Pavia was there—seemingly by happenstance—on the quay to receive us. "Welcome, friend," he said loudly, recognizing the prince, but receiving him as a commoner. "What business have you in Calais?"

"We are bound for Bruges," said the prince assuming the role of merchant, "but my shipmaster has fallen ill, and without him we are no more than a pile of spars on a waiting reef."

"You've leave to put in here till he recovers," said Aimery, "at least until the Feast of Epiphany."

"Gramercy, sir," said the prince with a smile. "You are a prince among men."

We entered Calais in the guise of tradesmen. Our weapons we smuggled in with little difficulty inside some pallets of cloth. The prince took up some petty conversation with the governor, playing his part with alacrity. He bemoaned the falling price of wool, and roundly cursed the rising customs that threatened to beggar him. He complimented the governor on the efficiency of the wharf and asked to view the prospect of the city from the vantage point of the walls. "As you wish," said Aimery, and in this manner the prince was able to see for himself the disposition of Calais's garrison and the state of the defenses.

Later, behind closed doors, the prince, Mortimer, Sir Walter Manny, and the tall, cloaked man whom I still supposed to be Chandos or Lancaster, met with the governor to discuss the details of how the ambush would be conducted. Charny, I learned afterward, had appointed the evening of the thirty-first to be the day of the exchange. As the sun rose on the first day of the new year, it would rise on a Calais that was French once again. But Charny, as the prince had averred, was no fool. He would need guarantees of Aimery's good faith, guarantees that he was not walking into a trap. The first demand was Aimery's son as hostage; Aimery was not an over-fond father and had already handed over the lad. The second demand was an inspection of the city one day prior to the exchange. Our reinforcements must remain well hidden if Charny's suspicions were to be allayed.

"There are too many of us," I said, when I heard of Charny's plans to scrutinize the city. "And the men—try as they might to card wool or loop fringe—are unmistakably martial. The game will be up before it has begun."

"Aye," said the prince, "and since we cannot hide what we are, it seems we must hide altogether. What think you of this?" he asked, and pulled a folded parchment from his pocket. There in rough lines was a design for a secret compartment on either side of the gatehouse. "Half the men will be entombed here. The other half mixed in with Calais's garrison or tricked out in peasant's garb."

I took the drawing and examined it critically. "And Charny's inspectors will be either so blind or so drunk that they will not notice these strange stone protuberances of such obvious novelty. Come, come! The stone will be three days old butted up against stone aged three hundred years—shiny, new hewn blocks lying side by side with mossy, timeworn walls. We would awaken less curiosity by building a great wooden horse to hide inside."

The prince smiled. "I own that I am much of your opinion."

"Then why this plan, highness? Was it your device?"

"No, not mine," said the prince, "but with whatever tools I am given, I will serve. And if Aimery proves as smooth-tongued as Sinon the Greek, then Charny will see no trap."

He set off to speak with Calais's master stonemason, and I watched him leave with a furrowed brow. If the plan liked him not, then why did he pursue it? Was it Aimery's artifice? Sir Walter Manny's? I shook my head at this silly stratagem and murmured a silent prayer for Mary's good favor. But as I said it, I blushed, for I could never implore Mary's favor without hoping instinctively for Margery's. And that were unseemly now, for I had determined that this trip to Calais was the last of my worldly adventuring. I would draw my sword one more time and then sheathe it altogether. The grapes my father planted had turned to wine, and it was a bitter draught, but I would drink it.

There are many ways to die; and for each man, brave through he may be, there is one way that frightens him more than others. Some men fear drowning, to struggle uselessly as the briny deep abolishes breath. Some men fear fire, to smell the roasting of their own flesh in the searing pain of flame. But for other men, a greater fear is that of an untimely burial, to be shut away in the earth before the soul has sped. Pity these men, for the two days that they spent entombed in Calais were nearly enough to drive them mad.

To construct our covert crypt, Aimery's stonemasons had built a thin wall around the perimeter of the gatehouse. The necessity of camouflaging the newness of this construction had occurred to others as well as to me. Within the walls of Calais stood an ancient church whose belfry tower was in an advanced state of decay. Aimery's workmen dismantled this tower stone by stone and transported the pieces to the gatehouse. There they laid the blocks in place but left them unmortared, for when the time came, our exit must be swift.

We talked but sparingly once the wall had gone up. It was dark outside, and inside the darkness was so thick that I could not see my hand before my face. The prince was on my left; I had taken good care to be near him so that I might serve him with water and victuals during our confinement. I knew not who was on my right, for the man spoke little and seemed not to understand me when I asked him his name and quality. However, I knew he must be a gentleman of note, for when I took out my bundle of food to serve the prince, his highness bade me serve the other man first. I did as I was told, and the man thanked me courteously in a voice that seemed familiar.

I never saw the outside of our tomb, but the stonemasons must have done their work cunningly. On the thirtieth day of December, a half dozen of Charny's men entered and inspected the town. They reckoned the garrison and looked over the town folk. They mounted every wall and scrutinized every tower. The new walls surrounding the gate house had been so cleverly faked to look like old work that Charny's spies suspected nothing of the vengeance that lurked within. When they had finished their exhaustive examination, they returned to Aimery almost disappointed, like spaniels who have prowled the heather but found no birds to flush. From behind our stony screen, we could just hear their interchange with Aimery as he let them out the postern gate. "My master will be pleased," said the leader and he gave Aimery the earnest money, a pledge of the twenty thousand crowns to be delivered the following night. "You will see us tomorrow when the moon rises."

The day passed slowly. Cramped and cold, the men grumbled intermittently. I wondered if those outside the wall could hear our muttering. "They must sleep," said the man beside me, "and marshal their strength for the evening ahead." Again, his voice seemed familiar, but again I could not discover the identity of the speaker. I would have known Chandos's voice, and Audley's deep croak was intelligible to any man.

"Aye," said the prince to the man on my right. As if on command, he repeated the words to the men about us, instructing them to lay aside their weapons and lay down their heads. "Sleep," the prince bade us, and he would brook no argument. The place was confined, but we all managed to contort our bodies into some semblance of recumbency. One by one we dozed off into a warmth and comfort that only sleep could bestow.

When I awakened, I saw a red sliver of light peeking through the mortarless masonry. The sun was setting. "Shall we arm?" I asked.

"Not yet," said the prince, but before the light had completely gone, he bade me fasten the points of his armor. It was a small space to buckle on plates, and I felt like a man trying to turn a somersault inside of a barrel. By this time, however, I was proficient in playing squire to his highness, for my lord was accustomed to be served by none but belted knights. I trussed his points with some small trouble, eased the embroidered jupon over his head, and received his gramercy.

While I turned my fingers to my own cuirass, the prince looked beyond me to the man on my right. "Friend," said he. "Shall I serve as thy squire?"

"With all my heart," said the unknown man, and stooping low, the prince performed for him the same office that I had just completed. He was a haughty man, my prince, and I wondered to see him serve another in this way.

We were all addressed now to meet our foe. We need only wait for the moon to rise, bright and far-reaching as a coastal beacon.

It was nearly midnight before the trap was sprung. In accordance with the agreement, sly Aimery had left the postern gate unlatched. A small French force slipped in, ready to raise the portcullis and admit the whole of their troop. From inside our makeshift masonry we could hear the grating squeal of the rising gate, strident and startling like the sharpening of knives on a turning stone.

"Stand there!" cried one of the garrison, for not all of Aimery's men had been apprised of the events that were to take place this night. Before the watchman could sound the alarm, a flock of arrows had buried themselves in his throat. Filing Frenchmen filled the courtyard inside of the gate. We could hear them tiptoeing and hushing one another, confidently unaware of the soldiery sequestered in the stones surrounding them.

"God's death! Let's have at these bastards!" murmured one of ours, and the men began to champ and rustle impatiently like horses before a race.

"Hold fast, or all is lost!" hissed the unknown man to my right, and the prince gave an order for no man to stir.

"We must draw them in," I breathed.

"Aye," said the prince. "It does no good to pull the lever before the foe is standing upon the trap."

The next three minutes abounded with stifled anxiety. The shuffle, shuffle of entering footsteps nearly unnerved me, but the prince seemed calm enough. "On my word of command, push forward with all your might," he said, and this instruction shimmered through the ranks like a flash of lightning. I set my left shoulder against the flimsy wall and grasped the pommel of my sword with my right hand. "Now!" shouted the prince, and his voice was as black as thunder.

"St. George and England!" cried the men, and giving a concerted shove, they toppled the unmortared wall with little more trouble than the Israelites had at Jericho. We were outside of our tomb. The moon shone clear; I could see it reflected in two hundred white eyes wide with surprise and terror.

"St. George!" I roared in fury and dealt a mighty stroke upon the basinet that stared at me. The man crumpled like a wilted flower, and I kicked him out of my way to face another Frenchman. By now, the enemy had drawn their swords, but they were bewildered and beleaguered on all sides and thought of nothing but making a hasty retreat. One of the French captains began to shout some orders. He had reckoned our numbers and seen that their force was equal to or greater than ours. If they could make a stand, Calais might still be theirs. Two thirds of their force remained outside the walls, and a steady trickle of men continued to pour into the court-yard like wine from a spigot. The prince, however, was determined to put a stopper in the barrel.

"To the gate! To the gate!" called the prince, and with a handful of us at his back, he pressed his way through the enemy hordes to the capstan that worked the port-cullis. "Turn the wheel!" he shouted hoarsely. Two men bent their backs to work the winch. I warded blows with sword and shield, fighting side by side with my lord. The creak of cold armor, the clash of brand against brand, and the grunts of intensity all contrived to drive the archbishop's rotting face, the flagellant's bloody flail, and my father's ghastly laughter out of my head. For the first time in months, I felt a kind of joyful freedom, like the feel of rushing wind upon the face.

"'Ware the left!" called the prince.

I wheeled to meet a new attacker, and met him foot to foot just inside the threshold of the gate. He was a ponderous fellow, with the strength of an ox in the swing of his sword. I barely deflected his blows with my shield. One penetrated my guard and, slicing through my pauldron, bit keenly into my left shoulder. "Aiee!" I cried, and struck out with all my might. Giant though he was, he stepped back beneath my onslaught, and in that moment the winch was unwound. The iron gate dropped to the ground. There my attacker lay, spitted through like a deer beneath the heavy portcullis.

"The day is ours," said the prince. The way was shut, and the invaders had been cut off from the rest of their force. Our men pushed the trapped Frenchmen together tighter and tighter till they were hemmed in on all sides. Dismay spread through their ranks like a ripple across a lake. Almost with one accord, they put down their swords and cried for quarter. Englishmen all around me scrambled to receive their submission. A noble prisoner would bring a noble ransom, and that could be the making of a poor man's hopes. The prince left my side, no doubt in search of Aimery. The Frenchmen would have surely paid him off when first they entered. Twenty thousand crowns! And where was it now? Throughout the fight Aimery had been invisible—perhaps secreting the money in hopes that his highness would have forgotten it.

Some of our men, however, had little thought of prisoners and plunder. The French were still without the walls and a swift sally would send them into inglorious flight. "To me, to me!" cried one of our English comrades, "Avaunt!" I looked toward the wall of the castle and saw a man beckoning fiercely with his weapon. It was the man who had come so heavily cowled upon the ship; it was the man who had knelt on my right all those cold hours in our stony cell; it was the man whose armor had been laced by a prince. The portcullis was shut, but he had opened the postern gate. Tall and proud he motioned for us to follow.

This was to be my last fight before I ended my days as a fighting man—all the more reason to leave reason to the wind; the French would remember the song of my sword before I sheathed it forever. "Lead on!" I called as I reached the gate. A dozen men-at-arms were at my back and at least as many archers. Following our unknown leader, we passed beyond the wall and onto the fen that surrounded the city.

"St. George and England!" cried our little band, and though we were but few, our voices carried the fervor of Gideon and his meager three hundred. Already alarmed by the wreck of their plans, the French feared total disaster from our sudden sally. Their army, a noble force of a thousand men or more, turned tail and fled with all the dignity of a startled rabbit.

This display of terror encouraged our small company. We gave tongue like a group of youthful hounds and pursued the fleeing French into the fen. You will remember that the terrain around Calais is mostly marshy. On the eastern side of the city, the ground is nearly impassable, so a causeway has been erected to allow safe passage through the quag. We had just approached the narrowing of the causeway, when the apparent rout lost its pell-mell momentum.

"*Tournez et vous defendez!*" boomed a Frenchman. On the causeway in front of us, a large Frenchman seated on a magnificent bay was brandishing his sword. The bright moon reflected on his steel sending shimmers of light like darts across the pavement. His voice was imperious and his mien was masterful. Hearing his words, the fleeing French stopped in their tracks like runaway horses seized suddenly by the reins.

"*Allons, allons! Montjoy et Saint Denis!*" they cried and swallowed their fear like a mouthful of pottage.

A great part of their army had already crossed the horizon, but nearly a hundred men turned to face us; the odds were four to one and far greater than I liked.

"Christ save us!" said one of the archers in the van. I despaired of victory, but determined to acquit myself as became a knight.

As the enemy narrowed the space between us, our unknown leader stood a space ahead of us upon the causeway, fumbling with his basinet. At last he had it off, and I saw his bare face etched darkly in the night air. "Hold fast!" he thundered, anticipating the retreat that was sure to whelm our wavering line. "I am Edward of Windsor, your commander and your king. Do your duty as men, and we will prevail."

With a swift motion, the newly-revealed king stripped the sheath from his sword and tossed it into the bog. "We must keep the causeway," he instructed, gesturing to the men-at-arms just where to stand. The causeway permitted no more than twenty men to walk abreast. If we held the causeway, then we would hold the enemy, for their fully armored men could not leave the road without sinking into the marsh. Half of our band was archers, however, and archers went unarmored. At a word from the king, they stripped off what little plate they wore and took up position in the fen. On tufts of grass, out of the way of our men-at-arms, they could shower arrows on the enemy's flank.

The French leader on the bay horse marshaled his men into a tight formation, and they advanced upon our resolute band. Calais had been theirs before it was ours, and they knew the dangers of the marsh as well as we. None of their knights or men-at-arms dared to depart the solid surface of the causeway. I hoped that they had not recognized the king, for although the revelation of his presence acted like an elixir to boost the courage of our men, it was also a fearsome responsibility. We were too small a bodyguard to be sure of his safety, and what if Edward should fall?

There was no time to think. They were upon us. Hand to hand we began to trade blows. My left arm had grown wooden from the wound I had received earlier, and my breath came shorter and shorter. They would have overwhelmed us with little trouble, had it not been for our dauntless archers. Standing lightly in the marsh, the archers refused to waste a single shaft. The presence of the king had impressed upon them how necessary it would be to fight well, and the enemy suffered sorely from the accuracy of English arrows.

The king fought like a lion. He warded and wheeled and hewed with ardor. I had never before been so close to him in battle, and I saw him now in all his bellicose splendor. But even a lion cannot hold back an unending horde of jackals. Slowly and painfully, the French bored a hole in the center of our line. On the left I had only five men with me to face two score. On the right I saw that the king was well nigh alone.

Four men had surrounded him. I could not tell the quality of each, but one bore the crest of Sir Eustace de Ribemont. The king lunged with all the fury of a baited bear. His uncovered head looked strangely vulnerable in the moonlight, and I redoubled my efforts to push through the enemy and reach his side. "A rescue! A rescue!" I voiced to the night.

No sooner had this prayer been uttered than I heard the pounding of hooves upon the causeway behind us.

An instant later they had joined the fray, a hundred knights led by the prince himself. His keen eye made out his father instantly, and with a few judiciously delivered blows, he drove off the pack surrounding him. "Rise, Majesty," he said, and dismounting quickly he helped the king to his feet (for the king had fallen onto one knee beneath the onslaught of our foes). "Take my horse," said the prince imperatively. Kneeling down, he heaved the king up into the saddle.

The battle had been lost a second time for the French. Their leader on the bay saw it. He would have fled if he could, but I blocked his path. I did not mean to harm his horse, but the truth of the matter is that I struck out blindly. The animal's knees buckled under him like a nervous bridegroom's. The knight toppled to the ground, slightly pinned by the fallen horse. An instant later I was bending over him with my misericordia at his throat.

"I yield me to your mercy," he said simply, and there was no anger and no shame to mar his voice.

I helped him to his feet and took the sword that he offered me. It was a fine, Spanish blade, perfectly weighted, and as I examined it, I saw that I had taken a man of some rank as my prisoner. "What is your name?" I demanded.

He smiled a little at my eagerness. "I am Geffroi de Charny, Sir Knight. I salute you for your courage; it seems that English valor has carried the day." Then he begged me to unlace his helm for him, for his head was bleeding a little from the fall although I had done him no scathe with my sword.

10

CAPTIVITY AND FREEDOM
January – August, 1350

All of Calais was awake with the news. Torches filled the streets as the townsfolk trickled out into the proleptic dawn. The sun had not yet risen, but the portcullis rose proudly to admit the returning victors. At the front of the procession was the king, bareheaded and battered, mounted on the horse that had been so seasonably provided by the Prince of Wales. He was in none of his royal attire, but word spread fast that the king himself had led the party to rescue Calais from the craft of the enemy. "Huzzah for His Majesty!" shouted a brass-faced urchin, and the folk around him took up his cry.

I saw now how the king's hand had been everywhere in this enterprise. It was he who had come over on the boat so heavily cowled, he who had insisted upon the construction of the hidden chambers around the gatehouse, he who had directed that the men sleep and held them back till the ideal moment for discovery. His desire to give the glory and management of this undertaking to his eldest son had been overcome by his own insatiable desire for command.

"I am glad to see you safe, Potenhale," said a voice, and I saw that the prince, on foot, had come up beside me.

"Not so glad as I was when I heard the hooves of your troop at my back. God's life, but it would have gone ill with us if you had not come!"

"Come now," said the prince with gentle raillery, "If I had not come, my father the king would have yet prevailed. He bears a charmed life, I think, and one Plantagenet is more than enough to beard a score of Frenchmen."

"Nay, your highness," said my prisoner who stood at my side, "If you had not come, I think there would have been one less Plantagenet and one more score to settle between England and France."

"Who are you, sir?" asked the prince, and he drew himself up coldly. Though he knew his own words to have been mere flippancy, it angered him to hear this Frenchman's bluff comments about his father's close encounter with mortality.

My prisoner returned the prince's stern gaze with frank consideration. "I am Geoffroi de Charny," he replied, "prisoner of this good knight you see before you."

"Ah," said the prince, "the leader of this wretched cabal." He squared his shoulders and looked the prisoner up and down. They were much of a height, the prince and Charny, but while the prince's younger sinews were taut with controlled intensity, Charny carried himself with the nonchalance of a man on a midsummer's stroll. The prince's jupon of blue and red was embroidered magnificently with thread of gold, but Charny's green surcoat was as simple as an open meadow. I watched their eyes meet, waiting to see my master's treatment of the prisoner so that I could modify mine accordingly.

"You are accounted an honorable man, Charny," said the prince, and his words swung sharply like a sickle through hay. "Tell me, how does this underhanded affair consort with the sworn truce between your liege and mine? Have not the French given their oath to forbear lifting arms against us while this pestilence prevails? Or perhaps your knightly word is but a child's bauble, easy to be tossed aside whenever you weary of it. Your master Philip will give you little thanks for today's work."

"Had I accomplished what I set out to do, I think that my master would have little cause for complaint." Charny's tone was grave, but a trace of soldierly humor peeped out of his gray eyes. I saw that the stern tone of the prince's speech had amused him far more than it had embarrassed him. "And as for my honor," continued Charny, "I think it can bear more stains than breaking a truce I never negotiated or infringing a peace I never swore to uphold. The truce between our two lands was sworn while I was away; I had no hand in its making."

I shrugged in silent agreement with his reasoning. In sooth, he had not been present at any of the peace conferences, and what Philip's vassals chose to do with their own men could not be strictly charged to Philip's account. Philip could not be accused of truce-breaking, and neither could Sir Geoffroi.

The prince glared angrily his lip curling like a wolf backed into a corner.

Charny continued to pursue the subject. "Should you not be more distressed with the dishonorable actions of your Lombard governor, highness?"

"How so?" demanded the prince.

"Why, as matters stand," said Charny, "I am accused of violating an oath which I never swore, while your governor has violated an oath which he declared to me with his own two lips. Aye, and with his two hands resting upon holy relics."

"But it would have been dishonorable for Aimery to deliver the city to you," replied the prince, "for he has pledged his word to my father that he would guard and keep it."

"And yet it was just as dishonorable for Aimery not to deliver the city to me," replied Charny, "for he had just as solemnly pledged that he would open the gates to my men."

The prince frowned. I could see his father's blood begin to stir itself. "How now, Sir Geoffroi! Surely you must agree that the first oath is more binding than the second?"

"Wherefore?" asked Charny calmly.

"It was an oath of fealty made to a king," replied the prince in exasperation.

"And should an oath to a king take precedence over an oath to a humbler man?" inquired Charny. I pondered his words. It was true. An oath was an oath. Aimery was as honor-bound to fulfill his oath to Charny as he was to fulfill his oath to King Edward—unless the second oath could be proved unlawful in some way.

The prince took up the same line of reasoning that my mind had laid hold of. "The oath to the king takes precedence, sirrah, because it was taken first, and thus it invalidates the second oath to you. Aimery could not lawfully swear to surrender the city to you because he had already pledged his honor to the English king to guard the city."

"But are you not forgetting," said Charny, "that before pledging his honor to Edward to guard the city, he had pledged his honor first to Philip to guard it. Aimery was France's servant before he was England's."

The prince opened his mouth to speak, then shut it again. The logic of Charny's case was indisputable. "You are a hard man to speak against, Sir Geoffroi. If it were possible, I would rather agree with you than argue anymore."

"Why then," said Charny in a conciliatory tone, "if Your Highness would agree with me, then let us agree on this: whatever the case, this Aimery de Pavia is a great rogue and not to be trusted."

"Amen to that," said the prince. "I have firsthand knowledge of that. When I went to retrieve the ransom that you paid for his perfidy, he was busy concealing it in a secret storeroom—for safekeeping he claimed. I insisted that Sir Walter Manny was the best safe to keep such a sum, and forced him to hand over the treasure boxes on the spot. Twenty thousand crowns! It is a large sum to lose, my good sir."

"Aye," said Charny, with a little bit of regret in his tone. "It is a large sum. I shall not see the like of it again in a hurry."

"A pity," said the prince with a smile that could not help being triumphant. "For if Potenhale has his wits about him, he will not ransom you for less than that price. And where is that to be come by? From your *roi Philippe*? No, my good sir, I think you shall be with us for some while."

The king, in his ordering of events, had not forgotten to give orders for a magnificent feast to follow the hard fought hours of the night. And so it was, that while the town folk were rising from their beds to pursue their daily labors, the king and all his men were sitting down to eat with their nocturnal work accomplished. The king himself sat at the head of the feast, bareheaded except for a chaplet of pearls. At the table on either side of him sat the most prominent of the French prisoners, knights of worth who had been captured in the failed enterprise.

With ironic hospitality, the king commanded the prince and all our English knights to serve food to the French captives before sitting down at our own table. "They thought to make servants of us tonight," said the king. "Let them not be disappointed." I smiled grimly as I carved the roast venison for our prisoners. Some looked ashamed as I placed a portion of meat upon their trencher, others declined the meat with ill grace, but Sir Geoffroi de Charny looked me boldly in the eye and gave me gramercy for the food.

When they had finished eating, the king stepped down from his chair and greeted his honored guests one by one. He commended them for their bravery, albeit misguided, and saluted their conduct in arms. When he came to Charny, however, his kindly look vanished. His tone changed color like an autumn leaf, and he would not give the French captain his hand. "I have little reason to like you, Sir Geoffroi," the king said coolly. "Last night you tried to steal from me what has cost me so much money and labor to gain. You thought to get it for twenty thousand crowns—cheaper than I did. But by God's help, you have been disappointed."

Charny said nothing; there was nothing to be said. Edward continued on down the table of French knights to where Sir Eustace de Ribemont sat. Sir Eustace was close in rank to Charny, and though his reputation was not as brilliant, his name was at least known to the king. He was one of the four knights that had surrounded Edward on the causeway, just prior to the timely arrival of the prince and his party.

"Ah, Sir Eustace," said the king in a voice markedly different than that which he had spoken to Charny. "You are the most valiant knight I ever saw. I never yet found anybody, who, man to man, gave me so much to do as you did today. I adjudge to you, above all the knights of my court, the prize of valor." With exaggerated courtesy, His Majesty removed the chaplet of pearls from his head and placed it on the brow of Sir Eustace. "I beg you to wear this for a year, Sir Knight, in whatever place you may go. And tell all ladies and damsels that I gave this coronet to you as a reward for your prowess. I release you from prison and ransom. You may leave tomorrow and go where you wish." The king finished with a meaningful look at Charny. "But not so the rest of you. You must bide in our hospitality across the sea until such time as your natural lord makes free to ransom you."

❖ ◆ ❖

The prince spoke true when he said that your husband would not be ransomed immediately. Indeed, it was well over a year before Charny returned to his homeland. In France, as well as in England, the ravages of the plague had lessened the number of laborers and raised the price of grain. Every nobleman's estate was hampered, and a ransom of twenty thousand crowns was too costly to be come by without the help of the royal coffers. But any appeal to the French king must wait till the season of mourning had passed. The year 1350 saw the death of French Philip, and as the kingdom tottered unsteadily into the hands of his son John, Charny was all but forgotten in his gilded prison across the Channel.

After our return to England, I made a pilgrimage to Canterbury. The plague had begun to abate in London and the surrounding areas, but though the plague had abated, my anxieties had not. The triple witness of my father, the flagellant, and Bradwardine sat heavily on my heart. I had resolved to enter the cloister after the rescue of Calais. I would keep my resolution. When I reached Canterbury, the abbot consented to receive me as a novice. He instructed me to make my farewells and dispose of my possessions as best I might and so I returned to Windsor where the royal household was lodged.

It was the prince who first told Charny of my plans. "I pity your reputation, Sir Geoffroi," he said. "In a month's time it will fly abroad that your captor in England is no more than a tonsured monk. What think you of this? Sir Potenhale means to leave my service and take vows at Canterbury cloister!"

"Is this true?" asked Charny, a look of surprise showing clearly in his open countenance.

"Aye," said I, expecting some words of remonstrance. My noble prisoner, however, kept his thoughts to himself, and unlike others who had sounded the current of my intention, he had no hint of ridicule in his eyes. The seeming folly of my plans was not lost on me. I had just captured one of the premier knights of France. Fame and fortune awaited me with open arms. Now—only now—was I worthy of Margery Bradeshaw. And now—only now—must I take the step that would push her from me altogether. But if it were folly to thrust aside this worldly glory, it were a worse folly to ignore the promptings of my soul. I could not continue to wear the heavy mantle of knighthood while it sunk me deeper and deeper into the miry abyss of the damned.

Charny refused to remonstrate with me, but as it came about, he was as concerned for my distress as is any abbot for the morals of his brethren. Later that evening, after the prince had retired, he sought out my company. I had gone up to the battlement to ponder my path. In former days I had shunned solitude, but of late I had acquired a penchant for it—what wonder when my thoughts were too ridiculous to be discussed, too foreign to be explained, and too incomprehensible to be understood. In the midst of my musings, Charny found me. He did not speak, but sat beside me as silent as the stone surrounding us. When he did open his mouth, it was not a question, but a simple statement about his past.

"I once thought to take holy orders."

"You?" I asked in a tone verging on disbelief.

"Aye," he said. "Is that so strange?"

"So strange that I hardly credit it," answered I. "But assuredly it was in your youth—before you were knighted and became the most peerless chevalier in all of France."

"Nay," said Charny. "It was not so long ago. I was in the prime of manhood and had fame and fortune already on my side."

"Why did you wish to join the cloister then?" I asked. "Was it fear?" I shuddered, for I could conceive of no other reason why a man would put aside this world, but fear of death, fear of doom, and fear of damnation.

"Nay," said Charny. "It was not fear, but love."

I begged him to tell me the tale, and wrapping his cloak tightly around himself, he began the story of earlier days.

"I was *en route* to the Holy Land, at Smyrna not far from Byzantium. I wore the Crusaders' uniform in those days. I see your surprise at that. Aye, the days of the glorious Crusades may be past, but some Frenchmen still have a passion to protect the holy places of the East. Duke Humbert of Viennois had raised a small force for that very purpose, and asked me to accompany him. I was curious—is that not reason enough?—and so I went with him as far as Smyrna.

"The Christians in Smyrna had just seized the city and stripped the minarets from the mosques. But the Turks were in no mood to be turned out. They came in force to regain the place. Outside its walls our little company met them, ready to strike a blow for Christendom against the ranks of the infidel. Duke Humbert is a good man, but his piety substituted poorly for a knowledge of Turkish tactics. Our little army was pushed back to Smyrna in trampled disarray. The walls were indefensible and the city could not be held. Before it fell we took ship for home, having broken the Turkish power not one whit. But though we gained no ground for Christendom, my time in the East was well spent. It was there in Smyrna that I came face to face with Christ."

"Face to face with Christ?" I echoed, confused how such a thing could be possible. And yet, I had heard that King Richard saw St. George in the Holy Land. "Was it a vision?" I asked.

"Nay," said Charny. "I saw him with these waking eyes. There was an old priest in Smyrna who had come from Jerusalem. It was he who showed me the Christ, giving me a gift I could never repay. I saw the weary brow, the wounded hands, the pierced feet. My soul went out to Him in love; I wanted nothing more than to renounce my arms and spend a life of holy contemplation of Him who was crucified so that I might live. On our return to France, I determined to take holy orders and so draw near the One who had revealed Himself so powerfully to me."

"But what happened then?" I cried out. "You are no monk today. Did this fire of divine love die within you?"

"Patience," said Charny, "and I will tell you all. It was on the return voyage that my mind was changed, but not through inconstancy as you may be imagining. The seas tossed roughly around the Aegean, and three times we were in peril of sinking. The Turks have pirate craft within those waters, and more than once they boarded us with hostile intent. The shores themselves boast no friendly harbors; one has as much to fear from the knife of an Italian *brigante* as the scimitar of the Saracen infidel.

"In the midst of these perils, death was possible, or even probable. I confessed my sins in terror and prayed for deliverance to the Almighty. It was then that a thought came to me: no man has so great a need for a clear conscience as the man-at arms. The religious folk may pray, and fast, and faithfully perform their vows, but for them the spur to holy living lies only in the rules of their order. It is the knight and the soldier who has sorest need to be right with God, for it is the knight and the soldier who is in sorest peril of death. The fear of death is the most powerful motivator toward divine love, and it is the fear of death that the cloister itself lacks. The cloister is full of complacent men, who say 'Tomorrow, tomorrow, and Christ will be here.' They shuffle their sins under the rushes of the floor and do not feel the urgent need to wipe clean the house of the soul. But the more a man engages in arms, the more he will feel the foulness of his sin and the urgency to be purified of it. 'Today,' is the word on his lips, for who knows whether his enemy's sword will send him that very hour before the great and awful Judge."

"But," I objected, "It is the fear of that Judge that I would avoid. I seek a way to rid myself of the terror of damnation! I wake at night and feel my face in flames, while my body shivers uncontrollably in a vat of ice. I toss about from side to side. And whatever side I turn to, I feel the prickings and the stingings of a thousand little imps intent on tormenting me for my sins. In the day my sufferings increase the more, for I lay up more sins to put me in terror when I go to sleep again. And always is the dreadful torment of uncertainty—not to know what greater terror awaits me beyond the grave! This is the anguish I suffer, good knight. And would you have me remain in this wretched state?" I halted my ramblings and looked at him appealingly.

"Come, Sir Potenhale, let me understand you: it is because of your sins that you are in fear of judgment?

And it is to keep from sinning that you would join the cloister?"

"Aye," said I, for he had put into words my very feelings.

"My counsel is this: it is far easier to keep from sinning if you do *not* join the cloister. Your soul will be safer in the constant peril of the battlefield than in the peaceful stagnation of a monastery. Remain a knight and keep your fear of judgment, for it is this fear that will keep your hands from doing evil, keep Christ ever present within your thoughts, and keep you on the path of salvation. Those who fear damnation will seldom stumble into it."

I shifted uncomfortably. Fear of judgment was the thing I had been fleeing from, running like a panic-stricken doe from the hunter in the forest; Charny bade me cease fleeing, turn, and embrace the thing that pursued me. And to what purpose?

"Sir Geoffroi," I said solemnly, "I grant you that this fear of damnation might be beneficial to a holy man, but how will it aid an inveterate sinner? If a man fears damnation and continues in his sin nonetheless, what benefit is that fear to his soul. It makes him more culpable, does it not? He knew the truth and trampled upon it."

Charny's brow furrowed. "I have observed you for many weeks, Sir Potenhale, and I cannot believe that you are so inveterate a sinner as you would make yourself out to be. What sins are these that you continue to commit—despite the violent terror which urges you to do otherwise? Perhaps your conscience is too tender in this matter. Are you certain that they are sins?"

I told him many things: of the looted houses in La Hougue, of the untrained farmhands cut down at Caen, of the starving fugitives who perished outside Calais. "But Sir Potenhale," said my prisoner. "You must not take the sufferings of the whole world upon yourself. All these things came about through the evils of war, and not through your own evil. These are calamities that befall us because of the use of the sword, and yet the use of the sword is not sin. When the disciple brought two swords before Our Lord, did He not approve of them by saying, 'It is enough!'? There are times when it is right and proper for a knight to strike with violence."

"What are those times?" I asked.

"A knight may fight to defend the inheritance of weak maidens and orphans."

"Truly, it is a good deed. But I have not done that."

"A knight may make war on the enemies of the Christian religion."

"A praiseworthy action! But I have not done that."

"A knight may defend the lives and property of his fellow countrymen when they are attacked."

"Well said! But it is the lives and property of others that I have always endangered."

Charny hesitated. "A knight may also use the sword to defend his own rights or the rights of his liege."

I looked him full in the eyes. "That I have done," said I, "and right heartily too. I have fought in all things for Edward and Edward's rights—though perhaps you French will not own my liege to have just claim."

"I will say nothing on that head," said Charny with a smile. "It is enough that you are reconciled to the justice of his claim. If the master's rights are disputable, that is upon his own soul. His men shall bear no blame for that wrong."

"Then there is no sin in what I have done?" I asked.

Charny clapped me upon the shoulder. "Nay, lad, I cannot answer that. I am no confessor to grant absolution or assign penance. I only say to you that there is not *necessarily* sin in what you have done. You have doubtless sinned as a knight, but you have not sinned by *being* a knight. The sins that you have committed are sins that you might just as well commit in a cloister. Pride, greed, envy, wrath, lust, gluttony, sloth—these are not peculiar to the knightly orders. But it is the knight who will put off these sins more rapidly since he must put on his armor and face imminent death."

I did not answer. Charny saw my turmoil, and instead of pressing me further, he left me to mull over the new thoughts he had created. I did not retire to bed. I spent the entire night in the cold January air on the numb stones of the wall. The battlement of Windsor Castle became the Garden of Gethsemane for me, and alone I prayed that this dreadful cup might pass from me. Little by little, I began to see that if your husband's words were true, it was a far, far harder thing to remain a knight than become a monk—each day to hold your mortality in the palm of your hand and each evening to consecrate your soul like the host of the holy mass. But though it was harder, could it also be holier?

As these thoughts besieged my mind, beating upon my resolution again and again with the force of a mangonel, a conversation from my boyhood arose from the halls of memory. I was twelve years old, nervous, foreboding. My grandfather, the old steward held a reassuring hand upon my neck. Before me stood a black-haired Chandos with a silver Virgin on his blue tunic.

"Can you fight?" he had said.

"A little," replied I.

"Can you read?" he had said.

"A little," replied I.

"Can you pray?"

"Aye," said I. "I can pray right well."

"That is good," said he. "Perhaps you have the makings of a knight."

And remembering this, I began to pray with a fervor that had never filled my prayer before. I wrestled all that wintry night, till my brow was wet with drops of sweat—or blood. At length, the morning watch came round by torchlight before the pale sun had dared to wake the world. "Ah, Sir Potenhale!" said the captain of the guard, recognizing the hollow-eyed face beneath the hood of my mantle. "Come down from this place, I pray you. The prince is searching for you high and low; he fears that you are gone away without a word of farewell."

"Nay, I am not gone," said I. "Bid the prince be easy on that score. I shall attend his highness anon, but first I must find my quarters and pen a letter to the good abbot of Canterbury."

"Are you not bound for Canterbury this very day?" asked the captain, for word of my proposed abdication had travelled quickly around the walls of Windsor.

"Nay," said I feigning a look of surprise. "The road to Canterbury is for pilgrims and gadabouts. A letter to the abbot will serve just as well as a journey. I must remain here at the prince's service."

The captain looked at me puzzled for an instant, but his quick mind soon apprehended the new state of affairs. "That is well," he said kindly, "for the prince has need of knights such as you. Word has come that the Castilians have turned pirate. We must all keep our harness bright if His Majesty intends to raise sail against Spain."

◆ ◆ ◆

Castile was the strongest of the Spanish kingdoms. She had long been courted by our sovereign. As a close neighbor of France, and especially of English Gascony, Castile's goodwill was something to be coveted. England could not afford to have an enemy on either flank of her foothold in France.

The surest way to ensure friendship with Castile was through matrimonial connection. Before Edward had ever set sail for France, he had broached a betrothal between his daughter Joan and Don Pedro, the Spanish crown prince. With customary Castilian cunning, King Alfonso hesitated, unsure whether his advantage lay in an alliance with France or England. Yet after Edward's successful siege of Calais, the scales tipped heavily in our favor. Alfonso sent word that his son awaited the arrival of Princess Joan, his promised bride.

Edward, a model of Plantagenet extravagance, spared no expense in equipping his daughter for her bridal voyage. He prepared a fleet of four ships to carry the treasures of her trousseau. One hundred and thirty ells of imported silk composed her wedding gown. Her riding suit was of crimson velvet, and even her corsets were embroidered with thread of gold. Her ship bore a portable chapel so that she might enjoy the masses of her own priest on the long journey from England to Castile.

The fleet proceeded from Portsmouth across the western portion of the Channel; but instead of continuing south through the Basque Sea, the travelers resolved to break their journey in Bordeaux. It was a fateful mistake to land in Gascony. The plague, which at that time had not yet cast its net over England, had already saturated the country of France. By the time the horrified princess fled the horror-filled city, the pestilence had already touched her. She perished outside of Bordeaux, a virgin bride gone to meet the greater Bridegroom.

King Edward expressed great dismay over the wreck of his political plans, but his pain over the death of his daughter was equally potent. I overheard Chandos condoling him when first the news was heard. "Pity and sorrow well become you, Majesty, but pity England, and not the princess Joan. These Spaniards are a cruel race. They put wives aside and take another, or refuse to put them aside, and take a mistress. King Alfonso has ten children by his paramour, and how long will it be before he divorces his second wife? The envoys say that Pedro is even as his father—nay, that he is crueler and less cautious. Far better for Joan to be sent ahead to Heaven to reign among the choirs of the virgins."

"Amen," answered the king piously, "and may she gladly intercede for our offenses before the throne of God Himself."

But though the princess Joan's eternal happiness was secured, England's foreign alliance was not. The king's chagrin at the failed compact with Castile was augmented by his inability to make alliances elsewhere. If Queen Philippa's fertility were the only factor, then England might have princes enough to wed with half the crown heads of Europe. But unfortunately, all such matrimonial negotiations had either proved barren or had perished in the womb before they came to birth.

At the age of eighteen, the prince had nearly gained a Portuguese wife. This had been another of King Edward's schemes to gain the goodwill of Castile. The royal houses of Portugal and Castile were so entwined that marriage with one nearly assured alliance with the other.

The plan to ally with Portugal began shortly after the prince's frustrated betrothal to Brabant's daughter. While the Castilian king was cautious, conniving, and wary of his own interest, the king of Portugal's chief quality was haste. He immediately consented to wed his daughter Leonor to the Prince of Wales. The English envoys, however, were not empowered to conclude the terms of the alliance on their own. Edward must ratify the agreement. Hazardous weather delayed the diplomats' travel back to England. When Edward finally received the favorable news, he set his seal to the proposed terms—but it was already too late. By the time the envoys returned again to Portugal, the hasty Portuguese king had grown impatient. Leonor was wed already, to one of the neighboring Spanish kings, the king of Aragon. This failed alliance with Portugal did nothing to advance our relations with her sister country of Castile. The prince, my master, was left a bachelor a little longer, and the kingdom of Castile wandered free as a loosed falcon, ignoring all of Edward's efforts to seize her by the jesses.

Of late, Castile had grown increasingly hostile toward her English neighbors in Gascony. Many English merchant ships harbored in the Gascon harbor of Bordeaux. When they sailed out with their cargoes into the Basque Sea, Castilian pirates buzzed around them like bees in a flower garden. Don Carlos de la Cerda was the worst of the predators. An admiral in the Spanish fleet, he knew the art of warfare well. No ships were as bold as his upon the high seas. In the summer of 1350, a large Castilian fleet led by Don Carlos overwhelmed the Gascon wine fleet entering the Channel. They looted the cargoes with murderous rapacity and tossed the crews over the side just as sailors will do with beer that has soured. Then they continued on to Flanders, their holds stuffed with the stolen wine of Bordeaux. The Count of Flanders, who had always been a foe to England, gave them harbor there.

Edward took this latest act of piracy with ill grace. No longer hampered by delusions of a future alliance with Castile, he acted with astonishing alacrity. He assembled both the English nobles and the English navy at Winchelsea with orders to man the fleet for war. The prince and I went thither immediately and invited Charny to accompany us—for you must understand that a noble prisoner in our land is treated with as much courtesy as a guest. Besides, the prince was unwilling for Charny to miss a military action that might redound to the glory of English prowess.

It was a grand company at Winchelsea: Henry, the Duke of Lancaster, the Earls of Arundel, Northampton, and Warwick, Sir Thomas Holland, Sir James Audley, and Sir John Chandos. Mortimer was there, but Montague was absent, for he had recently recovered from his passion for Lady Joan and had wed the sister of Mortimer. But even without Montague, there was a score of other noble names, among them Sir Walter Manny. That worthy knight had finally quitted his post in Calais for more pleasant pastimes in England. He crossed the channel just in time to join our armada.

"My lords," said Edward, when the nobles had all been gathered together, "Remember the manifold injuries these Spaniards have done to us in the past. We have for a long time spared these people, and yet they do not amend their conduct. On the contrary, they grow more arrogant, and it is for this reason that they must be chastised the next time that they pass by our coast. This Don Carlos has gone too far, and we will make him pay us back in blood for the wine that he has plundered." The nobles murmured in assent and pledged their collective support. The king sent messengers to the archbishops of Canterbury and York, apprising them of the Castilians' depredations and bidding them send up prayers for the victory of our enterprise.

The queen and her ladies had accompanied His Majesty to Winchelsea. There they waited in the safety of a convent for the expedition to set forth and return again. Joan of Kent had come with her husband, and I eagerly noted that Margery was in her train. I had not seen her since young Thomas's christening. At that time—my head full of hermits, hair shirts, and hell fire—I had refused to encounter her eye. Now, after I had reconciled myself to—nay, even embraced—the calling of knighthood, she mirrored my earlier coldness. She must have noted my presence, but she acknowledged me not one whit.

"Potenhale," asked the observant prince, for he too had his eyes on the company from Kent. "Is that not the lady who visited you in your tent at the Windsor tournament?"

"Aye, highness," said I, "but I seem to have lost her goodwill as soon as I gained it."

"Then you must win it back, my friend," said the prince, "for we must keep friends with that household."

I nodded but saw no way to fulfill the prince's injunction. It was easier to board a ship full of Castilian pirates than to approach Margery Bradeshaw when she was in a fit of pique. She persisted in her cold reserve; I relinquished my mute appeals and repaired to the fleet. The tide would turn sooner than Margery's head.

As soon as enough men-at-arms had been collected, the ships sidled out into the Channel. The king bade the shipmasters drop anchor at the midpoint between Dover and Calais. There we sat like a wolf at the mouth of a hedgehog's burrow. The gentle swells rolled quietly beneath our hulls and we kept sharp lookout toward the Flemish coast. Sooner or later, the Castilians would leave their safe harbor, and when they did, we would be waiting with open jaws.

11

AT THE STAKE
August, 1350

*I*t was a three day wait in the channel before the Spanish fleet appeared on the horizon. The king and his servants sat patiently aboard the ship, the *Cog Thomas*, while the prince and I passed much of our time aboard a smaller craft. We had fifty vessels in sum. Stationed close together in the gentle swells, the boats formed a small city. Noblemen and knights visited one another, passing from ship to ship with nearly as much ease as from street to street in London.

The greatest merriment was the dance that the king held aboard the *Cog Thomas*. He bade his minstrels play a song that Sir John Chandos had lately introduced to the court and ordered Sir John to stand up in the middle and sing the words. Sir John had a clear, sonorous baritone that would have served him well as a minstrel or troubadour. The sailors danced merrily to the lilting tune, and the king was diverted to no end by the jollity. Indeed, at such a time this, it would have been surprising to see the king in poor spirits. The Castilians had given him the very pretext he needed to engage their fleet. The anticipation of the conflict flowed through him like an elixir, brightening his eyes and quickening his step.

In his excitement over the expedition, Edward allowed his third son to leave the company of his mother and join the bellicose venture. The boy's given name was the same as mine—John. He was called John of Gaunt, for he had been born in that Flemish city and had come well-knit into the world like all the cloth produced in the Low Countries. At the time of our expedition, he was only ten years of age, but tall like his father and brothers, and indeed, like all of the Plantagenets. He conceived a particular affection for me over the course of our voyage, and as we waited in the channel I entertained him with matches of dice or backgammon.

On one of our evenings at sea, the prince challenged Charny to a game of chess. A small pavilion was erected on the deck of the ship and beneath it they played by candlelight. Young John of Gaunt and I watched the match with interest. I was unsure in my own mind as to which was the probable winner. The prince, I knew, had rarely met his master, but my confidence in Charny's powers had grown up overnight like a housewife's leavened bread. The French knight was endowed with a simple shrewdness that I could not fathom.

The prince advanced his ebony queen early, and Charny's pieces were soon hemmed in from all sides. His highness leaned forward intently on each move, stroking the short, dark beard on his chin and furrowing his brow. Charny reclined a little where he sat, the picture of a man at ease. He had lost a knight and a bishop now, but his demeanor remained unflappable.

In the midst of the match, a sailor entered; he told his highness of a party seeking leave to board our boat. The prince, in rapt concentration, waved me away to deal with the matter. I left the pavilion to greet our new guests.

"Ha! Potenhale!" said a thick voice, and I recognized the speaker immediately. It was my erstwhile adversary, the Earl of Kent. A bedraggled squire helped Holland over the side of the boat. He wobbled unevenly on the deck, and I saw that he had drunk much wine in the early hours of the evening.

"Sir Thomas," said I, forced into civility by my role as the prince's deputy. "The Prince of Wales bids you welcome. Will you join us on the rear deck?"

Holland grunted in assent. I returned with him to the pavilion. When I entered, I saw that of the prince's ebony pieces only the king remained. Charny moved his ivory queen, and the black king toppled tragically onto the checkered squares below.

"You have bested me," said the prince gravely.

"Nay, the Castilians have bested you," said Charny with a smile.

"How is that possible?" asked young John, the prince's brother, for we had not yet encountered the Castilian fleet.

"It is from a Castilian that I learned the game," replied Charny.

"I would like to meet that fellow," said the prince, "for truly, you play like a master at this sport."

"I should like to meet the man as well," said Charny with a shrug, "but he is dead these fifty years and more. He was the great-grandfather of the current Castilian king. His book, *Libro de los juegos,* poses problem after problem for the chess player; I spent many hours with it as a boy. Has your highness never heard of it?"

"Never," said the prince. "Thomas Bradwardine taught me what small skill I possess. I did not think it possible to acquire it from a book."

"And yet, nearly all knowledge may be imparted through the written word," replied Charny. "Name me a field of knowledge that may not be acquired in this way."

"The knowledge of knighthood," said the prince promptly. "That must be learned upon the field of arms."

"Do you not rather mean the skills of knighthood?" corrected the Frenchman. "For the knowledge of knighthood and chivalry may be fully set forth and expounded with ink on a dozen sheets of vellum."

"Ha!" said Sir Thomas Holland scornfully, and the prince—as if just noticing his presence—turned him a brief glance of recognition.

"Very well, Sir Geoffroi," said the prince. "Prove that the knowledge of knighthood may be learned in this way. Show me the book that teaches it."

"Grant me a year, highness, and I will place it before your eyes."

Sir Thomas, meanwhile, had set his large frame upon the bench beside his highness's young brother. "What do the French know of knighthood?" he said loudly. He leaned forward into Charny's face. "Look here, my good man, have the French anything of this sort?"—he fumbled with the garter on his leg. "Have the French anything like this?"—he held out the medal of St. George that swung from his neck.

"You refer to your English order?" asked Charny politely, "The Order of the Garter?"

"Aye!" said Holland, "Have the French an order that boasts so many fine knights and peers of the realm? Answer me that, Frenchman!"

"Nay," said Charny, "we have no such order now— although in past days many French knights won glory in the orders of the Hospitallers and the Templars."

Holland snorted. "Monkish men, the lot of them! What kind of vows are poverty and chastity for a knight? Bah!" He reached forward and nudged the prince familiarly. "I wager *you* could not keep such vows, highness." The prince glanced at him coldly, but gave no word of remonstrance, for he saw that the man was in his cups.

"But were not the Templars guilty of witchcraft?" asked John of Gaunt, for he knew the stories as well as the rest of us.

"Not so," said Charny, "The Templars were godly men in the main."

"Godly?" roared Holland in a surly tone. "Do you call it godly to deny Christ and trample on his cross? The French have a strange form of piety." The drunken earl began to wax obscene and called down imprecations on the defunct Templar order.

Ignoring him, the prince turned his attention back to Charny's claim. "I have never heard high praise of the Templar order. In sooth, the scroll of judgment is heavily charged with their blasphemies and perversions. If they were godly men, as you say, then why did your Philip the Fair take such great pains to uproot them?"

Charny sat silent for a minute, just as he had done several months ago on the battlement of Windsor Castle.

His silence at that time had been a prelude to his tale of the Crusade at Smyrna. I looked at him attentively and waited for the beginning of a new story.

• ◆ •

"Long ago," said Charny, "I had an uncle. He bore the same name as me, or rather, I now bear the name that was once made famous by him. He entered the Order of the Temple at the prescribed age—perhaps a little younger, for the preceptors often gave early admittance to young knights of promising quality. At the time of his entry, the Crusader outposts in Outremer were already in the throes of defeat. The Hospitaller Knights had just lost the city of Acre in a siege as bloody as Herod's slaughter of the innocents. Acre was the pillar on which the remaining Crusader cities leaned, and when she fell, all else tottered. Sidon, Haifa, Beirut, and Tarsus disappeared before half a year had passed, all prey to the implacable foe.

"In past times, the greatest enemy of the Crusaders was the Saracen. Your King Richard had much to do with Saladin, the prince of Saracens. That sultan was a cruel foe. He could slaughter a hundred Christian prisoners without a pang of remorse and frequently did so when a battle had been won. But he was also a chivalrous foe. When Richard's horse was shot from under him, he sent him two others to replace it. When Richard lay ill of a desert fever, he sent him fresh fruits and ice. They say that when a Frankish woman's babe was stolen from her, Saladin took the child from the slave market and restored him to her breast. There is a certain native nobility in the Saracen, and a man may take pleasure to fight such an enemy.

"But the nobility of the Saracen is entirely absent in the Mamluk hordes of Egypt, and there is no such pleasure in taking arms against them. The Mamluks were the slaves of the Saracens before they overthrew them and so there is little wonder to find them base. A slave is a man who has been taught that all men are beasts. His master has done his best to drive this thought into him by the sting of lash and tongue. What horror then, when the beast-like slave becomes in turn the master!

"You may wonder why the Crusader kingdoms toppled so easily before the Mamluks. Before Acre fell, the Crusaders had allowed the Mamluks to pass through our territory in the Holy Land. The intruders claimed that they only wished to do battle with the Mongols in the North. They pledged an oath that the Christian kingdoms would be left unharmed. But no promise binds an infidel. Once entrenched in our kingdoms, there the Mamluks remained. They attacked fortress after fortress, and in the heat of their fury, the Christian kingdoms of Outremer melted away like ice in the sun. By the time my uncle joined the Templars, only one small piece of Christendom was left in the East, the island of Ruad just off the coast of Syria.

"My uncle entered the order in a time of change. Jacques de Molay had been newly elected Grand Master. This man had commanded a troop at the siege of Acre and knew the rapacity of the Mamluks firsthand. At the time of De Molay's inauguration, the Templar headquarters sat on Cyprus in the Mediterranean. De Molay knew that Cyprus was too far offshore for launching effective strikes to regain the Holy Land; he moved immediately to garrison Ruad. My young uncle filled one of the posts on the island. It was not often that Ruad was free from attack, and he grew to manhood amidst the clash of sword and scimitar. For ten years, the Mamluks tried to take Ruad, and for ten years, the Templars held their island fortress.

"While my uncle Charny grew inured to danger on the battlements of Ruad, the Grand Master de Molay contended with other dangers that threatened the Templars. Pope Boniface was dismayed by the continual losses in the Holy Land. Assessing the situation from his seat in Rome, he determined that the knightly orders were too decayed and disorderly to retake Outremer. He suggested that the Hospitallers and Templars unite into one single order and combine their efforts against the infidels. Both orders balked, unwilling to give up their insignia, their prestige, and their autonomy. Surely there must be some other way to contend with the Mamluk besides merging the two orders into one!

"The Grand Master De Molay suggested cooperation with the Mongols. They harbored long-standing enmity for the Mamluks and might be willing to help the Crusaders. Full of hope for the enterprise, De Molay came to terms with the Mongol Khan in 1300. The Templars launched a sea-based attack from Ruad against Tortosa and waited for their allies to join them; yet despite many promises, the Mongol land force failed to materialize. By the time the Khan's tardy troops arrived, two months had passed and the Templars had already withdrawn. De Molay tried the same tactic the next year and the year following, each time with the same results. Meanwhile, back in Italy, the pope grew increasingly impatient.

"My uncle, by this time, had proved his worth at Ruad; beneath his redcross robe he had the sinews and the scars worthy of a defender of Christendom. De Molay recognized in Charny a leader of men and resolved to raise him to a higher position within the order. My uncle was remanded to France and took ship at once from Ruad.

"The transfer came none too soon, for the Mamluks had wearied of the Templars as one wearies of a persistent gadfly. A swarm of sixteen ships came from the Mamluk nest in Egypt and put in at Tripoli. From there, they surrounded Ruad and starved the Templar garrison into submission. When the Templar commander negotiated a surrender, the Mamluks agreed that the garrison could leave the island unharmed and take ship for the Christian land of their choice. But as the Templars—120 knights, 500 bowmen, and 400 servants both male and female—exited the gates of the rocky fortress, the Mamluks' mercy dried up within them like water in the desert sun. The infidels knocked arrow to string and struck down every Frank with a bolt through the heart.

"My uncle Charny arrived safely in France, and at de Molay's recommendation, filled the vacant position of preceptor of Normandy. It was an honorable post for a knight to hold but an unfortunate time for him to hold it. A new pope had taken office and had moved the papal see to Avignon. The changes in the papacy, however, did nothing to change the papal attitude toward the Templars. What is more, the pope's displeasure with the Templars had planted seeds of hostility within the fertile minds of the laity. Rumors began to hover and dart like dragonflies, skimming over but never quite dipping into the placid pond of truth.

"The Templars had always prohibited others from entering their preceptories, and now this very secrecy gave rise to speculation. What rites went on behind those closed gates? Whispers of impiety and perversion tiptoed among the people. The Templars, said some, had allowed the infidels to overrun the Holy Land because the Templars themselves had embraced the infidel faith. Inside their fenced fortresses they abominated the Christ they professed to adore, spitting upon the cross that should have been enthroned with honor. Along with forsaking their faith, they had forsaken the ways of nature. Ritual prostitution reigned in their halls, men with men committing what is shameful. So flared the flames of rumor, and try as they might, the Templars could not quench them.

"In these troubled times, my uncle continued to administer the preceptory of Normandy. Fewer and fewer young knights elected to enter the order, and the heads of the Templars were beginning to gray. The situation in the East had not improved. The loss of Ruad proved irreparable, and in the spring of 1306, the Grand Master de Molay returned from Cyprus to France. He awaited a meeting with Clement, the new pope, in Paris and asked Charny to accompany him thither. When they arrived in Paris, they found that the pope was not alone in demanding the conference. King Philip the Fair of France was behind the pope, and behind him was that viper de Nogaret.

"Guillaume de Nogaret was Philip's most trusted councilor and the keeper of the royal seal. It was de

Nogaret who had first advised Philip to tax the clergy and to ignore Pope Boniface when he objected to the levy. It was de Nogaret who had urged Philip to depose Boniface before Boniface could depose him. And it was de Nogaret who led the frustrated plot to kidnap Boniface. When Pope Boniface perished from the trauma of the attack, de Nogaret contrived the election of one of Philip's minions. Within a few years, he had effected the removal of the papacy from Rome to Avignon. Thus, it came about that Peter's See came into my own country in the reign of Philip the Fair.

"It was with de Nogaret's pope, Clement the Sycophant, that de Molay had to deal. When the conference commenced, the Grand Master found that Clement had the same wish that Boniface had earlier expressed, namely, to join the Templars and Hospitallers into one. But in addition to this, he had a second demand: Philip the Fair must be the Grand Master of the new, combined order. De Molay disagreed and denounced the proposal vehemently. As a lay leader, the king had no right to control a religious order. De Molay also questioned the king's motivations. The Templars were one of the richest societies in the world. As master of the order, King Philip would be able to control the nearly limitless wealth that lay in the vaults of the preceptories.

"De Molay and Charny spent three months in Paris as the Grand Master argued with Pope Clement over the matter and entreated him not to remove the papal blessing from the order. Almost—almost—Clement seemed persuaded. But whenever Clement showed signs of forgetting his lines, Guillaume de Nogaret lurked in the wings to prompt him with the words from Philip's script. Whenever the pope saw the wisdom of de Molay's protestations, de Nogaret dipped his spoon into the vat of rumor and ladled the malodorous accusations onto the pope's trencher.

"In the summer of 1307, de Molay demanded that the pope make an inquiry into the scandalous rumors that surrounded the Templar order; he saw that unless the rumors were dispersed, the order assuredly would be. De Nogaret, perhaps afraid that such an inquiry would reveal the groundless nature of the gossip, acted decisively to end the discussion. Using the pen of Philip, he ordered a mass confiscation of Templar property throughout France. The command was kept secret until it was carried out. One by one the preceptories were surprised by a force of Philip's ruffians. They stove in the gates, overpowered the knights, and rushed straightway to the money vault. Any Templar found within French domains was incarcerated on charges of blasphemy and perversion.

"Jacques de Molay and Geoffroi de Charny had been delayed in Paris as guests at a funeral for one of the king's cousins. When the preceptories were seized, these two men were seized as well. Philip imprisoned them in Paris and set his jailers to work on de Molay. If he could discredit the Grand Master by obtaining a confession of heresy or sodomy, he could discredit the whole order and thereby justify his seizure of the Templars' assets. By means of the rack and the *strappado*, the jailers extracted a confession from de Molay. He denied the charges of sodomy but admitted to blaspheming Christ and trampling upon a crucifix during one of the Templars' 'secret ceremonies'. This simple admission was not enough for

Philip, however. He brought de Molay out of the prison walls to make a public confession and then ordered him to draft a letter commanding every Templar Knight to admit to the same acts.

"Pope Clement heard these tidings with horror. Convinced of the Templars' guilt, he condemned Jacques de Molay, Geoffroi de Charny, and many other high ranking Templars to imprisonment for life. De Molay now realized that all was lost. Desperate to clear the name of his order, de Molay recanted all of the false words they had pried from him. In the face of new tortures he denied all accusations. Nothing that de Nogaret tried could alter his new stance. Charny was as immutable in his protestations as de Molay, and together the two of them were condemned to death, the death of a heretic.

"While awaiting the day of his execution, Jacques de Molay called down the curse of God upon all those who had judged his case. Clement, Philip, and Guillaume de Nogaret were the foremost named in his imprecations. When they brought him out to the stake, and tied him side by side with my uncle Charny, he repeated his words against them. They say that his last words were *vekam adonai*—'Revenge me, Lord.'

"A week after de Molay's death, Guillaume de Nogaret also departed this world. A disease came upon him suddenly, and when they found his body one morning, the face was horribly distended, the tongue straining from the mouth as if someone had tried to wrench it from the dead man's throat. Thus, the *advocatus diaboli* was punished, and in a fitting manner for one whose tongue had stirred up all manner of troubles.

"Pope Clement was the next to feel the Templar's curse. In the style of Pope Urban, he called a Crusade to retake the Holy Land from the Mamluks. But the Lord was unwilling to use such an unholy instrument to effect His holy purposes. The month following de Molay's death, Pope Clement died of sickness. As his body lay in state and awaited funerary rites, a great thunderstorm arose and lightning struck the church that housed him. The building caught fire as easily as men catch the plague, and Clement's body was consumed almost entirely by the flames.

"King Philip the Fair determined to carry on with the Crusade that Clement had called; but before he took ship, he fell from his horse in a hunting accident. Death followed on the heels of this fall, and before the year was out the king of France was no more. Philip left behind him three sickly sons who soon went the way of their father. The rest you know—how their cousin Philip of Valois assumed the throne and how his son John now holds it. Some might say that it is due to de Molay's curse that the English now seek the throne of France. For assuredly, if Philip or his sons had lived, your king would have no claim now to the French throne."

"Then God be thanked for the Templars!" said the prince with a smile, and I awoke as if from a trance. The prince's comment had no such effect on Holland who had snored loudly throughout the latter half of Charny's tale. John of Gaunt's attention had flagged as well. Long before the death of de Molay, the young lad had darted out onto the deck to play with a dog that the sailors had brought on board.

244 | I Serve

So much for my story," said Charny wryly, gazing at the Earl of Kent's sprawling form. "I intended it more as an apologetic than a soporific, but I fear that the latter has resulted."

"He sleeps from his wine, not your words," said the prince. "Potenhale and I have kept awake, however. You tell your story well, Sir Geoffroi, and what is more, I believe it. It is not beyond imagination that a French king should practice so cruelly on innocent subjects. My great-grandfather hardly believed the superstitions about the Temple Knights, and my grandfather was loath to drive them from our shores when Philip the Fair demanded it. I am sorry that the Templars do not still live, for they were fine knights and keepers of Christendom."

"But come," continued the prince, "it is time that we followed the example of Sir Thomas. The Castilians may be upon us in the morning, and it is not meet that we should be weary for the battle." I signaled two servants to remove the inert body of the sleeping earl, and we retired severally to our sleeping quarters aboard ship.

◆ ◆ ◆

The Spaniards were not sighted in the morning, and the king continued to make merry aboard his ship. The minstrels were still warbling when afternoon came, till a sharp cry was heard from the crow's nest. "Ship in sight! She looks Castilian."

The music halted abruptly. "Are there more than one?" demanded the king.

"Aye, one, two, three, four! So help me God, I can't count them all!" Brusquely, the king ordered the trumpeters to signal the remainder of the English fleet to fall in line. Then wine was fetched, so that the knights might refresh themselves before the battle. After drinking, they began to lace on their armor and attach their helms.

The Spaniards had the wind with them, and had they wished, their glutted sails might have pulled them southward to avoid our fleet. But Don Carlos de la Cerda was no coward; he bore down on us as eager for battle as we. As the Castilians neared, we saw that the forecastles of their ships were much higher than ours. This gave them an advantage, for they could bombard us from above when the ships were locked in close quarters. They had laid in a great store of stones and iron bars while they were in Flanders for exactly that purpose. Fortunately, however, their crossbowmen were no match for English archers. By dint of clever shooting, our archers could force the Spaniards to take cover behind their parapets.

The king, meanwhile, had transferred ships to the more formidable flagship, *La Salle du Roi*. Impetuously, he bade the helmsman ram the first Spanish ship that approached. It was like a clap of thunder when the two vessels met. A great shout went up as the Castilians lost their center mast. Their crow's nest castle toppled into the sea carrying half a dozen men with it. The English flagship was well joined and strongly made, but the shock of the impact split one of the seams. A voracious leak gulped in the ocean water. The ship had received its death sentence.

Knowing that it was conquer or sink, the king bade his men grapple with the next available Spanish ship. The grappling hooks sailed through the air like the talons of an eagle and latched onto the side of the enemy ship. The king's men lowered the plank; then, swarming aboard in a fury of desperation, they flung every single Spaniard overboard. No quarter was given. The spoils of war became the king's new battle station, and not a moment too soon. Leaving *La Salle du Roi* to founder, he crossed over to the captured ship and prepared to stage a new attack.

My ship, meanwhile, had encountered much the same peril. The prince had ordered us to grapple with a much larger Spanish ship. We had neared at too great a speed and hit the enemy's hull jarringly. Wide gaps opened up in our larboard seams too big for the carpenter to staunch. The king had solved this same problem by taking the Castilian ship and letting his own vessel disappear beneath the surf. We sought to do the same.

As our ship sunk lower and lower into the brine, however, there was less and less of a likelihood that we would be able to board the Spaniard. The enemy's bulwarks already towered high above us, and as our hull filled with water the disparity between the elevations of our decks became even greater. With arrows and missiles pelting us from above, we could not climb the steep sides of the Spanish ship to save ourselves from drowning in our own.

Fortunately, the other English ships were not unaware of our plight. "A rescue! A rescue!" shouted English voices from the other side of the Castilian craft. "Lancaster to the rescue!" Henry, the Duke of Lancaster, had maneuvered his ship parallel to ours on the far side of the Spanish attacker. Once he threw over the grappling chains, the Spaniards facing us were distracted and rushed across their deck to repel the new danger.

"Climb!" bellowed the prince, and seizing John of Gaunt by the collar, he forcibly propelled his young brother up the side of the enemy ship. So low was our ship in the water that my feet began to get wet before it was my turn to ascend the side. We reached the gunwale none too soon, for of our own ship nothing but the masts was still visible.

"England and St. George!" cried the prince, stepping firmly onto the Spanish deck. We drew our swords with that cry on our lips.

Surrounded on both sides, the Castilians fought fiercely, but they were no match for the combined forces of Lancaster and the Prince of Wales. Every man of them was thrown overboard, and the prince took possession of the new ship. The prince's brother acquitted himself remarkably well in the affair. He drew his sword like the rest of us, and though it was doubtless his first combat, he did not hang back against the railing. He was shoulder to shoulder with the prince and I when we fought our way through to Lancaster's party, and he was ready to keep hacking with all his might. "Enough, enough! These are friends!" said the prince as his brother continued to fight even though the battle was over.

"God's wounds!" cried Lancaster, catching one of John of Gaunt's fierce blows upon his own sword. "Here's a fierce cockerel in your highness's train."

"Aye, a cockerel who does not know which hens to peck," said the prince a little harshly.

"I beg pardon," said young John with a blush, and he put away his sword now that he saw the fighting was over.

"Nay, beg no man's pardon," said Lancaster heartily. "I like your spirit, sirrah. An' you were not the king's son,

I would engage you to be my man." John's face flushed again, this time with pleasure. Lancaster clapped him on the back and invited him aboard his own ship for the remainder of the fray.

"Watch him well," said the prince sharply, for his father had entrusted to him the care of his younger brother.

"As I would my own son," said Lancaster.

The prince set his coxswain at the wheel of the newly captured Castilian and turned her head toward battle. We grappled another ship, this time without injury to our own, and took her with little loss. As we slipped loose from our second prize, the sun slipped below the horizon. The sky began to grow dark. The Spaniards had lost fourteen of their fleet and with them their stomach for battle. Don Carlos ordered his ships to crowd sail; they sped to the southwest. The gathering darkness prevented pursuit, and we cast anchor until dawn.

On the next day, the king sent his sharpest eyed scouts into the crow's nests. They scanned the sea and saw nothing but sparkling water in every direction. The Spaniards had disappeared. "They have had enough of our English hospitality," said I with a grin.

"Aye, they are back to Castile with their tail between their legs," said the prince.

There was little hope that we could catch them and so the king ordered the fleet to put in again at Winchelsea. The queen, who had watched the battle from the soft downs of the shore, was much comforted to see her lord return safely. "I have ordered a banquet," said she, "with wine and dancing to welcome my victorious husband and his lords." The king gave her gramercy and the men-at-arms cheered; I was as pleased as any, for a banquet would give me the chance I needed to see Margery and perhaps have speech with her.

❖ ◆ ❖

The prince, as was his wont, bedecked himself for the banquet with as much splendor as the lilies of the field. He wore a yellow tunic, cut square at the neck and richly embroidered with birds and beasts in thread of gold. The tunic sheared off sharply at the middle of his thigh and beneath it he wore hose of brightest blue. Your husband, in contrast, had attired himself again in his plain green tunic. Its full fabric cascaded below his knees and it was gathered about him with a simple leather belt.

"Come, Sir Geoffroi," said the prince observing our guest's attire. "I will lend you this chain and enameled belt for the feast."

"Gramercy for your kindness," said Charny composedly, "but I will dress as I am. My dress sorts well with my station and I will not alter it through vanity."

"Nay, you are too modest," replied the prince, "or your station is higher than you know. You are the premier knight in France and guest to the king of England. You cannot dress too grandly."

Charny shook his head and I saw that his mind was made up. "A knight's dress is in his courtesy, his courage, and his skill at arms. These are his show to the world, and it is in these that he displays his true quality."

"You should have been a monk," said the prince disdainfully.

"Mayhap I should have been," said Charny simply, but he would not be goaded into wearing the golden chain or the enamel belt.

In the banquet hall, the prince sat at table beside his father and mother while Charny and I had seats at a lower table. Holland was on the other side of the hall with the lady Joan at his side. Margery came in later to take a seat at her lady's right hand.

I do not know how he came to notice—perhaps my eye followed her too closely as she moved across the room—but the meal had scarcely begun before your husband asked me Margery's name. "She is called Margery Bradeshaw," said I with a sigh. "She is waiting woman to Joan, the Lady of Kent."

"She is passing fair," said Sir Geoffroi with a smile, and I smiled back to have his approbation.

"She is indeed," said I and colored a little. "Though perhaps you think her dress too rich to be seemly in a maiden." For Margery had bound up her red hair with a gold fillet and her dress had a jeweled brooch below her throat.

"Nay," said Charny with a laugh. "I think you misunderstand me as completely as your master. I am no anchorite in a hair shirt and bare feet. I am merely for modest dress in men and not this overweening ostentation that speaks nothing of a knight's true quality. Leave adornment to the ladies for it is their proper pleasure. Men take up arms for war; women cannot do this. Men treat widely in society; women stay mainly in the home. And therefore, a woman should pay special heed to her apparel, her jewels, and her adornment, for it is through these things that she receives recognition. But a man receives recognition through his achievements. Those are his ornaments, his jewels, and his folderols. Fear not," said Charny, "I think your lady-love dresses most becomingly."

"She gave me a favor once," I said excitedly, and with barely an invitation to continue, I told him the whole story of the tournament and my disguise.

"And have you spoken to her since?" Charny inquired.

I hung my head. "Nay. At first, I had thought to enter the cloister and so thought a woman's company no place for me. And then, after you persuaded me that my soul would be best served as a knight, I thought to address her again. But she has turned as cold as a Virgin of lead, and whenever we meet by chance, she will not smile upon me or engage my eye."

"And are you so weak in the sinews that you fear aught of that?" asked Charny. "Come, come, Sir Potenhale. On the causeway at Calais you leaped in front of a fleeing horse and brought horse and rider to the ground with one swift blow. I have the scar upon my head to prove it. You are the favorite retainer of his highness, the Prince of Wales, and a valiant combatant in this latest sea battle with Castile. Does such a man tremble to hold converse with a maid?"

I nodded miserably.

"Then I shall play Pandarus to your Criseyde," said Charny. "I shall away to the lady and convince her so well of your good parts that she will never wish to part with you again."

Before I could protest, he had risen to his feet and sought the other side of the hall. I saw him exchange some good natured pleasantries with Sir Thomas and seat himself opposite the earl and the ladies.

The evening wore on. Ever and anon I would glance at Sir Geoffroi and see him in spirited converse. Margery's golden eyes shone with interest. She smiled at him, and laughed happily, and leaned her shoulders toward him with intimate closeness. I almost thought to be jealous of your husband and wondered if I had misplaced my trust in him to speak so freely of my lady. Charny was a man as I was, and even the wisest or most monkish of men are susceptible to female charms.

The banquet tables were emptied—still he paid his court. Holland and Lady Joan retired—still he lingered there. The prince, by now, had sought my company and bade me away with him to continue the evening's merriment. The victory of the previous day worked on him the same way that it did with his father. His spirits were high and he longed to revel in the martial triumph. "Brocas has arrived," said he, "and waits for us at my quarters. And if Mortimer comes as well, we shall have some sport indeed."

"And Charny?" I asked anxiously, unwilling to leave him at the banquet hall alone with Mistress Margery.

"Leave him be," said the prince. "He is no great addition to our revels. He will find his own way back."

I followed the prince out the doors and willed myself not to turn around as we passed the table of Margery Bradeshaw.

❖ ◆ ❖

Charny did not come when it grew dark and he did not come when the moon rose. At last, when the boisterous merrymaking had begun to die down and the prince ceased calling for another cask to be opened, I retired to my bed. I was awakened in the small hours of the night by a quiet knock on the panel outside. It was Charny, clad still in his green tunic.

"I did not think to find you asleep," said he.

"I did not think to find you returned so late," said I.

"Methinks your case is difficult," said Charny succinctly. I saw that he had completed his mission and was anxious to reveal the outcome to me. I invited him to sit and he began to tell me what he had learned.

"It took me some time," said Charny, "to gain the lady's confidence."

"Was she shrewish with you?" I demanded.

"She was *spirited*," said Charny with a wry smile, and I gathered that Margery had broken her wit upon him more than once or twice. "I began by praising your valor. I told her you were my captor and described your doughtiness at Calais."

"And what said she?"

"She made your courage of no account, and vituperated you strongly as a dissembler and a spy."

"Ah," I said with a groan.

"Following this, I praised your wisdom."

"Then what said she?"

"She said you had but shallow wit and your words were shallower still."

"Prithee, good sir," said I, my face flaming, "you may spare me her exact words."

"Why then, so it continued," said Charny, "and no sooner would I paint you kindly than she would call you cruel, and no sooner would I draw you gallant than she would name you false."

"It is as you say—my case is difficult."

"Nay," said Charny sagely, "I have not yet come to the difficulty of the matter. Her scorn is but a screen for a lovesick heart. My first wife was even thus, and she would sooner launch volleys of wit upon me than say she loved me; I daresay that when she delivered the first, it was her way of expressing the last."

"You think she loves me?" I demanded.

"I would swear to it," said Charny.

"Then wherein lies the difficulty?" asked I. "Did you tell her I have fortune? Did you assure her I have the prince's favor?"

"When the Earl of Kent and his lady retired, I had opportunity to speak more seriously with the young woman. She has served the lady Joan since childhood. Her mother was a distant cousin to the lady's family. It is in her close relationship with the Countess of Kent that the difficulty lies."

"Does the lady Joan mislike me?" I asked anxiously.

"Nay, nay," said Charny good-humoredly, doubtless becoming wearied of my constant interruptions. "She likes you well enough. It is her own husband that the lady Joan mislikes."

"Aye, she would have taken the veil rather than marry him," said I, remembering the prince and Montague's frantic appeal to the pope to dissolve the marriage between Joan and Sir Thomas.

"Time has done little to weather her dislike," said Charny. "She has born a child to him, but that has not made her love the father. She has become accustomed to, but not accepting of his crassness, and the maid feels her lady's distress even more keenly than the mistress."

"Then let her leave that house," cried I, "and become mistress of her own. I am of age. I am of means. I will wed her and take her out from under that roof."

Charny shook his head. "She does not wish it. She is—so she thinks—the sole prop of her mistress in her time of sorrow. She will not leave the lady Joan for any man. And that, Sir Potenhale, is why your case is a difficult one. My second wife was even the same. My sweet little Jeanne would not hear my protestations till her sister was settled safely in the grave."

I interrupted him with a groan. "Why did you not try to persuade her?"

Charny smiled sympathetically. "How many hours have I been gone, Sir Potenhale? You may pledge me a full cup that I have tried persuasion till my mouth was dry as sand. Enough, enough. We must let the Almighty have His will. He has frustrated your guilt and kept you a knight. He may yet frustrate her duty and make her a good man's wife."

And with that, my prisoner gripped my shoulder affectionately as a father might do to his son and wished me a dreamless sleep.

12

TRUE KNIGHTS AND TRAITORS
August, 1350 – 1354

The truce between our two countries that had been concluded at the fall of Calais was renewed several times, even after the death of the French king. John, the son of Philip of Valois, had inherited an uneasy country. The devastation of the plague was but a few years past, and shortage of labor had brought famine throughout the land. It was no wonder that John wished to maintain the truce and avoid open warfare with Edward.

In England, the situation was only slightly less dire. The shortage of serfs on manorial estates made the work of each laboring man more valuable to his liege lord. Farm workers, seeing their importance, began to negotiate with stewards, demanding more benefits to work their master's estate. Some lords—without men enough to work their lands—lured serfs from other masters with offers of higher wages.

To solve this problem, Edward enacted the Statute of Laborers in 1351. It forbade peasants to leave their native manors and enjoined masters to keep their wages at pre-plague prices. This edict, however, was largely ignored, and landholders continued to accommodate the demands of the laboring men so that the famine which beset France could be averted.

Though England and France were not ready to resume the hostilities, neither one was quick to make the concessions that could lead to a permanent peace. The pope, as was his way, urged a resolution of the quarrel and offered to mediate; both monarchs sent envoys to Avignon for a conference. Edward proposed a fair exchange—England would give up its right to the crown of France if France returned to England the full sovereignty of Guienne. That province, as you doubtless remember, had first come to England with the marriage of Queen Eleanor to Henry Plantagenet. At that time, the borders of English Guienne encompassed a full quarter of the territory of France. Since then, the extent of English Guienne had been much abridged, until little remained under English control save the territory of Gascony.

John of Valois found this offer unsatisfactory. The English claim to the crown, he contended, was a thing built of smoke and air, while the French possessions in Guienne were as tangible as earth and water. He would make no concessions of territory, and so conference continued on at a deadlock.

Edward, seeing that John was not to be moved by diplomacy, turned his energies to intrigue. He dispatched Henry, the Duke of Lancaster to discover dissension within the French court, or if finding none, to plant the seeds of it himself. If a man seeks a Ganelon, he will not have far to look; rogues like those are bred in every country. Lancaster was quick to see the troubled counte-

258 | I Serve

nance of the king's son-in-law, Charles of Navarre, and inquired discreetly as to the cause of his troubles.

Navarre, as you must know, is a small country about the size of Gascony. It is wedged tightly between Gascony and Castile, but its ties are more French than Spanish. In the days of Philip the Fair, Navarre had been without a king and therefore under the sway of the French scepter. But when the Fair Philip's sons died without male issue, Navarre declared itself independent. Having no royal line of their own, the Navarrese selected one of Philip's granddaughters to be their ruler, and when she breathed her last, the throne descended to her son Charles, that Charles of Navarre in whom Lancaster was so keenly interested.

Charles of Navarre, by right of his mother, was in nearly the same position as good King Edward of England. If inheritance through a female was acceptable, he was closer to the French throne than Philip of Valois. Unlike Edward, however, Charles of Navarre allowed the Valois seizure of power without any initial protest. Indeed, he was still in the womb when his parents acceded to the Valois claim. His infant bands in the following year made him more likely to cry for mother's milk than for misappropriated monarchy.

Charles was a year or two younger than the prince; when he came of age in the year 1350, he found himself master of not only Navarre, but also a generous part of Normandy. The Contenin, where we had landed four years earlier, had been bestowed on Charles' mother by the house of Valois as a thank offering for the repudiation of her rights to the crown. King John had succeeded his father Philip at about the time that Charles had assumed the Navarrese crown. He was at first anxious to keep friends with the young man. He united him to the house of Valois by giving him his eight-year-old daughter as wife and made him his lieutenant in southern France.

In a year's time, however, the novelty of Navarre's young king wore off and the French king became less assiduous in his attentions. King John omitted to pay the installations of the dowry that were due to Charles on account of his marriage. King John refused to bestow the County of Angouleme on Charles even though it had belonged to his mother in previous days. And King John forbore to advance Charles any further, turning his attention to a new favorite, Don Carlos de la Cerda.

Don Carlos, as you may remember, was the Castilian admiral whom we had defeated off the coast of Winchelsea just a year previous. In his youth, Don Carlos had spent much time at the French court, and in the Castilian dalliance with France, Don Carlos often played the role of ambassador. King John enjoyed the Spaniard's company and decided to reward him by making him a peer of the French realm. In a move of either extreme thoughtlessness or extreme provocation, King John bestowed upon Don Carlos the title of Constable of France and gave him the counties of Champagne, Brie, and Angouleme.

Charles of Navarre was outraged. Not only had Don Carlos received the highest title in the realm of France, but he had also taken possession of Angouleme, the county that belonged to Charles by right of his mother. This piqued not only Charles but also his retainers and immediate relatives. Don Carlos irritated them like a stone in the shoe, Don Carlos embarrassed them like a wooden collar about the neck, and Don Carlos angered them like a slap across the face.

It was Christmas of 1352 when the literal slap across the face occurred. King John was celebrating Christmas in Paris with his court. Charles de Navarre was not present, no doubt enduring a self-imposed banishment on account of his grievances. His brother Philip of Navarre was there, however, and also the new Constable of France—Don Carlos de la Cerda. As the Christmas feast was celebrated, the sixteen-year-old Philip of Navarre began to boast of his family's accomplishments and to belittle the Castilian admiral with every insolence and incivility that he could muster. Don Carlos, ten years older than this Navarrese pup but still young enough to feel the heat of blood, could stand no more of his impudence. Rising wrathfully, he gave the boy the lie in front of the assembled court. Philip drew his dagger. Don Carlos drew his. In a moment they would have been upon each other, but the king intervened and there was thunder in his brow.

"Enough, enough! I will have you be friends!" cried King John.

Philip of Navarre spat upon the floor. "Nay, you shall have us as friends when this one is dead." He turned on his heel to leave the court.

"You behave like *un enfant!*" said Don Carlos scornfully.

"Do I?" said Philip, casting a backward glance before he reached the door. "*Un enfant* is more dangerous than you know. Let the Constable be on his guard against *des enfants de Navarre.*"

It was no idle warning. On the feast of epiphany just twelve days later, Don Carlos was passing the night in a small inn at l'Aigle in Normandy. Charles of Navarre had spies everywhere. Cognizant of the Constable's presence, he entered the town the same night, bringing with him his brother Philip and a band of Norman nobles and knights. Charles' men waited till daybreak before they approached the inn. Then, forcing their way into the Constable's bedroom, they drew their daggers and gave him eighty wounds, most of them mortal.

Charles of Navarre, who had remained behind while his brother and his barons completed the butchery, busily drafted a letter to the Parliament of King John. "We beg leave to tell you that we have put Don Carlos of Spain to death. If the king is troubled by this, we are very sorry. Yet we feel that he ought to be greatly pleased by the matter when he thinks it over."

King John spent much time thinking over the murder, but his musings did not result in the pleasure that Navarre anticipated. For four days he kept to his room and would say nothing, and then on the fifth day he swore a mighty oath that he would never wear a light heart again until he was revenged upon his son-in-law. He prepared to attack the territory of Charles of Navarre.

It was with this Charles then, now surnamed Charles the Wicked, that Henry of Lancaster was resolved to intrigue. Even before the murder, Lancaster had apprized Charles of England's willingness to enter into a compact with him. Now, Charles sent word to Lancaster and offered him his unreserved support. Beyond this, the Navarrese knave wrote a letter to Edward himself, urging him to put the English forces in Brittany at his disposal. Allied with Navarre's Norman nobles, they could do such hurt to King John as from which he would not speedily recover. Edward, eager to renew the struggle with France, readily agreed with these proposals. He placed his troops at readiness and waited for the word from Navarre.

King John, however, was not eager to tangle with both Charles and Edward at once. Hearing word of the compact between the two, he humbled himself before his son-in-law. He promised the murderers of de la Cerda full pardon, he bestowed on Charles all the baronies that he wished, and he swore that he would never do him harm for the sake of the Constable's death.

Charles, having held the threat of England over King John's head like a cudgel, promptly dropped the cudgel when it was no longer needed. Now that his goal was accomplished, he cancelled the pending plans of attack. Frustrated, Lancaster reminded him of their agreement. Where were the Norman nobles?

Charles, instead of renouncing the accord altogether, gave Lancaster some hope that it was only delayed. Who knows how long the peace with King John would last? Lancaster grudgingly agreed to be patient. Those who treat with a traitor will often be tricked themselves.

While Edward and Lancaster continued their attempts to manufacture war with France, the prince kept me as busy as I would have been on a campaign. Christmas came quickly on the heels of the Spanish defeat at Winchelsea, and after that I bid farewell to Sir Geoffroi de Charny. His ransom had been set at twenty thousand crowns, the very price which he had sought to pay Aimery for the betrayal of Calais. The prince thought it unlikely that such a sum would ever be raised for the return of one knight. As you well know, the French country was in disarray, the plague had been replaced by famine, and Charles of Navarre had begun his machinations against the monarchy. That the sum of twenty thousand crowns was raised—most of it by King John himself—is a testimony of the high value which Charny's countrymen set upon him.

You must understand that I did not receive the whole of the ransom. No, soon after our return from Calais to England, the prince my master had redeemed Charny from me. He generously gave me a few thousand crowns as recompense for my service, and so it was that I became a man of means long before Charny's ransom had actually arrived.

The prince, though his devotion to Charny nowhere neared the level to which mine had risen, had become fond of your husband in his own way. The night before Charny's return to France, the prince threw a marvelous banquet replete with peacocks, pastries, and the best of Bordeaux wine. Charny, as usual, wore his simple green tunic, and I saw that little had changed for him since his arrival in England.

"Highness," said Charny, after thanking him for his kind attentions over the past year. "Some time ago you challenged me to use ink and vellum and set down in words what it means to be a knight."

"And have you done so?" said the prince, recalling the conversation that they had had aboard ship at Winchelsea.

"It is not finished," said Charny, "but it is begun, and God be willing, I shall finish it at last when I have reached my own land." He pulled out a sheaf of papers from the breast of his tunic and handed it to the prince to peruse.

"What subjects do you treat of here?" asked the prince leafing gently through the unbound papers.

"Why, I begin with the different deeds which a man-at-arms may do, commencing with the least honorable and proceeding on to the most honorable, then I defend knighthood as a worthy occupation in the service of God."

The prince handed back the sheaf of papers with a smile. "You should have given this book to Potenhale two years ago—he had great need of that defense."

I blushed, for I had never told the prince the part that Charny had played in my change of mind.

"But, tell me," the prince continued. "Do you treat of those who have gone before?"

"Aye," said Charny, "I speak of many worthy knights in my book."

"Ah," said the prince. "And who, do you say, was the worthiest of all knights?"

"Judas Maccabeus," replied Charny without hesitation.

"Wherefore?"

"Because in him alone could be found all the good qualities of a true knight. He was wise in all his deeds. He was a man of worth who led a holy life. He was strong, skillful, and unrelenting in effort and endurance."

"Is that all?" asked the prince.

"Nay!" said Charny, waxing enthusiastic upon the subject. "He was handsome above all others, but without arrogance. He was full of prowess, bold, valiant, taking part in the finest, greatest, and fiercest battles and most perilous adventures that there ever were. And in the end, he died in a holy way in battle like a saint in Paradise."

"I daresay that the Romans he fought against were worthy knights as well," replied the prince archly.

"Not truly, said Charny with warmth in his tone, "for they did not conduct themselves with true belief, trust, and hope in Our Lord. And besides, they fought to oppress a land that was not their own."

"So," said the prince slowly, and I was minded of the deliberate way in which his father would frame questions. "Are you saying that it is unworthy of a knight to fight for a land that he does not hold? That the only worthy knight is a knight who fights to protect his homeland?"

Charny smiled enigmatically, but I saw that he grasped the crux of the prince's question. "Nay, highness," he said. "A knight may make war to defend his own rights or the rights of his lawful master."

"Then why should you fault these Roman knights, who fought only to maintain the rights of their emperor against Maccabeus? In truth, there is no reason to say that the Romans were any less peerless than the Jewish knights."

I listened to the skillful interplay of their conversation and saw that we were no longer talking about the ancient province of Judea.

"Ah," said Charny, "but the rights of your Roman emperor must be examined. Did he indeed have just claim to the land, or was he merely a usurper, attempting to take by force what was not rightfully his?"

"The story is so old," said the prince, "that it is hard to winnow out the grains of truth. But for the sake of our discussion, let us suppose that the emperor was descended from the old king of that country, and that the Maccabees were from another line entirely. Yet because the emperor was far away and Judas Maccabeus near, he presumed to take the crown for himself. Are not the emperor and his knights, justified in invading that land and plucking the crown from the usurper's head?"

Charny smiled at the prince's thinly veiled description of the state of affairs in France. "But highness," said Charny, "let us also suppose that this emperor was of another race. True, he was descended on his mother's side from the old king of Judea, but he had not been raised in that land. He had his head full of other countries and conquests. Would not the people of the land be justified in wishing for a king who had lived among them? For a king who would honor their customs and maintain their ancient privileges?"

The prince's brows came together sternly. I remembered the first conversation between the prince and Charny, and how Charny had bested his highness in the debate over Aimery's perfidy. Then he had forborne to press the point, allowing the prince to retire gracefully without a total rout. Now he again showed his breeding by deferring to his highness.

"Perhaps the right of the matter remains to be proved, your highness," said Charny. "We know that God defends the right. If the emperor makes free to invade Judea again, we shall see whom God will defend."

"Agreed," said the prince. "And now, God speed you, Sir Geoffroi. I shall pray to the Holy Trinity for your safety."

"And I for yours," replied Charny. They embraced in farewell, the prince bedecked in silk and seed pearls, and Charny in his simple green tunic.

"Well, Sir Potenhale," said Charny to me, after the prince had left us. "If it were not for lack of two things—the French countryside and my sweet wife Jeanne—I would regret this stay in England not at all. You have been a most generous captor."

"And you have been a most charitable captive," said I. "I have much to thank you for. You have shown me many things."

"I would that I could have shown you Christ Himself," said Charny.

"You have shown me the path to seek Him," said I, "and that is as much as any man can do."

"If we meet again," said Charny, "I fear that it will be on the field of battle. I shall pray to the Holy Mother for your safety."

"And I, for yours," said I. "The Lord be with you, Sir Geoffroi."

"And with your spirit," he answered.

Those were the last words I ever exchanged with your husband. He departed for France immediately afterwards. In the months following, I received news of him several times.

"Have you heard?" exploded Brocas impulsively one day. "Have you heard what your Sir Geoffroi has persuaded King John to do?"

"What is it?" asked I, as eager to hear as Sir Bernard was to tell me.

"Why, he has stolen our king's notion of the Order of the Garter and made plans for a French order to imitate it!"

"But surely they do not use the garter as their symbol?"

"Nay, they call themselves the 'Order of the Star.' But you see how it is? These Valois kings cannot rest with taking the kingdom of France from our liege—they must also take every new idea that comes to him."

"And Charny is a member of this new order?" asked I.

"Aye," said Brocas. "They say the idea for it was his. He has written a treatise on knighthood as the rule for this new order."

"He showed me somewhat of that book before he left. It has much practical wisdom for being good knights."

"Ha!" said Brocas scornfully. "That is well, for King John has desperate need of good knights now. You've heard how he executed the Comte d'Eu last year, the Constable that Holland captured? Ah, he was a valiant man. King Edward gave him leave to take ship for France to collect the money to pay his ransom. But when he arrived to pay his respects to King John, that mighty monarch had his head hewn off. John claimed that the Constable was plotting with England to restore to us the territory of Guienne. But many men—and not just Englishmen—think that King John only wanted the Constable's title to give to his new favorite, Don Carlos de la Cerda. His own people mistrust him. Navarre plays on that mistrust. Aye, King John has need of good knights right now, for if King Edward doesn't contrive to dethrone him, his own people will."

The next news I had of your husband came nearly a year after his departure.

One cold February morning the prince entered my quarters precipitately; I saw that he had something to tell me. "Have you heard any news of Aimery de Pavia since Calais?" asked he.

"Nay, highness," said I, remembering the name of the man with the sharp, shiny face, "though it would seem that you have."

"Aye," said the prince, "and of our friend Sir Geoffroi as well."

"Is Aimery still governor of the town?" I asked, wondering whether Aimery had been so foolish as to double-deal with Charny again.

"No, no," said the prince. "My father would not tempt Aimery with such a responsibility a second time. True, Aimery did clear himself of treason by revealing the plot—but trust can only go so far. He was paid off and dismissed before we left Calais. My father gave him a small castle upon the coast of Normandy. There he enjoyed the fruit of his double dealing with English crowns lining his pocket and an English mistress hanging about his neck."

"Does he enjoy it still?" I asked.

"Nay, and that's the news I have to tell you. It seems your Charny takes a breach of honor most seriously— either that, or he will not allow a personal affront go unavenged. King John made Sir Geoffroi his deputy over all of Normandy when he returned—a difficult county to govern, full of many English sympathizers. A month ago Charny discovered Aimery's presence in his demesne.

He planned a night raid upon the place, this time the object being to seize the man and not the city.

"They say that Aimery was sound asleep in his mistress's arms when they took him. Charny's men rode him naked through the streets and over twenty leagues to their headquarters. I do not know what speech passed between the two of them. Doubtless Sir Geoffroi reproached the Lombard over his perfidy at Calais. Perhaps Aimery protested that he had had no choice but to reveal the plan. But in the end, Charny struck off Aimery's head, quartered his body, and put it on display."

"And are you sorry for it?" I asked.

"Not one whit," replied the prince. "There are few men that deserve such an end, but Aimery was one of them. I should have done the same in Charny's place."

"Indeed," said I. "So you would have."

Navarre had played us false once, but the king still had high hopes of bringing him over to our side. Lancaster continued his negotiations. Once Navarre turned, war would be inevitable and immediate. In view of this, the king began to make spiritual preparations for a new campaign. Accompanied by the prince and many of his nobles, the king pursued a pilgrimage throughout the holy sites within the kingdom.

We went first to see the Holy House of Our Lady of Walsingham. The building there is a replica of the home where the angel first told Mary that she was with child by the Holy Ghost. Nearly three hundred years ago, the Madonna appeared to an English lady at Walsingham and recounted the tale to her. The shrine was built to commemorate that appearance. A statue of the Virgin with her Child marks the exact spot where her holy feet stood. Sir Chandos made especial prayers at that place, for the image of the Virgin was always close to his breast.

In Suffolk, we went to St. Edmund's Bury. The abbey there houses the grave of good King Edmund; he was killed by the Danes long before Norman William came to English shores. Many holy miracles had taken place at his tomb, though we did not witness any during our stay there.

At Reading, we viewed the cathedral and beheld a fragment from the very cross of Christ. "It looks much the same as any other wood shaving," remarked Sir James Audley impiously.

"Hold your tongue!" said Chandos. He reverenced the reliquary before us, and I followed his example with joy and trembling.

"But is it not strange," asked Audley doubtingly—for he, like many others of a cynic's humor, was given to unbelief—"that such an inconspicuous sliver of wood should find its way all this distance from the Holy Land into merry England?"

"The Lord works many wonders," was Chandos's reply.

"Aye," said William Montague, the Earl of Salisbury. "Indeed He does. I have heard that the very shroud in which Christ was buried in has found its way to France— so it is no hard thing to believe that this piece of the holy rood could be brought to our own land."

"And how do they know it is His shroud?" demanded Audley.

"They say it bears the marks of his passion," responded Salisbury.

"Humph," said Audley suspiciously.

"I would that I could see the cloth!" said Chandos.

"Mayhap you will," said the prince with a smile, "for we shall be in France ere long. Once we take the crown off King John's head, you can search for relics at your leisure."

After Walsingham, Suffolk, and Reading had been visited, we went at last to Canterbury. The tomb of Thomas the Martyr at Canterbury had always held a special significance for the prince. He had visited it often, and I had often accompanied him there. It was Thomas the Martyr who had first ordained the day of the feast of the Holy Trinity. The prince himself was a passionate devotee to the cult of this martyr and the cult of the Trinity; it was the name he glorified after every battle. We venerated the Martyr's tomb inside the church, kissing the flagstones upon which his blood had spilled and thus finished our pilgrimage at the holy site of Canterbury.

Canterbury is located in the English province of Kent. The lady Joan, as you may remember, brought the title of Kent to her marriage with Thomas Holland, and it was in that county that she held most of her estates. When the king learned that Sir Thomas and his lady were at home, he halted the royal pilgrims to break their journey there.

Joan received us graciously. Her beauty had not diminished, and one could see from the roundness of her garments that she was great with child and soon to be delivered. She had two lads already by now. Their eyes were bright with excitement to see such magnificent guests, and the prince and I took them out of doors to the stables to show off the fine horses that we had ridden upon.

The eldest of the boys was godson to the prince, and his highness, as was fitting for a godfather, brought a pretty present for the child. It was a wooden dagger, gilt with gold and inlaid with precious stones. Little Thomas had no sooner seen the gift than he seized it with two hands and began to brandish it wildly. His brother, little older than a baby, soon received the full brunt of the blunted blade upon his head and began to cry plaintively.

The prince, taking the crying child into his arms, chastised his young godson roundly. "How now, Thomas! You must not strike your brother who is so much smaller than you!"

"But I am to be a knight!" replied little Thomas cheerfully. "I must learn to strike hard no matter how small my enemy. I will be the greatest knight in all the world just like my father."

"Oh?" asked the prince curiously. "Is your father the greatest knight in all the world?"

The lad cocked his head thoughtfully. "It seems to me that he is," said he. "For he has a great, loud voice such as a knight should have. And I have seen him cuff one of the servants so hard that the man could not rise. I should like to be as fine a knight as my father."

"And should your mother like that?" the prince inquired, treading—I thought—on perilous ground.

"Nay," said little Thomas with a giggle, "for women know nothing about fighting. She says that I shall not be a knight at all, but shall stay always with her and keep her company."

We had shown the lads our horses by this time; the prince lifted both the boys onto the saddle of his mount and led them benevolently around the courtyard. "Look there, Potenhale!" said the prince gaily. I lifted my eyes up to the house and saw a lady walking toward us with hair of red and gold.

"God give you good den, sirs!" said Margery.

"Well met!" I replied, and I became acutely aware of the soft red glove that I held always in the bosom of my tunic. I wondered if she still had the mate to it, the glove that a charlatan monk had left in the stands of a long ago tournament.

"My lady sends word that the feast is prepared. I am to take the young gentlemen from you so that you may wash and go up to the hall."

"No, no!" cried the young Hollands, unwilling to leave the saddle of his highness's jet-black charger.

"Leave me the lads a little longer," said the prince winningly. "I shall bring them to their mother safe and sound in a quarter hour's time. But there is no reason to keep Sir Potenhale. Prithee, lady, as he is a stranger here, of your kindness show him the path to the hall."

"As you wish, your highness," Margery said, and curtseying deeply she led me away.

We had no sooner left the courtyard behind than she addressed me abruptly. "I see you are not dressed in holy orders today, sirrah."

"Nay," said I, sensing the tremulousness in her tone, "though when you saw me in them three years ago, I was indeed trying them on for size. At the time, I had thought to become a monk. But soon after I repented of it and refrained from taking the Benedictine vows."

"And what caused you to refrain?" asked she.

"It was not the hope of your favor," said I shortly, "since you've given me little enough cause to hope for that."

"Then what?" asked she.

"Someday I shall tell you, perhaps," said I, and lapsed into silence. We walked on past the storehouses and the plum trees.

"Did you send Sir Geoffroi to press your suit for you at Winchelsea?" she asked after a little space.

"Aye," I replied, unashamed to admit as much, "I sent him. I trust that he used every means of persuasion with you?"

"Indeed, he did," she replied.

"Then a man can do no more," said I.

"Nay," she answered, a little sadly, it seemed.

We walked on.

I could bear it no longer.

"Margery!" I cried, and I seized her about the waist. "For the love of Christ, I must speak again though it is to no avail! Do you not love me?"

"Aye," she said and her eyes brimmed over with tears sparkling like cut gemstones.

"Then wed me!" said I, pressing her to my breast.

"But—what of my lady?" she said mournfully.

"I will ask her to free you from your service," said I. "She will not refuse such a boon."

"You are right," said Margery. "She is too kind to refuse me. And for that reason, I will not ask. I love you much," said she, "but that does not make me love my lady any less. What kind of faithless wench would you have me be to abandon my mistress in her hour of trial?"

"If it were only an *hour* of trial!" I said exasperatedly. "But nay! It is a lifetime of misery that your lady undergoes. Her husband is a brute, and her home is a hell—and yet, God knows why two should languish there instead of one! Her trouble is too great. You can do naught to help her."

"That is not true," she said, pushing me away from her but not hard enough to loosen my grip. "I may comfort her in her suffering and give her the courage of mind to stand against his wickedness. I alone knew of her secret marriage to Holland. I alone bore the anguish of her soul when she was betrothed to Salisbury. I alone stood beside her in the birth of her children. Whither she goes I will go, and her people will be my people."

"You take too much upon yourself," I said angrily. "Such devotion to an earthly mistress is unnatural!"

"Would you leave your prince if I bade you?" she retorted.

"Yes, a thousand times yes!" I answered. As the words left my mouth, I knew they were false.

We halted at the door of the hall.

"Then stay behind when your master leaves," she said. She looked me full in the eyes, and then came closer to stroke my face with a sudden burst of passion. I tried to pull her into my arms, but she turned and fled the other way.

Entering the hall, I sat down to eat; the food was as dry as chalk within my mouth. At the high table, the king complimented Sir Thomas on his well-managed estate and predicted that Joan's imminent childbirth would produce another son. The prince entered anon and joined his father at the high table. He greeted Holland with civility, and the two exchanged perfunctory conversation on the state of affairs in France.

Margery did not come in to supper that night, and I did not go to seek her afterwards. The red glove was still in my bosom, but I knew now that neither I nor its owner was willing to give up our masters for the sake of each other. Margery's challenge had showed me that much. As long as my prince required my service, I would follow the pennants of war. And as long as Joan needed comforting, Margery's love for me would bow to the dictates of duty.

We retired early to sleep, and on the morrow I saddled my horse to ride back to London beside my prince. The rest of the household was still abed, but Sir Thomas came out to bid us Godspeed. His body had become exceedingly fleshy in recent years. Great jowls hung down from his throat, and his round belly sagged beneath his broad tunic. The savage leer that his eyes once held had softened a little into a self-satisfied smirk.

Holland made his obeisance to the king, and raised his hand in farewell to our entourage. My eyes followed him morbidly as he turned to enter the manor house. "This man here," said I to myself, "is the cause of all our suffering."

The morning was cold, and the ground was icy; I watched Sir Thomas slip on a glassy puddle that stood before the door. He reached out a hand to recover himself, but it was some time before his ponderous weight could regain its balance. "If only he had fallen a little harder," thought I. "Many a man has broken their neck ere now on an icy day."

I wondered what it would be like to fight him in tournament now. I would wager a hundred crowns that the old bull could no longer turn and charge as he used to. My mind flitted back to the melee at Westminster when Sir Thomas had come directly in the path of the prince. He had as much reason to wish Holland dead as I. Why had he avoided him? Why had he not struck? Another had done it. I saw the image of myself—King Edward in Potenhale's armor—rising up in the stirrups to deliver a buffet upon Sir Thomas's helmet. Again and again the sword descended! I remembered how Holland had swooned from the fearsome blow of the blunt blade. But how if it had been sharp instead of blunt? I imagined blood cascading down Holland's fat face. I watched his body jolt heavily onto the ground, never to rise again.

13

THE RETURN OF THE CONQUEROR
1355 – September, 1356

O ur souls had ample time to grow dusty again after the cleansing that the holy sites had provided. King Edward's pilgrimage proved premature. The invasion of France was postponed yet again. A second squabble between Charles of Navarre and King John had seemed promising, but the quarrel had been hastily patched together, ending almost as soon as it had begun. King Edward was forced to wait a while longer for a suitable opportunity to invade France. In the early months of the next year that opportunity came—but not in the form of the Navarrese alliance.

England, as you know, possessed three main outposts in the continent at that time: the city of Calais, a small strip of Normandy, and the province of Gascony. The area of Gascony, a tattered and diminished relic of what used to be the country of Guienne, has no strong ties to France. The people themselves speak a different dialect, the *langue d'oc*, and have no desire to be ruled by a Parisian king. The Gascon nobles are comfortable with

English rule, and when that rule is threatened, they are the first to complain to the English king.

It was approaching Easter of 1355 when an embassy arrived in England from the Gascons. Jean de Grailly, the leading noble of the region, was petitioning His Majesty for aid against the incursions of the French. De Grailly, whom you may also know by his honorary title *le Captal de Buch*, confirmed what we English had already heard rumored. King John's French lieutenants had been steadily working to pare down the size of Edward's continental domains, trimming the borders off Gascony as one trims the rind off of a wheel of cheese. The Comte d'Armagnac was the worst of these predators. His ruffian knights constantly patrolled the Gascon border, terrorizing peasants, ousting manorial lords, and seizing castles. And all things they did in the name of d'Armagnac so that King John could not be accused of truce breaking.

The Captal de Buch outlined the predicament with all the suitable histrionics. He was a small, wizened man, with long moustaches that came down below his chin. He was theatrical—a typical Gascon trait—but well respected by all for his sagacity and valor. He had been one of the first to receive the Garter when the order began.

"And I tell you," said de Grailly before the council of His Majesty and English lords, "that if you allow d'Armagnac to carry on like this unhampered, he will carve off the best parts of our fair Gascony and leave only a bare skeleton for Your Majesty's table."

Edward heard his words in silence, then bounded to his feet and paced about the room. "We must take action, my lords. But how?"

"A full invasion!" urged William Montague, the Earl of Salisbury. Like the prince, the earl had grown surer of his own judgment with the passage of time. His disappointment over the thwarted marriage with Lady Joan was as distant as a childhood memory. "Let us have Crecy all over again and remind them that English mettle is not to be toyed with."

"Aye," said Sir John Chandos, my old master, "but let us strike this time from Gascony, and use Normandy as the counter feint."

"A reversal of tactics!" boomed Audley, for in the expedition of nine years ago, the king's force in Normandy had been the main army, while Lancaster's force in Gascony had been a mere diversion.

"Sire," said the Earl of Warwick, who had helped the prince in his first command at Crecy, "give me the command of the Gascon force. I will make for Bordeaux immediately and make this Comte d'Armagnac repent that he ever laid hands on Your Majesty's demesne."

"No!" said a voice, loud and clear. The chair directly in front of me resounded with it. All eyes turned to the prince as he stood and assumed the center of the room. "Give *me* the command in Gascony, my liege. Let it be my command—all mine—and I will show you what sinews you have bred in me. It is an honorable thing for a knight to defend his own rights or the rights of his lord. Let me have this honor, and let me have it in Gascony among worthy men with a worthy cause."

The Captal de Buch looked at the prince with shining eyes. His moustaches waggled with emotion and he pumped the prince's hand vigorously. "God bless you, your highness, for we Gascons will surely pray for your soul."

The king fingered his beard in consideration. I marveled that he did not agree at once with the prince's request. "Would it not be more prudent to send Lancaster again to Gascony?" he asked the prince. "He has the experience of the territory there. And you, my son, have the knowledge of the Norman coast."

"Not so, not so!" said the Captal de Buch wildly, forgetting all decorum as he contradicted the king. "The prudence of the matter is entirely the other way around. Think you how greatly it will encourage the spirits of my people to see the prince—Your Majesty's eldest son!—at the head of the Gascon forces. It has been seventy years since an English king or his son has set foot in the land of my fathers! Seventy years! And will you now deny us the presence of your son when he begs this command of you? We must have him, Your Majesty! Do not deny us."

The king smiled beneath his beard, and I saw that he was well-pleased with both the audacity of this Gascon and the resolution of his heir. "What more can I object?" he said to the Gascon lord. "You run at me like a fighting cock, de Grailly, and I must acquiesce or be pecked to death." He turned to the Prince of Wales. "The command is yours, my son. May God be with you in this endeavor and bring you swiftly to victory."

❖ ◆ ❖

The prince, though he was determined to be the sole commander, desired company on the expedition to Gascony. Warwick, who had requested the command himself, he invited to come along, as well as Salisbury, Chandos,

Audley, Brocas, and others. He had twelve lords in total in his train, though Holland was not among them.

One part of me wished he was—it is easier for a man to lose his life in the fields of war than the in the fields of peace. Of late, I had a growing fascination with the idea of Sir Thomas's death. How much misery would be ended if his life were cut short! But Sir Thomas did not go out with our expedition, and it was useless to dwell on the accidents that might befall a man in battle.

While the king busied himself with procuring a force for Lancaster's diversionary army, the prince and the lords who accompanied him made shift to assemble their own army. The prince put together a company of a thousand men, a combination of men-at-arms and archers, while his nobles together produced the same amount or more. It was a mere handful compared to the force that Edward had brought to Normandy nine years ago, but it did not need to be any larger. "Your army is only the grain of sand in the oyster," the Captal de Buch had said, "and our Gascon men will cluster around it till it becomes a pearl of immeasurable value."

"He has a high opinion of himself, that Gascon!" Audley had complained later. "We the grain of sand, and his men the pearl!"

It was not until the ninth of September that the fleet was ready to sail. It had taken several months both to collect and to arm the men. The prince, whose estates had produced poorly in the years following the plague, was forced to contract a great deal of debt to provision the company. He had mortgaged his lands up to the hilt; should he die on the venture, they would go to his creditors instead of to his family. "No matter," said he, "for if I die, I die wifeless and childless, and my father has land enough." Though the lack of an heir from his own body might have been disheartening, the debt itself was not. The prince blithely assured Warwick that the French plunder they would take would more than repay the costs they had incurred.

It was the third time that I had left the shores of England for the land of France. The first time I had gone as a beardless squire. The second time I had gone determined to become a Benedictine. And now, the third time, I went as a knight in the full strength of my powers. I was twenty-five years old. The Prince of Wales trusted me as his companion-at-arms. I had made a name for myself with the capture of Geoffroi de Charny. What further glories lay in store?

By the time our army had reached Gascony and set up a base in Bordeaux, the first signs of the winter chill had already appeared. Whatever was to be done must be done quickly before the weather circumvented our purpose. The day after our arrival the prince swore an oath before the nobles of Gascony that as the king's deputy he would observe the rights, liberties, and customs of all citizens of Guienne. Then, assured of his commitment toward them, the Gascon nobles and merchants wholeheartedly committed their vassals and goods to the prince. A council of war commenced.

Warwick was for striking northward against the domains of King John; but the Captal de Buch insisted that since the Comte d'Armagnac was the one who had violated the borders of Gascony, the Comte d'Armagnac must be the one to feel the fury of the English (and Gascon) army. The prince agreed that the interests of the Gascons must be put first. In two weeks he found his army augmented by four or five thousand Gascons ready to press forward into the territory of d'Armagnac.

The army, once it passed over the border of Gascony, was separated into three parallel groups by its commander. Nine years ago the prince had watched his father's army march from the Contenin to Calais, and he had not forgotten the manner of its marching. Fanned out along the Garonne River, our army cut a wide swath through d'Armagnac's territory, burning and plundering everything in our path. The three armies, marching side by side, met town after town, castle after castle, stronghold after stronghold. Most were taken and destroyed with barely half a day's halt.

One town, a place called Bassoues, belonged to the archbishop of Auch. The town surrendered as did the others, but the prince would allow none of the army to enter it for plunder. "We fight against France, not the church," said he. The prince put a small sum of money into the hand of Sir John Chandos and bade him enter the town to seek supplies. The prince knew that Sir John Chandos was a pious man, and that the property of the church would suffer no scathe from his intrusion.

In one incident, the prince resolved to spend the night in a captured citadel. The soldiers were so eager to fire the town the next day that they applied the torches before the prince and I had awoken and taken to horse. "*Allons!*" shouted Brocas rushing into my room. "Hurry if you don't want to be roasted!" I had barely time to throw on my clothes and snatch up my sword before the fortress was filled with smoke. It was a Gascon company who had fired the town, and the prince minced no words when he berated the company commander for his incompetence. From this time forward on the campaign, he always made a point of sleeping in the field, and I roundly cursed the Gascon stupidity that forced me to sleep inside of a tent when there were beds enough to be had in the cities.

Wherever we went we met with only shallow resistance. The Comte d'Armagnac had hidden himself away in the fortified city of Toulouse. Aware of the prince's arrival in Gascony, he had provisioned and garrisoned Toulouse to withstand all assault. The prince was unwilling to besiege such a well-fortified city, so he continued his depredations on the countryside. The Comte would be a shabby suzerain indeed if he did not come out of hiding before all of his fief was in flames.

Carcassonne, though not as wealthy as Toulouse, was as populous and prosperous as the English city of York. The prince spent two days there laying siege to the castle before he gave up and set fire to the town. The destruction of Carcassonne failed to adequately stimulate the Comte so we pressed forward toward the even richer city of Narbonne.

The people of Narbonne fled from us as if from a crowd of lepers. They quitted their thatch-roofed homes and retreated into the castle, sending frantic messages to their liege to succor them. These cries finally produced a response. D'Armagnac, who would not encounter us on his own strength, had received reinforcement from King John. He exited Toulouse and drew near to Narbonne to draw off our army from thence. "He's left his den at last," said the prince eagerly. Casting Narbonne aside as a boy does with a nut he cannot open, we turned about to face the Comte D'Armagnac.

Though the Comte had spent much time marshalling his forces, those forces had spent little time marshalling their courage. Our alacrity in accosting them dismayed them; they took refuge behind the river and cut down all the bridges to prevent us from crossing. It took us a day to repair the bridges, and when we crossed, we found that they had drawn back even further into a little town. We advanced and camped for a whole day in front of the town waiting for our adversary in full battle array. No one came. On the morrow we entered the town and found that the French had withdrawn yet again.

When it became apparent that the Comte's men would do no battle with us, the prince called a council to decide our course of action. "It's nearly Christmastide," reminded Chandos, "and the weather's been louring of late."

"Aye, highness," said the Captal de Buch regretfully. "Let's retire till spring, and if those *bâtards* of D'Armagnac will meet us then, we'll have a proper battle."

The prince acquiesced to their wisdom, and we returned to Bordeaux for the winter. Although the Gascons were happy to see the Comte D'Armagnac punished for his depredations, the prince's extensive raid had done little to improve the English holdings on the continent. Lancaster's foray into Normandy had been as ineffective as ours. Realistically, the expedition had commenced too close to winter to accomplish anything significant. But the new year held brighter promise. The king approved of the prince's plan to wait in Gascony till spring. And so we stayed.

The winter months passed slowly. While the weather was too unpredictable to stage a large-scale assault, dry spells often afforded opportunities for swift sallies. Raiding parties led by the Earl of Warwick, by Sir John Chandos, or by the Earl of Salisbury crossed into French territory and illuminated the night sky with their fires. On one occasion, when the prince's warband approached a small town, the inhabitants sent out a bishop to buy us off with a chest of gold.

"What do I want with your money?" the prince replied in scorn. "The king of England, by God's grace, is rich enough to supply for my needs. I will not take gold and silver for such a cowardly arrangement. No! I will do what I came to do—to chastise, discipline, and make war on all inhabitants of this duchy who are in rebellion against their father! If you men of Guienne will not recall your former allegiance, I will make you recall it by force of arms."

It was a grand speech, gallant in its defiance. But for all that, I was wondering if it were not better to take the bribe. The prince's coffers had run very low indeed; and though he boasted that his father was well able to supply us, that boast carried more bravado than verisimilitude.

A rainy spring followed the cold winter and we continued to wait for the weather to clear. One day in early May, a ship put in at Bordeaux bearing orders from King Edward. That was not all the ship bore. I stared open-mouthed at the emissary the king had sent— Thomas Holland, the Earl of Kent. While the prince, the Captal de Buch, Chandos, and Audley closeted themselves with His Majesty's letter. I was left to see to the accommodations of the bearer.

"So, Potenhale," said Holland, walking beside me a little unsteadily. "I see you have not quitted your master's service."

"Certainly not," I replied. "I shall always remember my duty to him."

"It is well you have a good memory, sirrah," retorted Holland. "I hope you have not forgotten that drubbing I gave you at Windsor."

I looked up at him sharply. His fleshy form no longer inspired the same dread it once had. I remembered the prickly drops of sweat sliding down my face and the sticky apprehension in my mouth when he had first challenged me to joust. I had no such tremors now. I folded my arms across my chest. "Yea, I remember Windsor right well, my lord. You had the advantage of me then. But if you would deign to break lances with me again, I will show you what mettle has been forged in me. You will not take my horse and arms so easily this time, even with such a jade's trick as an unlaced helmet."

Holland looked me up and down. I had come into my full height since the tournament at Windsor, and though I was an inch or two shy of the prince's stature, I was reckoned tall by many. My shoulders were as broad as Holland's but knit with younger sinews. My arms and legs gleamed like pillars of bronze. I wore a black scalloped tunic with my silver chevron emblazoned across my taut chest.

"Ha!" said Holland scornfully, but I sensed a note of hesitation in his voice. "An' we had time to fight a tourney, I would remind you how it feels to be unhorsed. But we must be about the king's business, not our own. Leave me, boy. I must rest."

I learned the contents of the king's letter later that night. In it Edward had enjoined his son to make no move from Gascony until Lancaster had time to receive reinforcements in the North. Then Edward desired the two commanders to muster their men, advance toward each other, and meet in the center of France where the two armies would fuse together like bars of molten steel. Our instructions beyond this point were uncertain. Possibly our united forces would then march on Paris. Or possibly we would encounter King John and best him in the field with a second Crecy.

At the end of the letter the king hinted that he himself might be coming to join Lancaster and to take charge of the expedition. "What response will your highness make to that suggestion?" I asked.

"A most filial response," replied the prince. "I shall write how my heart yearns for his presence, and yet deplores the thought of him suffering such care and trouble. I shall lament the hardship he will undergo and express fervent prayers that his health would not suffer in this campaign."

"Will that stop him from coming?" I asked.

"Who can tell?" answered the prince.

◆ ◆ ◆

It was not until the middle of the summer that our plans matured. Lancaster had roused himself in Normandy and was bringing his force down to the Loire valley. The Gascons and we would go up from Bordeaux and meet Lancaster near the city of Orleans.

Edward, as it turned out, had been distracted by affairs in England and could not cross the Channel to join the army—although he continued to promise his presence later in the season. The prince showed no improper emotion at the receipt of this news, but I doubt not that his highness was glad of his father's absence. The autumnal raiding party of the previous year had given him little chance to prove his mettle as sole commander. The summer boasted greater promise.

Holland, having no such pressing affairs in England, had remained with our company in France. "If it pleases your highness," he had said to the prince, "I shall lead a company in the summer campaign."

I listened eagerly, waiting for the prince to refuse him. But my master received Holland's service with equanimity, or even enthusiasm. "Aye, it pleases me well," said the prince. And thereupon, he set Holland over a company of two hundred men-at-arms. It was a sound tactical move; Holland had proved himself many times to be an able commander of men. But the matter did not please me. I could not stand to see his highness give preference to Holland, the man who blocked my matrimonial desires like an iron portcullis.

As in the previous expedition, our English army was augmented by an even larger force of Gascons. The Captal de Buch would have joined us at their head; however, spies brought word that the Comte d'Armagnac had mobilized his forces once again. "Viper!" boomed Audley. "He'll come slithering into Gascony the moment we turn our backs."

"And for that reason," said the prince firmly, "de Grailly must stay behind."

"But your highness!" pleaded le Captal de Buch, his moustaches wagging in pathetic remonstrance. His excitement over the upcoming campaign was second no man's. "Have we not fought together these many months? Are we not brothers of the sword?" His eyes brimmed over with tears at the thought of the prince leaving him behind in Bordeaux.

"Aye, we are sword brothers," replied the prince kindly. "Yet you are also the seneschal of Gascony. You must serve where you are called, not where you wish. My heart is sore to forego your company, but you must remain at your post to deal with d'Armagnac when we are gone. It would be a pretty folly to report to His Majesty that we had moved our forces to the Loire valley, only to lose the heartland around the Garonne."

I saw then that the prince rejected the Captal de Buch's company for the same reason that he had received Holland's. He had found the place where each man might best serve, to the end that he himself might render better service to his father.

Once we received word that Lancaster was on the move, the prince struck north immediately. In the raid of the previous year, the prince had tolerated some of the natural disorderliness of the men—not so on this expedition. In words as firm as granite, he commanded the men to keep to their ranks. "I forbid any man to wander about the countryside unarmed," said he. "At all times, you will keep the armor of leather and steel upon your breast, and the armor of penitence and the Eucharist upon your soul. At all times, you will be ready to fight those who have rebelled against the rightful rule of my father. And at all times, you will live in worldly honor so that dying you may enter eternal honor."

I took the prince's admonishments to heart. There was a comfortingly familiar ring to them. Here were the same precepts that Sir Geoffroi de Charny had enjoined me to follow. Here was the code that keeps the soul of a fighting man in brighter polish than the soul of a monk. As the pace of our northward journey increased, I increased the frequency of my confessions and strove to purify my mind of evil desire.

But though I succeeded in ridding myself of many sinful passions, there was one passion too fiery to be quenched. Try as I might to be at peace with all men, I could not eradicate my rancor toward Sir Thomas Holland, the Earl of Kent. In earlier days, the sting of his scorn had often lashed me into a fury of indignation. Now, the indifference with which he treated me cooled my anger not one whit. When in confession, I prayed fervently that this malice might pass from me. When out of confession, I hoped just as fervently to see Holland meet his demise in this campaign.

The prince himself took meticulous charge of the camp. Each morning he supervised the camp's dismantling and ordered a forward march once the road had been deemed safe; each evening he oversaw the camp's placement and erected measures for defense. During the nights, the prince saw that the watch was kept. Frequently, he went around from station to station, ensuring the vigilance of the sentries, and assuring his own mind that there were no gaps in the defense.

The prince appointed Sir John Chandos and Sir James Audley as scouts for the army. With their companies of trained knights, they rode ahead of us each day, scouring the woods for ambushes or signs of the enemy. It would be ill fortune to meet with the French army before joining our forces with Lancaster.

Under the prince's strict shepherding, our army of nearly seven thousand men, passed quickly northward through the counties of Berry and Poitou; for nearly four weeks we marched. We took what supplies we needed from the countryside, burning as we went, but deviated little from our set path in search of plunder. It was near the end of August, when we halted alongside the noble city of Bourges to take stock of our position.

The prince had called a council of war in his pavilion. Brocas was there, Salisbury, Holland, and me. Others continued to trickle in after they had seen to the defenses in their sector of the camp. We sat on makeshift chairs around a large unrolled map. The faded vellum showed the soft outline of France. The rivers and their crossings, the cities and larger towns were labeled with the blue and gold lettering of Gothic script. A tall chess piece—the queen from the prince's ivory chess set—stood regally in the middle of the map. It marked our position in the land of France.

The tent flap opened to admit one more. "No word from Lancaster," said the Earl of Warwick glumly. He threw himself wearily into a chair within the inner circle. His words unfolded slowly like the petals of a flower. I could not tell if his hesitation came from doubt or exhaustion. "Will your highness continue north?"

The prince was silent.

"We must continue north!" said Holland vociferously. The rigors of the campaign had redeemed some of his flaccidity, and he spoke with his former forcefulness. "Lancaster is waiting for us, and we must not disappoint him. United, we can advance on Paris. Without him, we can do nothing."

"But we have gone nearly two-thirds of the distance between Bordeaux and Normandy," argued Warwick. "Surely, Lancaster, if he were able, would have met us before now. There is no doubt in my mind—he is beset, perhaps even destroyed."

"Even so," contended Sir Holland, "there is still the king!" For Edward continued to dangle possibilities of landing a third army on the northern coast.

"Well, highness?" said the earl of Salisbury preemptively, before Holland and Warwick's discussion could gain more momentum. "These two say no more than what we all already know. It is for you to decide what must be done."

"I am loath to cross the Loire without news of Lancaster," said the prince slowly. "If we continue north, then cross it we must. Lancaster may not be there to meet us, but I daresay the French will be; then we shall be trapped between the river and their swords."

"Well said!" commended Warwick, and Holland grunted in acknowledgment of this concern.

"But I will make no decision without the advice of my scouts," continued the prince. "Potenhale, did you not summon Chandos and Audley to my tents?"

"Aye, highness," I replied. "But they are not yet returned from their foray. You must remember that you gave them orders to range afield as far as the town of Aubigny today."

"That is not so far from here," said the prince. "They should have returned before now."

His words acted like a conjurer, for he had no sooner spoken than the tent flap parted to admit the two grizzled scouts. In their company was a third man, bigger than both. Like the scouts, he wore full armor, but his surcoat was bespattered with mud as if he had fallen from his horse. His gray hair curled voluminously like the coat of a ewe, and I learned later that this had earned him the sobriquet *Grismouton*. I saw at once that he was a Frenchman and surmised that he must be their prisoner.

"Your highness," said Chandos formally, "allow me to make known to you Sir Philip Chambly."

Sir Chambly bowed in a courtly fashion.

"Welcome, Sir Chambly," said the prince courteously, and he gave him his hand to kiss. "How come you to be in the company of these gentlemen?"

"Through the mischances of war," he said, shaking his woolly head ruefully. "My company was deployed to Aubigny and your captains surprised us there. *Mais par le sang Dieu,* it was a hard battle! There are eighteen of my company brought into your hand, as many more dead on the field—and Christ knows whither the rest have flown!"

The prince turned to his scouts. "So you have taken Aubigny?" he asked with a gleam in eye.

"Aye, highness," said Audley in a tone of satisfaction. "We've taken her, torched her, and left only blackened rubble in the place."

Chandos, his black hair lined with streaks of gray, nodded in concurrence with Audley's words. There was

a slight stoop in his shoulders that I did not remember—
but then it was nearly ten years since I had served him
as a squire.

The prince resumed his questioning of Sir Chambly.
"You say you were deployed at Aubigny—who sent you
there, and from what place?"

Sir Chambly hesitated. He dropped his eyes before
the prince like a sheep who has stumbled into a clearing
and found himself face to face with a wolf.

"There is no harm in telling his highness what he
asks," said Audley roughly. His stocky arms gestured
contemptuously. "I have already questioned your men
and they say that you come from Orleans. King John is
there in arms, with a grand company of pennants *en route*
from Chartres."

"Sweet Mary!" said Brocas with a sharp intake of
breath. "He's at the Loire waiting for us." And indeed, it
was so. Your French king had chased Lancaster to and fro
across the southern border of Normandy till the harassed
commander had retreated to the coast of the Contenin.
Now, having peremptorily prevented our army from con-
verging with our comrades, he straddled the river like a
mighty colossus waiting for us to swim between his legs.

"It's just as I said," said Warwick triumphantly,
although it was an unhappy happenstance to triumph
in. "Lancaster's overturned. There's only disaster if we
continue north."

"It's not confirmed!" objected Holland sulkily,
unwilling to give up his position in the argument. "If we
can get across the Loire we can still get to Lancaster—or
to His Majesty's landing party."

298 | I SERVE

"And how might we do that?" demanded Warwick, "with the entire garden of French chivalry planted in Orleans at the crossing?"

"Well, what do you propose?" Holland blustered loudly. "You would have us turn tail and run back to Gascony like a frightened child who's shitted his breeches!"

Warwick turned an inarticulate shade of red.

"Come now, milord," Salisbury remonstrated with the Earl of Kent. "That is something too round of a description."

The prince held up his hand before the wrangling could begin afresh. "Gentlemen," said the prince calmly. "I have made my decision. It was in my mind to do this ere now, and this new intelligence only confirms me in my resolution."

All eyes turned to the prince.

"We go west," said the prince. His long fingers closed around the ivory queen upon the map. He picked her up and moved her three inches to the left. "*Tours*," said the blue lettering with leaf of gold. A serpentine line sliced through the city name like a scimitar. The map marked rivers as well as cities, and Tours lay just south of the Loire.

The prince calmly surveyed the council of captains and nobles, his subordinates in rank and blood but superiors in the matter of military experience. He did not need them to approve his decision. He would not change it if they frowned upon it. "We move on the morrow, milords," said he. And rising from his chair he exited the tent with strong, purposeful steps.

The others lingered a little longer in the tent to discuss his highness's decision. "So we are abandoning

Lancaster then!" said Holland. "We are circling round to return to Bordeaux."

"Perhaps," said Brocas archly. "Or perhaps we are merely sidestepping the French army to continue north. I believe that one can cross the Loire at Tours as well as at Orleans, can one not, Sir Chambly?"

"You English are well informed," said our French prisoner wryly.

"Nay, we'll not be traveling north again," said Audley. "That's not the prince's intent. Tours itself is a rich enough reason to turn to the west. If we can sack that city before returning to Gascony, our summer's foray will not have been in vain."

"She's as rich in fortifications as she is in funds," remarked Chandos. "We'll not see the inside of that castle easily."

The talk rambled on to the battlements and breastworks of Tours. Our guest, having ridden all day on horse, yawned, shook himself, and showed other signs of fatigue. "Come, Sir Chambly," said I. "I will show you to your quarters."

"Gramercy, young sir," said the great ram inclining his wooly head toward me. "I think these gentlemen would retire to their beds as well if they knew how hot my king is to catch them and do battle. *Sacre dieu*, they will have need of their strength when next they see our Oriflamme."

14

THE FALLEN FLAGBEARER
September, 1356

O ur English army cut a wide westward swathe of destruction as we left Bourges and made for Tours. We paused for five days at Romorantin to besiege the castle there. Warwick gritted his teeth at this, for Romorantin sat closer to Orleans—and to King John's army—than was to his liking. Holland, also, chafed at the delay. He still hoped that the prince intended to continue north from Tours. He knew we must arrive there before the French anticipated our plan.

Romorantin surrendered, but only after we used siege engines to set fire to her keep. In the meanwhile, our scouts brought word that the Comte de Poitiers was fortifying Tours against our imminent arrival. "We must hurry!" said Holland brusquely, "before he destroys the bridges across the Loire." The prince agreed to increase the army's speed, but by the time our seven thousand men reached the outskirts of Tours, three more days had passed. The Comte de Poitiers, just as Holland had feared, had acted both expediently and expeditiously. He dismantled the bridges across the river like a boy tearing the wings off a fly. Then he retreated behind the walls of the city to gloat proudly over our advancing army.

Holland cursed loudly. His chagrin was compacted by the news that the evening watch brought in. "Campfires," said Brocas loudly. "My men saw lights across the Loire last night. It looked like the campfires of a small host."

"Sweet Jesus!" said Holland blasphemously. "It's Lancaster at last, and we've no way of getting to him."

"Or mayhap it's King John," said Audley gruffly, determined to be contrary to the Earl of Kent. "We've no way of knowing whether the fires are French or English."

"Nay," said Chandos more coolly. "It could not be King John's army. They were at Chartres when we encountered Chambly—a week behind us or more."

"We must begin rebuilding the bridges at once," said Holland. He slapped his thick thigh with an open palm.

"And how shall we do that?" demanded Warwick. His clear eyes encountered the prince as he voiced his objection. "We cannot put a bridge across the narrows without coming within bowshot's length of Tours. It is not safe to build!"

"It is not safe to dither here!" replied Holland.

"You are right," said the prince simply, "Both of you. And that is why we must take Tours immediately."

The prince sent Audley and Chandos to fire the town. I went out with the latter's company, eager for some activity after the oppressive atmosphere within the camp. The wrangling of the commanders had disseminated to the men-at-arms. The nearer that the French army came, the more fractious grew the ranks.

"We should have turned south at Bourges," I heard one squire say to his friend. They were polishing their master's cuirasses, a chore I had frequently performed for my master Chandos—I had my own man to do such a task for me now. The squire coughed unhealthily; he wiped his mouth with the back of his hand and continued his strictures. "To come west all this way only puts us farther into the hands of the French."

"Aye," replied his fellow. "But the prince is too green to know when to cry halt. If it were only his father who had us in hand, we would be safe in Gascony again."

"Ha!" I said scornfully, and they looked up at me in some confusion. "Return south at Bourges?" I demanded. "Is that what you think the king would have done?"

"Aye," said the first squire saucily. His chin jutted out like a coxcomb's crest. "And so says my master."

"Then, more fool him!" replied I. "Think you—how would we have provisioned the army? The countryside's burned from Bourges to Bordeaux. *You* lit the fires that kindled the crops. *You* drove off the cattle and slaughtered the rest. Go south from Bourges? Go to! You are a fool."

The squires murmured beneath their breath; I knew I had not convinced them. Their mistrust in the prince's leadership was symptomatic of a sickness beginning to spread throughout the army. We were seven thousand men trapped at Tours! And who knew when King John— with his tens of thousands—would be upon us?

September had settled in with vengeful wetness. The roofs on the houses of the suburbs of Tours were thatch, and flammable in theory; but our attempts to set fire to the wet straw failed miserably. Without fire, we could do little harm to the place. We spent three days there, praying like pilgrims for the weather to clear. The castle of Tours, with its newly erected defenses, was as impregnable as Calais had been ten years ago. We did not have twelve months to siege her into submission. We did not even have that many days.

Lancaster, we learned from our scouts, was camped a mere sixty miles away. But the river still stood between he and us, and he could find no satisfactory crossing to unite with our army. The Valois king had no such trouble. After we had lain outside of Tours for three days, the scouts brought word that King John had left Orleans, crossed the Loire, and was rumbling toward us like a giant boulder.

"How many men?" the prince asked. It was the question on every man's lips.

Audley grimaced. "It is hard to say, highness. Forty thousand—perhaps more."

Salisbury let out a slow whistle. "Five to one," said he.

"Six to one," said Holland, "for his forces increase as he comes to us."

"It is a large discrepancy," said the prince. "We must not engage him if we can avoid it. We shall strike camp immediately and retreat to the south."

I saw then that he had given up every hope of uniting with Lancaster. I stared in disbelief. Unwittingly and perhaps unwisely I had placed my confidence in that very thing: that despite all opposition, the prince would prove his mettle by locating Lancaster and forging our forces into one mighty brand of steel. That hope was dead, and with it died a part of my confidence in this Plantagenet prince. The raid was over. We were homeward bound, having accomplished even less this summer than in the *chevauchée* the previous autumn.

The disappointment in the army, and in the prince's own inner circle, radiated out like heat from a bowl of stew. My face was warm with it. The prince, however, betrayed no dismay at this setback. He continued to give orders with inflexible resolve and indefatigable courtesy. In one instance only, did he acknowledge the gravity of our position. "Let prayers for our safety be offered to the Holy Trinity," he ordered me tell his chaplain, "For without the aid of heaven, King John will assuredly find us before we reach Bordeaux."

◆ ◆ ◆

Heaven, it seemed, had set itself against us. Two days after we left Tours, Chandos' men brought word that John was at Loches, less than twenty miles to the east. Spurring on the men and their mounts, the prince brought us twenty-five miles in one day. We encamped at Châtellerault, and on the next morning the prince sent out Audley to reconnoiter. It was imperative to know whether the French had paralleled our southern progress or had continued west toward our old encampments.

Sir James Audley was gone the whole day. He returned with the setting sun and dismounted without a word. I escorted him to the prince's tent. The old knight sat down, removed his helmet, and called for wine and food to be brought. His voice was none too gentle.

The prince watched him eat in silence, and even filled his flagon for him. Ever and anon one of the other commanders would enter, as skittish as a foal in their anxiety.

The prince held up his hand and bade them hold their questions until Audley had supped. "Well?" he asked when the scout had finished. "What news?"

Audley put his hands on his gray head and rubbed the cropped hair furiously. "No news, highness."

"What do you mean?" demanded the prince. The strain of the forced marches was telling on him. His jaw pulled back sharply, as if his will had bridled his tongue from using some harsher language.

"Precisely that," said Audley roughly. "I have no news of King John. I have no news of his army."

"Come, man, said Brocas exasperatedly. "How can you have no news of forty thousand men? Where are they camped?"

"In God's name," said Audley wildly. "I do not know! We've ridden sixty miles today—east, west, north, south—I do not know what's become of them!"

"Have they retreated to Tours?" asked Chandos kindly. The worried frown on his face was as benevolent as the blue Virgin Mary upon his breast.

"Perchance," said Audley. "But I know nothing for certain. No one has heard. There are no signs. There are no rumors. They've disappeared like phantoms into the mist!"

The lords pressed him further, but Audley could say no more. The prince walked to and fro in some agitation, then dropped into his chair and stroked his bearded chin in thought.

"Shall we continue south?" asked Warwick, anxious for the prince to make a hurried decision.

The prince cocked his head. "It is better for a blind man to sit still than to walk about near a precipice. We shall stay here till we have news of the French."

"By your leave, highness," said Audley, desperate to remedy his failure. "Grant me permission to lead out my company again tomorrow. I will put my nose to the ground and search them out. You shall have word by midday, my liege."

The prince nodded his permission, and Audley took his hand to kiss. Then, rising from his knees, the barrel-chested old knight strode to his quarters to commission his company for the morning's ride. They left before daybreak.

It was past vespers when Audley's horses rode back into camp. The thunder of their hooves was quiet compared to the thunder on Sir Audley's brow. He went straight to his own tents. His highness sent me to inquire how his mission had fared; I approached Audley's pavilion with slight trepidation. One of Audley's four squires bolted from the tent flap bearing his master's helmet, his own cheek red from a recently received cuff.

"I come on the prince's behalf," I said with pursed lips.

"Enter at your peril," said the breathless young man. "Sir James' temper can rival the devil's own fury."

I grimaced and slipped inside the flap of the tent. Sir Audley had tapped a great cask of Burgundy wine and filled a flagon with it. "Ha, Potenhale!" he said loudly, and there was an ugly look in his eye.

"I've come to share a drink with you, Sir James," said I. "They say that your wine is as good as the prince's."

"Aye, that it is," he said with a harsh laugh, and beckoning to one of his bachelors, he soon provided me with a brimming goblet. He bade me sit and refresh myself, "though you must pardon me if I stand awhile," he said with a sneer, "for I've been long in the saddle today."

"And you're like to be long in the saddle again tomorrow," said I, "when the columns advance." I took a large swallow of the Burgundy. "What news of the French?" I asked succinctly.

Audley grunted. "I found a goodly number of the infantry encamped east of us at La Haye."

"How many?"

"Ten thousand, perhaps fifteen."

"And King John?"

"With the remainder of his men, no doubt."

"Where is the remainder?"

"Aye, there's the rub," said Audley. He cursed and tossed his empty flagon at one of his squires, ordering him to fill it again. "I found neither tooth nor claw of them. They've not retreated to the north, they're not east of us in La Haye, and I rode five miles south without word of them. They've disappeared."

I set down my flagon and rose to leave. "I shall alert his highness of the news."

Audley snorted and looked the other way. It is a melancholy thing to fail in your duties to your sovereign, and Audley felt it more keenly than most.

When I arrived at the prince's tent, I found him striding about briskly—barking orders at his servants and at Warwick and Chandos as well.

"Your highness," I said, "Audley says he found the infantry east of us at La Haye, but the rest of the French...."

"...Are twenty miles south of us," said the prince.

I looked about me bewildered. "It's true, lad," said Chandos. "Holland's brought the news."

"You sent Holland out as well as Audley?" I asked sharply, losing some of the respect due to a prince in my distaste at hearing Holland's name.

"Aye," said the prince crisply. "I bethought what I would do if I were Valois—I would contrive any way I could to get ahead of my enemy, to cut him off from his base. I would strike south with all the speed I could muster. And so, while Audley darted about like a wren, I sent the Earl of Kent on an eagle's flight ahead of us, with orders to soar southward until he encountered the French forces."

"But twenty miles ahead of us!" I exclaimed. "How is it possible that John could have come on so fast?"

"Did not you yourself just tell me that he has left the infantry behind at La Haye? He has brought forward only his knights, and his mounted men-at-arms. The loss of the infantry is no great matter to that army—their arms still triple ours in number."

"What now?" I asked.

"We break camp in the morning," said the prince, "and then we march south toward Poitiers and Bordeaux. If God be for us, we shall slip through John's fingers like a handful of minnows. But if He wills otherwise, we shall engage the French in battle like men, and prove my father's claim with our bodies and our lives."

◆ ◆ ◆

Poitiers was a two-day march from our position at Châtellerault. For most of that march, we glimpsed no sign of the enemy, though the Earl of Kent vociferously insisted that King John and his army lay behind every bend of the road. On the afternoon of the second day, the forward company of our army—led by Chandos— came across the rearguard of the French battalions.

Outnumbered, Chandos ordered his men into the woods, falling back to the safety of the main army. The French followed eagerly, unaware that the lone wolf they had surprised was leading them back to the snapping jaws of his pack. The prince, seeing that our men vastly outnumbered the French rearguard, gave his commanders free rein. We ambushed the approaching cavalry, overthrew them, and took many knights—as well as two high-ranking counts—prisoner. The skirmish lasted until nightfall and prevented us from reaching Poitiers that night. We encamped in the forest, just a few miles outside the city, and waited until morning with the knowledge that King John's army was close at hand.

The next day was a Sunday. The prince celebrated an early mass and left his confessor to take to horse. The scouts rode in just as the sun was rising. They brought word that King John had drawn up in battle order just outside the city of Poitiers. His army blocked our road to the south. We could not in all honor ignore the challenge.

The prince cast about immediately for suitable ground on which to entrench his army. At Crecy, King Edward had made sure that he held the advantage of the terrain. He had positioned us on a hill, protecting our flanks with a river on one side, the village on the other; Edward, however, had the luxury of arranging himself for battle prior to the arrival of his opponent. The prince found his enemy already established and must make do with the ground that was left to him.

King John had pitched his army on a plateau outside the city. Below him dipped a small valley, about a quarter mile in length. On the other side of the valley stood a cultivated hill with a fortified manor. This place, the prince determined to occupy.

"If only they give us time to entrench!" said Warwick hopefully.

"Unlikely," snorted Audley. "Their rearguard was only too eager to give chase. Your highness had best prepare for battle to be joined immediately."

The advice was good, but Audley had not reckoned with the officiousness and interference of the Holy Church. Before the sun had reached its zenith, the cardinal Talleyrand of Périgord crossed the valley between our forces. His scarlet cassock shone out like a juggler's costume and proclaimed that he came on papal business. As the pope's emissary it was his duty—and fervent desire—to forestall the bloodshed between our two armies and to promote sweet concord between the rival sovereigns of France and England. He was an old man, near sixty years of age. His hair was white as milk, and his face wrinkled like parchment left in the sun. The prince greeted the holy man with reverence but bade him be brief in his discourse. "Now is the time for swords, not sermons, father."

"Ah, my son," said the cardinal, and there were tears in his faded blue eyes. "I have come from the camp of the French king. If you had seen his army and formed a correct idea of its size, I am sure you would allow me to arrange terms between you. It is not too late for peace." The old man's hands shook a little as he laid them on the prince's arm. "Young prince," said he, "take pity on all these noble men who might lose their lives here today in this great conflict. Are you sure that you are not in the wrong? If you would make an agreement with the king of France, God and the Holy Trinity would reward you for it."

The prince took the old man's hand in his, and I saw that he was moved with pity at his tears. "Indeed, good father, we know that what you say is true, and it is in the Scriptures. But we maintain that our quarrel is just and true. You know that it is no idle story that my father, King Edward, was the nearest heir. He should have held the throne of France, and all men here should have done allegiance to him; however, Philip of Valois conspired to seize what was not lawfully his, and thence comes the source of all this bloodshed.

"But, nevertheless," continued the prince, and I saw that his mind was working quickly to turn this cardinal's visit to our advantage. "I do not want it to be said that so many brave men died here because I was proud, nor do I ever mean to hinder peace between Christian brethren. It is not in my power to conclude terms of peace with the House of Valois—that is for my father alone to determine. But I can hold back my men if King John desires to enter into deliberations on the matter. Whatever terms we make must be ratified by my father before England accepts them. And yet," said the prince, his eyes glittering like polished obsidian, "if the French pretender does not want to entertain negotiations, make it known to him that I also am ready to await God's verdict. However much my heart may yearn for peace, our quarrel is so just that I am not afraid to fight."

The cardinal took this caveat with good grace. "Bless you, my son," he said. He wrapped his mantle around himself and prepared to mount his donkey. "I shall tell King John that you are eager to come to terms, and if the Holy Trinity will soften his heart as well, this may be a day of rejoicing instead of bloodshed."

"Go with God, father," said the prince, and he inclined his head to receive the pontiff's blessing. In truth, his very presence had been a blessing from Christ, for this cardinal would buy us the necessary time to fortify our position on the hill.

King John, though he was doubtless loath to enter into negotiations when he held us like a flea between his thumb and forefinger, could not refuse the remonstrances of the papal see. He promised to respect the sanctity of the holy Sunday by refraining from any warlike disturbances. He also pledged to treat with the Prince of Wales, although it was unlikely that the parley would produce much fruit.

As a result of Cardinal Talleyrand's mediation, commanders from each army descended into the valley below to resolve the dispute *sans* bloodshed. On the English side came Warwick, Chandos, and Audley. On the French side appeared Sir Jean Clermont, the Comte de Tancarville, and my old friend—Sir Geoffroi de Charny.

The prince had deputized his commanders with extraordinary powers of concession; these were owing to the extraordinary circumstances in which he was placed. Our provision wagons were as bare as a widow's cupboard; we were hedged in behind and before; our army was outnumbered with disheartening odds. "Tell King John," said the prince, "that I will give up all towns and castles that I have captured during this campaign, I will set free all prisoners without requiring ransom, and I will refrain from taking arms against him for seven years. All this I will do if he will allow our army to pass unmolested to Bordeaux."

Warwick, as chief spokesman of the English emissaries, presented the prince's offer in the most winsome language. It mattered not. Sir Jean Clermont, the mouthpiece of the French, was deaf to the earl's eloquence. He had his own proposal from the French king, and Warwick brought it back for the prince's consideration.

"King John is willing to allow our army to retreat unmolested, but only upon these terms: your highness, and a hundred of your knights, must surrender unconditionally to him. He will do with you and the hundred as he wishes, but the rest he will send away free."

The prince furrowed his brow in silence.

I jumped to my feet. "No! A thousand times no! What man of honor could live with such shame?"

"So say I!" echoed Brocas.

"Gentlemen, I am of your mind," said the prince. "I have but one death to die, and I had rather put it to the hazard than live in such disgrace. Take back our answer, good sirs, and bid the French prepare their souls for battle."

314 | I Serve

It was well nigh an hour before the commanders came back again. When they did, Chandos' face flamed red as a peony, and his usual good nature was as ruffled as a windswept pond.

"How received they our reply?" asked the prince curiously.

Warwick shrugged and allowed Sir James to tell the tale. "The cardinal wept," croaked Audley, "till his cassock was stained with tears. The French knights sneered—all except Sir Geoffroi de Charny. He said your highness had answered as a prince and a gentleman must, and commended you for it. And he proposed a second way of averting the battle. He asked that we should field a century of our knights against a century of the French. They would fight a melee, but with sharp points. If our men win, we depart for Gascony as free men. If the French conquer, we yield ourselves as King John's prisoners.... It was a promising offer, highness. I was minded to clap hands with him and accept it before your ears had heard it."

"Why, that is the same offer he made us at the siege of Calais!" said I in amazement.

"Aye," said the prince with a smile. "And my father's commanders scoffed at it there. They thought it a trick to take away our advantage. But here he offers it again when our spirits are drooping, and when it is decidedly *to* our advantage to accept. A noble heart and a noble gesture! You did not accept this, Sir James? Wherefore? I could find it in my heart to hazard our safety on the swords of a hundred knights."

"Tell on!" said Warwick quickly, urging Audley to finish relating the conference before the prince formed a plan on a false impression.

"As you say, highness," said Audley, "the proposal was decidedly to our advantage, and the other French knights recognized that immediately. Sir Geoffroi had imparted the offer apart from their counsel, and they castigated him roundly for it. The Comte de Tancarville withdrew the proposal as soon as it was uttered, and Sir Jean Clermont impugned his fellow ambassador as *un grand fou*."

"And that ended the negotiations?" asked the prince.

Audley hesitated and glanced sideways at Chandos. "The formal negotiations came to an end, though there were more words exchanged between Sir Clermont and Sir Chandos."

Sir Chandos flushed. "Nothing of import, your highness."

"Come, come," said the prince. "I must know what has come to pass to discompose you, the most placid of all my generals."

"If you must know," said Sir Chandos stiffly, "I called out Sir Clermont for his abusive language toward his own countryman and fellow-at-arms. I have always found Sir Geoffroi most true of heart and fair of speech, both when he was sojourning in our country and when he has met me in the field. I rated Sir Clermont poorly for his offense toward Sir Geoffroi, so he heaped the same obloquy on me as he had on his companion."

Sir Chandos would say no more. Later, Warwick and Audley explained the matter more fully. It seems that the arms of Sir Jean Clermont were similar in color and style to the arms of Sir John Chandos. They both bore the face of the blessed Virgin on a field of cerulean blue. When Chandos rebuked Clermont for his discourtesy toward Sir Geoffroi, the French knight roughly abused Sir Chandos for wearing a livery so similar to his own. "Since when have you taken to wearing my emblem?" Sir Clermont had demanded.

"It is just as much mine as yours," Sir Chandos had said, for he had adopted the coat-of-arms out of particular reverence for the Virgin.

"I deny that," said Sir Clermont sharply, "and if there were not a truce between us, I would show you here and now that you have no right to wear it."

"Indeed, sirrah?" Chandos had said coldly. "Well, there will be no truce tomorrow. You will find me more than ready then to prove by force of arms that this emblem belongs to me as much as it does to you."

The Comte de Tancarville and Sir Geoffroi de Charny had tried to pull their comrade away, but Clermont could not resist a parting shot at Sir Chandos. "That's just the sort of pompous boast you English make!" he had cried. "You can never think of anything good yourselves, but anytime you see something good in France, you try to steal it!"

The prince laughed a little at this story. "I hope my dear Chandos will make his boast good tomorrow. It would do my heart good to see this fellow Clermont fall. But look!—here comes our benevolent cardinal! And behold, his tears continue to flow."

Cardinal Talleyrand of Périgord was approaching our encampment once again. Hearing the failed outcome of the peace conference in the valley, he had besought the French king to extend the truce beyond a day so that further parleys might be held. The French had angrily told him to go back to Poitiers or it would be the worse for him. "My son," the old prelate said, placing a hand on our leader's shoulder, "do your best, for I fear you will have to fight. The king of France has not the slightest desire to make an agreement with you."

"Nor I with him, if truth be told," the prince answered cheerily. "But be not downcast, father. The God of battles will defend the right. Get you to Poitiers, for I would not have you caught here in the thick of the thunder that will roll through this valley tomorrow."

✦ ◆ ✦

Though the cardinal's interference gave our army time to set up defenses, it also allowed the French time to gather reinforcements. We learned later that King John, scrambling to position himself south of us, had left behind a large portion of his infantry and ridden forward with his best mounted knights–you will recall that Audley had sighted over ten thousand of these stragglers at La Haye. The Sunday delay allowed many of the slower Frenchmen to regroup with their sovereign and so the army that faced us the next morning held a larger number of lances than it had the previous day.

Upon arriving outside of Poitiers, the prince had positioned us on the hill opposite to King John's plateau. Between our two armies stretched a deep, marshy valley through which a river ran. Our hill was entirely surrounded by fences and ditches, its slopes covered with bushes, pastureland, vineyards, and sown crops. The prince resolved to stand against the French on the heights, forcing them to come up to us as King Edward had done at Crecy. He sent all the wagons and carts of the baggage train to one side of the hill to protect our flank. This was Salisbury's division. The other flank he bestowed on Warwick, where the bend of the river brushed past the old Roman road; and there he stationed the archers. Many of these were the same men who had performed such faithful service ten years ago. "We must pray that they have not lost their skill," said Warwick grimly.

The sun had already risen—and passed behind the clouds—when we heard the French trumpets summoning their lords to battle. The prince rode a length or two ahead of us to survey the enemy's battle line, a stern, solitary figure against the gray backdrop of sky. There was the French cavalry stretched out across the horizon, straining at their jesses like hawks at the sight of a hare.

"Holy Mother of God!" said Brocas, overwhelmed by the sheer number of their pennants. "It will be a slaughter. This is death, my friend." I nodded in agreement and crossed myself convulsively.

"Silence!" said the prince in a voice as hard and black as the coat of mail he wore. His horse wheeled sharply about. "It is blasphemy to say such things while I am still alive."

"Then I must do penance for my impiety," said Brocas. He held his helmet underneath his arm; his curls lifted a little in the light wind. "And right soon, too, for unless I say my *paternosters* straightway, I shall not live to mumble them."

"Nay, my friend," said the prince. His nostrils flared with anticipation. "Cast aside these morbid thoughts. Fasten your helm, draw your sword, and ride beside me. I swear to you, by the name of the Holy Trinity, that if—nay, *when*—we come through this battle victorious I shall grant you any boon you may desire."

Brocas pulled the basinet over his brow. "I shall hold you to that promise," he said, and the visor closed over his face.

"Fellow Englishmen!" said the prince in a loud voice, for the time had come to speak to the assembled army. "In days gone by you have proved your worth. Under the lead of my father and of my ancestors, the kings of England, you have shown all Christendom that for Englishmen: no task is unconquerable, no land too rough to cross, no castle impregnable, no enemy too formidable, no hostile ranks too great in size. Your fathers tamed Frenchmen and Saracen. They subdued the stiff-necked Scots and Irishmen.

"Today I exhort you to tread in the footsteps of your fathers. Occasion, time, and danger can make even the timid brave. Honor, love of country, and the rich spoils of France—more than any words of mine—will put courage in your hearts. Follow your banners! Keep your bodies and your wits intent upon the orders of your officers. Then shall life and victory walk hand in hand.

"But if envious Fate—God forbid!—should drive us upon the last road of all flesh, these gentlemen"—here the prince gestured to Chandos, Audley, and the other peers surrounding him—"and I will drink this same cup with you. There is danger in fighting the French nobility, but a danger wrapped in glory. There is danger of defeat, but it is a danger free from shame and makes a man's soul tingle. We prosecute a righteous cause! Whether we live or die, we are servants of God. He that shall persevere unto death shall inherit eternal life; and whoever shall suffer for righteousness' sake, theirs is the kingdom of heaven!"

The English ranks mustered all the spirit they could to cheer the prince's words. As if on cue, the French lines before us began to advance. On the plateau across from us, the Oriflamme moved forward. The great orange flag dipped in the fitful breeze. Its fiery tails half-concealed the crest of its bearer, and I did not learn till later that your husband was leading the way with the standard.

The French advanced in far better order than they had at Crecy. King John sent a company of pikemen to take the left side of the hill where the manor house stood. The French footsoldiers trudged manfully through the marsh and made their way up the incline over fence and hedge. Our men sent up a great shout as they approached. "St. George and Guienne!" they cried, and Salisbury led out his knights to engage the French there. Pikes fell to the ground as the overpowered French sought to yield or flee. Salisbury's knights pressed the fliers back to the march and began to mount their own attack on the opposing plateau.

On the right side of our defenses, a wave of French cavalry led by Sir Jean Clermont attempted to cut through our lines; however, the archers stationed at the bend of the river applied their skill to such good effect that the attack was stemmed. The French stallions screamed in anguish and their riders collapsed amid flailing hooves. I saw the standard of Sir Clermont fall and was glad in my heart for Sir Chandos.

When the French king saw that the two wings of his army had failed to cut through the English defenses, he advanced the center of his forces *en masse*. Strangely enough, they had all dismounted; this, we later learned, was due to the advice of a Scottish knight who was close to King John. Yet even without the added bulk of horses, the French forces were imposing enough.

The prince's company, which held the center of our line, had become overly enthusiastic from the small victories on either flank. Some of our men had wandered off like distracted children, eager to join Salisbury's cavalry or Warwick's archers in the bloodletting. Behind me I saw gaps in our line. In front of me I saw the glittering spears of the French host, rolling forward like a tidal wave. My eyes opened wide in terror, and the bloody reek of battle poured into the back of my nostrils.

The prince himself must have felt the same overmastering fear, for as King John's men crossed the marsh and began their ascent, he dismounted and fell to his knees on the battlefield before the eyes of all. Then he, who had never knelt to any man save his father the king, cried out: "Almighty Christ, I believe that You are king of all kings. I believe that You are truly God and truly man. I believe that You willingly endured death on the Cross to rescue us from hell. By Your most holy name, protect me and my men from harm, for You know that our cause is just."

With these words said, he rose to his feet, and a squire helped him regain his saddle. Chandos and Audley, as was their wont, rode close beside the prince and me. "Highness!" said Audley as the French knights began to close the distance between our forces, "I have made a vow that I will be the first of your company to break lances with the French. Give me leave to go." It occurred to me that Sir James Audley was desirous to redeem his earlier failure in scouting out the French king's movements.

"Do as you wish," said the prince, and thereupon, Audley set out a lance's length in front of his troop hurling himself on the enemy like a thunderbolt. Our own horses did not linger far behind. I entered the battle at the prince's side, and after this it was all confusion.

❖ ◆ ❖

Audley disappeared after the initial collision; I feared he had fallen. Chandos rose high in his saddle to deliver a mighty buffet with the sword. The prince smote about like a madman. He hacked a path with steel through the enemy lines leaving devastation in his wake.

Above the left side of the French line, the Oriflamme danced high, attracting Englishmen eager for the prize of bringing it down. "Those stars will fall today!" bellowed a great voice. I saw Thomas Holland, the earl of Kent, pursuing the orange banner with a score of the minions in his train. A cluster of French knights ranged themselves around the standard, but Holland trampled them like a bull, tearing out innards and hacking off limbs. "Holy Mary!" said I, "it is Sir Geoffroi!" Only then did I realize that the Oriflamme waved proudly in the hands of your husband.

I pulled my charger away from the prince's flank and galloped toward the orange banner. French foot soldiers impeded my progress. One grabbed my stirrup trying to pull me from the horse, but I gave him such a blow with the hilt of my sword that he spat out his own teeth. I neared Sir Holland right as he cleared the field of Charny's protectors. Holland's own men had been pulled away in the tide of battle, and he faced Charny alone—

THE FALLEN FLAGBEARER | 323

or as alone as two men could be in the melee of battle. Sir Geoffroi had planted the butt of the standard in the soft ground and stood beside it sword in hand.

Holland, no longer seated on his mount, lunged at the Frenchman, clipping the corner of his pauldron. Charny swung his own blade and made the earl fall back a step. I reined in my horse several paces behind Holland's large frame, unsure how to proceed. The exigencies of honor insisted that I aid my countryman against our common foe. The dictates of friendship demanded that I intervene on Sir Geoffroi's behalf. Yet paradoxically, it was neither of these two concerns that prompted my confusion.

As I stared at the dull finish of Sir Thomas's backplate, an insidious thought crept through the chinks in my visor and lodged in the crannies of my mind. There he stood— the bitter water in my cup, the fly in my ointment, the bar to my happiness. His whole attention was engaged by Sir Geoffroi, for your husband was a redoubtable match for any swordsman. "Here is the one," said my thought, "who is the wreck of so many lives. Would it not be just and proper for me to remove him from the way?"

"Nay," said a second voice within my head, smooth, clear, and silvery like the voice of your husband. "A knight may defend the widow and the fatherless, a knight may defend the rights of his liege, but it is sin to take vengeance in this way. If you were to die with such blood on your hands, then might you truly fear the judgment you have striven so hard to evade."

"But did not you yourself take vengeance!" the insidious thought argued back. "You hunted down Aimery of Pavia, pulled him from his bed, and slew him for his betrayal at Calais."

"That was an act of war, not treachery," said the voice calmly. "He was not my comrade-in-arms."

"And neither is Holland mine!" said my thought, repudiating the obvious reminder that Holland's shield—with the outline of England on it—carried.

I couched my lance, dropping the point on a level with Sir Thomas's back. The prince had spared him in the lists at Westminster; I would not be so forbearing. I kicked my heels into the side of my horse. The faithful beast jumped forward with alacrity. I aimed for the weakest place on the backside of the armor, where his helmet nearly joined with his backplate. My lance was two seconds away from threading through Holland's neck like a meat spit through a hare.

Holland was oblivious to my approach, but his adversary's eyes flickered sharply as I lowered my lance. Charny saw me and knew me, doubtless from the silver chevron on my shield. His own helmet had been torn off in the struggle; his uncovered head nobly crowned the green surcoat he wore. He looked me in the eye, as directly as if I had no basinet upon my brow. In that instant, my innermost intentions were revealed to him; I felt the same shame of nakedness and guilt that first overtook Adam in the garden.

Then, in one deft, deliberate motion, Sir Geoffroi lowered his sword arm and left open his guard. Holland lunged to the left to finish him with a stroke, leaping out of my path with as much rapidity as if he had been cognizant of my intentions. My lance swung wide of its mark, and my horse thundered by him into the thick of the French lines.

The next few moments enveloped me in a struggle for survival. French swords flailed fiercely about me, and I fought hard to keep from being unhorsed. When I gained breathing space enough to turn my head, I saw that the orange standard had fallen, as had its bearer. Charny's green surcoat lay trampled upon the ground, housing the poor clay of the noblest knight in Christendom.

I fought on. The battle, it seemed, had begun to lose its intensity. A few French knights cast anxious glances over their shoulder hoping to flee if enough of their fellows were like-minded. By dint of vigorous strokes, I gained the prince's side again.

Chandos, who had shadowed the prince throughout the battle, spurred his horse forward till he was level with the prince's mount. He saw the signs of imminent rout in the faces of the French. "Ride forward, sire!" he cried. "The victory is yours. Today you hold God's favor in the palm of your hand. Let us make for your adversary, the king of France—that's where the real business lies."

"Is he retreating?" I shouted.

"Nay," said Chandos. "He is too brave to run away. By God and St. George, he will be ours!"

The prince's eyes kindled. "Come on, Potenhale. No hanging back now!" He called to his banner-bearer with imperious enthusiasm, "Advance, banner, in the name of God and St. George!" The golden lion of the Plantagenets moved ahead with majestic ferocity. The French lilies lay just beyond us, and beneath them the pretended king of France.

King John, as Chandos had remarked, was a brave man. When he had ordered all his knights to dismount for the advance, he had done the same. Wielding a double-bladed axe, he planted himself firmly in the thick of the battle. However strongly the English gale might blow, he refused to be uprooted.

This resolution, however, was not held with such fervor in the hearts of the French troops. An epidemic of fright swept through the French ranks. Whole companies of King John's men took to their heels. The cries of *"Montjoy!"* and *"St. Denis!"* faded from the field of battle. Before the prince's company had even reached King John, the standard with the French lilies fell to the ground. St. George had won the day for England.

15

PEACE AT LAST
September, 1356 – December, 1360

The English men-at-arms pursued the fleeing French down the hill, through the marsh, and up to the gates of Poitiers. Those gates the city of Poitiers had wisely resolved to bar against fugitives from the battle. As so often happens in a rout, more French died in flight than had perished during the actual engagement. Up to the very walls the French were butchered, or made prisoner by Englishmen greedy for ransom.

All the field was littered with broken armor, basinets, swords, knives, lances, shields, flung away in desperate flight. Dead horses, dead men, and dying men lay tangled up with pennants, trumpets, arrows, and saddles. Welshman wandered about with their long knives, picking up valuables and giving the quietus to soldiers too poor to be ransomed.

The prince pursued the fleeing French as wholeheartedly as any man, with Chandos and me in his train. At length, as the shadows began to lengthen, we fell under the grip of exhaustion. The prince cried a halt. Chandos remarked that the men, in pursuit of the foe, had scattered very widely about the countryside. Even though there was no danger of the French re-forming, it would be good to rally the men to the prince's standard.

Ordering the trumpets to be sounded, the prince took off his helmet. Blood covered his face in grimy streaks. "Great God!" said Warwick, leading in some of the men from his battalion. "Salisbury and I competed to spill the most enemy blood, but you have outdone us all, prince."

I helped the prince disarm, and ordered refreshment to be brought immediately. The servants who had stayed with the baggage during the battle rushed to erect a small pavilion. The prince sat down wearily and drank a little wine. One by one, the English lords returned from the pursuit, their companies swelled with booty and prisoners.

King John had not been taken by the prince's own hand. Sir Denis de Morbecque, a French expatriate who had fought on our side, had received his surrender, and it was that knight who now brought him before us. John was of slender build. A large, Gallic nose protruded beneath his thick mane of thatch-colored hair. He was eleven years the prince's senior, and had reigned as king for the past six years.

John's conduct in the battle had been courageous and honorable, but we English had little other reason to praise him. He had begun his reign by autocratically executing his constable; then he had bestowed that high office upon a Spanish pirate, Don Carlos de la Cerda. He had mismanaged affairs with his son-in-law Navarre, alternately showing pitiful weakness and highhanded tyranny. Yet although the Valois king's reputation was as checkered as a troubadour's tunic, the prince received him with as much regard as if he had been his own father. "Welcome, dear sir," said the prince courteously. He offered John a stoop of wine and, rising himself, volunteered to act the squire and help the prisoner disarm.

The French king waved him off. "Nay, cousin," he said in a sad tone, acknowledging their common ancestry from the house of Capet. "Do not trouble yourself, for I do not deserve such esteem. In sooth, you have won more honor today than any prince before you!"

"My lord," answered the prince frankly. "God has done this and not us; we must thank Him and pray that He will grant us His glory and pardon this bloody victory which our hands have wrought." With that, the prince sent orders throughout the congregating host that prayers of thanksgiving should be said by all men-at-arms, giving glory, laud, and honor to the Holy Trinity for the doings of this day.

Poitiers, now certain of the victor, threw open its gates and invited the Prince of Wales to take possession of her; the prince, however, determined to lodge in the field. "How many of my countrymen lie fallen here?" he asked. "I will sleep here beside them until the earth is turned over their faces."

Chandos, ever faithful as the eyes and ears of his master, received the solemn duty of reckoning up the dead. I begged leave to follow his squires. We combed the field making note of the slain nobility on both sides. Darkness fell before the count could be completed, but the length of Sir Chandos's tally for the enemy indicated that the finest flower of French chivalry had died that day. The spirits of six thousand Frenchmen had fled, a tenth of which were belted knights.

Sir Jean Clermont was among them, his blue surcoat with the Virgin Mary pierced through by half a dozen arrows. Sir Geoffroi Charny was another title in the list. The orange ensign had been stripped from the pole beside him and carried off by an eager plunderer. I found one corner of it in the folded fingers of his cold hand. I took it, dear lady, as a memento of your husband.

Besides the dead, there were nearly as many prisoners to account for. Coming back from the pursuit and clustering round the prince's banner, the English found that their prisoners were at least as numerous as they. Some of the French knights paid their ransom then and there. Others gave their parole that they would surrender themselves at Bordeaux by Christmas, or else deliver the payment there.

The nobles, whose ransom was set at a higher figure, would linger a little longer in our care. There were thirteen counts, five viscounts, twenty-one bannerets, and a score of other prominent knights. Besides these, we had King John and his youngest son Philip. The prince invited them all to a feast that night, procuring provisions from Poitiers to supplement our scanty supplies.

I sat at table with our Gallic guests. Salisbury was there, Chandos, Warwick, and Holland, but Audley had not come in with the others. "Where is Sir James?" I asked Chandos in lowered tones.

"I do not know," replied the knight, lines of worry forming on his brow. "I have sent more men to comb the field for him, but alas! I fear the worst."

The prince seated King John in the place of honor at the banquet, but for his own part refused to sit. He carried out the dishes like the veriest servingman, and carved up portions to place on the trenchers of his guests. When the French king protested that it were unseemly for the conqueror to wait tables on the conquered, the prince only shook his head with a smile. "Do not make such a poor meal!" he urged, commenting on the French king's abstemiousness. "God has not heard your prayers today, but rest assured that my royal father will show you every mark of honor and friendship. You have good cause to be cheerful, for today you have won the highest renown of a warrior, excelling even the best of your knights."

The prince presented King John with a palm and a crown, proclaiming him the bravest paladin on the field that day. I looked to my right and to my left and saw approbation in the face of the French. Their worried faces relaxed, and I heard one count murmur that our Prince of Wales was the most magnanimous victor he had ever encountered.

As the feast continued, a squire entered precipitately and whispered something in Sir Chandos's ear. "Highness," said he, rising and brushing the crumbs from his lap. "My man brings word that Sir James Audley has been found. Grant me permission to go to him, for he is yet alive."

"You have my leave," said the prince. "And I must beg leave of this company to depart as well. Forgive my brief absence, gentlemen, for Sir Audley is a man that I would not lose for all the world."

Slipping from my place, I joined the prince and Chandos outside of Audley's tent. The men had carried him there on the face of a broad shield; Audley's four squires shuffled their feet, uncertain whether he should be moved again. "Come, you!" said the prince briskly.

"Strip off this armor and lay him in a soft bed." The squires scurried to obey.

Sir James's eyes were closed like the shutters of a prison; his breathing was faint but steady. Once inside the tent, the prince took Audley's cold hand in his and pressed his lips to the old knight's face. Gradually, the wounded man recovered his senses enough to recognize the prince. "How went the battle, highness?" he asked in labored tones.

"The day is ours," said the prince proudly. "Your charge led the way to victory."

Audley's blood-spattered face split into a broad grin. "The pope may be French," he said weakly, "but Jesus Christ is English to the hilt!"

Chandos and I laughed with relief. This sardonic comment was proof that Sir James would live to see another campaign. The prince hurriedly described the rout and delighted Audley to no end when he told him that we had King John in custody.

"I would not credit it," said Audley, "if any man but your highness had told me that piece of news."

"Believe it and thank the Virgin!" said Chandos fervently. "John's capture will do England more good than the keys to a hundred castles."

"Aye," said the prince. "He is the hostage that will give us everything we desire. His ransom will be Guienne, and his price the treasury of France. My father will hold again the lands that the Conqueror held and all the lands that Lackland lost."

❖ ◆ ❖

The next morning, after making the necessary funeral arrangements for our fallen comrades, the prince set out for Bordeaux. There was no need to stop on the way in search of plunder; the riches we had ransacked from the French camp were enough to fill every man's saddlebags and all the wagons besides. The prince had gathered a quantity of jewels, King John's costly crown, and his insignia from the Order of the Star. Out of his own spoil, the prince bestowed upon Sir James Audley the yearly pension of five hundred marks. It was a fit reward for his bravery. Audley, who had never cosseted his underlings, showed surprising magnanimity by bestowing the prince's gift on his four squires. The prince applauded him for his generosity, for liberality was a quality that the prince admired in others as well as in himself.

The news of our triumph went ahead into Gascony. When we reached Bordeaux, the city welcomed us most nobly. The clergy came out to meet us in procession, carrying crosses and chanting prayers. Ladies, girls, and maids lined the streets and windows, showering late summer flowers on the heads of the heroes.

The Captal de Buch held a feast as extravagant as his panegyrics to the prince. One hundred courses loaded down the tables in leisurely succession. A roasted peacock, with its feathers replaced and its beak gilded, looked live enough to strut across the table. Pork meatballs coated in green batter fooled many into thinking them apples. Skewers threaded through dried figs, dates, prunes and almonds—though belied by their smell—looked for all the world like savory boar entrails. Meat, fish, fruit, vegetables, creams, and puddings replaced our memories of empty bellies outside the town of Poitiers.

There was wine enough to wash it all down—and good wine to boot, for the wine of Bordeaux is renowned throughout Europe.

It was late September when we reached Bordeaux. The prince resolved to winter there with his prisoners. He sent word of the battle to his father, asking for speedy conveyance home in the spring. King Edward rejoiced exceedingly at the news of his son's conquest. The capture of King John added a sweet plum to the pudding. As Sir James Audley had ironically remarked, the triumph proved to all that though the pope was French, Jesus Christ was English through and through! Divine favor had delivered France into the hands of our people.

When the winter storms subsided, His Majesty sent a flotilla of ships and barges to bring the victors—and their prisoners—home to England. As the prince and I left the Captal de Buch's residence to board the boat, I caught a glimpse of red-gold hair coming down one of the gangplanks in the harbor. I stared dumbfounded at the sight of Margery Bradeshaw. In her arms she bore a little girl child with hair the color of smooth honey and bright, violet eyes. At first, my heart misgave me that the child might be Margery's; a closer look convinced me that Margery only played nurse, for the child was an exact copy of her mother Joan.

"What is this?" I demanded of my companions. "Is the lady Joan come to Bordeaux?"

"Aye," said Sir Brocas knowingly. "The king has appointed the Earl of Kent to be captain general over his affairs in Gascony. Holland's family has crossed the channel to be with him."

I looked at the prince for confirmation; he nodded dispassionately then turned his attention to the harbormaster. I wondered whether his indifference was real or feigned and schooled my features to adopt the same iron-hearted cast.

"Here come my lads!" bellowed a loud voice from behind me. Holland had arrived to the wharf to greet the arrivals. Two small urchins whizzed past my legs like excited puppies and wrapped their arms around the great red doublet that Holland wore. Their nurse Margery followed more sedately with little Joan. Holland patted the baby's head clumsily, and I recollected that—since he had been with us in Bordeaux since last summer—he was seeing his newest offspring for the first time.

"A blissful reunion," remarked Brocas sardonically, and then turned aside to join the prince.

"Amen to that!" said Holland loudly. "Though it seems my lady wife is not as keen to greet me as her brats are."

Margery's pale cheeks glowed red to hear her mistress's feelings discussed so frankly in full hearing of the wharf. "There were several parcels to be arranged with the shipmaster, sir," she said meekly. "Lady Joan bade me come ahead with the children."

I winced to hear her submit so tamely. Was this the same woman who had berated me for losing the prince's letter? Was this the same woman who had bidden her mistress defy Holland and marry Salisbury? Was this the same woman who had given me her red glove at a long-ago tournament? I forgot my feigned indifference and searched her face eagerly for some sign of recognition. There was none. She neither met my eye nor avoided it.

"Sir Potenhale and I have been comrades-in-arms," said Holland, noticing my gaze fixed on Margery. His one eye rolled about mischievously. "You were beside me—yes?—when I killed Charny and felled the Oriflamme?"

I gritted my teeth and grunted. Yes, I had been behind him, beside him, or somewhere in that vicinity.

"It was a strange encounter," Holland mused. "For a great part of it, I was sure that Sir Geoffroi would get the better of me. He met stroke after stroke with ease and delivered them back again with interest. But after I began to worry a little, he suddenly ceased his blows and stood to attention. His face was unhelmed; I saw his piercing eyes stare beyond me like a man who sees a vision. In that instant, he let down his guard, and—praise the saints!—I skewered him through his armhole."

"I am sorry for that," said Margery softly. I remembered the time that she had conversed a whole evening with Sir Geoffroi.

"He was your friend, was he not?" Holland asked me.

"Aye, more than you know," said I. Sir Geoffroi had been the truest of friends, never moreso than on the battlefield at Poitiers. The Earl of Kent had no knowledge of the deed my hand was poised to do that day. He could not see the lance head on a level with his neck. He did not understand that when Sir Geoffroi let down his guard that day, it was to guard Holland's own life, and—what is more!—to guard the soul of an insignificant knight from Herefordshire. The flagbearer had fallen so that Sir Potenhale's honor might stand. Sir Thomas Holland did not know the thanks he owed to Sir Geoffroi de Charny.

Through the creaking of pulleys and lapping of waves, I heard a voice calling my name. I made my adieus to the Earl of Kent and gave a curt nod to Margery. She dropped her eyelids like a washerwoman worn out from a day's labor. I strode quickly down the wharf until I found my friends stationed by the largest of the cogs.

"Come, Potenhale," said the prince crisply. "The tide has turned, King John is aboard, and the shipmaster says we must embark."

"Your cousin Joan is still disembarking," said I. "Perhaps you wish to greet her ere we depart."

The prince looked at me quizzically. "And miss the tide? Nay, Potenhale, I'll not dally here to exchange pretty pleasantries. We have been away from our dear England too long. The sooner that we can bring King John face to face with my father the better. We shall see what terms France is willing to give us, now that we have lopped her lilies a little."

At home in England, the king arranged our arrival with as much pomp as a Roman triumph. An honor guard of twenty earls and barons met us at the harbor and rode beside the prince on his path to the city of London. Playacting also formed part of the pageant. On one leg of our travel, five hundred men dressed in green sprung from the forest in mock ambush. The prince, much to King John's confusion, attacked these actors with gentle, good-natured blows, whereupon the men "surrendered" themselves to the all-conquering Prince of Wales and congratulated his latest conquest in France.

When we reached the gates of London, the mayor came out to meet us surrounded by guildsmen from every trade bedizened in the insignia of their guild. The narrow streets were made narrower still as the inhabitants of every house came out to watch our procession. In the avenue between the goldsmith shops, two glittering birdcages dangled, each one holding a fair damsel to scatter gold and silver leaves on the cavalcade below. We passed St. Paul's cathedral; instead of Flagellants, the bishop himself came out to meet us, and a procession of patriotic clergyman. At the palace of Westminster, many, many lovely ladies showered their attention on the prince and he received praise from all quarters. There was dancing, hunting, hawking, jousting, and feasting, just as in the glorious days of King Arthur's reign.

The presence of so many fine French knights in England, albeit as prisoners, provided an excellent excuse for a series of tournaments. I gained honors at Smithfield and Windsor, though none of the awards for tilting moved me like the red glove which I had been awarded at a previous tournament. None of the applause from the stands exhilarated me since the face I wished to see in the crowd was across the channel in Gascony.

Though my master, Prince Edward, invariably gained the highest honors at these tourneys, there was another young man, also wearing the Plantagenet lion, who distinguished himself above his peers. "By all the saints," said Audley, watching John of Gaunt unhorse his opponent, "he is the very image of his highness, the Prince of Wales, the day we landed at Crecy."

Young John was sixteen now, dark-haired and long-limbed like his brother, his father, and their progenitors.

His beardless jaw was set with the same indomitable hauteur, and his eyes glinted with the same insatiable hunger for glory.

"I hear His Majesty's ready to send the boy to his marriage mass," said Roger Mortimer knowingly.

Audley raised an eyebrow. "Lancaster's daughter?"

"Aye, little Blanche," replied Mortimer. "Lancaster, of course, is pleased with the match."

"By all the saints!" said Brocas in mock despair. "I had my eye on the maiden for myself. Lancaster has no sons—or at least none on the right side of the kitchen door. The earldom will fall to whomever Blanche weds. A pretty prize, that!" He turned to me and demanded my attention. "Think you, Sir Potenhale, that it is right for a callow youth like John of Gaunt to marry and get children before seasoned warriors such as ourselves have bedded a bride?"

I shrugged.

"Ask your friend, the prince," said Mortimer. "He's of an age with you both. Tush! The man's a monk. He rejects every matrimonial alliance that his father and Parliament propose. Will he ever marry?"

Brocas and I exchanged glances. "Indeed," said Brocas jocularly, "when King John offers to give him his daughter with France as a dowry, he'll enter the banns as quickly as an arrow flies. But until then, no. The man is wedded to the sword."

"A pity," said Mortimer with a shake of the head. "For if he's to be king someday, it were well that he should have sons of his own."

❖ ◆ ❖

340 | I Serve

The prospect of King John offering his daughter's hand with France as a dowry, was appealing, but highly improbable. King John, while he still reclined in his gilded cage in Bordeaux, had agreed to sign a preliminary truce. Now that he was in England, the talks of permanent peace protracted over several months. Our English demands were not unreasonable. King Edward forbore from pressing his claim to the French crown. Instead, he asked only for the restoration of Ponthieu and Guienne, the dowry that Eleanor had brought to his Angevin ancestor. In addition to the land, he also required four million florins of ransom. If the French agreed to these terms, King John would be returned to them.

King John, after multitudinous cavils and conditions, formally accepted the terms a year after his arrival in England. His own country, however, was even less ready to render up the ransom than he was. You yourself could relate the state of affairs in France at this time far better than I. Beset behind and before by the intrigues of Navarre and the outrages of rebellious serfs, the dauphin and the French assembly balked at ratifying the treaty. King John was left to languish in England while his son strove to keep the Paris guildsmen from proclaiming Charles of Navarre the new king of France.

The delays had exhausted Edward's patience. Since the French assembly would not conclude the peace, he resumed his plans for war. Sending Lancaster on ahead to Normandy, Edward put together an invasion army. He publicly announced his route and objective; the dauphin heard it and trembled. Edward Plantagenet intended to land at Calais and march to Rheims where he would compel the bishop to crown him king of the country of France. Your French kings have all been crowned at Rheims. With the holy oil of Saint-Rémy on his brow, Edward's authority could be denied by none.

The prince provided a large company to take part in the campaign. Contracting heavy debts to the merchants of London, he mustered nearly fifteen hundred men. Chandos, Audley, and I accompanied him. I was nearly thirty years old at the time; my lightning bolt crest had begun to be known by a few, and I took on two squires who desired to serve under a seasoned knight.

What more shall I tell you of this campaign? It was only a year ago that we landed. Lancaster, the king, and the prince commanded the three divisions of the army. We rode like devils to Rheims and found that the dauphin had fortified it against us. We tried a siege; Rheims held out. The miserable weather in France and the insurrections of the peasant laborers had left scant crops for the taking. The men complained and despaired till Edward abandoned the siege. Frowning at our failure, Edward swung southwest in a path like the curve of a scimitar.

My company passed by this very village of Lirey not a day's ride away. Sir Chandos wished to stop here, for he had heard of some relic worth seeing in the vaults of Lirey's church. The king, however, had no time for such detours. He ordered the columns on, and I thank the Holy Trinity that you were not harmed by our soldiers.

We halted at Auxerre while King Edward negotiated with the Duchy of Burgundy. Roger Mortimer died there, killed on a foraging raid. Burgundy paid us off, to keep us from invading his county, and the king rolled out maps and charts to plot our next move.

With characteristic reluctance, the dauphin had refused to come meet us in the field, so the king determined to draw him out from his den. Edward brought the army north to Paris. The dauphin, who had only lately quelled the uprisings in the city, set fire to all the suburbs lest we English should take shelter in them. We camped in the charred rubble outside the city. Tumultuous Paris was in no condition to withstand a siege.

Unfortunately, our army was in no condition to lay one. The worn-out men woodenly waited beneath the walls, in as much danger of starvation as those we hoped to starve. We lingered there to no avail; the dauphin still declined to meet us in the field.

Frustrated, King Edward marched our bedraggled battalions south to Orleans. The March weather, which till now had been as fair as any could wish, turned ugly with the ferocity of a wolverine at bay. A violent hailstorm raked our ranks followed by a night as cold as death. Our bruised, emaciated horses fell by the road, and some men died in their saddles. Much of the baggage train was abandoned.

"How much longer can we go on?" I cried in despair. We had been seven months in France. We had taken no great towns. We had fought no pitched battles.

"Patience, Sir Potenhale," said Chandos calmly. I had interrupted his devotions to the Holy Virgin. His dark silver hair fell forward over the shoulders of his blue surcoat. "His Majesty has met reverses in this campaign, but we are still a great enough force to be reckoned with. Have patience. The dauphin will either fight or come to terms."

As usual, my old master had wisdom on his side. When we reached Orleans, we found an embassy from the Holy See awaiting us. In her accustomed capacity as intermediary, the Church had arranged a peace conference just north of the city at Bretigny. For twenty-one days conditions were batted back and forth like balls in a tennis court. In exchange for complete sovereignty of the territory of Guienne, Edward agreed to give up his claim to the French crown and to renounce his hereditary rights in the counties of Normandy and Anjou. The city of Calais he refused to part with, and the dauphin grudgingly let it stand as an English enclave in the midst of French-controlled territory. Edward generously agreed to reduce King John's ransom to three million florins, in consideration of the famine, unrest, and marauders that were currently crippling the French treasury. The peace was concluded at last.

I returned with the prince to England to assure King John that his deliverance was at hand. He had been three years in our country and had many adieus to make. The summer had nearly passed by the time we brought him from London to Canterbury—for the prince longed to lay an offering on the holy martyr's shrine—and from thence to Dover where we took ship for Calais. The removal of garrisons and the transfer of territories took several more months. In October the first installment of the ransom arrived. King John rode out of the gates of Calais, a free man once again.

Edward sailed home, devoid of the crown he had come to assume, but assured that he would never be required to pay fealty for the southwestern quarter of France. The prince and all his retine crossed the channel soon after. I begged leave to remain longer in France. The prince granted my wish, and so here I am come to Lirey at last.

You must pardon me, dear lady, for the length of the tale I have told. I heard the bell toll for Compline some time ago. My sole excuse must be that I have only done what you asked. You bade me to begin with my knighthood, and I did not wish to omit any instance that would illuminate my relationship with your husband. Will you take my gift? It is my dearest remembrance of him.

16

THE SACRED CLOTH
December, 1360

The afternoon light had disappeared completely by the time the knight finished his tale. Jeanne de Vergy's eyes had never wavered from his face as she listened in rapt, almost reverent attention. She took the box that he offered and removed the ragged piece of the Oriflamme from it. The candles in the apse illuminated the fire in the fabric and it burned a brilliant orange as it must have on the day of its last battle four years ago. "You have come a long way to bring a scrap of cloth to a dead man's widow," she said softly.

"What better way to honor him," said the knight, repeating his words of three hours ago, "than to give the one he loved the most the thing that he honored the most."

"I think," she said slowly, "that you have mistaken him, even as your master the prince did. I am not the one he loved the most, and this is not the thing he honored most." She paused a minute. "You have given me your treasure and remembrance of him, Sir Potenhale. It is meet that I should give you a glimpse of mine."

She rose from the bench where they sat and approached the reliquary that occupied the niche. Reverently, she removed the box from the wall and opened the lid. She raised the object inside and unfolded it.

The knight looked openmouthed at the sheet of linen that she had laid gently over the pew. The face of a thousand Byzantine icons, stared out from the light-colored fabric, the piercing eyes, the weary brow, the kingly hair and beard. Below the face was an impression of the man's entire body, hands clasped modestly over his groin and legs pressed tightly together. The traces of ghastly wounds could be seen on his hands and feet and the dark henna color of blood long since dried.

The knight crossed himself instinctually and fell to one knee before the cloth. "It is our Lord," said he, "the face of Christ that your husband saw in Smyrna!"

"Aye," said she. "You remember! Before he abandoned the Crusade and took ship, Geoffroi met an old priest in Smyrna who lay upon his death bed. The priest was by himself. His flock and his brethren were too terrified of the Turks to stay in the city. You know my husband—he would not leave a dying man to die alone. He stayed with him to the end. In the waning hours of his life, the priest revealed that he was a descendant of Joseph of Arimathea, the Jew who owned the tomb where Christ was laid. With him, however, the line of his fathers would perish; and having no heir, the old priest entrusted into my husband's keeping the cloth that you see here. It is the very shroud in which our Savior Jesus Christ was enfolded. It is the very blood from the wounds that our Savior bore. And it is the very likeness of our Savior— impressed upon this shroud when he was resurrected, when the apostles found naught but the grave clothes in an empty tomb."

"I see such suffering in His face!" cried the knight.

"He suffered so that you might not," said the woman.

"And yet such love upon his countenance!" The knight sighed. "And has it been granted to me to see such a marvelous vision of our Savior? What man could see this shroud and not believe in the love of God for Adam's race?"

"What man, indeed?" said the wife of Geoffroi de Charny; she folded the cloth and replaced it in the reliquary.

The knight watched her silently, then beckoned to the smaller box on the pew. "And what of the Oriflamme?" he asked. "You were right to spurn it. It is of no account beside such a relic as that you have shown me. Shall I cast it away?"

"Nay," she said looking at the tattered remains of the royal ensign. "It has some value. It is a symbol of the place my husband attained in this world through the love of his Savior Jesus Christ. He loved God, and God loved him. He served God, and God rewarded him for it. He feared God, and God made him secure from his enemies. He honored God, and God gave honor to him.

"Come, Sir Potenhale, you shall keep this cloth, as a reminder of the other cloth that I keep. Keep it, and remember that if you ask of Him, you will receive much from Him. If you pray to Him for mercy, He will pardon you. If you call on Him when you are in danger, He will save you from it. If you pray to Him for comfort, He will hold you in His bosom. Believe totally in Him, Sir Knight, and He will bring you to salvation in His sweet paradise."

When the lady had finished speaking, she took the orange cloth that was in the box and bound it about Sir Potenhale's arm. And ever after, though he was a knight of lowly parentage, he wore the wreck of the Oriflamme about his arm as proudly as if it were the symbol of the Garter Knights, and as reverently as if it were the grave clothes of Our Savior Jesus Christ.

Jeanne de Vergy would have kept him longer. She entreated him to stay till the new year. But Sir Potenhale had performed his duty to the dead and must be back to render duty to his living prince. He tarried for the night in the wayside inn, and on the morrow departed again for Calais.

◆ ◆ ◆

"Ho there, it's Potenhale!" said Lord Brocas waving jovially from an upper window at the weary traveler entering the streets of Calais. Sir Bernard's merry, chestnut curls framed his face, and his face glowed warmly in the December air.

"Well met, Brocas," said Potenhale with a smile. "I did not think to find you in France, but in England with the prince. Have all his highness's friends left him alone at Christmastide?"

"Nay, it's the other way around," said Brocas. "He would have left me alone at Christmas—but I followed him here to Calais, like a faithful hound despite all his kicks and curses."

"What brings the prince to Calais?" asked Potenhale, dismounting and handing off his horse to a servant.

"You've not heard the news?" asked Brocas. He smiled gleefully like a young boy who has all the sweetmeats to himself. "Come up, come up, and I shall tell you all."

Potenhale entered the house, which he recognized as belonging to Sir Walter Manny, and removed his travel garb before searching out Brocas. He had been riding in the cold, wintry air all day, and he entreated Brocas to let him get warm before he filled up his ears with nonsense.

"You'll wish you'd listened sooner when you hear what 'tis," said Brocas knowingly, "for the news concerns you as well as his highness."

"Well then, tell away," said Potenhale with a grumble. "What is it that I must hear?"

"Why, it is namely this," said Lord Brocas. "The king's captain-general in France has died and gone to heaven—at least that's what his well-wishers say. I'm inclined to think that he's gone to a far smokier place."

"The king's captain-general," repeated Potenhale. "But that is none other than Sir Thomas Holland!"

"Exactly," said Brocas smacking his lips like an old woman who has just sucked the marrow from a bone. "Sir Thomas Holland is no more."

"How?"

"Taken on his sickbed—as could happen to any man, even to one of such a robust constitution as Sir Thomas."

"And his wife?"

"She remains in Gascony still with her children but will soon emigrate, no doubt, to the more congenial shores of our own land."

"The prince?" asked Sir Potenhale, hardly able to catch his breath.

"Like a madman," said Lord Brocas shaking his head. "First, he locks himself in his room; then he takes ship for Calais swearing he will find you and go on to see the lady in Bordeaux. And now, once he's in Calais, he locks himself in his room again and swears he will leave you here and take ship once more back to England."

"So he has not seen her?"

"Nay! He says he will not go!" Lord Brocas clenched his fist in exasperation. "And yet, how many years has he waited for this hour? If he persists in this folly, I shall take harsh measures with him."

"What can you do? You know him as I do. His highness cannot be cajoled."

"But he can be coerced."

"By you?" Sir Potenhale looked incredulous.

"Nay, by his honor," said Lord Brocas. He smiled slyly. "Wait and watch, Sir Potenhale, and you will see my wonders."

When the prince heard that Potenhale had come, he made no move to leave his room. The newly arrived knight brought him his supper and sat down to table with him there. They talked in a desultory fashion till the meal was over. Then began Sir Potenhale, "Lord Brocas says...."

"I'll not hear him," said the prince wearily. "It passes all understanding how that man's tongue can prattle so long."

Sir Potenhale was silent for a moment. "So we are for England, then?"

"Aye, we leave on the morrow," said the prince in a tone that brooked no discussion.

But, as events turned out, their voyage on the morrow was destined for a province far south of English shores. Sir Potenhale awoke from his sleep just in time to hear Brocas's encounter with the prince in the courtyard.

"Highness," said Brocas. The prince would have turned away, but Brocas shouted—"Grant me at least an audience for friendship's sake."

"Very well," said the prince shortly. "For friendship's sake."

"Do you remember that time at Poitiers when I doubted your leadership?"

"Aye," said the prince. "You would have fled the field had I not brought you to your senses."

"And do you remember that you swore to me that day that if you brought us alive out of that battlefield you would grant me any boon that I should ask."

"Aye."

"As God is my witness," said Brocas, "I have never asked you anything from that day till this, and still I have a boon promised me."

"You speak truly," said the prince suspiciously. "What would you ask of me?"

"Highness," said Brocas, cocking his head to one side. "I have grown up beside you as a boy and fought beside you as a man. We begin to grow old together, and still there are none to come after us. I have already seen thirty summers come and go, and methinks it is time that I get myself a wife."

"You?" asked the prince. "A wife?"

"Aye," said Brocas, "I have been thinking to do as much for a long time now, and I have settled at last upon the lady. But she is a great lady, and I know not whether she will accept my offer."

"I wish you well of it. How does this matter involve me?"

Lord Brocas looked him full in the eye. "I would have you broker a marriage between myself and the lady Joan of Kent."

Silence fell across the courtyard, awful and mysterious like the silence of a sacred grove. Men have been struck dead for intruding into such a silence such as this, and Sir Potenhale knew better than to enter the courtyard.

"You know not what you ask," the prince replied hoarsely.

"I know very well," said Brocas. "I ask that you go to Bordeaux and plead my case with the lady there. Your cousinly persuasion will doubtless soothe any qualms the lady might have, and by Eastertide I shall be your cousin by marriage, sweet prince."

The prince stared at Brocas. "So," he said at last, "this is the boon you are asking of me?"

"Aye," said Brocas.

"So be it," said the prince. "You shall have your boon, my dear friend. Send a messenger to the harbor to tell the shipmaster we have changed directions. We are no longer for Dover, but for Bordeaux."

◆ ◆ ◆

The journey to Bordeaux was pleasant so far as winter sailing may be. The prince went at once to greet his old friend the Captal de Buch. Sir Potenhale, who had been dispatched to inquire about the widow of the late captain-general, found that she had removed to the abbey at *l'Eglise de Sainte Croix*. The good monks had taken in both her and her four children until she could make arrangements to return the household to England.

The prince had made his arrival incognito, but he did not want to approach Joan unannounced. He remained behind at the residence of the Captal de Buch and sent Potenhale ahead to proclaim his presence to his cousin.

The knight found his way to the abbey with no difficulty. "Is the lady Joan here?" he asked the watchman who sat at the cloister gate.

The watchman looked Sir Potenhale up and down, disapprovingly it seemed. "Aye, she's here," he said, "but she is in mourning and will take no visitors."

"I am sure that my message will be of interest to her."

"No visitors," said the watchman, pursing his lips in disgust.

"Well then, is there a lady named Margery in her company?" the knight asked.

"Aye," said he in a surly tone."

"And is she in mourning too?"

"Nay."

"Then I adjure you, my good man, tell the second lady that Sir John Potenhale is without and desires speech with her."

The watchman grunted and left to do the knight's bidding, but before he left, he warned him against crossing the threshold in his absence. "An' you fear God, you'll not set foot inside this gate!"

The knight, though sorely tempted, followed these instructions. He waited a goodly amount of time before any answer came, but when it came, it was in the form of the lady herself.

"Sir Potenhale!" said the lady in a voice of earnest pleasure. "It has been long since I laid eyes upon you."

Sir Potenhale smiled at her from outside the gate. "Your watchman would barely let me send word to you, and it seems I must stand outside if I wish to hold any conversation with you."

Margery laughed and stepped forward lightly to lift the latch upon the gate. "In sooth, he is a well-meaning soul," she explained as Sir Potenhale walked forward into the open grounds of the cloister. "No sooner had Sir Thomas been in the grave a week than a dozen suitors began buzzing around my lady like flies to honey—every swain is fain to court the loveliest lady in England. She's had much ado to send them packing. It is out of consideration for her that the watchman has proved your foe."

"He'd have been wiser to fend me off more forcibly," said Sir Potenhale mysteriously, "for I fear I'm pack and parcel with the rest who have been beating down your door."

"Why, what do you mean?" asked Margery, and a blush caught her ears and spread down to her ivory cheeks. "I know you too well, sir, to think that you come as a suitor yourself."

"You know me far less than you think," replied Sir Potenhale. "But I shall press my suit when it suits me, and at present it does not. My errand now is as the herald of a suitor, or rather the herald of a herald."

Margery looked at him in bewilderment. "Explain yourself, sir."

"The prince my master has arrived in Bordeaux and would call upon his cousin tomorrow."

"The prince!" said Margery eagerly. "Is he the suitor of whom you speak?"

Sir Potenhale hesitated. "A suitor of sorts," said he.

"He will be welcome," she said, and ran off hurriedly to inform the widowed lady of Kent.

The prince was no laggard. He arrived on the heels of his messenger's departure. The gatekeeper, who had been warned of his coming, admitted him with suitable courtesy.

The south of France is mild even in the winter, and the prince found his cousin sitting outdoors in the garden adjoining the cloister. Lady Joan's golden hair was obscured by a mourning veil, but the cheerful blue of her dress and the glistening gold of her embroidery belied the magnitude of her bereavement. She rose to meet the prince and curtsied.

"Welcome, cousin," said she. "You are kind to visit." Her face was older—her cheekbones had lost the round- ness of youth and her eyes the naivety of earlier years— but, nonetheless, it was beautiful still. The prince stood silent a moment with his eyes upon her.

She bade him sit and they talked of Christmas, of the treaty, of Calais, and of her children. Neither spoke of the reason behind her veil of mourning, and the prince was glad of that—it is difficult to offer condolences for an event one has so long desired. When all these subjects had been exhausted, they came at last to the reason for his coming.

"Cousin," said the prince, "as much as I delight in your conversation, I must bid you attend to mine a little, for I have somewhat to say to you." The Lady Joan fell silent and looked on him with shining eyes. The prince wavered a little with a trepidation that he had never felt since his first campaign. "The words are not my own," he said. "I come as an emissary to plead a case for another."

"Who dares to make a diplomat out of a prince?" said Joan with lifted eyebrows.

"A friend may dare all things," said the prince, "and Lord Brocas is one such friend. He is the suppliant, and I come before you at his behest. If you hold me dear, sweet cousin, you will not deny his asking."

"I cannot deny a request that I have not heard," replied Joan, "but neither can I grant it. Say on, dear cousin. What would the good Brocas have?"

"He would have you," said the prince shortly, "to wife."

Lady Joan breathed in sharply. "Ah," said she. "And for this purpose you are come to beg?"

"Aye."

She stood up suddenly and walked a few paces away. Then turning back to him, she smiled disarmingly. "Why, cousin, what folly is this! I must speak plainly, I see. I have made a vow that I shall not marry again, but shall live chaste, even as the good monks here in this cloister. I regret but that Lord Brocas must be disappointed."

"You shall not marry again?" asked the prince.

"Nay," she laughed. "I have married twice—or very nearly twice—and that is more than enough for one woman. I have four children. My little Thomas is ten years old! What can I want with another husband?"

"But cousin," said the prince, reaching out for her hand and pulling her gently back to the stone bench, "*Belle Cousine*! You must marry." He smoothed back the veil that covered the sides of her face. "You cannot let those great beauties with which Our Blessed Redeemer has endowed you be all for naught. Upon my soul, if you and I were not of common kin, there is no lady under heaven whom I should hold so dear as you."

At this, the lady's smile disappeared. She fell forward and leaned upon his shoulder as bitter tears ran down her cheek. The prince stroked her face gently and tried to comfort her, but her tears continued to fall like summer rain. He kissed her brow, and still she wept. He kissed her cheek, yet she cried on.

"Lord Brocas is a good man!" said the prince in anguish. "He will make you happy, my dear one."

"Ah, your highness," said Joan reproachfully. "For God's sake forbear to speak of such things to me. I have made up my mind not to marry again; for I have given my heart to the most gallant gentleman under the firmament. For love of him, I shall have no husband but God so long as I live. It is impossible that I should marry him, and yet, for love of him, I wish to shun the company of all other men. I am resolved never to marry."

The lady cast down her eyes as she said this, but the prince lifted up her chin. He asked her tell him who was this gentlemen to whom she had given her heart. The lady shook her head sadly. When he persisted, she fell to her knees before him. "My dear cousin," said Joan. "For Christ's sake and for the Holy Virgin's, I entreat you to forbear from asking me."

"Nay, I shall not forbear," replied the prince, and his voice shook with some of the thunder that it carried at Poitiers. "I have been your friend, dear lady, but if you do not tell me here and now who is this gallant gentleman that holds your heart, I shall be forever your most deadly enemy. Tell me, Joan. Tell me his name!"

She wiped a tear from her eye and looked straight into the dark eyes below his threatening brow. "Very dear and redoubtable lord, how can I hide it from you any longer? It is you who are the most gallant gentleman. And it is for love of you that no gentleman shall lie beside me. Since I cannot be your bride, I shall be the bride of Christ."

The prince raised her kneeling figure from the ground and held her firmly in his arms. "Lady, I swear to you that as long as I live, no other woman shall be my wife."

"But it cannot be!" said Joan. "We are kin!"

He stopped her mouth with a kiss. "Then I shall build an abbey for the Holy See. William the Conqueror did the same for his Matilda, and in consequence of that the pope said nary a word of condemnation."

"But he did not have to deal with a French pope," objected Joan, perversely parading every protest now that the prince had made his protestation of love to her. "Mayhap an abbey will not appease him?"

"Then I shall march an army to the gates of Avignon!" replied the prince in good natured exasperation. "I have outwitted conspirators at Calais, I have sunk Spaniards aboard their ships, I have captured kings at Poitiers— and shall I fear the cry of "Consanguinity!" from a caitiff pontiff? Come, cousin, have done with your cavils and say rather that you will have me as your husband."

At this the lady demurred no longer, but placing her hands in his, declared herself entirely willing to forget her cousinly scruples and trust in the better judgment of her *beau cousin, le chevalier le plus galant dans tout le monde.*

◆ ◆ ◆

When the prince returned to his quarters several hours later, the early winter evening had already chased the sun from the horizon. The Captal de Buch had retired to bed, as old men are wont to do, but he found Brocas and Potenhale wide awake and playing at chess before a warm fire.

"How went my suit?" demanded Brocas with a devilish gleam in his eye.

The prince shook his head, "Poorly, poorly. It seems the lady likes you not."

"Alas and alack!" cried Brocas. "But did you seek to persuade the lady by itemizing my better parts?"

"I used every means of persuasion, my friend, but the lady swears she loves another."

"Another?" asked Brocas in mock despair. "Who is this wretch? Tell me his name that I may throw my gauntlet in his face."

The prince shrugged. "What can I say? I am he."

Brocas rose slowly from his chair. "I could be angry at you, methinks. I asked you to get me a wife, and you have dealt most feigningly with me."

"I also could be angry," replied the prince. "For against my will, you have thrown me in the way of my cousin and forced me to make love to her."

Then they both dispelled their pretended displeasure and grinned broadly. "Gramercy, my friend," said the prince. "You have served me better than you know."

"God bless you, my prince," replied Lord Brocas, and he clapped him on the shoulder with strong emotion.

Potenhale, still sitting by the fireside, smiled wryly to hear the prince discuss his new plans for the marriage. There was no fear that his father would object. The man who had taken a kingdom had the right to take his own bride. They would live in Guienne, perhaps in that self-same city of Bordeaux—for the king had promised to make his firstborn the ruler of that province. The prince thanked Brocas again. He would have led him away to the wine cellars when he remembered that he was, after all, still the herald of another suitor. "Potenhale," said he, for there was one more piece of news to relate.

The prince's time in the cloister had not been spent exclusively in Joan's arms. After the newly-betrothed couple had wasted many words on tender endearments, Joan called the children to come meet their future papa. She also called Margery, anxious to share the happy news with the maidservant who had shared her every sorrow.

Margery curtsied and felicitated her mistress. Her bright eyes sparkled with genuine joy. Considerately, she stepped back to leave the couple alone, but the prince stopped her and asked her to stay a while. He had pleaded his case with her mistress, and now he had some conversation to hold with her. Margery scanned his face in bewilderment. What could the Prince of Wales have to say to her?

◆ ◆ ◆

"Potenhale," said the prince. "This was her only word." And pulling a crimson glove out of the breast of his jerkin, he tossed it to his faithful servant. "God give you joy."

Selected Bibliography

Appelbaum, Stanley, trans. and ed. *Medieval Tales and Stories*. Mineola, NY: Dover Publications, Inc., 2000.

Barber, Richard. *Edward, Prince of Wales and Aquitaine: A Biography of the Black Prince*. Great Britain: The Boydell Press, 1978.

————, trans. and ed. *The Life and Campaigns of the Black Prince: from contemporary letters, diaries and chronicles, including Chandos Herald's* Life of the Black Prince. Great Britain: The Boydell Press, 1979.

Creighton, Louise. *Life of Edward the Black Prince*. London: Rivingtons, 1876.

Froissart, Sir John. *The Chronicles of England, France and Spain*. Translated by Thomas Johnes and edited by H. P. Dunster. New York: E. P. Dutton & Co., Inc., 1961.

Froissart, Jean. *Chronicles*. Translated and edited by Geoffrey Brereton. London: Penguin Books, 1978.

Geoffrey of Monmouth. *The History of the Kings of Britain*. Translated by Lewis Thorpe. London: Penguin Books, 1966.

Hallam, Elizabeth, ed. *Chronicles of the Age of Chivalry: the Plantagenet dynasty from 1216 to 1377: Henry III and the three Edwards, the era of the Black Prince and the Black Death.* London: Salamander Books Ltd., 2002.

Houston, Mary G. *Medieval Costume in England and France: the 13th, 14th and 15th Centuries.* Mineola, NY: Dover Publications, Inc., 1996.

James, Francis Godwin, ed. *The Pageant of Medieval England: Historical and Literary Sources to 1485.* Gretna, LA: Pelican Publishing Company, 1975.

Kaeuper, Richard W. and Elspeth Kennedy, trans. and eds. *The Book of Chivalry of Geoffroi de Charny: Text, Context, and Translation.* Philadelphia, PA: University of Pennsylvania Press, 1996.

McKisack, May. *The Fourteenth Century: 1307-1399.* London: Oxford University Press, 1959.

Muhlberger, Steven. *Jousts and Tournaments: Charny and the Rules for Chivalric Sport in Fourteenth-Century France.* Union City, CA: The Chivalry Bookshelf, 2002.

Sedgwick, Henry Dwight. *The Black Prince.* New York: Barnes and Noble Books, 1993.

Tierney, Brian. *Western Europe in the Middle Ages: 300-1475,* Sixth Edition. USA: McGraw-Hill College, 1999.

Made in the USA
Charleston, SC
09 July 2011